HOUSE OF PAIN

BOOK ONE

KAROLINA WILDE

First paperback edition December 2022

Cover Art and Design by Lena Yang

Map by Anastasiya Li

Developmental Editing by Lauren Humphries-Brooks

Copy Editing by Lauren Humphries-Brooks

Proofreading by Beth Attwood

Illustrations by Dara Illarionova

ISBN (paperback) 978-1-7391129-0-5

ISBN (hardcover) 978-1-7391129-1-2

ISBN (ebook) 978-1-7391129-2-9

www.karolinawilde.com

To my Family.
Without the trauma, I wouldn't have been able to write these characters.

DISCOVER THE REALM OF INATHIS WITH THE FREE NOVELLA

INATHIS IS THE REALM OF MAGIC FULL OF DANGER, ADVENTURES, AND WICKED WITCHES.

One night. Two academic rivals. A mystery to solve. What can go wrong?

When Lorelei Moonfall returned to the town she grew up in for one last fun Litha celebration, the last thing she expected was to see her high-school academic rival, Rune Cedar. Let alone have to work with him to save their friends' little sister.

But when the child goes missing on one night of the year when children disappear to never come back, Lorelei and Rune have to put their differences and old wounds aside and work together to uncover the centuries-old mystery that will change their lives forever.

On their way to solving the mystery, Lorelei and Rune find themselves confronted with their feelings for each other. And both are surprised when their mutual dislike turns into something either expected least.

If you're looking for a spicy one-night story packed with the tension between two academic rivals fighting each other and their attraction for each other, then download the Children of the Wicked for free: https://www.karolinawilde.com/ newsletter

CONTENT WARNINGS

Before reading the book, please check the trigger warning list below:

- Mutilation (carving of flesh for magic purposes)
- Sexism and misogyny
- Dubious consent
- Profanity
- Explicit sexual content
- Bullying
- Physical, emotional, and psychological violence
- Blood
- Molesting (hints and mentions, no explicit content)
- Sexual harassment (no rape or anything explicit)
- Suicide (hints)
- Self-harm (hints)
- Eating disorder (hints)
- Drug and alcohol use
- Toxic relationships (no cheating) and friendships

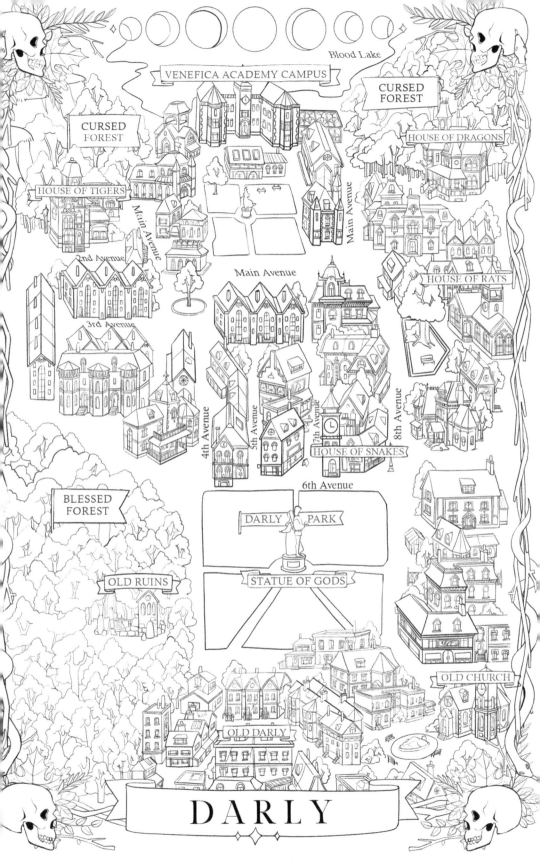

The relief of giving in to destruction.
—*Kafka*

I. DEADLY HEARTS

1

During this year's Game, hearts would break.

Loud thunder rumbled in the distance, the dark night's sky bright with the blues and the reds of the wild lightning bolts hiding behind fluffy clouds. The sound of it almost killed the blaring music under Alecto's feet.

A light giggle drew Alecto's attention away from the sky to the dimly lit room where five of them were standing in a tight circle.

Val, keeping the smoke from escaping, passed the blunt to Jolene, who brought it to her mouth.

Alecto licked her lips at the sight; she wasn't sure whether it was because of the blunt or the way Jolene's deep violet lips parted to accommodate it.

"Say it, bitch," Val urged Jolene, her dark eyes glittering with mischief. "Say it loud."

Jolene released a large cloud of smoke, letting it rise to the ceiling, gray tendrils swirling over their heads, despite all the open windows that should have pulled it all out of the room.

If not for their *magic*.

"Let his smile be as charming as Heath Ledger's, with a dimple in one cheek," Jolene said. Alessandro snickered while Blaze closed his eyes and nodded in agreement. "Let his hair be as dark as night itself, eyes deeper than the fucking Mariana Trench, and let his cock be long and beautiful and capable, just like every fucking bitch deserves."

"Ah, you're just describing me right now," Blaze chimed in.

Val giggled, biting her lip as she met Alecto's gaze.

Jolene flipped him off before dropping the black rose petals she held in her free hand into the bowl that sat in the middle of their little circle. They all hollered in agreement, Val tilting her head up to howl like a wolf.

Even Alecto laughed, the sound foreign on her lips. The uneasiness of what their group was doing tonight was becoming just a distant memory the longer she breathed the intoxicating air.

Her whole body tingled with excitement now. The black petals in her palm were soft and tender as she gently rubbed them, just like she would caress her lover's skin.

Taking over the blunt from Jolene, Blaze said, "Let him be tall as a tree, broad-shouldered, have a lean waist—"

"Looking to conjure some competition here, *Blazy*?" Val teased him, her sensuous mouth curling into a wicked grin as she ran her tongue through her teeth.

Blaze only smirked in response. "Let him have lean, strong muscles over his dark skin and let his touch be as intoxicating as the taste of any drug. Let his body be painted in the history of the whole witchkind and his dark past."

With that, he sucked in a sharp breath, the very tip of the blunt burning bright red, and the circle cheered on.

Another bundle of black petals landed in the bowl.

Alecto couldn't stop herself from rolling her eyes at Blaze as he passed the blunt to her. He was so extra and dramatic. For no fucking reason.

What does "painted in the history of the whole witchkind" even mean?

There was a challenge in his gaze before his black eyes traveled to where their fingers touched as Alecto took the blunt from him. A sharp electric current zipped through her fingers before she took her hand away.

Whenever he got a chance to show how much he disliked Alecto, he always took it. Blaze wouldn't miss an opportunity to abuse his power, using it for his own amusement as if it were a little toy and not something that could kill if used carelessly.

Of course, Alecto knew Blaze wasn't trying to stop her heart.

He only intended to play with it.

At least she hoped that was the case.

All eyes settled on Alecto as she drew the blunt closer to her lips.

With her heart racing, she inhaled the sweet, thick smoke, letting it fill her lungs until she couldn't breathe anymore, then she tilted her head backwards, closing her eyes.

Warmth spread from her lungs to her chest and further to the very tips of her limbs. When every muscle in her body relaxed, only then did she release the smoke.

"Let him be smart enough to hold a conversation that doesn't include boobs or sports," Alecto said, cocking her head. Alessandro and Jolene giggled. "Let him be charming as one of the demons from Hel. And let him know exactly where the fuck the clit is and what to do with it."

Another round of shouts and giggles went around the circle, and Alecto dropped the petals in the bowl, immediately missing the softness against her skin.

If they were going to summon a Guardian to help them win the Game, she was going to make sure he was decent. There were already enough useless men around them. Men who didn't know what to do with women. Who were clueless and selfish.

Alecto shuddered as she remembered her last hookup, Gabe from the House of Tigers.

There were rumors spread since her first day at Venefica Academy about the size of his cock, and all the girls whispered of it like he was a legend.

Naturally, Alecto was thrilled when she finally got his attention at the end of her first year. A mere first-year student—a half witch at that—getting the invitation to hang out with the legendary Hulk, as they called him.

She liked a man with a big cock as much as any other girl, and when he bent her over and slammed into her from behind, back at the boathouse by the Blood Lake, it was divine.

It was a *real* thrill.

Until he finished right before Alecto could fully get into it. Once again, she was left empty, unsatisfied, only with his jizz streaming down her thigh as he zipped his jeans.

Disappointing.

Men were disappointing, big cocks or not.

"Hold hands," Val instructed, and they all obeyed, lacing their fingers together. This time, Blaze kept his power to himself. Val closed her eyes, and they followed. "*Grantisio immane.*"

3

A tingly, warm feeling washed through Alecto, and from the gasps around the circle, she guessed the others felt it as well.

But it was gone as suddenly as it appeared. When Alecto opened her eyes, the room was quiet and still, even if the air remained electric from the storm coming their way.

Val's crimson lips curled into a wicked grin. "Let's go to the party, bitches."

2

"Give me a fucking break," Jolene murmured as she downed one jelly shot after another.

Her pretty brown nose scrunched, and she shivered at the taste of alcohol.

"What?" Alessandro shrugged, lifting his palms in defense. "I'm telling you, those whores from the House of Rabbits didn't need their daddies to buy their grades. They fucked the professor. I saw it with my own two eyes."

"You're full of shit, Andro." Even Blaze didn't believe him. "There is no way they could have fucked Professor Darcy. He barely looks at his students during class, as if we're too beneath him to even spare us a glance. It doesn't matter that our parents are the ones who pay his fucking salary."

Blaze would know all about it. His parents were one of the most prominent Alumni after all. Of course, so were Andro's, Jolene's, and Alecto's families. But Blaze's parents were the ones who owned half the buildings on Venefica's campus.

"Well, what difference does it make?" Alecto asked, rolling her eyes. "Correct me if I'm wrong, but weren't you the one to fuck Professor Goldfinch last trimester to get a better grade for your Enchanting for Witches class?"

"It was a completely different story," Andro scoffed, brushing a hand over his dreadlocks, his face twisted with distaste.

"Is it now?" Alecto arched a brow.

"How the fuck is that any different?" Jolene chimed in.

"It was a dare," Andro explained. "It's not as if a better grade was the goal here. It was a mere bonus to Professor Goldfinch's long, perfect cock."

Alecto and Jolene exchanged a glance and burst into laughter.

"Your little dare got Mr. Long Perfect Cock fired," Blaze reminded Andro, his dark eyes intense over the rim of his glass.

Alessandro didn't look even one bit regretful. "Well, it's not my problem he broke one of Venefica's laws and fucked a student now, is it? And anyway, since when do you care about the well-being of our professors, *Blazy*?"

"I don't," Blaze replied, swallowing a big gulp of his drink.

Blaze shifted his attention to the room behind their backs, where the party was in full swing.

"So, wait, did you say you saw it with your own eyes?" Alecto blocked out Jolene's and Andro's voices as she followed Blaze's gaze to the wide leather couch at the end of their living room.

Their House was built somewhere in the mid-1800s, and for the most part, still carried the old Victorian spirit throughout it. The large modern couch Val dragged out of Gods know where didn't fit the wall moldings or the expensive crystal chandelier hanging from the ceiling.

But it oddly made sense.

Right now, Val was spread out on the leather couch with two boys under her—Hendrix Monterey from the House of Dragons and Killer Jenkins from the House of Rats. Val had been teasing them along for months now, during the summer break, which drove their Houses insane.

Dragons and Rats couldn't be seen together sharing the girl from the House they all loathed the most.

Alecto found herself repulsed yet compelled by Val's behavior. She envied Val's determination to do what had to be done to secure her social standing. If only Alecto had even a fraction of that, her life in Inathis would have been easier.

Alecto brought her glass to her lips, tasting the scorching clear liquid on her lips as her eyes followed Val's hands, one of them slipping inside

Hendrix's unzipped pants. As Val's hand moved, Hendrix's head fell on the back of the couch, revealing the tall column of his golden throat.

"She *won't*," Alecto whispered more to herself than anyone else, but Blaze heard the words.

"Oh, she definitely will." His voice was husky and rough, and when Alecto looked at him, she found his gaze focused on Val and the boys. "Wanna bet?"

His moon-pale face was blank of any expression, but his dark eyes glittered with unmistakable desire, and if Alecto had moved her hand to cup the front of his black jeans, she was sure she would find his cock hard.

Something about the thought of it twisted her insides, but she pushed the feeling away, leaving her unfazed right before his gaze shifted to her. Blaze arched a brow.

"The ritual we performed today requires sacrifice. That's why Val chose this weekend," he reminded Alecto. *Patronizing asshole.* "And sex magic works better than anything else. So you better believe she'll fuck them both."

"Yeah, but maybe not in public," Alecto scoffed, taking another sip of her vodka. Blaze huffed a laugh and moved closer.

She could *feel* the heat from his body.

Alecto ignored the shivers and the way her body reacted to Blaze's presence. It took her long enough, but at the end of last year, she finally managed to convince herself that Blaze wasn't attractive.

Not even one bit.

"Oh, you are such a prude," Blaze said, his voice mocking.

Alecto refused to look at him, at those intense obsidian eyes that could swallow her whole. "We could help her seal the deal, you know? Joining in the *fun.*"

Heat surged to Alecto's cheeks. She straightened her back, her heart thrashing against her rib cage.

He's just fucking with you.

Blaze's long finger touched her cheek, brushing strands of her long white hair away and then returning to caress the line of her jaw.

"You know, I've been thinking about something, *Alecto.*" The way her name sounded on his tongue made her toes curl. Alecto wasn't sure Blaze had ever been this close to her. Let alone fully focused on her. She stole a sideways glance to find Blaze's eyes hot as coal, lips curled into a dark smirk. "How does it feel to know you can never compare to one of us when it comes to your magic?"

Blaze's tone was a gentle caress, sending tingles down her spine. Yet the words that spilled out of his mouth were full of venom.

Flames licking at her cheeks intensified and Alecto stepped away from Blaze. He tilted his head back and barked a laugh, clearly satisfied with his own nastiness. Oh, humiliating her was probably making his dick hard. That's how much Blaze seemed to enjoy it.

Alecto searched her mind for something, for a clapback that would sting just as much, but her mind was empty. Shame took over everything else.

"She's fucking crazy." Blaze's words snapped Alecto from her thoughts, and she followed his gaze to where Val still was with the boys.

They were almost naked now, Val's top long gone, small breasts hovering over their faces as she stroked their cocks in long, teasing motions.

"*Gods*," Alecto breathed out, her jaw falling open.

But the nakedness and public sex wasn't even the craziest part.

Right then, Val took her athame out of the pocket of her jeans and brought it to Killer's defined V line. His eyebrows furrowed when the dagger pressed into his skin. But he didn't stop Val carving out the pointy first letter of her name in his flesh.

Then, Val did the same to Hendrix and passed her dagger to Killer, pushing her jeans down and turning the side of her hip towards them.

As Killer brought the knife to her soft flesh, she hissed and then giggled. And when she lifted her dark eyes to meet Alecto's, she winked before returning her attention back to the boys, carving their own initials into her flesh.

"She's using *blood* magic," Andro hissed. "This bitch is going to get us all in trouble."

A tremor passed through Alecto's body as her anger rose.

Val was out of line.

Public sex, fine, it's her prerogative.

But using blood magic, in such a public manner when their enemies were around them, *under* her, was beyond everything.

She was risking the Snakes' reputation, their legacy, and their damn future with such behavior. There were lines even witches couldn't cross.

"*Or* she's just making sure that we win this year's Game." Blaze's voice was calm and collected, which only made the fire inside Alecto burn brighter. "Mixing blood and sex magic will get us the results we need."

"If the Dean finds out about our little ritual, we're fucked," Alecto said through clenched teeth. "If he finds out about the ritual *and* the blood magic, we're going to be expelled. Nobody's exempt from breaking the blood magic rule. Not even *legacy*."

Alecto spat the last word, willing as much anger into it as she could muster. Blaze liked to think that being legacy made them invincible.

"Nobody is going to find out. Val is known to have a taste for wild sex. Nobody will even guess a little bit of carving of the flesh is part of blood magic."

I bet you would know all about it, Alecto wanted to snap at him, but she swallowed the bitterness and turned back to Val.

"Well then, let's hope she fucks them senseless."

3

The next morning, Alecto found herself sitting on the monthly Liaison meeting, her hangover making her wish she was anywhere *but* here.

"You cannot *not* participate in the Game," Garcia announced, her sharp face set in stone as she glanced at Mariana sitting on the opposite side of her by the massive round oak desk. "These are the rules for all Houses on campus. You either participate in the Game, or you lose the right to call yourself one of the Houses."

Alecto sat on Garcia's left, trying very hard not to lose her shit at the argument that's been going on between the Pigs and Goats for what seemed like forever.

You would think that two Houses that were supposed to be compassionate, gentle, and calm wouldn't waste everyone's time with petty arguments. But apparently today they woke up and chose to be a pain in everyone's ass.

"Last year, we lost three witches because of the stupid Game," Mariana complained, shifting her thick black-frame glasses higher up her nose. "If the Rats hadn't slaughtered our members in order to win, we wouldn't be struggling with the new pledges this year."

"Don't blame this on us, sweetheart," Killer snorted. After yesterday's party, Alecto didn't think he would show up to the meeting. "If your witches can't protect themselves against a few loose spiders, then maybe you shouldn't even be at Venefica. And by the way, you can't throw accusations like that on other Houses. Not unless you want to get sued."

"It's public knowledge that it was the Rats who removed the enchants on the cages holding the Hollowa spiders that attacked *my* witches," Mariana argued. Alecto could almost see the steam coming out of her ears. "You set the trap because you knew those pledges will be in the possession of the Book that night. That's how you took our Book and won the Game. So don't give me this nonsense, *Jenkins*."

Yeah, how unfortunate that win was. The Snakes were so close to acquiring the Book from the House of Tigers and winning. But the House of Rats were faster.

Alecto and the rest of the Snakes still held the grudge.

That's why they were determined to win this year. So determined, in fact, that they used their magic to create a magical Guardian to help them cause havoc amongst other Houses and used blood magic to seal it.

Alecto still wasn't sure how she felt about the whole thing.

"Listen," Garcia said. "Shit happens. Any one of us can die at any moment during the Game. Just deal with it. As I said, you're either participating in the Game like all the other Houses, or you're going to lose your privileges. I can't wait to see you explain that to the Dean and your Alumni."

"Yeah, *Cantini*," Killer teased Mariana. "Daddy's not going to be so happy if he spent all this money and his girl ruined his legacy."

Mariana flipped him off, only drawing more shouts and laughter from the other assholes around the table, all trying to lick their way up Killer's ass.

Morons.

"So, is that all?" Alecto asked, sitting straight in her chair. "Some of us have to prepare for the Ceremony tonight, you know?"

Garcia awarded Alecto with a sideways glance, clearly aware of the subtle dig at the House of Goats, whose performances always sucked, but then smashed her wooden hammer into the table, indicating that the meeting was over.

"Thank the Gods," Alecto murmured to herself as she rose from her seat and walked towards the large double door.

Right outside the entrance, Val was leaning against the stone wall, half her face covered with large sunglasses even though there was no reason for it—the sky was still gray and cloudy.

Blaze stood by her side, his head lowered to Val's ear, a smirk tugging at the corner of his mouth as he whispered to her.

Alecto ignored the weird feeling pushing at her chest, the way Val's tongue dragged over her lips as she listened to him speak, the way she cocked her head backwards and laughed.

It would be easier to forget that Blaze was mean if Alecto didn't have to see him being decent with other members of the Inner Circle.

"What are you doing here?" was all Alecto asked as she approached them.

Blaze's gaze snapped to her, taking her in with a glance as he leaned one shoulder against the wall.

"We've come to take you to breakfast," he said, voice flat. "The others are already in the cafeteria, saving us the spot."

"So kind of you," Alecto deadpanned, forcing a fake smile.

The other Liaisons all left the meeting building, streaming past them to either lectures or the cafeteria. The campus was half-empty at this time of the day, the wind rustling in the already gold-turning leaves of birch trees scattered around.

"So, anything interesting happened in the meeting?" Val asked as they fell into step, walking the long stone path through the main field towards the large cafeteria building south of the center of the campus. "Anything I need to know about?"

Val was the leader of the House of Snakes, Blaze her Second. She might have been a crazy party girl with weird sex habits, but she was damn good at her role.

Another thing Alecto envied.

"Nothing important, really." Alecto shrugged. "Just the usual nonsense and blabbering about what's fair and what's not."

"VAL," a voice came from their left as they reached the crossway where four different paths meet, with the tall black marble statue of Venefica's founder in the middle. Galia Rathone, the High Priestess of the Rats, was storming their way, her blond bob bopping with each step.

It took Alecto one look at her face to see that she was pissed. *Royally* pissed.

"Oh, hi there, baby girl," Val drawled, a smile spreading on the small portion of her face still visible despite the sunglasses. "I'm sorry I didn't invite you to the party last—"

Val didn't get to finish the sentence. Galia's palm connected with her face with such intensity, people at the other end of the campus probably heard the slap.

"You *skank*," Galia hissed, shaking her hand in the air. "You think you're so smart carving up one of my Rats as if he's yours?"

Alecto blinked, glancing between Val and Galia.

Val's hand cupping the cheek that just got slapped slid down, revealing a red patch. Alecto hoped Blaze would be smart enough to step in between the two before things escalated.

But to her surprise, Val barked out a laugh.

"Jealous, Galia?" she asked. "Is it that you're jealous that you're never going to have two men falling for you enough to let them carve your name into their groins, or is it that you would have loved to be the one under my knife?"

Galia's face turned red. She took a step towards Val. Alecto stepped in front of her before she could do any more damage and attract any more attention from the students on the campus.

"How about we try to be civil, Galia?" Alecto asked, her voice calm. "We all know Val has a taste for some seriously fucked up shit. But I was there last night, just like half the student body, and let me tell you, Killer was more than eager to get himself *marked*."

"I know what you're doing, bitch," Galia spat, looking over Alecto's shoulder at Val. "Your stupid mind games don't work on me. Don't even for one minute think I'll let you win. This year, the House of Rats are going to be the winners *again*. And sooner or later, we're going to crush you to dust. No Queen or King rules forever. Remember that."

With one last glance at them all, Galia turned on her heel and strode up the path, her blond bob moving with each stride.

"I hope you know what you're doing, bitch," Alecto said, turning back to Val. "Because it doesn't look as if Galia's going to fall for what we have planned for her."

"I do," Val assured her. "And trust me, Black. She's gonna be on her knees, begging, when we're done with her."

Alecto's heart thrashed against her rib cage at the sight of the cruel, wicked grin blooming on Val's face. Wordlessly, they fell back into step, strolling towards the cafeteria.

T he cafeteria was packed when they entered, all the students crammed around large tables, clearly separated by their Houses. You'd never see an Ox sit with a Rat, or a Pig sit with a Rabbit.

Even if last night you fucked in the middle of a party, for the whole student body to see.

Val and Blaze went straight to their usual table, at the very end of the old Victorian hall, perched by the arched window overlooking the Dean's building. They exchanged a few whispers, Alecto trailing a few steps behind them.

It was Alecto's second year at Venefica. Her second year being a member of the House of Snakes and the Inner Circle. Yet, she still didn't quite fit in. Not enough to be the one Val shared her secrets with.

Alecto left her bag on the chair between Andro and Jolene and went straight to the bar, hoping that there would still be a cinnamon bun left for her.

She needed something sweet to kill the aftertaste of vodka still lingering at the back of her throat. Some happy hormones would have also been nice this dreadful morning.

When she took her place at the end of a long line of students all trying to pack their plates with breakfast food, Alecto's appetite wavered.

There was some coconut porridge this morning and fancy-looking avocado toast available from the small list of food she could stomach, but none of it was appealing.

Cinnamon bun and black coffee were the way to go.

"Is that going to be all, Alecto?" A forest sprite dressed in a tiny green dress made from already yellowing leaves jumped up from the other side of the counter.

"Yes, Kaliad. That's going to be all for this morning," Alecto said, passing a card to the sprite.

Kaliad was a small one, so the card was almost half her size. But she took it in her tiny hands nonetheless and swiped it through the cash registry.

"I heard someone got slapped today in the middle of the campus," Kaliad said, her voice a whisper. Alecto couldn't miss the shine of excitement in her eyes.

Kaliad wasn't a fan of Val. Most people at Venefica hated Val. She had that quality about her. And some days Alecto wished she was one of those people.

"Yeah. Galia really tried her best," Alecto said, a small smile tugging at the corner of her lips.

"I'd be careful if I were you, Alecto." Kaliad's words came as a surprise, but Alecto shuffled that emotion down.

"What is that supposed to mean?"

A shrug of tiny shoulders. "You're a nice girl. Val's exact opposite. Don't let her change you."

Alecto left Kaliad behind without another word. Kaliad didn't say it to Alecto's face, but the meaning behind her words was obvious. Val was a full-blooded witch and Alecto wasn't.

You're a nice girl.

Alecto wanted to scream. She would have rather been anything *but* a nice girl. Nice girls didn't get to survive at Venefica. Or anywhere else in Inathis, for that matter. And Alecto wanted to survive.

No, that wasn't right. Survival wasn't enough. Alecto wanted to thrive.

"So, when are we going to find out whether our little spell worked?" Jolene asked in a loud whisper just as Alecto approached their table.

She glanced around and over her shoulder, but there was nobody there.

"How the Hel am I supposed to know?" Val just shrugged, biting on a piece of burned bacon. "It doesn't say in the Book the exact date and hour of when the Guardian is supposed to show up. But I'm sure we'll know when he does."

"Should we even call him a Guardian though?" Andro took clear lip gloss out of his pocket. He slowly traced his plump lower lip, spreading the thick, sparkly liquid evenly. "It would be more fitting to call it a sex monster."

Val barked out a laugh before she took off her sunglasses to reveal red-rimmed eyes. "A very fitting Guardian for the House of Snakes if you ask me."

Their House was famous for using sex magic for centuries now. Alecto wasn't sure why she was surprised that that's exactly what they decided to do to win this year, creating a sex god who would wreak havoc amongst rival Houses.

Havoc that was supposed to help them steal another House's Book and win the Game.

Alecto bit into the fresh cinnamon roll, the sugary taste filling her mouth. She barely kept herself from moaning and her eyes rolling to the back of her head.

This was what meadows probably felt like.

After a few more bites, she washed down the sweetness with the hot, bitter coffee. Sadly, it didn't make her feel any better. The hangover was a bitch. And right now, it was twisting her stomach into knots.

"Rough hangover?" Andro asked, bumping his shoulder into hers.

Alecto just hummed as she took another sip of her coffee.

"You know that our girl doesn't do well the morning after," Jolene teased.

Alecto awarded her friend with a middle finger. "Eat faster, fuckers. Shouldn't we be rushing to finish preparing for tonight's Ceremony?"

"That's the spirit, Black," Val said, smiling her signature predatory smile. "Have you changed your mind about participating in the sex ritual this year?"

Alecto despised their yearly ritual. There was nothing worse than public sexual exhibition. Except for a public sexual exhibition *with* a group of people. And if that wasn't enough, she'd have to deal with her father being here.

It was normal for all the parents to come to support their children, even if that might seem weird according to mortal standards. Alecto's mother would have never signed up for a thing like that if she was still alive.

Maybe that's why he got rid of her at the end.

Somehow, Alecto managed to keep her face straight and chin high as she said, "No."

Blaze huffed a laugh, shaking his head as if he didn't even expect another answer from Alecto. Andro simply nodded, seemingly not bothered by Alecto's reservations. But it was Val's next words that made Alecto's stomach sink.

"I suppose not," Val mused, eyeing Alecto. "Half witches don't have it in them to be shameless with their sexuality." She paused as she rose to her feet. "Neither do they have it in them to be cruel or merciless."

As Alecto left the cafeteria after breakfast, she couldn't stop thinking about Val's dark glare when she said those words.

Would she be able to prove Val wrong?

The fire burning inside her indicated that there was nothing she wanted more.

4

There were many things that Blaze would have rather been doing right now than standing on the side of the massive stage at the back of the green field stretching behind the Dean's building.

The view wasn't bad, overlooking the crimson lake surrounded by thick pine forest, the sun lazily hanging on its last threads before it plunged and disappeared behind the rigid horizon.

But the program for tonight was boring as fuck.

It was Blaze's third year participating in the Ceremony. While the first year was exciting and intricate, with weird and different rituals he had only read about in books, the second year was way less exciting, and once the sex ritual part was over, the night just seemed to drag on forever.

By the third year, even the sex ritual had lost its appeal.

It wasn't as if Blaze couldn't get a good fuck elsewhere.

He scoffed to himself, adjusting the loose sleeve of his wide shirt. There was a streak of black glitter on the white silk, probably from when he dragged his hand over his hair and smudged the paint on his face.

Ah, well. Smudged it is.

The Pigs were almost at the end of their performance, and after them, it was going to be the Snakes' turn, followed by the other main Houses.

Blaze fidgeted in his spot, his muscles aching for a comfortable bed and a long blunt to put him to sleep.

Maybe he shouldn't have gotten so drunk at the party last night.

"I'm going to die of boredom," he muttered, turning to Andro.

The boy next to him was deeply interested in his nails right now. A matching white shirt hung from Andro's tall and lean frame. But instead of black, gold glitter was streaked atop his high brown cheekbones.

"I know, right," Andro said. "I don't even know why they bother with the other eight Houses. They're so dull and boring."

Blaze nodded, even though it wasn't what he meant.

He didn't really care for any other Houses except the Snakes. And even then, he only cared about the Snakes enough to keep on his father's good side.

Just barely though.

Blaze's survival instincts were *lacking*, to say the least. So it wasn't a surprise that he enjoyed taunting his fate more often than he should have.

Right then, a familiar platinum blond head came into Blaze's view. He tipped his head to the side—just slightly—to have a better view of where Alecto stood, blue eyes darting around the crowd.

Well, maybe tonight didn't have to be *that* boring after all.

Without second thought, Blaze made his way towards Alecto, brushing past people carelessly in the crowd.

Blaze didn't like Alecto.

On certain days, his dislike could be considered borderline *hate*. But there was something that forced him to gravitate towards her.

Maybe it was the way her eyes flickered, angry and sharp as daggers whenever he teased her with all the intentions of being mean and cruel for the sake of his own entertainment.

Or maybe it was the fact that Blaze was looking for someone to sink his claws in.

Someone to play with.

And who was a better victim than a lonely half breed?

Blaze found himself towering over Alecto, a crooked smile tugging on the corner of his lips as she lifted her gaze to meet his.

The way her eyes sparkled with icy rage indicated that he had made the right choice.

Ah, sweet.

"What the fuck are you looking at, pleased as a cat?" Alecto snapped but kept her voice low.

"Well, why wouldn't I be pleased to be in your company?" Blaze drawled, lazily dragging a finger over her naked shoulder, tracing the line of a rose tattoo—one of many—gracing her left arm.

Her skin was soft.

He ignored it.

"I'm not in the mood for your games, Blaze."

Bingo.

"And why is that?" he mused, grinning wider. "Not a fan of a little bit of public affection, Black?"

Alecto turned her face away, focusing on the stage where the Pigs were finally done with their pathetic ritual, leaving the stage at the other end.

Val, standing at the front of their group, started barking out commands.

"Mind your own business, *Leveau*."

An idea popped inside Blaze's mind then—something that would definitely make this evening less dreadful.

He had noticed the weird hesitation Alecto had with public affection of any kind. Especially when it came to sex. The way she always refused to participate in any sex rituals the Snakes performed.

Blaze was aware of her sexual escapades. This girl was no prude amongst the witches. So it fascinated him that she was so against something that was so natural for their kind.

Is it her mortal side?

He recoiled inside himself at the thought, remembering once again that Alecto was, in fact, a *half breed*.

Yet, she was still *legacy*.

Still an equal member of the House of Snakes. Even if she didn't deserve it.

Ignoring the bitter sting in his chest, Blaze slid his hand down her arm, looping their fingers together. Alecto jerked her hand, but Blaze didn't let her slip away.

"How about we have some fun tonight, *baby*?"

Alecto didn't have to know that the only one having fun would be him.

Humiliation was Blaze's forte after all.

And he knew exactly how to humiliate *dear* Alecto to bring him the most satisfaction.

Right then, Val called out—it was time for the third years to go up to the stage. Blaze moved, tugging Alecto with him before she could refuse.

As he passed Val, a question shone in her eyes about him disobeying her and bringing the second year out of line. Blaze simply winked and took the first step up onto the stage.

To his surprise, Alecto didn't fight him, trailing after him to the stage, lit up only with a massive number of candles scattered at the edges. As more and more Snakes filled the space on the stage, the candlelight flickered higher, more aggressively.

Blaze led Alecto to the end of the stage, black and pink rose petals scattered under their feet, wings of white doves flapping over their heads as the creatures made circles.

Even though they were at the very corner of the massive stage, the other members of their House shielding them from the crowd of spectators, there wasn't anywhere to hide as Blaze came to a stop and turned to face Alecto.

Her eyes were shooting bullets as she warned, "Don't you even think I'll fuck you on this stage. I don't—"

He placed a gentle finger over her lips. Blaze had to bite down on his lower lip to stop the laugh, but his heart was singing seeing Alecto so openly suffering.

As if he would ever fuck her against her will.

As if he would ever fuck her *at all*.

"Don't worry," he whispered, lips brushing past the shell of her ear. He could have sworn she shuddered under his touch. "I want our first time to be special."

Her whole body went still, but just for a moment. Then, she grabbed the front of his shirt, curling the silk in her fist.

Which surprised Blaze greatly.

Alecto hadn't stood up to him before. Not once.

"Keep sweet-talking me, and you'll regret it." Her voice was a warning.

There was nothing Blaze enjoyed more than a challenge.

What was the worst this girl could do to him? Stare him to death with her icy blue eyes?

Please.

When Val's head appeared on the stage, Blaze snapped his attention to their group.

The fourth and third years were all at the front, standing in a circle, where the second years kneeled obediently in the center. Blaze tugged at Alecto's hand, dragging her after him to join the circle.

Alecto was supposed to be inside, kneeling with the rest of second years, getting ready to find another witch to kiss, because she refused to have sex for the sake of her performance like the rest of them.

But what fun would that be for Blaze if they followed the rules?

Val's intense gaze indicated that she wasn't happy with Blaze's disobedience.

But while she was their leader, and for the most part, Blaze respected that, he was her Second and *legacy*.

Blaze was allowed to break some rules of hers, and Val didn't get to say anything about it.

If she was pissy about it later, Blaze knew *exactly* how to coax her back to a pleasant state.

Besides, Blaze was sure Val would appreciate a little bit of humiliation on Alecto's part.

Finally, lyrical music filled the stage, dramatic notes traveling through the air with such intensity, they tickled his skin. Right then, three first years —their newest pledges—appeared on the stage, long white cloaks flowing down their bodies and covering their faces as they took their spots around the stage.

Alecto's hand stiffened between Blaze's fingers, and he stole a sideways glance at her face.

She was probably freaking out by now, even though it didn't show on her perfectly composed face. *Good.*

Just a little bit more taunting, and then it's going to be over.

Blaze wasn't completely heartless—he wouldn't torture Alecto for too long.

Just long enough.

Soon, the chants started as the third and fourth years around the circle started swinging to the rhythm of the music. Blaze joined in, tipping his head back and closing his eyes, allowing himself to get lost in the music just for a moment.

The music rippled through him, caressing his skin, the tingly feeling of his magic awakening inside his chest, spreading further to the very tips of his fingers.

Someone on his side gasped, and he cracked his eyes open to meet Alecto's bewildered gaze, her rosy lips parted as she stared at him.

Blaze offered her a lazy grin as he straightened himself. Then, he wrapped a hand around her waist and pulled her closer.

Alecto tried to resist, but her efforts weren't fertile. Soon her shoulder was pressing into his chest.

The chanting was getting more intense, making Blaze's skin hum with anticipation. He had forgotten that once you get on that stage, once you stand there with magic making its way to the marrow of your bones, boredom dissipates.

And all that's left is the pit of bottomless hunger for power and destruction, thirst for things their kind was created for.

The second years in the middle of the circle were midway through the action, their mouths connected, sliding from one sloppy kiss into the next one, bodies pressed tight together as if they were trying to melt into one.

It was intoxicating to watch, and Blaze's leather pants were suddenly too tight.

He swallowed hard, dragging his attention from the middle of the circle to the girl still pressed to his chest.

Alecto met his gaze and narrowed her eyes. Grinning, Blaze wet his lips and then ducked his head down, his lips grazing hers.

At first, Alecto jerked backwards, but he held her firmly in place, swooping her hips into his palms. Unsurprisingly, she relented.

From time to time, Blaze liked to tease Alecto, making sultry remarks, watching her squirm.

Just like the other night at the party.

It brought him so much satisfaction.

Especially when he always got to strike her down by reminding her that she was worthless.

Lesser.

While Blaze was a whore, sleeping around with witches like it was his full-time job, he never truly intended on seducing Alecto.

Did he ever think of her when pleasuring himself or fucking other girls?

Maybe.

But that wasn't anything to bother himself with.

But as their lips slid together, as Alecto's mouth responded to Blaze's teasing and gentle coaxing, something was not right.

Something *felt* very, very wrong.

Blaze pulled away, meeting her eyes once more. There wasn't any anger in them anymore. *No*, there was something else entirely.

Blaze blinked. This wasn't how this was supposed to go.

Before he could gather his thoughts and gain his composure back, Alecto's nails dug at the back of his neck. She dragged his mouth to hers with such force he had to try very hard not to lose his balance, sending them both on the floor.

Alecto's lips were insistent, tongue grazing the seam of his lips, asking for permission, and the Gods be damned, Blaze granted it.

There was a sound rumbling deep inside her, or was it coming from his chest? Blaze wasn't sure.

But he pulled her hips closer to his, pressing their bodies together as her nails dug into his shoulders, the piercing pain making his body come alive.

Alecto was the first to break the kiss, her lips traveling down to his jaw, leaving a trail of soft kisses along the side of it as she traveled lower to his exposed neck.

The chants and music and the sounds of people moaning and gasping were all tied together, enveloping them in the electric blanket that sent spikes of pleasure through Blaze's body, prickling at his skin that has gotten rather sensitive.

That's why he hissed, digging his fingers in Alecto's flesh as a sharp pain pierced his neck. It took him a moment to realize that it was Alecto's teeth sinking into his neck, her soft lips sucking on his skin, leaving a mark behind.

His hips bucked forwards of their own accord. Blaze had to fight the urge to whirl her around right then and there and bend her over so he could fuck her from behind while he tugged on her silky soft hair.

But he didn't get a chance.

Alecto pulled away, catching his gaze from under her thick lashes as she brushed a thumb over her lip. Blaze blinked, his eyelids heavy.

Alecto looked away, Blaze following her gaze to Val. Their leader put two fingers in her mouth, and a sharp whistle pierced the music.

 A moment later, the gasps and moans started winding down, music turning more intense, dramatic, pressing over them.

And then, one first year lifted a hand towards their mouth, pressing a small flask to their lips. Their mouths moved as the chant formed, and when they blew into the air, the raging purple fire shot to the sky.

The other two new pledges followed one by one, letting the flames rise over their heads as the others were finishing off, primal sounds of pleasure still ringing in Blaze's ears.

A new, unfamiliar heaviness had settled on Blaze's chest.

He had gotten more than he bargained for trying to humiliate Alecto.

Something he hadn't expected.

Something he didn't like.

5

Alecto wondered if it was possible to roll her eyes all the way to the back of her skull at Andro.

"I'm telling you, the best fuck I've had in weeks," he gushed, looking behind his shoulder where Gael, one of the second years, stood with a bunch of his friends.

Andro always said exactly the same thing about every guy he fooled around with.

Oh, he's my new obsession for this season.

"Oh," Andro said. "He's my new obsession for this season."

"Right," Jolene said, laughing.

Yes, believe me when I say that I will make it my mission to have his cock in every possible way.

"Yes, believe me when I say that I'm going to make it my mission to have his cock in every single possible way. And then some that seem impossible."

Alecto was just glad that the Ceremony was over. Only a few more hours of mingling with the faculty and the parents, and she'd be able to get into a hot bath and wash it all off.

"*Mm-hmm.* Those second years have a flair for surprises," Blaze murmured, his dark eyes on Alecto.

She couldn't read his face or his blank expression.

It made her stomach twist, the skin on the back of her neck prickling at the intensity of those black eyes.

That bastard had the audacity to kiss her on the stage. To drag her into the middle of the ritual and lay his filthy lips on her. The memory of it made her shudder, but she refused to wonder whether it was disgust or pleasure.

The rest of the Snakes didn't think Alecto had it in her to stand up for herself. Blaze thought he could play with her like his personal doll.

No. Alecto had had enough.

Alecto had to show Blaze that she would not be messed around. Not anymore. If he wished, Blaze could kiss her, humiliate and hurt her. But Alecto would bite back.

Hard.

"There's my sweet little girl." Alecto's father's voice came from behind them. With a stiff back, she turned to greet him.

His hand wrapped around her waist, pulling her into a fatherly embrace that would seem so affectionate and kind to the eyes on them now.

Galliermo Leveau, Blaze's father, was right beside him, his dark eyes boring into Alecto with anger or mistrust. She couldn't tell.

Alecto was used to Galliermo being just as big of an asshole as his son.

Guess the apple really doesn't fall far from the tree.

What still startled her to this day was how Blaze's mom, Auburn, who was so sweet and kind, could have settled for a man like Galliermo.

But then again, how had Alecto's mother settled for a man like her father? Alecto hoped it was magic. It would have been so much easier to know that Alatar Black put a spell on her mother, taking her as his mortal bride.

If she were here against her will, then maybe it would be easier to understand why she had chosen to take her life, leaving Alecto in the grip of this cruel man who called himself her proud father. But nothing in life was as easy as that, was it?

"The House of Snakes really put in the effort this year," Alatar said, turning to face the rest of the group, his eyes falling on Val. "You really smoked the other Houses with your performance. I'm sure everyone agrees."

Val offered her most pristine smile and bowed her head. "We're here to win, Mr. Black."

"Good to hear," Galliermo said, his voice hard. "At least someone is taking our legacy seriously."

Blaze didn't even bother lifting his gaze to meet his father's withering stare, glancing around the party with a bored expression.

Anger bubbled inside Alecto as she glared at Blaze. That bastard had the whole world at his feet, yet he didn't seem to be even one bit grateful for any of it.

Val scooched closer to Blaze, placing her palm over his naked chest as she smiled at Galliermo. "Let me assure you, Blaze is taking his responsibilities as my Second very seriously. When we win this year's Game, it's going to be thanks to him."

The sweetness of Val's voice, clearly artificial and meant to coax the Alumni to her side, was making Alecto sicker than her father's hand resting on her waist.

If the Snakes won this years' Game, it was definitely not going to be because of Blaze. He cared about their House less than any of them.

Galliermo didn't say anything else, eyeing his son before he turned to Alecto.

Alecto's back stiffened even more as she remembered that her face was probably streaked with black glitter from the kiss she shared with Blaze.

From the way Galliermo's eyes flickered, it seemed that he remembered that kiss on the stage as well.

"Alecto, I heard that this year you're going to be gunning for the main role in *Carmen*?" Auburn chimed in, her voice sweet and familiar. Too similar to Alecto's mom for her comfort.

Alecto's mother and Auburn used to be friends. Her mom would take her to the Leveau penthouse as a child, and they would spend afternoons in their nursery, surrounded by dozens of plants that Auburn tended to herself, sun rays streaking through the thick wall of leaves.

Those were a few scarce memories Alecto had of her time with her mother.

"Yes, Mrs. Leveau." Alecto nodded, forcing a smile. The woman was nothing but sweet to her. The least she could do was return the favor. "I'm going to be attending the audition next week. Fingers crossed I land the role."

"Of course you will, sweetheart," her father said, pulling away to turn to

Auburn. "She's just shy, my girl. Did I tell you that she spent the whole summer in the acting camp? I didn't even have to lift a finger to get her in. Her talent and wit were enough on their own."

"That's wonderful, dear," Auburn gushed, covering her mouth with her elegant palm. "I think you'd be perfect for Carmen."

The only thing Alecto could do was smile brighter, swallowing the bitterness down. The praises and the sweet-talking, followed by rewards and lavish gifts, were something she was used to by now.

Father of the fucking year.

"She's not a redhead," Blaze murmured into his whiskey glass.

He slowly met Alecto's gaze, his black eyes hot as coal. Alecto's cheeks burned with shame, and she was grateful she opted for a thick layer of foundation to hide her skin tonight.

"That's just a small detail a little bit of magic can easily fix," Auburn said, offering a reassuring smile. "It's about the talent and the charisma. That's something no amount of magic can grant."

"And my sweet pumpkin has it all," Alatar said, his face beaming. "All of it from her mother, of course."

Auburn chuckled. "Don't be so modest, Alatar. We all remember the times from Venefica when you were pulling all the witches who crossed your path."

If she had to listen to them reminiscing about their glory days, she was going to pop her eardrums.

"That's not how I remember it." Another voice came from behind them, and Alessandro's parents joined them, their hands linked together.

The Weirs were the couple of the goddamn century. Alecto always looked at them and wondered what it would feel like to have a love like theirs, to walk through life with someone who viewed you as an equal, a partner by your side.

From the looks on Jolene's and Val's faces, it was clear that Alecto wasn't alone in wondering.

Rufus Weir's brown face beamed with a dazzling smile at her father as they shook hands. Then, Alatar took Octavia's hand and gently lifted it to his lips, planting an elegant kiss. Galliermo offered a grave nod to each and let Auburn do the greeting.

The elite of Avalon Hills was a bunch of rich assholes, with their fake greetings and soft kisses, expensive elderberry wine, and clothing made of gerberry silk.

Alecto looked around the field, bringing her glass of bubbly wine to her lips as she tried to come up with a good enough excuse to run away.

There were a couple dozen Crahens, entities conjured from clay and magic to serve their needs, roaming the field, carrying large silver trays with drinks and canapes.

The bubbly wine was bitter on her tongue, nothing like the champagne she had tasted in the mortal world. Despite that, she gulped the glass down and reached for another one as the faceless waiter passed them.

As Alecto turned back to their little group, she caught Val's gaze.

It wasn't malicious or angry. Yet it was intense and blazing as if Val was trying to drill a hole in Alecto's skull.

It was hard not to miss the way Val pressed her tiny body against Blaze's lean, hard figure, the way she traced one finger over the defined muscles of his naked chest, as if to show everyone he was her property.

Alecto didn't care. Why should she?

Val could have Blaze and then some. They were very fitting for each other—both soulless and mean, a match made in Hel.

There wasn't much Alecto wouldn't have done to be one of them.

"Dad." Andro's whine brought Alecto back from her thoughts. "Stop it."

"What, child?" Rufus huffed a laugh. "I'm telling Alatar the truth. Your rockey game has gotten weak since you started the piano class again."

Andro's brown face was flushed as he glowered at his father.

"Well, honey, it's normal," Octavia said, smoothing the wrinkle of Rufus's white shirt with her small hand. "It'll take some time to adjust to the new routine. But you know damn well our boy is capable of keeping his grades high while still being the star player."

"Yes, that's probably true. Blaze, are you ready for another season? Being the captain for the second year in a row is an honor. You're following in your old man's steps well."

Blaze met Rufus's gaze, briefly nodding as he dragged a hand over his dark hair, long tips of it falling right back on his forehead and temples.

"If he manages to pull away for long enough from drinking and women, then he should be able to lead the team into another winning season," Galliermo answered for Blaze, throwing a quick glance at Alecto before turning back to his son. "Will you, Blaze?"

"Yes, Father," Blaze replied gravely. "Of course."

Everything was handed to him on a silver platter, and yet, he failed to notice how lucky he was to *belong*. Blaze belonged in a way that Alecto never could, and for that alone, she hated him more every day he spent wasting.

6

History of the Sexuality of Witches was Alecto's favorite class at Venefica.

Not only because it tackled the issues of femininity and sexuality amongst the witches, but also because Professor Fallo was the only professor who didn't seem to get off humiliating and degrading her students.

It was a safe space.

The room where their lectures took place was bright and welcoming, the walls draped in creamy silk curtains, covering the old wooden panels that covered the majority of the academy's interior, still there from when all the buildings were built back in the eighteenth century.

There were pine shelves with dozens of books, green plants scattered between them, and everywhere else you could find a space—on the windowsills, on the professor's desk, and even on the polished hardwood floor.

Professor Fallo herself was damn eye candy, with her wide hips and plump thighs always covered with silk skirts reaching her elegant calves, her round breasts hidden behind delicate matching shirts.

The woman looked maybe in her mid-thirties, with barely any signs of aging on her deep brown skin, except for a few light lines along her lips and in the creases of her eyes. But Alecto was sure that she was way older than that—Professor Fallo's signature was on the Venefica founders' agreement.

"Let's start by going over your thoughts from last week's reading," the professor announced, leaning her hip against her desk, careful to not disturb the plants.

Her gaze traveled around the class, no hands rising to volunteer.

Alecto could have been the one to answer. She did the reading and even wrote down ten thoughts that the text had prompted before the party last Friday, but Alecto wasn't a teacher's pet.

She was not going to speak unless asked.

"I see," Professor Fallo said with a sigh. "I know it's terrible and unfair to have a class on Monday mornings when all the good parties take place over the weekend. I get it. But I thought that reading some good erotica would put you in a mood for a good week ahead, don't you think?"

A bad thing about Professor Fallo treating them as equals was that most students took advantage of it. Yet, at her words, a few heads around the class that were just lowered snapped up, eyes wide.

"Erotica?" Garcia asked, blinking.

"Yes, Miss Torth. If you had read what I gave you, then you would know that we're reading the *Diaries of Hell Galliano*, the infamous courtesan who was responsible for starting the war between humans known as World War I."

Now Professor Fallo had the attention of the whole class.

Alecto lowered her head, opened her notebook with her notes and plenty of tiny illustrations everywhere around the text, and prepared to take notes. But Professor Fallo didn't get to explain too much about their reading before there was a knock on the door.

When the door opened, an electric current passed through Alecto.

She slowly dragged her gaze to the door to find a pair of deep amber eyes staring at her. A breath hitched inside her throat.

He was real.

The Guardian they conjured last Friday night was real.

And right now, he was standing in front of the whole class, dressed in Venefica's crimson uniform, two buttons of his white shirt loose, the tie hanging over his shoulder casually. There was a book in his hand, and while his stance was casual, face bored, his eyes were scorching fire.

He was also not alone. The Dean's secretary, Miss Bellthrove, stood right beside him. She passed a paper to Professor Fallo, who read over it as she walked to her desk.

"We have a late newcomer, I see. Rogue Smolder," the professor said, writing something down in one of her notebooks. "Take a seat, Mr. Smolder. You're just in time for the new reading we're starting, so I'm sure it'll be easy to catch up with the rest of the class. And your classmates will be more than happy to help if you have any questions."

Like Hel they would.

One glance at the classroom was enough for Alecto to see all the eyes turning towards him as he advanced further, strolling through the narrow paths between desks.

Everyone, even the boys, looked at him as if he was one of the Gods walking the earth.

He sure as Hel looked like one.

Too late, Alecto realized that he was striding towards her, to the only free seat left in the whole classroom. His book landed on the table first, and then the Guardian slid behind the desk, his presence sucking out the air around them.

The smell of the forest pine filled Alecto's nostrils, and she had to grip her pen very hard to not lose her shit. Val, Jolene, Blaze, and Andro were all staring at her over their shoulders, their eyes wide.

Finally, Val's lips curled up, and she winked before turning her attention back to Professor Fallo, who stood by the chalkboard writing something.

There was something in Blaze's eyes that made Alecto's stomach turn, but she turned away, ignoring him. Rogue's gaze lingered on her, so she turned her head to the side.

"We're going to be partners for this class." His voice was rough and deep, rumbling from the depths of his chest, and Alecto's toes curled inside her shoes against her will.

She cleared her throat. "So it seems."

A wicked grin raised one corner of his lips, and a dimple appeared. "You don't look so happy about it."

He wasn't real, was he?

He couldn't be real—just a bundle of magic.

But the boy next to her seemed real enough. And he smelled real.

Flesh and blood, bone and muscle right beside her.

"It's too early to say" was all Alecto said before turning her attention back to the professor.

7

Alecto flinched when Blaze pushed the Guardian against the wall next to the sink. *Hard.* "What the Hel do you think you're doing?"

Immediately after the class was over, Val led them to the common bathrooms next to Professor Fallo's classroom.

"This is not what we fucking bargained for," Andro said, gesturing with his long hands.

A Guardian showing up at Venefica as one of the students was *definitely* not how they planned the whole thing.

Val walked closer to the Guardian and placed a hand on Blaze's shoulder. Immediately Blaze backed off, walking away from the creature, allowing Val to take the lead.

"Rogue Smolder," Val mused, tilting her head to the side. "It wasn't written in the Book that Guardians get to choose their own names, let alone attend an academy of their own accord."

The Guardian huffed a laugh, leaning the back of his head against the tiled wall, seemingly not bothered by being cornered.

"A Guardian?" he asked, arching a brow. "I'm no Guardian."

"You're the *exact* copy of the Guardian we summoned," Jolene said.

"Well, to be fair, we haven't checked the—" Andro began, but Val shut him up by lifting her palm.

"Who are you then if you're *not* the Guardian we summoned?" Val asked.

That damn dimple appeared as he smiled. "I'm the demon summoned to serve at your will."

Rogue lifted one arm, tugging the crimson school jacket up to reveal three black lines wrapped around his forearm. The lines that indicated the bondage between a witch and a demon from Hel they summoned to do their bidding.

"Shit" was all Alecto could muster.

Alecto's heart leaped in her chest as the door to the bathrooms opened. Two girls stopped in the doorway the moment they took in the view of them cornering Rogue.

"What the fuck are you staring at?" Andro scoffed, coming to stand in front of them.

Val pushed past Andro, getting into their faces. "Go. Get the fuck out of here," she barked. "If I catch you staring like that at either of us on campus, I'm going to rip your eyeballs out and make a necklace of them."

The girls whirled on their heels and hurried outside without another word or a glance.

Alecto bit down on her lip to stifle a laugh.

"What the fuck, Val?" To Alecto's surprise, Blaze was the first to snap at their leader, his eyes blazing. "A *demon*? Seriously? What the fuck were you thinking?"

"I didn't do shit," Val said, turning towards them. "We used the spell that specifically calls for a *Guardian*. Even I'm not crazy enough to summon a fucking *demon*."

"Yet here I am," the demon drawled, his eyes sparkling with amusement.

Alecto had never met a demon before. They were dangerous and deadly, so witches kept their distance. Demons were supposed to rip witches' hearts out when summoned or trap their souls and drag them to Hel.

Rogue didn't look like any of the monsters in their textbooks. Neither did he look particularly vicious or interested in their souls.

In fact, he appeared to be somewhere in between light amusement and casual boredom. Which, of course, unsettled Alecto greatly.

"How the fuck did this happen?" Andro hissed. "And how the fuck is he bound to us?" He turned to Rogue, eyeing him carefully. "Are you really bound to us?"

"Yes, the binding is real," the demon said with a heavy sigh. "I'm bound to the witches who summoned me to serve them by blood until I'm released from my service."

"Blood!" Jolene shrieked, pointing a finger at Val. "I bet it happened because you used blood magic to empower the spell."

"Bitch, don't point your finger at me," Val sneered. "And that's not true. There is no way using blood magic summons—"

"How the fuck do you know?" Alecto interrupted, spreading her arms. "We haven't had an introduction in blood magic. Only the fourth years have the lectures. So we could have triggered something without even knowing."

"*Or* someone from the other Houses could have done that for us," Blaze suggested, his finger tracing the line of his sharp jaw as he eyed Alecto. "There were a lot of students at our party that night."

"*What?*" Alecto snapped at him. "Even the fourth years from the House of Dragons wouldn't be stupid enough to pull something like this. Calling a demon for a Game is a risk."

"Wouldn't they now?" Blaze challenged, arching a brow.

"Well, it doesn't matter now," Val interrupted, walking over to sit on the corner of one sink. She fished out a pouch from her pocket and started to roll a new blunt. "What matters right now is that we have an actual demon in our possession. A demon who's willing to do our bidding for us."

Alecto's stomach turned at the pure wickedness of Val's smile.

"You can't be seriously entertaining this, Val," Jolene said.

"You're going to get us all expelled," Andro agreed. "Or he's going to get us killed."

Alecto's head was going to explode. As if the fact that she was hungover wasn't enough, as always the Inner Circle were determined to argue with each other. She sighed, rubbing her left temple.

"I can't kill or harm the witches I'm bound to in any way," Rogue chimed in, rolling his eyes.

Alecto bet he found their little bickering amusing. For them, it was their futures on the line. Their lives.

The Game was serious. The future of the House of Snakes lay with their generation now. And Alecto wanted to win badly. She *needed* their House to win. If they lost another year, they might not be in the top four for much longer.

If the House of Snakes were not in the top four, their power would dwindle. And the prestige and protection that came with it.

The only reason why Alecto even agreed to go to Venefica was because she belonged to the House everyone feared. If nobody respected the Snakes her life might as well be Hel. Even more than it was already.

"Be smart about it," Val continued, her voice surprisingly calm. Her tongue slid down the length of the paper, wetting the sticky strip right before she sealed it. As she lit the blunt, sweet smoke filling the air, she added, "We're guaranteed to win the Game this year with his help. And anyway, it's not as if we can go to the Dean and say that we have a demon we didn't summon on our hands. He won't believe us. So the only way I see is going along with it."

Alecto didn't want to admit it, but of course Val was right. It was a slippery slope, and a game so dangerous Alecto wasn't sure any of them would be able to play. But maybe…

"Can anyone guess that you're a demon?" Alecto asked Rogue. "Can anyone *sense* you? The Dean or one of the professors?"

A wolfish grin graced his face. "Not unless I want them to."

"Are you seriously entertaining this, Alecto?" Jolene asked.

Alecto just stared at her.

"You can't be fucking serious," Jolene growled, turning her back to them. "You're the last person I expected to be on Val's side in this madness."

Neither do they have it in them to be cruel or merciless.

It was easy for Jolene to object, when her life wouldn't change if the Snakes lost. Maybe Jolene, just like the others, didn't believe Alecto had the guts to do what needed to be done.

It was time Alecto proved them all wrong.

"Why don't we give it a spin, mm?" Blaze asked, leaning against the wall next to Rogue.

"I vote for giving it a little spin," Val said, lifting her hand with the blunt in the air.

Alecto also raised one hand, Blaze catching her gaze before lifting one of his.

There was no mistaking the smirk dancing at the corner of his lips or the way his eyes flickered.

Alecto bet he also didn't believe she had it in her to stand up for herself and her House. To actually do something that went against the rules to help them win.

"Fine," Andro said, sighing heavily as if the burden of the whole world weighed on him. "Let's see where this gets us. But I'm warning you right now—if the Dean finds out, I'm throwing you all under the carriage."

Alecto snorted. Of course Alessandro would be the first one to bolt.

There was only one more vote left.

"Jolene?" Val drawled, her voice sweet as honey as she started singing the old mortal song. "Jolene, Jolene…"

"Please just agree before she sings more of that goddamn song," Alecto said, placing her palms over her ears.

Alecto hated mortal country music.

Val continued to sing the next line.

"FINE," Jolene almost screamed, lifting her palms in the air. "I'll agree. Just stop fucking singing."

"Oh, shut up. You love it when I sing," Val shot back.

So it was set.

They agreed to carry out their plan with an actual demon instead of a Guardian.

When Alecto once more met Rogue's deep amber gaze, there was something very intense in it that made hairs rise on her arms and neck.

There could be only trouble when it comes to Rogue. It was written on his smooth golden-brown forehead. Alecto could only hope that trouble found other Houses and not theirs.

"How are we going to deal with him being around though?" Jolene asked.

"Simple," Val said, hopping off the sink. "I'm going to let one of the new pledges go, so there will be one spot left free. Rogue is going to take that spot and officially be property of the House of Snakes."

As always, Val had it all covered.

8

Val rapped her knuckles on the chalkboard floating in the air, drawing Blaze's attention back to her. The chunky piece of white chalk was working hard scribbling something on the board.

Blaze hadn't even noticed how his attention had wandered from the meeting to Alecto, who was folded in a leather chair in the corner of their home library. With her chin propped on her hand, she eyed Val intently.

All thirteen members of the House of Snakes—Rogue included—had gathered for their monthly meeting that took place every full moon without any exceptions.

Even if you were missing a limb, on the verge of bleeding out, you still had to be at the meeting on time, or Val, the High Priestess of their House, could expel you.

"Rogue Smolder," Val announced. "He's new to Venefica this year. Transferred from Hollowbay University. And he just joined the Snakes." She paused, eyeing the witches. "We had to say goodbye to that first year, whatever her name was, to make space. Which should remind every one of you that if you're not legacy, your place here is never guaranteed."

Blaze barely held a laugh in.

How funny it was coming from Val, who pointedly was *not* legacy.

Of course, nobody said anything. Just a few nods and they were moving on to the next topic.

"Anyway, today we need to discuss our Game strategy for this year," Val continued. The piece of chalk was finally done with the scribblings. Val's magic grip loosened, and it plopped on the floor. "Last year we were real close to stealing the Tigers' Book. But we were not fast enough. This year, we can't afford to make the same mistake."

A few nods in agreement went around the room.

"Our target House this year is the House of Tigers. Again. So I wanna hear all ideas for—"

Blaze ignored the rest of Val's tirade as he dragged a finger over his jaw, eyes darting between Alecto and the chalkboard.

That kiss at the Ceremony was a bit more than Blaze anticipated. He was supposed to humiliate her in public.

Yet, that's not what happened.

Blaze could still feel the way Alecto's teeth sunk into his neck. The way her lips sucked his skin, leaving the mark behind.

Blaze was in control. Until suddenly, he wasn't anymore.

It absolutely annoyed the fuck out of him.

Who the fuck did this girl think she was?

To make matters even worse, Galliermo had to remind Blaze how big of a fucking shame he was, while Alecto's father praised her to the Gods, even though she was a fucking *half*.

When Blaze returned home for the dreaded family dinners next weekend, he wouldn't stop hearing about it.

Alecto's and Blaze's fathers were business partners and old friends, going all the way to when they both were members of the House of Snakes. How come Alecto's father looked at her with stars in his eyes, while Blaze's father couldn't wait for a moment to humiliate him?

What a massive bag of shit.

"Why don't we try one of the smaller Houses?" one of the girls asked. "The House of Monkeys or the House of Oxen surely have less protection around their Books."

Blaze recognized her face, being from the same House and all, but he couldn't recall her name.

To Blaze's and everyone else's surprise, it was Alecto who answered the girl. "Because we're one of the big four. We don't steal from lesser Houses if we want to continue being in the big four."

Ah, how interesting.

Alecto's eyes were icy cold as she glared at the girl, making her shrink into her seat by the bay window.

The tiny snarl curling her lips amused Blaze more than he would have liked.

Since when was Alecto Black so vicious?

"That's right." Val eyed Alecto with a pleased smile, tilting her head to the side. "Blaze, how's the preparation for the first attack?"

It took a moment for Blaze to drag his attention away from Alecto and realize it was his time to talk.

Blaze cleared his throat. "We're going to perform the locator spell on their Book. As we know they like to change location due to their protection wards being weaker." He paused and Val nodded. "I'm going in to steal the Gorms we need for the ritual from Professor Gabetown. Once I have it, we'll be ready to go."

Val jerked her chin. "Is anyone helping you with that?"

Blaze pouted, shaking his head.

His original plan was getting the newest pledges to steal the Gorms they needed from the Herbalism in Witchcraft professor. But they proved to be rather pissy about breaking into a classroom after hours to steal something their first week on campus.

Those motherfuckers were going to drive Blaze mad. All the boundaries and tiptoeing around the rules as if they were scared little does.

They were supposed to be the ruthless *and* fearless House of Snakes.

"Take Jolene with you," Val instructed.

"I'm *not* going to go anywhere with him," Jolene shot back, crossing her arms.

Blaze pretended to collect the tears from the corners of his eyes in his palm, but he couldn't hold the chuckle back.

"For fuck's sake," Val said, rolling her eyes. But she didn't push Jolene to agree. Instead, she turned to Alecto. "How about you? You have a good relationship with the professor. If Blaze fucks up, you can help smooth the situation."

Blaze was about to open his mouth to argue against such foolishness, but then an idea bloomed inside his mind.

An idea so wicked that Blaze almost leaped out of his chair with a happy yelp.

This would be a perfect opportunity to get back to Alecto for that hickey action.

Blaze's own personal revenge.

"I don't think—" Alecto said.

"Wonderful idea," Blaze cut her off. When she shot him a deadly look, his smile only widened. "I'll take Alecto with me, and we'll be done with the preparation by the end of this week."

"That's what I wanna hear," Val agreed.

Clearly Alecto had forgotten her place. It was time Blaze reminded her.

A fter the meeting was over, instead of going to the town for drinks with the rest of the House, Blaze decided to retreat into his room and spend the rest of the afternoon catching up on sleep.

Blaze's room was on the third floor of their brownstone. He occupied one of the two rooms taking over the whole floor, the other belonging to Val.

When she took over the leadership position from the old leader, Cassandra Valenti, and made Blaze her Second, she convinced him it was appropriate, knowing their status.

Blaze didn't argue, mostly because it offered a quiet and isolated corner for him to work on his craft when he wasn't in practice or drinking.

Once he slammed the door behind him, he shrugged off his black short-sleeved shirt, dropping it on the leather armchair sitting by a large wooden bookshelf covering the whole side of one room.

Walking over to open all the windows, he took the tucked-in white tank out of his skinny black jeans and let it hang out messily.

In one of the antique nightstands standing by his large king-size bed, he fished out a pack of cigarettes and an old metal lighter with a skull that Andro got him from the mortal world as a present last Yule.

Blaze popped a cigarette between his lips, sitting on one of the windowsills, the view through his window opening up to the park that separated the Old Darly from the New Darly, or as locals simply called Darly these days.

Just as he was about to exhale the smoke, his door cracked open, a black head appearing.

"What do you want?" Blaze asked, turning back to the window as Val slipped inside his room, closing the door behind her.

She stayed silent for a moment, lurking by the door.

"Have fun last night?"

Blaze shrugged, leaning his head back against the wall. "It was as boring as I anticipated."

Val's heels made a dull sound as she walked from the door to the window. Slowly, she leaned a shoulder against the wall opposite Blaze.

"Then what was that all about?" she inquired, her voice dangerously sweet. "Bringing Alecto out of line, standing with the third and fourth years instead of being where she was supposed to be?"

Now Blaze turned to face her.

"Why do you care, Val? It's not as if that ruined your fucking performance."

She straightened her spine, pulling her shoulders back. "People noticed."

"Val, get the fuck out of my hair. Nobody fucking did."

"Your *father* did, asshole," she hissed.

Ah, of course.

"So what? He hates her just as much I do, if not more. In his eyes, she's just a half breed."

"And I'm just a filthy street rat," Val sneered, lowering herself on the windowsill. "We had an agreement."

Blaze would barely call what they had an agreement.

Val wanted his father's recognition and access to him because he owned half the fucking Avalon Hills, and the only thing Val ever wanted was to go into politics. Having the support of Galliermo Leveau would guarantee her a career in the city.

Blaze couldn't tell her that he didn't hold any power over his father and his decisions. So he just let her trail with him, which was more than enough to satisfy her.

For Blaze, this loose agreement guaranteed him a date to all the charity events and balls his father and mother dragged him to, not having to always look for a pretty whore to dangle by his side.

Val knew the people, she knew how to talk, she knew how to act. He just had to show up and not piss off his father too early in the evening.

"We still have an agreement," Blaze scoffed, rolling his eyes. "Just because I decided to play around, it doesn't change anything."

Val's eyes flickered with obvious dissatisfaction, but she didn't say anything else. One of her hands landed on Blaze's thigh, black nails digging into his flesh.

Warmth surged through him, gathering right at his groin, and he swallowed hard.

"I don't really like you being with Alecto in front of your father," Val said, her voice sweet as honey as her hand massaged his thigh with those skilled fingers. "What if he and her father suddenly come up with the idea that you two would look great as an *item*?"

Blaze snorted, turning his face away to the window.

Val was fucking crazy, worrying about something that would never happen.

Blaze's father would have rather drowned him than let Blaze marry a half breed, a witch without pure blood, even if she was the daughter of Alatar Black.

And it's not as if Blaze would ever entertain such an idea.

But it was getting rather annoying seeing Val so territorial of him. She didn't want him. She wanted the power that came with being a Leveau, with being at the mercy of his family.

It didn't bother Blaze. At least he didn't think it did. But it also didn't give her the right to fuck his brain with her stupid insecurities.

"Don't piss me off" was all he said, flicking the butt of the cigarette out the window, watching it fall to the stone path that rounded the house.

"Mmm," Val hummed, her hand moving higher, body leaning forwards. "Someone's in a mood today. How about I fix that for you, honey?"

Blaze met Val's gaze, a familiar wicked smile gracing her beige face as her fingers found the zipper, sliding it down. When she gripped his cock in her hand, it was already rock hard.

Blaze was still horny as fuck after last night's ritual, even if Alecto ruined his mood completely.

Because of it, he couldn't get himself off with one of the many girls so eager to ride that sweet Leveau dick, so a few touches and his cock was hard, straining against his jeans.

Val chuckled as she freed him from the tight pants, gripping the base of his cock harder as she popped her tongue out just a bit and licked the very tip of it.

Blaze's dick twitched in response, and he released a long breath as he watched her take the tip fully in her mouth.

Val was many things—psychotic, a control freak, and sometimes totally batshit crazy. But if she was exceptionally good at one thing, then it was sucking dick.

Blaze's muscles tensed as she bobbed her little head up and down, moaning and gasping over his dick, sending waves of intense pleasure through him.

"Ah, *shit*," he hissed as Val threw herself on him, his dick hitting the very back of her throat before she retreated, inhaling wet air.

Well, there were also the blow jobs that Blaze got out of their agreement.

He never asked for it, but Val was a girl with initiative. She was ready to do whatever it took to get what she wanted.

And Val had her eyes on Blaze since their first year at Venefica.

What a score it must have been for her to find out that the Leveau in her grade was *fuckable*.

Val worked her tongue around him like a pro, sucking and licking and moaning to the Gods, one of her hands gripping the base of his cock hard while the other one played with his balls.

Blaze closed his eyes, his abs tensing as his release was getting closer, warmth gathering in his groin, ready to erupt.

As if knowing he was close, Val leaned forwards again, taking him in until she was choking on his dick. Blaze grabbed her short hair, pulling her back, and then unloaded himself with an involuntary grunt.

Val stayed close, leaning on her hands as she found his gaze. She opened her mouth to reveal a mouth full of him before gulping it down, not forgetting to lick her lips as if she'd just had the most delicious dessert.

She winked, smiling at him, and Blaze reached out a hand to caress her cheek.

"Still the most delicious dick I've ever had."

If Blaze didn't know it was all for show, a part of her careful manipulation, he might have been impressed. He might have even believed that she enjoyed sucking him just as much as she acted.

But Blaze wasn't stupid. And neither was he naive.

It didn't stop him from getting good head on a regular basis though.

Without another word, Val rose to her feet.

Blaze hummed a tune under his breath, another cigarette already resting between his lips as he tucked himself back in. His gaze followed Val to the door, turning back to the window only when she silently slipped through.

He had long lost any ideas of anyone staying after, spreading comfortably on his bed for long, lazy conversations.

It's not as if he ever gave anyone a chance anyway.

9

Alecto had three lectures on Wednesday, but because of the large gaps between them, she ended up getting back home well after eight in the evening.

When Alecto entered the brownstone, she bumped into someone's hard chest.

When she lifted her eyes, opening her mouth to apologize, it was Rogue glaring down on her.

"Excuse you," he said, cocking a brow.

"Yeah, excuse you."

Rogue didn't move. He stood there in the narrow corridor, blocking her path to the stairs.

"You have something to say?" she asked.

A smirk appeared on his brown face, and Alecto's stomach flipped at the way those sensuous lips curled.

"You seem to not like me," he said. She blinked. "I just can't figure out why."

"I don't dislike you," Alecto assured him. "I barely fucking know you. And excuse me if I don't go drooling after you, knowing that you're a literal *demon* from Hel."

Alecto was drooling over Rogue, just like all the other witches. How could she not? He was handsome with his dimple, intense eyes, and muscles straining hard against all of his shirts.

But Alecto would never give him the satisfaction of knowing that.

Rogue huffed a low laugh, shaking his head, and his short curls bounced playfully.

"You seem to be the only one bothered by the fact that I'm a demon," he observed. "I won't hurt you. Nothing to be afraid of."

Alecto smirked, pushing past him to climb the stairs to her bedroom.

The last thing she was interested in was bonding with their personal demon errand boy. Alecto might have agreed to use him for their own gain in this year's Game, but it didn't mean she liked it.

The Inner Circle were surprised when she was with Val on it. And that pleased Alecto. It meant that she was on the right track.

When Alecto opened the door to her room, she almost jumped out of her skin. Blaze was spread out on her bed on his back, casually playing with something in his hands.

That *something* being her silver bullet vibrator.

"What the fuck are you doing here?" Alecto rushed towards him. "And what the fuck are you doing going through my drawers?"

She climbed on the bed, reaching for the vibrator, but Blaze was faster, jumping off the bed with a satisfied smirk.

"I was just looking for a lighter because mine was dead," Blaze replied, shrugging. He glanced at the silver bullet resting between his fingers, glittering in the dim light of her bedroom. "That's something you only find in a mortal world. How fascinating."

Alecto scrambled off the bed, anger mixed with embarrassment heating her cheeks. She grabbed for Blaze's hand, but he lifted it over his head.

"Give it back, you asshole," she growled.

Blaze only laughed, wild and untamed. Alecto didn't think she had seen him as amused as he was right now. At least not with her.

"Oh, you naughty little witch," he teased. There was a challenge in his eyes. "Come and take it from me."

Alecto jumped, but it wasn't any use. Blaze was way taller than her, and she had to climb a fucking ladder to reach that far over her head.

Alecto jumped again, but instead of reaching for the toy, she threw herself at Blaze. Caught off guard, he lost his balance for a moment, stumbling backwards. His back and head hit the wall, and he cursed under his breath.

For a moment, he lowered his hand, and that was enough for Alecto to snatch the toy out of his palm.

Alecto pushed herself away from him, leaving him leaning against the wall, and shoved the bullet back into her drawer, slamming it shut and pushing her thigh against it.

A wicked grin spread across Blaze's face as he stepped away from the wall, scratching the back of his head.

"So savage." He tsked. "Tell me, does it really work as well as everyone claims?"

"How about you get one yourself and find out?"

She wasn't about to tell Blaze that it worked *better* than everyone claimed and that it was basically the only thing that could get her off.

"It's already after sunset. You're late," Blaze announced, glancing at the watch on his wrist, tangled together with a gazillion silver bracelets and cuffs.

Alecto threw her crimson uniform jacket on the bed, the imprint of where Blaze just lay still fresh on her white sheets, and went around it to the dresser.

"I had three lectures and large gaps between them. I got here the moment my class was finished."

"Well then, let's roll," he insisted.

Alecto threw him a mean glance and went into her bathroom, slamming the door behind her.

Blaze was an entitled asshole. It made her blood boil having to go anywhere with him. Why would Val think it was a good idea to assign them to work together?

Alecto growled in frustration, stripping out of her pleated uniform skirt and white shirt, kicking off the black knee-high boots. Then she pulled on a tight black turtleneck and a pair of flared black jeans.

Without much thought, she put her boots back on. They had a heel, but Alecto didn't think they'd need to run anywhere, so it wasn't a risky business.

After Alecto pulled her hair back with a tortoiseshell clip, she returned to her room to find Blaze leaning against her desk, looking bored as ever.

When his eyes landed on her, he cocked an eyebrow. "Ready?"

The only answer he got was a roll of her eyes.

Their Herbalism in Witchcraft lectures took place in a massive greenhouse built like two centuries ago, with the glass fogged up and dirty from the age. It stood on the northern side of the campus, right on the edge of the rockey field.

As Blaze and Alecto made their way through the campus, neither of them spoke, Blaze striding in an easy step, hands shoved in the pockets of his black jeans, only occasionally humming something to himself.

Alecto tried to push the weird feeling of embarrassment prickling at her chest as they got closer to the greenhouse, but it was so fresh, her cheeks were still hot. She was grateful that the night hid her shame. Blaze would probably find a way to use it against her.

As soon as they reached the main path leading through the large garden to the greenhouse entrance, Blaze snatched her wrist, tugging her after him off the main path to the smaller one going around the greenhouse.

"What the fuck are you doing?" she hissed.

Blaze turned back to her, stopping as his gaze met hers.

"Are you seriously thinking of going in to steal something from the professor through the main entrance?" he asked, arching a brow. Alecto blinked. He had a point. "Yeah, thought so."

She followed him in silence, her heart hammering in her chest.

Alecto wasn't a problematic child growing up. She was raised to be a lady, always polite and considerate of her behavior.

It was just appropriate for a girl from a family like hers.

Even as Alecto grew up into the young woman she was today, she never stopped being the pristine daughter her mother would be proud of.

But she had to learn to navigate the cruel world of the witches to survive. Which, she learned recently, sometimes involved doing rather questionable things.

Like breaking into a classroom after hours and stealing from the professor.

Finally, they reached the back of the greenhouse where the path ended, the bushes of black roses spreading around them. Blaze let go of her hand, dipping closer to the greenhouse, his long fingers trailing the edges of the glass panel.

Alecto stood beside him. She doubted anyone would see them, even if they were at the garden at this hour. It was pitch black, and the cloudy sky hid all the stars and the blood moon.

For a moment Alecto wondered whether Blaze pulled off a few spells to make sure that the sky stayed dark and angry tonight.

There was a quiet thud, and Blaze grunted as the glass came off in one piece. He took it off the metal frame, leaning it on the side against the greenhouse.

Then, he straightened, looking back at Alecto.

"Ladies first," Blaze said, gesturing at the opening in the greenhouse. Alecto couldn't see his face well, but she was certain there was a smirk at the corner of his lips.

She didn't allow herself to hesitate, ducking inside the greenhouse.

The glass panel opened a way to a little observatory. Alecto stopped in the middle of the path, large tables lined with different plants, flowers, most of them sleeping in the darkness, perched on both sides of it.

Before Alecto could complain about the lack of light, Blaze shoved something into her palm, his hard chest so close to her back it warmed her even through all the layers of clothing.

Alecto's muscles tensed, but she refused to step away. Instead, she turned to him, their faces so close they shared a breath.

In her palm rested a long, thin glass stick. Alecto gripped it tight and started shaking it, Blaze doing the same with the stick in his hand.

They were standing in the dark for a moment, both shaking their glass sticks until Alecto's started warming up in her hand.

Soon, the illuminating glow appeared, softly lighting up enough space for them to find whatever they needed. The humming from the firebirds trapped inside the glass stick wasn't loud enough to wake the plants or attract other types of attention.

Alecto whirled on her heel, striding down the long path from Blaze towards the main part of the greenhouse, where Professor Gabetown's classroom was.

"Leave it to you to wear high heels to steal something in secret," Blaze snorted.

Blaze was right. It was careless of her. In the dead silence of the night, Alecto's high heels were very much the only thing anyone would hear.

Fucking idiot.

She wasn't used to sneaking around in the classrooms after hours; how was she supposed to know? And either way, high-heeled boots were the only shoes that went with her flared black jeans. She would have needed to change the whole outfit if she wanted to wear combat boots.

Finally, they reached the double glass door, and Alecto carefully opened them. She took two steps down and turned to Blaze.

"Well?" she asked. "Do you know where the professor keeps the Gorms?"

Blaze strolled past her, his shoulder almost brushing her chest, and Alecto barely stopped herself from taking a step backwards.

"It should be here," he mused, going over the large glass terrariums lining the only exposed brick wall in the room.

Alecto tugged at her turtleneck. It was stuffy and hot inside the green-house, even at this hour. There was probably a spell cast that kept the temperature perfect for the plants even when the nights got colder, especially in the fall.

"Ah," Blaze's voice came from the very end of the shelving unit, and he looked around. "I need a container of some sort."

Of course Blaze came unprepared.

Moron.

Alecto looked around, trying to figure out where Professor Gabetown could possibly keep glass containers he liked to use in the class for experiments.

She went through his desk, searching each drawer, before turning to the console by the other wall. There had to be something in there. She doubted the professor had another place for his storage apart from what was in the room.

When she finally opened the last door, a large array of glass containers lined the shelves.

"Bingo," Alecto muttered, grabbing for a mason jar with a metal lid.

Suddenly, the light in the room went on.

"Miss Black?" There was no mistaking Professor Gabetown's voice.

Alecto straightened, slowly turning to face him. She stole a glance at the terrariums, but Blaze was nowhere to be found.

"Care to explain why I've found you in the middle of the night in my greenhouse?" the professor asked, his eyes calm but clearly disappointed.

Alecto blinked, looking around, still clenching the glass jar in her hand.

Blaze had dipped. That motherfucker had left her.

Alecto opened her mouth to explain, but no words came out.

"I suppose it's for the Game, isn't it?" the professor inquired with a heavy sigh. "I'm afraid, Miss Black, rules are rules."

She exhaled, anger burning her chest, but nodded.

"Yes, Professor," she mumbled.

"Please put the jar back in place and come with me to the Dean's office," he instructed. She obeyed, putting the jar back and closing the door. "A month of detention will be a suitable punishment, don't you think?"

She was going to kill Blaze.

10

"You really didn't have to do it," Andro said, shaking his head as they strode through the campus towards the rockey field. "We're supposed to go against other Houses, not members of our own House, you dumb fuck."

"I had a score to settle with Alecto," Blaze replied. "I don't understand what the big deal is."

Blaze barely registered Andro's hand grabbing the front of his T-shirt and whirling him around, his back slamming the stone wall of the cafeteria hall. Blaze blinked at Andro's face just a few inches away.

With all that sass and glamour, it was easy to forget Andro had the muscles to beat anyone's ass.

"What the fuck is wrong with you?" Andro hissed. "I love you like a brother, you know that. But Alecto is one of us. One of our Inner Circle. I'm not going to stand by and watch whatever the fuck you and Val are trying to pull off here."

Blaze pushed Andro back. "Why do you assume Val's involved?" Blaze dragged a hand over his hair. "This one is actually all on me."

"Well, congratulations, dipshit. You're being an asshole all on your own!"

Blaze growled, straightening his T-shirt, but Andro didn't seem to be backing down.

"Leave her the fuck alone," Andro warned. "I'm serious. Whatever the fuck is going on between you two, you need to solve it quickly, or the other Houses are going to figure out that something's up. And you know damn well what they do when they find a weakness."

Yes, Blaze knew well enough.

He was the one who could usually sniff out other people's weaknesses and use them against them.

Everyone remembered Genevieve LaBronx from the House of Dragons. She was Blaze's proudest work to this day.

The girl had to leave Venefica last year after Blaze and the Inner Circle were done with her.

"You just like to ruin my fun, don't you?" Blaze murmured as they fell back into step.

"If that's your idea of fun, then I must say that you have some serious issues, brother."

Well, Andro wasn't entirely wrong.

But still, in Blaze's book, getting Alecto a few afternoons in the detention was just a means to put her back into her place. To get back the power he had lost that day at the Ceremony.

Now, they were even, back to square one. Blaze was again in control.

"Leveau!" Coach called for Blaze the moment he and Andro stepped foot on the field.

Blaze left Andro by the bench, jogging towards where the coach stood, his broad shoulders and six-foot-five figure as intimidating as it ever got with men.

"Coach." Blaze came to a stop.

Coach's glare was trying to drill a hole in his head.

"You remember what we talked about at the end of last season?"

Blaze nodded.

How could he ever forget the conversation he and his coach had, with his father present, of course, because the only thing Galliermo cared about when it came to Blaze was his professional rockey career?

Don't drink, don't smoke, don't party anymore, the coach had said that day. *You need to be in top shape and keep up your grades so the Dean won't have a reason to not let you play.*

"Then you know what I'm going to tell you right now." Coach's brows rose all the way to his hairline. "I want you leading practice every morning.

At sunrise. I don't care how busy you think you are or how important the Game is. You're here every morning before lectures, or I'll find a new captain."

Blaze squared his shoulders but only gave a curt nod.

It was tempting to say fuck you and walk off, leaving the field behind and never playing rockey again.

But it would only hurt Blaze.

Rockey was the only thing Blaze had for himself. All the glory and worship were due to his skills and abilities on the field and not because of his name.

It was the only reason he still showed up every day, despite hating the future his father had in mind for him as a professional player in the Premier League.

"Also," the coach added, taking a step closer. "Lay off the booze, Leveau. If I see you with a drink in hand, I'm going to send you to detention on the weekends so that you won't have time to get wasted. Am I making myself clear?"

"Yes, Coach."

Coach grunted, clasping a hand over his shoulder, almost sending Blaze sprawling down to the ground.

"Go warm up now," he instructed, glancing back at the field where the rest of the team was stretching already. "After we're going to look over the new players and see which ones are fit."

Without another word, Blaze jogged off to where Andro was sitting on the grass, stretching his legs while still managing to engage in some serious flirting with one of the newbie players.

"Get on your feet, ass hat," Blaze said, tugging at one of his dreads. "Let's run some laps."

Andro slapped away his hand, quickly getting to his feet, and soon they fell into a jog side by side.

"What did Coach want?"

"The usual," Blaze said, rolling his eyes. He dragged a hand over his hair, pushing it off his face. "Don't drink, don't do this, do that."

Whatever.

Blaze knew exactly what he needed to do to win this season, to be just good enough to keep up and keep everyone else off his back.

"Oh, and practice every morning at sunrise," he told Andro.

"He fucking hates us," Andro whined as they finished their first lap around the large field.

Blaze huffed a laugh.

Some days it seemed as if the whole world hated them.

When they finished the second lap, Gabe from the House of Tigers and one of his lackeys joined them.

The Tigers were the weakest House out of the big four, in Blaze's opinion.

Yet they were the most fucking annoying.

"It's looking like the Snakes are not in the best shape this year," Gabe said, smirking. "I guess losing the Game for the first time in over fifty years last year was a huge hit."

Blaze threw him his most dazzling smile, only increasing his pace.

"That was our first loss in half a century. When's your first win?"

"Yeah, dick bags," Andro said. "How about you worry more about keeping your Book safe and less about what we're doing."

Gabe's lackey barked a laugh. "*You* should worry about keeping your Book safe this year. You won't even know what hit you before it's too late."

Blaze snorted. "Doubt it. If you really *had* game, you wouldn't be talking about *having* game. Am I wrong, *Hulk*?"

"I don't know, Leveau." Gabe shrugged. "I thought Alecto would have told you all about it. That sweet piece of ass didn't seem to be complaining as I fucked her bent over the balcony at the boathouse."

Gabe bumped fists with his lackey, and they ran off laughing.

Blaze's chest swelled with hot rage, eyes tracking them as they moved further away.

It would be a pleasure breaking Gabe so bad he would beg Blaze to spare him.

"I think we need to talk with our High Priestess about that plan of hers." Blaze dragged a hand over his hair once more, increasing his speed. "The House of Tigers seem to be *begging* for extra special love this year."

11

Alecto's father was going to be *thrilled* when he found out that his precious little daughter had detention for the next month because she broke into a classroom after hours.

Oh, she wished she could tell them Blaze was also there.

She didn't know much of his relationship with his father. But something told her that Galliermo wouldn't be happy with his son being in such petty trouble.

Leveau men were above it all. Above getting caught for breaking in. They came in and took whatever they needed without consequences nor remorse.

But Alecto wasn't a snitch.

With a heavy sigh, Alecto opened the first two buttons of her white shirt and loosened her tie. She glanced around the library, then threw a glare towards a pile of dusty old books waiting for her.

She supposed having to work in the library for a month, a few hours a day, wasn't the worst thing to ever happen to her. At least they didn't make her clean the toilets or work in the kitchens.

Alecto would have thrown a tantrum.

She would have called her dad and pulled her precious daughter card to get her out of it, no matter what it would cost her later.

Just as she was about to start dusting the first book, the door to the library opened, and Miss Bellthrove entered, two tall figures coming in after her. She smiled at Alecto, glancing at her over the top of her round glasses.

"Well, dear, good news," the Dean's secretary announced, all chipper. "I have two gentlemen over here who are going to be joining you."

She gestured for the guys behind her back to come closer before she whirled on her kitten heel and, without another word, strode out of the library, leaving Alecto and the two men alone.

"Well, Rogue Smolder and Matias Santos," Alecto mused, crossing her arms. "Just when I thought my life couldn't get any better."

Rogue narrowed his eyes, taking in the view of the library and dusty books behind her. Matias cracked a smile, his tongue playing with his silver lip ring.

"Well, my life for sure just got so much better," he said, wiggling his eyebrows. "What did you do to get here, Black?"

"Oh, you know, the usual—smoking, drinking, fucking, sucking…"

"Stealing," said Rogue. She narrowed her eyes in a way that indicated that he should shut his mouth before giving anything else away.

Matias was a member of the House of Tigers. And he was Gabe's best friend.

The Tigers couldn't know about their little shtick because it would reveal Blaze's prank and what was about to happen. No matter how much Alecto hated Blaze, she wanted their House to win more than anything.

"Oh, yeah?" Matias asked. "What did you steal, baby girl?"

"Your heart."

That made Matias laugh, and Alecto didn't miss the way his eyes flickered as he rubbed his chin.

"So, how are we going to do this?" Rogue asked.

Alecto gestured to the books on the desk. "I suggest starting with dusting the books off, then we will be able to categorize them according to their genre and then by alphabet. After that, we'll only need to put them onto the shelves."

Rogue nodded, pouting, and started towards the other table on the left.

"Whatever the lady insists," Matias said.

They sorted through the books, wiping the dust with the cloth from each one, mostly in silence. Alecto kept shooting glances at Rogue, who was sorting through the books like a good little student. Which was, of course, very weird, because he was a demon. You'd think a creature like him wouldn't bother with such petty tasks, even if he was bound to the Snakes.

While Val seemed to have moved on from the fact that they summoned a demon instead of a Guardian, Alecto still didn't trust Rogue. He was too content with his current role for Alecto to feel comfortable.

"Don't they like have spells for shit like this?" Matias finally asked, tossing the book he finished cleaning on the desk with a loud *dunk*.

Alecto waved a hand at the massive dust cloud that rose in the air.

"Do you mind?" she hissed, closing her watering eyes. "Some of us have allergies."

Matias huffed a laugh. "Oh, right. I keep forgetting you're a half mortal with your weird little quirks."

It was kind of him to refer to Alecto as a half mortal rather than a half breed.

Pure-blooded witches never had things like allergies.

"I'm pretty certain they don't use magic to sort through the books so that students like us would have something to do when we get in trouble," Alecto said, pushing one book aside to the "cleaned" pile.

"I really don't see a point," Matias complained. "It's not as if dusting books and organizing shelves will stop us from doing it again."

Alecto arched a brow. "Well, well, do tell—what got you here, Santos?"

"Gabe and I egged the Rabbits' House."

Alecto laughed. "That's so fucking basic."

"Oh, you think?" Matias asked, leaning on the desk, drawing his tanned face closer to hers. "It might be basic, but it's very effective. It still stinks, even though they managed to clean most of the junk off."

"Rotten eggs?" Alecto widened her eyes. "That's just evil."

"You bet your tight ass." Matias winked, prodding his lip ring with the tip of his tongue.

Alecto narrowed her eyes on him but couldn't help the smirk.

Matias was a handsome guy, and she knew damn well that he had abs for days, being a swimmer *and* a rockey player.

Maybe this detention didn't have to be a punishment after all.

From the mischievous flicker in his brown eyes, it seemed he shared the sentiment.

12

"Do you think Jack's gonna fall for Rogue?" Blaze asked. "I feel like I haven't seen him enjoying the company of a man in a long time."

Val pouted as she considered his words.

"Have you seen Rogue?" she finally asked. "Everyone's gonna be panting over him the moment they see him."

"Yeah. We truly summoned the most handsome demon in Hel," Andro chimed in.

They reached a busy crossroad in the middle of Upper North Side in Avalon Hills, large pumpkin-shaped carriages gliding through air like fucking crazy. One whizzed so close to them that the wind ruffled Blaze's hair.

Bristled, Blaze raked a hand through his hair.

"Sure. Some might find him attractive." Blaze wasn't a fan of Rogue. Something was way off about the guy, something besides the fact that he was a demon. He just couldn't figure out what.

Val clicked her tongue. "Listen, next weekend I'm gonna walk into the Tigers' party with Rogue on my arm and every bitch will do anything in their power to have him. Purely so they could take something away from me."

Val had a point.

Witches were twisted like that.

Everyone was worth more when they belonged to someone else.

"Look at that," Andro chirped once they reached a skinny redbrick building with brown window shutters, perched between two luxurious white stone homes. "We came in at the perfect time to Gill's!"

Blaze took hold of the long brass handle, pulling the heavy wooden door open. He waited for Val and Andro to walk inside before following them.

Gill's was the most prominent custom spell shop in Avalon Hills, hence the location on the Upper North Side, where all the prominent witches of the city resided.

Though, from the *humble* look from the outside of the building and the way the inside didn't look even one bit better, you'd never guess that.

The interior was…lacking. Old, barely held together pine shelves were perched in every single corner of the shop. From the way they were leaned against the walls, it wasn't quite clear whether the walls held the shelves in place or the other way around.

Skulls of birds, cats, snakes, and Gods knew what hung from the concrete ceiling on thin ropes, and Blaze and Andro had to duck their heads unless they wanted the bones to keep hitting them in their faces.

Maybe that was the whole point…

At this time of the day, the shop was empty, with not a single soul inside. Two large ravens the size of Blaze's head sat on the counter, their black eyes wary.

"Oh, Gill," Val called, tapping her hand on the counter. One of the ravens croaked at her.

"What the fuck do you want?" Gill's smoky voice came through the archway into the back room. They didn't appear though.

No, Gill was going to make them wait.

So, Blaze wandered off, the shelf with the glass door on his left piquing his curiosity.

It was the only shelving unit that didn't look pathetic, and behind the glass lay an array of black silk cushions, beautiful, handcrafted jewelry pieces resting on top.

The shiny gold, the polished silver, and the whiteness of the mother-of-pearls were blinding all at once, so Blaze blinked, rubbing his eyes.

One piece in particular, a dainty pearl choker with a clasp shaped like a heart, drew Blaze's attention.

He was sure he had seen one exactly like this one before—

Ah, Alecto Black owned this same necklace.

How interesting.

It didn't escape his attention that Alecto had been completely ignoring him.

As if Blaze didn't even exist.

It had been a week since Blaze left Alecto in that greenhouse, since she got into trouble just as he had engineered, and she hadn't said a word to him ever since.

Blaze made sure that Professor Gabetown would get a message that someone had broken into the greenhouse, and he timed his retreat perfectly, so that she was occupied enough for him to sneak out before Professor Gabetown walked in on her.

Ah, it was worth every moment of her icy rage and silence.

Yet while Blaze was satisfied that he had gotten what he wanted, somehow he still managed to be annoyed. He just wasn't sure what about.

"Step the fuck away from the shelves, Leveau." Gill's croak jarred Blaze away from his thoughts, and he whirled on his heel towards the counter.

Finally, Gill decided to grace them with their presence.

They wore their grey hair in long, thin braids, cascading down their shoulders, all the way to the base of their back. Gill's deep brown eyes were almond-shaped, and when they landed on you, it seemed as if they were reaching right into your soul.

Blaze fought the shudder as he walked closer, reaching a hand to pet one of the ravens.

The bird's beak snapped, nearly taking off Blaze's finger.

Gill chuckled.

"Keep your limbs to yourself unless you're ready to say goodbye to them," they mused, one corner of their full mouth curving up.

"I'm happy to see you too, Han," Blaze murmured, watching the raven tiptoeing towards Gill.

They offered their arm, and the raven took it, swiftly climbing up to Gill's shoulder.

"Why the fuck are you here?" Gill asked. "You don't have anything better to do than to interrupt me?"

Val smirked, unbothered by Gill's rudeness.

Gill might have been rough around the edges, and they might have chased the Snakes out of their shop multiple times in the past, but everyone knew that Gill loved them.

Well, maybe not loved, but at least Gill *liked* the Snakes.

"You know why we're here, Gills," Val drawled. "Like every new academic year, we're in need of your best protection enchants for our House."

Gill scoffed, rolling their eyes.

"Why do you fuckers have to bother me every year with it?" they scolded. "I give you the best I've got, and yet you keep coming back and back, ungrateful, spoiled witchlings."

A sudden cough rattled Gill's chest.

But they just croaked, waved their hand, and resumed like nothing happened. "Maybe I should send my flock of ravens after you and see how fast you can run for wasting my fucking time every single September."

Val exchanged a glance with Blaze and Andro.

Andro's eyes were wide, but he didn't speak. Blaze had to rub his thumb over the corner of his mouth to hide a smirk.

"Listen, Gill," Val said. "We know you're the best of the best. That's why we're here. And don't tell me that you haven't found a better spell, a more improved spell from last year?"

Gill cursed them in a language Blaze wasn't familiar with as they disappeared into the back room.

"They scare me shitless," Andro whispered.

Blaze couldn't hold the laugh back. Val joined him, leaning her forehead into Andro's shoulder.

"How many lungs do you think a witch needs to survive?" Gill asked after they returned a moment later.

Blaze shrugged, guessing, "I'm fairly certain one would be enough, isn't it?"

Gill's wrist flickered so quick none of them registered it until Blaze was toppled over, heaving as the pain in his chest burned through him.

"You're right," they said, face blank. "So why don't you volunteer your lung for me, Leveau, huh? I've got a new spell I'm working on that needs a witch's lung. They're hard to come across."

Copper taste filled Blaze's mouth, and he closed his eyes, riding out the wave of pain, trying to stop himself from inhaling the air his lungs were desperate for.

Somehow, he managed to huff a cough, blood trickling down his lip onto the hardwood floor.

A moment later, the pain stopped.

Blaze straightened and brushed blood from his lip with the back of his hand.

"Here is the spell for the best protection ward I've got in my shop," Gill said, placing a golden card holder in front of them on the counter. "It's new, this year's making, so don't fuck my brain."

"And it's gonna protect against physical and nonphysical treats?" Val asked, picking up the cardholder and slipping it in her pocket.

Gill's eyes were not too kind. "As always, High Priestess. But it's gonna cost you more. You know, the better the spell you require each year, the more work goes in, the higher the price."

Val smirked.

She fished out a checkbook from her other pocket and swiftly penciled something in it. Without a word, Val turned the checkbook for Gill to see.

"Add one zero to that" was all Gill said.

One of the perks of being part of the House of Snakes was money.

"Pleasure doing business with you. As always," Val said and turned to leave.

"See you next year, Gill," Blaze called over his shoulder.

"Fuck off." Gill's voice carried to them right before the door slammed shut.

13

"Red," Matias guessed. He sat on one of the desks, legs swinging. His mouth was lazily working a piece of gum, eyes intently watching Alecto.

"Guess again, pretty boy."

Matias hummed.

Alecto had been laboring over the books in this library for almost a week now, and she couldn't be happier that it was almost Friday.

The good thing about her detention was that she had time to actually think about what she was going to do to get back at Blaze for leaving her in trouble. Last year, Alecto would have left it alone. She would serve her time and then pretend it didn't happen.

For the sake of their House.

But it was not about their House. It was about Alecto standing up for herself. She was done playing nice.

If she didn't show Blaze that she was not to be messed with, then Blaze would think that he could do whatever he pleased with her. And with that boy, there were no limits. Alecto was sure of it.

"If it's not black, not red or white, then what other color could it be?" Matias mused.

The mystery of what color underwear Alecto was wearing today.

She chuckled. "You seriously don't know any other colors apart from those three?"

Matias finally glanced at her, a half smile on his face as he looked her up and down. Then, he shrugged. "These are just three of my favorite colors for underwear."

"Sorry to disappoint."

Matias flashed her his most dazzling smile, all white, straight teeth. "You could never, sweet cheeks."

If Alecto were honest with herself, he was the reason why she hadn't complained about her detention too much. They had fun. Flirty, innocent fun that put Alecto in a good mood.

Matias might not be the brightest, but he was smooth, and he made Alecto feel wanted. Which was perfect because she wanted to feel this way, and it'd been a while since she last had sex.

"Are you two going to work today, or are we going to sit here until midnight?" Rogue asked from the desk behind them.

Alecto whirled. "Are you in a rush, *Rogue*?"

He met her gaze. "I don't know about you, but I wouldn't want to miss a party."

Of course, Rogue had to be at tonight's revel at the House of Tigers. Val wanted to test the waters for the first time since they had summoned the demon.

"Are you coming tonight, Alecto?" Matias asked.

"Maybe."

He cracked a smile. Alecto picked up a stack of books and rounded the desk.

"Will you help me real quick?" she asked, cocking her head towards the shelves.

Matias didn't need to be asked twice. He jumped off the desk and followed her deeper into the library.

Alecto stopped by the ladder leaning against one of the tall bookshelves. She threw Matias a glance over her shoulder. "Hold the ladder for me, will you?"

She climbed the first step as Matias came to stand right behind her. His fingers wrapped around the ladder, closing her in a cage.

It didn't bother Alecto. She arched her back, making sure her ass brushed his chest as she climbed higher, keeping the books to her chest.

As Alecto put the books back in place, on the very top shelf, the antici-pation inside her grew. She was high enough for Matias to get a good view up her skirt, and it made her even more excited.

She bit her lip, shifting her weight from one leg to the other, making sure her hips shifted as well. A low growl came from the bottom of the ladder, and Alecto's toes curled.

"I think I have a new favorite color underwear," Matias announced, voice low and thick when Alecto finally came down the ladder.

He kept her locked in the cage, her back pressing into the ladder.

"Oh, yeah?" Alecto asked, voice light. "It's good to broaden your horizons."

Matias toyed with his lip ring as his eyes darted between her eyes and her mouth. The darkened expression on his face right now was making Alec-to's heart hammer in her chest.

She leaned forwards, flicking her tongue over the lip ring, which was cool to the touch. Matias stilled, and Alecto took his lip between her teeth, biting it hard enough to get a groan from him.

With a flip of her hair, Alecto slipped away from his grip, striding back to the main area of the library. She made sure to swing her hips, knowing damn well Matias's gaze was locked on her.

That was what true power felt like.

Tonight was the night for the House of Tigers to show off their might. When Alecto opened the iron gate to their front garden, it was obvious that they went all out for tonight's party.

The music was blaring with full volume, bass so strong the windows were vibrating. There were people already standing on the stairs and around the little front garden that had only a small patch of artificially preserved green grass.

Jack Riverblood, the High Priest of the House of Tigers, stood by the door, a whole array of glitters and paints propped on the small foldable table by his side.

"Ladies," he greeted Alecto and Jolene with a nod as they approached him. His green eyes greedily took in Alecto's outfit, lingering longer on her naked legs.

For tonight, Alecto wore high-waisted short leather shorts with a zipper going down the front that left a huge part of her ass exposed. The white tank top Alecto chose to wear with nothing underneath let her nipple piercings be the stars of the show.

"Riverblood," Alecto acknowledged. They locked eyes.

Most witches were fucking crazy according to mortal standards. But Jack was crazy even for witches.

"What do you have here for us?" Jolene chirped, leaning closer to look at the table by his side.

"Tonight's a special night," Jack teased, his voice low. "Need to look the best. Not that you ladies lack in the looks department tonight."

He emphasized his words by shamelessly looking over them both, biting on his lower lip.

"You're cute." Jolene chuckled. "But no amount of flattery will change which team I play for."

Jack only cracked a half smile. "Lucky girls, what can I say. Pick any paint or glitter you're feeling like rocking tonight, ladies."

Alecto glanced around at the assortment of all sorts of magical paints and glitters swirling inside the pots, dancing to the beat of the music.

Without much consideration, Alecto pointed at the deep crimson pot with black chunks of sparkle, and Jack took it in his hand. Then, he stepped closer to Alecto, slowly dipping two fingers in the pot. When he slid them out, the crimson paint covered his fingers, not a single drop dribbling.

Jack dragged the paint over her right cheekbone, then the left one, his touch light as a ghost over her skin.

His eyes dipped lower then, and he trailed his fingers down the middle of her throat, right until he reached the small crevice in the middle where her collarbones met. One finger lightly traced the line of her right collarbone, and Alecto barely held the shiver back at the touch.

Jack read her body, and a small smile settled in the crevice of his mouth. He slowly repeated the motion on her other collarbone and then stepped aside, looking her over as if admiring his handy work.

Alecto blinked, feeling the skin under the paint warm up, tingling.

"What the fuck is that?" she demanded, trying to look down at the paint on her chest.

"It's something special to make things more exciting," Jack explained, moving over to take the pot of blue glitter that Jolene picked.

The glitter paint was warm and pleasant on Alecto's skin. Too pleasant. It made Alecto's nipples hard. She scratched the back of her neck, fighting the sensations as the warmth spread through her whole body.

Of course the Tigers had to pull something like that. Surely, it was some sort of spell to make everyone more excited or crazy or whatever the fuck else that would cause havoc amongst the partygoers tonight. The Tigers were known for their subtle manipulation after all.

Alecto sighed, seeing Jolene getting dowsed in the blue glitter.

Once her friend was satisfied, they headed inside the House, making their way towards the kitchen where Alecto hoped they would find drinks.

Andro and Blaze were already there, leaning against the kitchen island.

Gael stood by Andro's side, Andro's hand resting on his waist casually, and Blaze wasn't alone either—two gorgeous twins, Izzy and Lizzy from the House of Oxen, were pressing their half-naked bodies close to his tall frame.

"Right on fucking time!" Andro screamed when they approached. He sent multiple air kisses, and Alecto laughed. She caught one in her palm and placed it on her lips.

"We're always on time," Jolene screamed back. It was the only way to communicate when the music was so loud.

Alecto tried very hard to pretend that Blaze didn't exist, only greeting the twins with a smile and a nod.

"Where's our leader?" Alecto asked, coming over to stand by Andro and Gael.

"She's in the living room," Andro snorted, rolling his eyes. "Probably fucking someone already."

Alecto laughed, remembering how their last party went down; it wouldn't be a surprise to anyone.

Jolene pushed a rocks glass into Alecto's hand.

"Drink, bitch," she commanded, tipping her head and downing her drink. "We're already behind."

Andro howled, clapping as Alecto gulped hers, vodka burning her insides like a bitch. Jolene didn't waver and refilled their glasses, this time doubling the liquor.

"Careful, you might outdrink us all if you keep up this pace," Blaze teased.

Tonight, he looked wickedly stunning. Straight black pants flowed down his long legs and a black short-sleeve shirt made of lace was wide open, showing his carved-out chest and the top of the flat plane of his stomach.

Alecto averted her gaze, breath hitching in her throat as she took another sip of her vodka.

Blaze was a fucking bastard. Alecto shouldn't have found him attractive.

Maybe I just need to get laid.

Without another word, Alecto left the Inner Circle behind, making her way through the crowd to the living room. There, people were lounging around on the green velvet couches and armchairs in the middle of the room.

As per usual, some students were in the middle of steamy action, while others were simply chatting.

Val sat in the middle of one of the velvet sofas, Rogue by her side. One of his arms was draped over her shoulder, his thumb drawing circles over her naked shoulder.

So, the first phase of the plan was in motion after all. First, they were going to parade Rogue as Val's latest toy. And then Val was going to let him go after Galia and Jack.

Right then, something warm and hard pressed against Alecto's back.

"You came." Hot breath tickled Alecto's ear, and she whirled around, meeting Matias's gaze.

A smile curved her lips, and she placed a palm over his chest, the heat from his body coming through the cotton T-shirt with the House of Tigers' sigil.

"Of course I did," she replied, leaning in to whisper in his ear. "I wouldn't have missed a good party for anything."

"You look like a snack," Matias teased.

When he retreated, his gaze dipped lower to her neck, painted collarbone, and breasts that were sure as Hel very much on display, her nipples hard and visible through the material.

Matias raked his bottom lip through his teeth. Alecto took a deep breath that caused her chest to brush his.

She was going to do it.

Alecto came here to have fun, and *fun* was standing right in front of her, staring at her as if he were about to devour her whole.

Without another word, Alecto took hold of Matias's hand, leading him out of the living room to the stairs in the foyer of their House. He didn't stop her, following her into the foyer and up the stairs.

Alecto brought her glass to her lips, tipping her head back. Out of the corner of her eye, she caught Blaze's moon-pale face by one of the walls.

Her gaze locked with his as she climbed the stairs, navigating the bodies sprawled under her feet. Blaze's black eyes were hot as coal as he stared at her, Izzy's *or* Lizzy's head burrowed into his neck, while the other one worked his mouth.

Hairs on Alecto's neck rose, her heart quickening at the intensity of his gaze as he licked his way into one of the twins' mouths. Alecto should have looked away, but she couldn't.

Only when they reached the top of the stairs and Blaze disappeared from her view was she able to look straight and finish her drink.

Matias pushed past her, leading her down the corridor to what she hoped was his bedroom. She left her empty glass on one of the side tables along the wall and entered the room after Matias.

It was messy and dark, dim light illuminating the large bed with gray sheets. Before Alecto could say anything, Matias pushed her against the closed door, and his mouth closed over hers.

Alecto parted her lips, allowing him to deepen the kiss, arching her back to give him full permission to explore her body, use her and worship her.

Matias's palms hovered over her ass, squeezing it hard, and she hooked one ankle over his leg. Immediately, he lifted her, his hips bucking into hers as he groaned.

Warmth traveled to Alecto's core, her clit throbbing with anticipation as he shoved her on his bed. His eyes were dark as the night, glittering in the dim light as he shrugged his T-shirt off, hands moving to unbuckle his belt.

"Take it off," he instructed, voice husky.

Alecto hesitated for a moment but then yanked her tank top over her head. Then she unzipped her shorts, shimmying them down her hips.

When Matias noticed the red lace of her thong, his hands stilled. One corner of his lip curled up, and he lurched forwards, impatiently snagging her shorts down before his head ducked for her breasts, taking one of her nipples in his mouth.

He sucked on it, hard and fast, and Alecto moaned, letting her head fall back on the bed.

Matias was better than Gabe already. He moved from one nipple to the next, letting his hand knead the flesh as he sucked on the sensitive peak. Alecto squirmed under him, gasping and whimpering.

Before she could submerge in the pleasure completely, Matias retreated. His large palms grabbed Alecto's hips and flipped her on her belly.

Without a word, he lifted her hips in the air and slipped her thong down her thighs. Slowly, Matias dragged a finger over her length before slipping one inside. Alecto bit her lip at the sudden harsh movements but kept her mouth shut, swinging he hips to the sides.

"You're so tight," Matias whispered. "I'm clean. And I'm taking the brew."

"Me too."

A low growl escaped him as he pumped his finger in and out of her in slow motions. Warmth built inside her again, and Alecto rocked her hips, chasing his hand.

But then his finger slipped away, and a moment later she felt the tip of his cock at her entrance. Matias groaned as he slid inside, and Alecto moaned in the sheets as he stretched her, a slight burning making her whimper.

Ah, it was too early. Fuck.

Matias's hips rocked, his dick sliding in and out of her almost fully and Alecto gripped the sheets with her hands, burying her face in the mattress.

After the initial discomfort finally died down, the pressure was once more building inside her belly, and she rocked her hips, meeting each of his thrusts eagerly.

Another growl rose from Matias's chest, his fingers gripping Alecto's hips harder. He quickened the pace, only the sounds of their naked bodies slamming into each other filling the room. Alecto reached out one hand to touch her clit as the pressure inside her intensified, heat waves rolling down her thighs.

She whimpered, rolling her head to the side to catch a breath, and Matias increased the pace again.

"You like that, huh?" he groaned, his hips slamming into her hard. "Yeah, you like that, you little slut."

Alecto ignored his dirty talk, letting him grumble and murmur whatever the fuck he wanted. She learned early that boys liked to call her slut, whore, and all the other colorful names during sex. It turned them on. It got them off. So, Alecto ignored them.

She wanted to please them after all.

Another moan escaped her, and Alecto cried out, her fingers around her clit moving frantically. She was so close to the edge now.

Matias groaned, his body behind her tensing, and after two more hard thrusts, he slid his dick out of her with a grunt. Alecto lifted her head, getting ready for a position change, but that wasn't what happened next.

Instead of Matias flipping her over, something warm and wet slid down her back, and Alecto realized that he had finished.

She jolted as Matias slapped her ass. The mattress faltered as he got off the bed, striding into the bathroom connected to his bedroom.

Slowly, Alecto straightened her back, still kneeling on the bed. Her body was cold now, despite the soreness and hot ache between her legs. She rose to her feet, grabbing the cotton T-shirt to wipe his jizz off her back.

Quietly, Alecto dressed. She sat on the bed to retie her boots when the door to the bathroom opened, and Matias emerged, pleased as a cat.

He came over to where she sat, cupping her cheek in his palm. One of his thumbs brushed her lips, and he whispered, "You're a hot piece of ass, Black, you know that? Did you finish hard?"

Alecto blinked slowly. "Yeah."

Matias only smirked and turned away to get dressed.

Without another word, Alecto went over to the door, leaving him in his room as she made her way back downstairs.

It was rich of her to expect that Matias was going to give her what she wanted.

Maybe she should just give up on having sex with men. It didn't look as if they knew what the fuck they were doing anyway.

Or maybe Alecto was indeed broken, unable to have an orgasm with another person involved.

"Bitch, where have you been?" Jolene's scream welcomed her as she descended the stairs.

Jolene stood by Blaze and the twins, still in the same spot by the wall, a bottle of whiskey in her hand.

Alecto strode towards them and grabbed the bottle from Jolene. She tipped her head back as she took a few massive gulps of whiskey.

Jolene laughed, "Atta girl!"

Alecto gave Jolene the bottle back and wiped her lips with the back of her hand as she locked eyes with Blaze. He smirked, his eyes flickering with challenge or amusement; Alecto couldn't tell.

Well, if Alecto couldn't get fucked tonight, at least she could get fucked up.

14

There were two things that were annoying the fuck out of Blaze.

First was his hangover, or the lack of it.

He hadn't drunk enough last night to completely ruin him today, and because of it, he was stuck in this groggy state, where his mind was slow as a snail, and he wanted to die, instead of being pleasantly buzzed during lectures until he finally sobered up in the afternoon.

The second was that Alecto still hadn't spoken to him.

Yesterday at the party, she at least looked at him. Even if it was just to throw a few icy glares.

But it was getting completely out of hand.

Yes, Alecto was often pissed off. If Blaze were honest, she was almost *always* pissed off. But this was just unacceptable.

How was Blaze supposed to play when Alecto was not responding to his games?

How fucking boring.

Blaze snorted, drawing Val's attention. She arched a brow as if asking whether he had lost his mind, but he ignored her.

They were sitting in the Defensive Artistry class. It was Blaze's last lecture of the day, and he was so over it all. A joint and a bed were all he craved.

Yet, Professor Felix didn't seem to give a damn.

"Mr. Leveau, would you mind coming over to the front of the class to demonstrate this spell?" the professor asked, looking at Blaze over the top of his thick brown glasses.

Blaze sighed heavily, rising from his seat.

He didn't even have the energy to argue and debate with the professor, so that he would just give up and find it easier to get another student to perform the fucking spell instead.

Blaze took the steps down the auditorium, striding to the long table in the middle of the platform where they usually came to perform spells, the professor's desk shoved in the corner.

"Just like any other magic, your defense spells require either the ritual to fuel it or one of five magic types' sacrifice," Professor Felix explained, coming to stand by Blaze's side. "Blood magic, which you don't have the permission to practice at Venefica, might I add."

He said the point as if they didn't know the rules already. Blaze rolled his eyes, which drew a few laughs.

"Blood magic will require a decent amount of blood depending on the strength of your protective shield. The stronger the spell you want to cast, the more blood you'll have to use. And the more potent the source of the blood will have to be."

"So, like, if I kill you, Professor, and use your blood to cast a protective spell over myself, the police won't be able to get to me to arrest me because the spell will be too powerful to overcome?" Andro inquired, drawing a few more laughs.

Professor Felix nodded. "Yes, that's right, Mr. Weir. If you killed me and used the blood from a pig to protect yourself from the police, I'm afraid you wouldn't be able to get away with your crime."

A wave of laughter went over the class.

"Witches who choose to wield death magic will have to use the remains of the dead or spirits in order to fuel their protective spell," the professor continued, walking over to the edge of the platform. "Sex magic will require an act of sort to be performed, bone magic will rely on the bones of the First Ones to empower the spell, and nature magic will draw from the witch creating the spell themselves, draining their life source."

"But what will happen if I need a super-potent protective spell and I'm using nature's magic to fuel it?" Jolene asked, leaning forwards in her seat. She was a naturalist who refused to use any other magic but nature and sex. "Would the spell drain all energy from me to create the potent shield?"

"Let's hope you don't have to find out, Miss Frone," the professor said simply, turning his back to the class to walk over his desk.

A few more students chuckled at the look on Jolene's face.

It was beyond him why some witches and warlocks used their own life source to practice their craft when they could just channel the power from someone else.

"But actually, it's an excellent question, Miss Frone," Professor Felix added after a moment. "If you find yourself in a situation where you can't fuel the spell with one of the five magics, then you can use the ritual circle to fuel it."

The professor leaned on his desk, crossing his arms over his chest. He then jerked his chin at Blaze.

"Mr. Leveau, please start mixing the ingredients in the bowl," the professor instructed. "Let's create a shield around you so you can see how the spell works."

Blaze glanced at the bowl and many glass jars in front of him with different herbs and berries.

"Frog's tail, green rose petals, dried midnight lily, and three dashes of Sea Monster's tears," the professor said. "In that order, Mr. Leveau."

It took Blaze a while to gather all the ingredients, his brain and fingers working exceptionally slow, but he managed. Once he dropped the last tear of Sea Monster in the bronze bowl, he glanced back at the professor.

"Say *isolentus mixortis* and conjure the shield of energy stretching around you inside your mind."

Blaze closed his eyes.

As his lips moved, whispering the chant into the air, his mind worked to conjure the image of soft white tendrils swirling around him, joining together to come into a united formation.

Almost immediately, electric current zipped through his body to the tips of his fingers, and his hands shook at the power gathered in his palms.

Blaze took a deep breath, his muscles going taut, but he didn't let go, continuing the chant and keeping his focus on the image.

It would be worse than embarrassing to mess up a simple protection spell in front of the whole class.

Only when a few gasps reached his ears did Blaze dared to crack his eyes open. The view of the class in front of him was distorted, a barrier of some sort making the sight fizzy.

It was the shield he had conjured in his mind, the white smoky tendrils swirling together in a cocoon around him.

"Nicely done, Mr. Leveau," Professor Felix said, coming to stand closer to Blaze. Then, he spoke to the class. "The same protective shield will look different for different witches and warlocks. It all depends on how you imagine it in your mind and bring it to life."

The professor walked around the long table, grabbing something from one of the jars.

"This particular spell is designed to protect you from any physical damage," he explained. Blaze barely caught the movement of his hand as the professor threw a dried elephant beetle at the shield.

There was a light sizzling sound as the beetle turned to dust the moment it touched the shield.

"If you find yourself in a pickle where another witch is trying to hurt you in a nonphysical way, this protective shield won't do you much good," the professor added.

He turned back to Blaze and murmured something under his breath.

In a flash, a sharp pain pierced Blaze's mind. He groaned, grabbing his head with his palms. The shield he held in place dropped in an instant, and the pain was gone just as fast as it appeared.

The whole class was gawking now.

"Just as each witch can determine how their shield is going to manifest, they can also learn to manipulate it, so it's more bendable and not so obvious," the professor said, strolling to his desk. He glanced at his watch. "But we're going to discuss that and all the other types of protective spells in other lectures this year. You're free to go. Your homework will be in your notebooks by the end of the day. I suggest you don't miss out on completing it as homework will be 30 percent of your final mark for this year."

All students rose, shuffling out as the professor continued giving his instructions on the grades and homework and whatever else.

Blaze strode back to his seat, picking up his books, glad that the only thing standing between him and his bed was a ten-minute walk.

"I'm having a meeting with some of the members," Val said as they were leaving the classroom. "Want to meet me later for a drink?"

Blaze shook his head, lighting a cigarette the moment he walked out of the building.

"I'm off to bed," he said, stopping to wait for Andro. "I need my beauty sleep before tomorrow's game."

"As you wish." Val walked off, leaving him alone as students streamed out of the building, rushing to different parts of the campus.

"Well, that was some skilled witchcraft," Andro said, finally emerging from the building with a wide smile. "Mr. Leveau, you look good in a shield."

Blaze laughed, shaking his head as he let the smoke escape his lips. They walked casually around the main building where most lectures took place, towards the main path leading outside the campus.

As they rounded the corner of the building, a fountain emerged. Gabe and his lackey sat on the edge, chewing on some brightly colored candies.

Blaze threw them a glance and kept walking.

"I have it in a memory orb," Matias said, snickering. "Unlike you, I actually managed to get her in my bedroom, right where I needed her to seal that sweet ass getting railed inside the orb."

"Fuck off," Gabe spat. "That doesn't make you the fucking hero."

Matias shot back, "It does when it's Miss Black we're talking about."

The moments those words left Matias's lips, the blood froze in Blaze's veins. He stopped abruptly.

Blaze exchanged glances with Andro, who clearly had heard the same thing, his eyes blazing fire.

"What the fuck did you just say?" Blaze snapped, whirling and striding back to the fountain.

Matias cracked a wide smile. Gabe crossed his arms, a pleased smile spreading on his angular face.

Blaze wanted nothing more than to wipe that smug grin off his ugly face with one of his fists.

Or both.

Preferably both.

"You have a habit of listening to other people's conversations?" Gabe snorted.

"It didn't sound as if you were trying to be discreet," Andro countered, coming to stand at Blaze's side.

Blaze's heart hammered in his fucking ears as his fingers curled into fists.

"What, Leveau? Mad that I fucked your girlfriend last night and saved a little memory for the future?" Matias teased. "My boys will be happy when I show them how good Alecto Black is in the sheets."

Blaze's sight went red, and before he could think better of it, he lurched at Matias, grabbing him by the collar of his shirt and drawing his face close.

"You give me that memory orb right *now*. Or I'm going to make sure you shit blood for the next month," Blaze spat.

"I don't think I will, Leveau. It's just too valuable to have such a thing in my possession. Not every day you get something on a Black. And I intend on keeping it as a souvenir."

Matias didn't even react as Blaze's fist slammed into his jaw. Blaze let him fall backwards as Gabe jumped him from behind. Blaze ducked and smashed his elbow into Gabe's groin, making him groan with pain.

Before Blaze could straighten himself, a fist collided with his face, sending him backwards. Matias jumped Blaze.

Matias threw another punch, and Blaze's skull rang with the impact. But Blaze wasn't going to give in, and he managed to swing a punch back, sending Matias onto his side.

Blaze rolled over Matias, straddling his body as he swung one punch after another, cracking Matias's nose.

"Blaze, STOP." Andro's voice was somewhere in the distance as someone's hand wrapped around his neck, choking Blaze and dragging him off Matias, who rolled on his side, spewing blood.

"You fucking dick. I'm going to break your legs so you can never play rockey again," Gabe growled in his ear. Blaze's eyesight went black at the corners.

Then, suddenly, Gabe's grip was gone.

When Blaze whirled, he found the guy on the pavement, out cold. Alecto stood behind him, gripping a cloth bag in her hand.

"You're going to pay for this, Leveau," Matias drawled, trying to get back on his feet.

Blaze glanced around at the small crowd that had started gathering around them. Andro stood wide-eyed, panting heavily as he took in the attention as well.

"Let's go," Alecto said, grabbing Blaze's hand, then Andro's, and dragging them away into the nearest building.

Before leaving, Blaze kicked Matias in his chest, knocking the wind out of him and sending him down on his knees as he wheezed.

Getting the Tigers' Book wasn't going to be enough during this year's Game. Blaze was going to make the Tigers bleed in every way he could.

"Come on!" Alecto snapped at him.

Alecto led them into a small classroom with no windows, with only one desk and a chair perched in the corner and a dirty chalkboard lining one of the walls.

Blaze leaned against the desk, his head pounding, jaw hurting. He wasn't even sure where the pain had started and ended.

"What the fuck was that about?" Alecto scolded them, crossing her arms.

"They've got a memory orb of you and Matias," Andro said carefully. "From yesterday's party. From what I can tell, they were going to use it to blackmail us or some shit."

Blaze turned his head so he could see Alecto's face better. Whatever he expected to find, it wasn't there, her face completely blank.

She didn't even blink. "The Tigers are going to be very sorry this year."

Blaze and Andro exchanged a glance, nodding their heads.

"First though, I'm going to have to go and do damage control," Andro said, sighing heavily. "Alecto, can you help him clean his wounds and make sure he doesn't get into more trouble while I try to cover this incident up?"

Alecto nodded, and Andro left them alone. Blaze blinked at Alecto as she hurried around the table, opening the first drawer and taking out a pouch from it.

A moment later, she returned to Blaze, unzipped the bag, and took out the washcloth.

Then, she locked eyes with Blaze. "You're a fucking idiot, you know that?"

15

Alecto couldn't believe Blaze would get in a bloody fight with Gabe and Matias. She couldn't believe he would do it in the middle of the campus, in the afternoon when everyone was around to see.

And she couldn't believe she had used her magic to knock Gabe out cold so he wouldn't strangle Blaze to death.

She had cussed him enough since they came in here, and now Blaze sat on the corner of the desk, silent, letting her clean his wounds.

"You would think witchy boys wouldn't need to use their fists in fights," Alecto murmured, pressing the washcloth to his face, trying to scrub away the blood starting to dry around his right temple.

"What's the fun of a fight if you don't get a lil' bit physical?" Blaze's dark eyes didn't leave her face, not even for a moment, tracking her movements like a hawk.

Alecto ignored him.

She was grateful that her hands didn't tremble, even though her whole body was taut with tension.

Why would Blaze do that? Why would he—of all people—be so reckless as to get into a fight when he clearly didn't like Alecto?

She cleared her throat, wiping the last smear of blood over his eyebrow.

"You didn't have to do it," she said.

He blinked slowly, still silent.

Alecto could have taken care of it herself. She didn't care about getting her hands dirty. In fact, it was clear to her that she'd have to cross the line this year to show the Tigers that she was not to be messed with.

They were in the possession of the memory orb, and Alecto was going to have to get it back. Soon.

"But thank you."

Blaze's gaze dropped from her eyes to her lips.

Those black eyes of his were heavy-lidded, darker than she had ever seen before, and then, he leaned forwards slightly. Alecto blinked, glancing between his lips and eyes, her body still as a stone, afraid to move.

What the fuck was going on?

Was he...going to kiss her?

Just as a breath hitched in Alecto's throat, Blaze blinked, the haziness evaporating almost as quickly as it appeared.

"You know, you should really start picking your lovers better," Blaze announced.

"What?"

"I said you should choose your lovers better," he repeated, rolling his eyes as his hand moved to touch his swollen jaw. He winced and dropped his arm back into his lap.

"Are you really shaming me for sleeping around?" Alecto asked, still unable to clearly understand what just happened.

Or rather, what *didn't* happen.

"I'm not slut-shaming you for fucking around," Blaze replied. "I'm shaming you for your poor choice in lovers."

"Fuck you."

"Tell me I'm wrong. Tell me that Gabe or his friend, whatever the fuck his name is, was a good fuck. Tell me that they at least managed to give you a few orgasms for all this trouble. Because you sure as Hel seemed to get back from his bedroom very quickly."

Alecto snapped her mouth shut and threw the washcloth at Blaze. He caught it in the air before it hit his face.

"That's none of your fucking business," she said.

"Ah, but your reaction tells me everything I need to know. I can't say I'm surprised that fucker didn't make you come."

Alecto took a step backwards, unable to stop her cheeks from heating up.

This was not a conversation she'd planned on having with Blaze, or anyone else for that matter.

It was confusing and embarrassing navigating her issue with orgasming with men. She didn't need the biggest asshole at Venefica knowing anything about it.

But her silence was a mistake.

"Why are you blushing?" he asked, voice amused.

Alecto only smirked, rolling her eyes.

He can fucking suck it.

"Oh, don't tell me—" Blaze said, eyes suddenly wide, lips parted in shock. "Don't tell me you've *never* had an orgasm with someone else before."

Alecto remained silent.

"*Oh.*" A smile spread across his pretty face, and Alecto had an urge to slap it right off. "Well, that's what you get for choosing lousy lovers, Black."

"Yeah, right." Alecto rolled her eyes. "As if you're Mister Orgasm Giver yourself. Give me a fucking break."

"Well, I never leave my ladies unsatisfied," Blaze said, shrugging. "Don't believe me, ask around. They're going to tell you all about it."

"They already have," Alecto shot back. "I know all about your skills *or* lack of skills, rather."

"*What?*"

Alecto could have basked in that surprised, hurt, prideful look on Blaze's face all day long. She could have sealed it inside a memory orb, always keeping it with her just so she could revel in it anytime she needed to lift her mood.

"Oh, you know what I'm talking about, *Blazy*," Alecto teased, smiling. "Your little issue with giving head."

Blaze frowned, clearly confused and unsatisfied with where this conversation was going.

Fine, if he was going to pretend, Alecto could play this game.

"You don't go down on girls."

Blaze looked taken aback by her words as he blinked, lips parted.

"*What?*"

"I know that you don't go down on the girls you sleep with. Every girl on campus knows it," Alecto repeated. "I don't care how good of a fuck you think you are, that is a red flag in a guy, and you shouldn't glower about being an amazing lover."

"So, that's what you've heard about me? And you're so quick to believe the rumors without even giving me the benefit of the doubt?"

Alecto sucked on her teeth but remained silent, keeping his gaze.

Blaze slid away from the desk, throwing his hands in the air. "Un-fuck-ing-believable. That is some straight-up high-class bullshit."

"Why did it get you so heated if it's not true?" Alecto asked, crossing her arms, not able to hold back a satisfied grin that only seemed to enrage Blaze further.

For a long moment, he just stood there, his tongue poking his cheek as he stared at Alecto.

"Oh, I've got an idea. How about we find out whether the rumors are true, *baby*?" Blaze stalked closer.

Alecto wasn't sure what it was that prompted her to say what she said. Was it the way Blaze's eyes flickered with something dark and sinister? Was it the adrenaline from seeing him smash a fist through Gabe's face in defense of *her*?

Or was it something else entirely that prompted Alecto to lift her chin and say, "Bring it on, fuck boy."

Blaze closed the distance between them in a stride, and Alecto took a step backwards, her back colliding with a wall. His hand landed on the wall beside her head, face coming dangerously close to hers.

"Actions do speak louder than words, don't they?" he drawled, gaze snapping between her eyes and lips. Alecto's heart skipped a beat, palms getting sweaty, but she refused to stand down.

Alecto didn't answer.

Blaze dipped lower, dropping to his knees in front of her.

She gasped as his hands gripped her thighs, spreading them apart. For a moment, Alecto wasn't sure what the fuck was she doing, what she was allowing him to do. It all started to seem like the best and the worst idea ever. "Blaze—"

"Shh," he murmured, slowly massaging the soft flesh, sending ripples of warmth up to the very center of her. His gaze shot up, meeting hers.

Slowly, Blaze's fingers traveled higher up her thighs, disappearing behind her pleated skirt. Alecto inhaled a sharp breath when his fingers traced the line where her leg met her hip, skimming the sensitive skin and then finally, sliding over the band of her black lacy panties.

Blaze didn't rush, taking his time as he brushed a finger over the band, sending spikes of pleasure down to her core. Alecto tried very hard to stay still.

The gentle touches were something she didn't expect from someone like Blaze, who was always erratic and unpredictable, fiery and explosive.

Those nights she imagined him between her thighs, he took her hard and fast, making her beg for her release. *Apparently* the reality was quite different.

Blaze wet his lips as he finally dragged her panties down, sliding them all the way to the floor. He then glanced up at her, waiting for her to step out of them. Alecto obeyed, barely breathing.

To her surprise, instead of throwing her panties to the side, he stuffed them in the pocket of his school jacket, the other hand moving up her thigh.

"Lift your leg for me, baby," Blaze whispered, his voice hoarse and thick, and she let his hand guide her leg over his shoulder.

Alecto was utterly exposed, so, so naked and at his mercy.

She hated it.

Yet, she couldn't stop herself from craving more.

Blaze lifted the skirt, pushing it all the way to her waist, and a low moan escaped his lips.

Alecto couldn't look anymore, so she pressed the back of her head to the wall, closing her eyes shut as her hands curled into fists by her sides.

She had never had a guy go down on her. Barely any guys ever suggested it, and she never knew how to ask.

It made her uncomfortable, having a man between her legs, so close and intimate with her most sensitive part. Alecto could never relax, for the love of Gods.

Blaze's fingers traced her length, stopping to circle her clit and then going down again, just to come back up and tease her some more.

Alecto gasped, biting on her lower lip, still keeping her eyes closed.

"You know, it's going to be much more pleasurable if you relax," Blaze whispered, his warm breath tickling her clit, turning her blood into molten lava. "Don't you trust me?"

Alecto huffed a laugh, opening her eyes to meet his scorching gaze.

"Not one bit."

Blaze smirked. "That's smart."

Then he dove for her, soft lips closing over her clit, eyes keeping on hers, and Alecto gasped, her toes curling.

She was fire.

Her fucking body was fire.

Blaze's tongue moved in slow, lazy circles around her clit, teasing her, coaxing. Then he moved lower, exploring the rest of her with such hunger Alecto thought she might faint.

Breathe, my fucking Gods, breathe.

With much effort, Alecto took a few breaths, watching Blaze work her, and when his mouth once more closed over her clit, he moaned, sending her body into a sea of pleasure.

Alecto leaned her head back against the wall, exhaling. *"Fuck."*

"What did you say?" Blaze asked, retreating just a few inches. "Did you say you want more?"

The only thing Alecto could do was nod her head. Frantically.

He chuckled. She *felt* him chuckle and kiss her one more time.

Alecto moaned, digging her nails into her palms as the familiar pressure started building inside her. She allowed him to explore her, lick her whole, her legs trembling uncontrollably when his tongue found her entrance and darted inside, teasing.

"Mmmm," Blaze moaned, returning to her clit. He retreated once more. "You're absolutely fucking delicious, did you know that?"

Alecto shook her head, sucking her lips in as her neck and face heated from his words.

Why would he say something like that?

She was burning. Burning with pleasure and shame.

One of his fingers slipped inside her, and she bucked her hips forwards. He slowly pumped it in and out, caressing her from the inside, making the flame burn brighter in her belly.

"Oh, fuck."

"You know what I would like?" Blaze asked, his finger still moving in and out of her.

Alecto rolled her hips together with his finger, chasing every bit of pleasure, and that drew a smile from him.

"I would have you locked in my room for days," Blaze said, his voice low and thick, eyes darker than the night as they met Alecto's gaze. "I would tie you to my bed with a silk tie I keep only for special occasions."

He leaned in to plant a soft kiss over her clit, sliding another finger inside her.

Alecto was flushed, overwhelmed with sensation.

"And you know what I would do then?" Blaze asked. Alecto shook her head, her hips chasing his fingers more desperately now. Her body's reaction seemed to please him. "I would feast on you for hours, letting you get to the very edge, before retreating back, leaving you hanging."

Alecto whimpered as her core burned. She could feel her hot wetness on her thighs, and that didn't escape Blaze's attention. His eyes widened as he wet his lips once more.

"You'd like that, wouldn't you?"

Alecto didn't say anything, clamping her lips shut, but in her mind she was screaming, *Oh, Gods yes!*

"I would eventually let you come," he admitted, leaving a trail of soft kisses over her length, his fingers never stopping pumping inside her. "But not before I had you dripping all over my sheets, cheeks flushed as you're begging me to finish you off."

Oh, dear fucking Gods.

Blaze was going to drive her mad with those long, skilled fingers, those lips, and those damn filthy words that made her cheeks heat up with shame.

What the fuck was going on with her?

"Would you beg?"

Alecto nodded, biting on her lip. She was getting dangerously close to the edge, and right now, it was all she could focus on.

"*No,*" Blaze said, tsking. "I need you to use your words."

"Yes," Alecto managed, her words coming out breathy.

Blaze took hold of her hands, still curled in fists by her sides, and guided them one by one to his shoulders.

And then, he dove back into her.

Alecto whined and whimpered under his mouth. It was hard to keep quiet or still. Yet he didn't let her move, his strong hands holding her hips in place as he feasted.

The tension building in her belly was growing warmer, spreading to her core, and her muscles clenched. Right as she thought she was going to explode into million pieces, his lips retreated.

Alecto whined, opening her eyes to meet Blaze's heavy gaze, a smirk gracing his glittering lips.

"What?" Alecto panted, her breathing erratic.

"Say it," Blaze whispered, his warm breath tickling her. Alecto squirmed, chasing the sensation of his mouth on her.

Her reaction only drew out a chuckle from him, but he pressed a thumb over her clit, moving in gentle, lazy circles.

Alecto was going to lose her mind if he didn't stop teasing her. She was so close she could feel the very edge of the orgasm.

"Say it, *baby*," he repeated, leaning in to plant a kiss over her clit, and her hips bucked forwards.

Oh, fuck it.

Fuck him and everyone else.

"Please," Alecto breathed out, grabbing a bunch of his hair in her fist as she leaned her head back against the wall. "Please, please, please—"

She gasped as his mouth once more collided with her, licking and sucking harder than before, his tongue moving so wickedly, she didn't know it was possible.

The spike of her orgasm was so sharp and hot, spreading from her core where Blaze's tongue was to her thighs and even the very tips of her toes. Alecto grabbed his hair harder, a cry escaping her lips as her body trembled with the release.

If it weren't for his hands holding her, she would have lost her footing because her legs didn't seem to belong to her anymore.

Blaze carefully set her leg draped over his shoulder down and rose to his feet, still offering his support.

Alecto's eyes fluttered open to meet his, glazed like the night of the Ceremony after their kiss. He glanced around her face, both their chests rising and falling in deep breaths.

There was slickness on his lips, slickness from her, and that sent shivers down her back. Alecto pushed his hands from her hips, taking an unsteady step out of his embrace.

"See you around, Black," Blaze said, amusement back in his voice as if what just happened was just some sort of game for him. Then he left, leaving Alecto alone in the classroom.

She closed her eyes, exhaling.

Fuck.

16

That was eating pussy out of spite.

Definitely.

No doubt about it.

Blaze couldn't let the absurd rumors of him being a lousy lover spread. It was beyond him how anyone would come up with shit like that in the first place.

It was not common for Blaze to give a fuck about rumors. If he cared about what other people said, he wouldn't be able to sleep at night.

Most rumors were hilarious anyway. Like the one where people talked about him and Val carving each other and drinking blood during sex, like the little sex monsters that they were.

Blaze scoffed at those absurd stories because they weren't real. He wasn't even fucking Val, not that anyone ever bothered asking him about it.

But this rumor hit different because it was true.

Partly.

It was not that Blaze found eating girls out repulsive, not at all. But it was just something he had to be in a *special* sort of arrangement to do.

Except for this time with Alecto.

What the Hel was he even thinking?

That was definitely out of spite. It had to be.

Alecto provoked him. It was nothing but her fault that Blaze felt the need to prove her wrong. Blaze loved a good challenge.

But then why was his cock hard as a rock, pressing to his pants as he strode through the campus towards the Main Street, her sweetness still lingering on his lips?

In his mouth.

The sensation of Alecto hot and wet wrapped around his fingers almost made Blaze growl with unfulfilled need as he crossed Main Street, the memory of what just happened so fresh in his mind it was hard to think of anything else.

Get it together, Leveau.

Hate fucks always left him feeling a certain type of way. This must have been the case.

The solution was to go find someone else to fuck.

Blaze still had a boner and was feeling horny. Fucking someone right about now would help, and it would take the edge off just right.

Finally, he rounded the corner of Main Street and turned onto 7th Avenue, where the House of Snakes stood at the very end of the street, close to the park that separated two parts of Darly.

Blaze strode up the stairs in a few long strides, opened the unlocked front door, and went straight for the stairs, ignoring other members of the House along his way.

In a few more moments, Blaze was on the third floor, but instead of opening the door to his room, he went into Val's room without knocking.

She was sitting by her desk, and some other girls from their House were sitting around the room. And all their eyes were now on him.

Val rose to her feet, her eyes wide as she noticed the bruise on his jaw and the split lip that Blaze had completely forgotten in the heat of the moment.

"What the fuck happened—"

Blaze didn't let her finish, glancing at the girls as he said, "Get out." A moment later, he added, *"Please."*

Without as much as a whisper, girls rose, and one by one left the room, leaving Val and Blaze alone.

"Blaze, what the fuck is wrong with you?" Val asked, crossing her arms. "I was in the middle of something, you know? And what the fuck happened to your face?"

Blaze didn't listen to her tirade, closing the distance between them in two strides. He cupped her cheeks in his palms and smashed his mouth into hers with such force that Val stumbled backwards.

She didn't hesitate, though, immediately raking her hands through his hair, wrapping an ankle over his leg, and pressing her body closer to his.

Blaze could count on Val for many things—having his back, playing the role of a proper witch when he needed, and pretending to care about him when he craved it.

He could also count on her to keep his mind off things he didn't want occupying it.

II. WICKED GAMES

17

Alecto could barely sit straight in her seat. Just this morning she woke up hungover and sore after last night, the unfulfilled ache from sex with Matias plaguing her. It didn't last long though.

Right now, Alecto's thighs were still tingling where Blaze's fingers touched her, her cheeks growing hot whenever her mind wandered to that dark classroom.

Alecto yawned and cracked her neck, waiting for the acting class to start. A few low chuckles two rows down drew her attention. Three girls from the House of Tigers whispered to each other, throwing mean glances Alecto's way and then snickering.

So, the whole House knew about Alecto and Matias. About the damn memory orb. They might even have watched the whole thing, laughing and giggling as Matias boasted about his abilities in the bedroom.

Anger surged in Alecto's chest, burning so hot it was hard to breathe. She needed to get that fucking memory orb back and destroy it.

Finally, Madame Raquel strolled into the classroom, her black robe flowing like a river down the sultry curves of her body.

"Ladies and gentlemen, come, come," Madame Raquel called, waving one elegant hand for all the students in the auditorium to come forwards. "I want to see the best performance from each one of you today. I'll be immediately deciding who gets what role for *Carmen*. You only get one chance. Alecto, you go first."

A breathy curse escaped Alecto's lips as she rose from her seat and walked over to the stage.

She'd never had a fear of performing. She loved being on the stage, in front of the lights and other people, taking on the role of someone else. It came as naturally as breathing.

"Half-breed slut," one of the girls taunted as Alecto passed them. The whole auditorium heard it because a wave of laughter went around.

Ignoring the slamming headache in her right temple and the dread suffocating her chest, Alecto took her place in the middle of the stage, bright lights blinding her.

"You recite the lines of Carmen, and I'm going to read Seville's lines," Madame Raquel instructed.

Alecto nodded, rolling her shoulders as she briefly closed her eyes.

She took a deep breath, letting the air fill her lungs and even her belly before she exhaled. When she opened her eyes, she wasn't her anymore.

She was Carmen.

"Oh, my lover, dear precious lover, will you come to me and take me with you?" Alecto drawled, letting her hand brush her hair behind her shoulder.

"I'm right here, Carmen. I never even left. There isn't a force stronger in the world than my attraction to you. Only the army of demons from Hel or the Goddess herself can stop me from living the rest of my life with you in my arms, my Carmen," Madame Raquel read in a low voice.

Alecto took a step to the side, dropping her gaze to the ground, tugging a strand of her hair behind her ear.

"Your words are somber and promising, lover. But I've heard them before, oh so many times. How am I to believe that you mean it when you've not even looked my way since we came here?" she said, her voice quiet. She lifted her eyes as if she were glancing shyly at her lover.

"Your words break my heart, Carmen. How could you ever doubt me? I've had countless nights where sleep evaded me, refusing to take me to the land of peaceful dreams. How could you doubt my admission of love when the food I eat when you're not around is as bland as ash on my tongue?" the professor read, louder.

Alecto huffed a laugh, her hand coming up to her mouth to cover it.

"Words, words, words. Another ocean of meaningless words. Dear lover, I'll give you that—you know exactly how to coax your way to my heart, whispering sweet nothings in my ear whenever my heart aches for a taste of you," Alecto said, more enthusiastically now, letting the heat of passion fill her veins as she stepped closer to the edge of the stage.

"My Carmen…my dear, lovely Carmen, don't question my feelings. Not like this, not now."

Alecto's whole body trembled as she placed a hand over her chest, inhaling a ragged breath before turning away from the stage and walking to the side. She turned her head to the class again, her eyes stinging with tears.

"You've promised me the night's sky full of stars, the world beyond these walls, the sun rays on my cheeks in the middle of the spring. And yet, all I have so far has been a cage of stone and empty words," Alecto said, voice trembling, and then she dropped her glance to the floor, one tear rolling down her cheek right before she stepped off the stage.

"Excellent, dear!" Madame Raquel cheered, clapping as she rose from her seat.

Alecto sniffled, brushing the tears away, and awarded her professor with a smile. Madame Raquel was beaming.

"Next," the professor announced, throwing a glance over her shoulder. Another student rose from their seat. Turning back to Alecto, she said, "You're going to be my Carmen this year, dear. Don't doubt it."

Alecto pulled her shoulders back, bowing her head lightly, pleased to hear Madame Raquel say it.

"We're going to need a spell or two to make you a redhead with dark eyes," she continued, letting a strand of Alecto's hair fall through her fingers. "But ladybug, I'm going to need you to eat a little more. You're very scrawny and thin, and Carmen is supposed to be plump and luscious. Can we work on that?"

Alecto swallowed hard but nodded. There had to be a spell for that. If she couldn't find one in the Book, she'd have to pay a visit to Gill's.

Alecto would be the best Carmen any of them had ever seen, Gods be damned.

"Also, keep in mind that a big role like Carmen comes with a lot of attention," the professor said, her voice falling a few octaves. Her eyes were serious when Alecto met her gaze. "You're stronger than you know, ladybug. And you'll need to draw from that strength very soon."

Then, just as fast as it appeared, the seriousness was gone, and Madame Raquel flashed one of her coquettish smiles before settling back in her seat, turning her attention to the other student on the stage.

Alecto stalked back to her seat at the back of the auditorium in silence, letting the professor's words sink into her hungover brain. She could only hope Madame Raquel was right.

While Alecto was performing on the stage, Rogue had settled a few seats away from her. Their eyes locked, his amber gaze steady and serious. A few more giggles reached them, and Alecto's cheeks burned with shame, but Rogue didn't seem to pay them any attention.

Alecto took her seat, dropping one leg over the other. A moment later, Rogue moved to the seat next to her.

His voice was low, barely above a whisper when he spoke. "You know, I know a spell to make them shut the fuck up. *Permanently*."

Despite herself, Alecto's mouth curled up. She glanced at Rogue on her left, his eyes flickering with mischief.

"Do you also know a spell that would turn back time and stop me from making a mistake?"

Rogue smirked. "Sadly, no."

Alecto smiled, not a happy smile, and turned back to the scene in front of them.

"But there is something I *can* do for you," Rogue added. Alecto turned her attention back to him. "Use me, Black. You're a smart girl."

For a moment, Alecto considered Rogue's words, mulling them over in her mind. *Use me.* He was right. Rogue was bound to them, and he was here to do their bidding. He could help Alecto rectify this situation.

"Are you able to get the memory orb back for me?" Alecto asked.

Rogue's face broke into a wolfish smile, his canines longer than regular witches'.

"Consider it done."

18

"What's up, bitch?" Val greeted Alecto as she stepped out of the auditorium.

"What do you want, Val?"

Alecto didn't stop. Val didn't hesitate, falling into step beside her, and they both made their way through the old foyer to the outside.

"Let's go get lunch with the rest of the Inner Circle," Val insisted, looping her arm through Alecto's and tugging her towards the cafeteria building.

There was no point in arguing, so Alecto let Val lead her through the campus. She wasn't sure whether her hangover would allow her to stomach anything more than a cup of coffee, but at least she'd get that.

"How is detention going?" Val asked.

Alecto shrugged. "It's manageable. *Dusty.*"

Val barked a laugh.

"Rogue mentioned that you've been sneezing like crazy."

"Did he now?"

They rounded the corner, and Val waited until they were alone on the pathway before she spoke again.

"Why haven't you talked with your dad about it?"

"About what?" Alecto frowned.

Val rolled her eyes. "About getting off detention. I'm sure Daddy can pull a few strings. You don't have to serve the whole fucking month."

Alecto hummed. Of course, Val was right. One call would be more than enough to get her off for good, no more libraries and dusty books.

But there would be a price to pay, an extra dinner or event to attend, or worse—going back home for a weekend. Alecto would rather choke on the dust in that library for however long it took her.

Realizing that Val was still waiting for an answer, she shrugged. "It's not the worst detention ever. I don't mind."

Val narrowed her eyes but only nodded. "You're not thinking about getting back at him for it, are you?"

Ah, so this was what it was all about. Blaze and protecting his ass.

Alecto cracked a smile, meeting Val's dark gaze.

"I have better things to do."

"Good girl." Val smirked. "Loyalty to your House is what ensures the win."

Someone crashed into Alecto's shoulder, almost sending her to the ground if it weren't for Val steadying her by her side.

"*Whore*," Rebecca Moon from the Tigers sneered.

Alecto wasn't sure what came over her in that moment, but her mind acted before she knew it.

Neither do they have it in them to be cruel or merciless.

Rebecca was about to turn away, but Alecto grabbed her by the throat, slamming her into the nearest wall. They were on one of the secluded paths between the buildings, the shortcut to the cafeteria from the auditorium.

"Say that again to my face, *bitch*," Alecto sneered.

Rebecca lifted her hand to slap Alecto or push her away, but Val was there in a heartbeat, slamming her hand into the wall. *Hard.*

The girl winced, and Alecto strengthened her grip around her lean neck. Rebecca's eyes widened with shock as she choked.

"Not so brave anymore, are we?" Alecto teased, her eyes roaming Rebecca's face.

Alecto bet Rebecca didn't think she would react this way. Rebecca probably thought she could bully Alecto like all the other witches on campus did, and she would take it silently. Most of the time, Alecto ignored the bullies, minding her own business and swallowing the insults because fighting back wasn't worth it.

But not fucking today.

Val chuckled. There was a clicking sound. A blade appeared in Val's hand and she lifted it to Rebecca's face.

"Oh, she's probably on the verge of pissing herself. Aren't you, Becks?" Val teased, cocking her head to the side, a wide smile on her face.

"You're fucking crazy," Rebecca choked out, her free hand gripping Alecto's wrist, digging her nails into her skin. "Let me go, or I'll go to the Dean and—"

"And what?"

"You're going to cry to the Dean about Alecto Black pushing you against the wall in a dark alley on your way to class, huh?" Val drawled. "You're going to against *legacy*, and you think you'll win?"

Rebecca's eyes darted between Val and Alecto.

"Please—" she pleaded, but Val cut her off.

"Let's say you do win in this case, and Miss Black gets into trouble for getting physical with another student," Val mused. Alecto could barely hold the laugh back as Becks's face grew ashen with fear. "You fuck with a member of our Inner Circle. Do you think the House of Snakes are not going to come after you? Oh, darling, it would be Genevieve 2.0."

"And that was messy, wasn't it?" Alecto pouted, shaking her head. "I don't think you want to deal with all of that, Becks."

"No, I don't think you do," Val agreed.

"I don't—" Rebecca started.

"That's right." Val cut her off again, her eyes turning malicious. "Next time you come at Alecto, threatening, remember that I'm going to ruin you. How's Helena doing?"

Rebecca's body stilled, eyes growing wide. "I don't know who you're talking about."

"Let me refresh your memory for you—Helena, the pretty blonde, gray eyes, tattoo of a butterfly above her pubic bone. Does that ring any bells, Becks?"

"I think it does," Alecto chimed in, cracking a smile.

Alecto's heart was racing, her breathing shallow. It was a feeling weirdly foreign and…addicting.

"Listen, I don't know what you know or what you think you do. It's not what it looks like," Rebecca said, stumbling over her words.

"Oh, we've seen your little performance backstage," Val said. "In fact, we found it so good, we sealed it in a memory orb, didn't we, Alecto?"

"Oh, yes, we did. It was quite a show. Who could blame us?" Alecto's smile widened as Rebecca's face lost all its color. Alecto could feel the hard swallow under her palm.

"What do you think Damon would say about his bride being not so pure if he found out?" Val asked. "I don't think his family would be happy about that."

"So, sweetheart, think long and hard before you once more say a word to Alecto, glance her way, or even think of her," Val warned, her face turning serious as she pressed the knife against Becks's cheek. "Stay in your fucking lane, or I will show Damon what his fiancée loves to do when he's not around. Am I making myself clear?"

Rebecca swallowed once more and nodded.

Right then, Alecto let go of her throat. The moment Rebecca was free, she ran away from them as if her ass were on fire.

"Getting a bit protective?" Alecto asked, turning to Val.

Val shot her a smile. "Nobody calls my bitch a whore." Alecto barked a laugh, falling back into step with Val on their way to the cafeteria. Val draped an arm over Alecto's shoulder, whispering sweetly into her ear, "You have potential I didn't see before, Black."

It might have been the sweetest thing Val had ever said.

19

The next evening, Alecto and Jolene made their way to the lockers before the first rockey game of the season. Alecto's heart raced, her chest heaving with anticipation and fear.

Jolene had helped Alecto conjure a little spell that would make Blaze's game tonight a little bit slippery, and it didn't take Alecto long to learn that revenge did taste better than peace.

Jolene's fingers linked with Alecto's as they rounded the corner. A few whistles followed them as they passed a bunch of guys from the House of Rats.

"Fucking first years," Jolene said, throwing them a middle finger over her shoulder. "They don't seem to realize that we can turn them into actual *rats*."

Alecto chuckled. "How fitting that would be."

Of course, it was no surprise that boys were drooling as Jolene walked past them.

Tonight, she had half of her long, dark hair pulled up into two horns, letting the blue locks shine as they waved down her back. Jolene opted for a black dress similar to Alecto's, but hers was made of velvet and not silk and had a very high cut, going almost all the way up to the nook where her thigh connected with her hip.

And if that wasn't enough to get people's hearts going, Jolene wore a golden chain dangling from her neck to her waist and then connecting around her exposed thigh.

Jolene always knew how to dress to own everyone's attention.

"You have the amulet?" Jolene asked as they stopped before the door to the lockers. "I'm so fucking excited you don't even know."

Alecto laughed, pushing the door with her shoulder, and they entered the room full of witches getting ready for the game. As they made their way towards Blaze's locker at the very back, many heads turned their way.

Neither Gabe nor Matias dared to look up as Alecto walked past them; the bruises on their faces were still fresh. It gave Alecto an unholy amount of satisfaction seeing them like this.

Oh, that's nothing compared with what I have planned for you.

"Alecto?" Andro couldn't hide the surprise as Alecto and Jolene approached.

Blaze next to him arched a brow, leaning against the door of his open locker. Perfect position for what Alecto needed.

Jolene immediately walked forwards, wrapping Andro in her arms.

"We came here to kiss you for good luck," Jolene announced, all cheery. Then, she grabbed Andro's face in her palms and brought her lips to his, giving him a wet smooch.

Andro laughed, pulling her in close and burying his face in her neck. Jolene squealed and laughed. "It tickles! Androoo!"

Blaze's eyes flickered as Alecto met his gaze. "Did you bring me a kiss for good luck as well, baby?"

They hadn't seen each other since the incident in the classroom. Since Blaze was on his knees in front of her, driving Alecto out of her mind with his tongue.

Coming closer to him, Alecto forced a tight-lipped smile. Blaze's muscles tensed. Alecto didn't give him a moment to prepare as she pushed him back into the locker door, placing a palm over his chest.

Blaze's moon-pale skin was hot under her touch.

Alecto bit her lower lip, bringing her lips to his, and it was very hard for her not to laugh at the sudden frightened expression on Blaze's face as she pressed her mouth to his.

It wasn't a kiss. Not really.

Alecto nipped at his lower lip, dragging it through her teeth before pulling away.

The expression on Blaze's face was priceless—fear mixed with shock, mixed with something darker. Something Alecto had seen twice before when he looked at her.

With a smirk, Alecto pulled away, smacking a wet kiss on Andro's cheek before turning to walk out of the locker room, Jolene right behind her.

Let Blaze think Alecto came here driven by what had happened between them. She needed him distracted, and while she was sure Blaze hated her, for whatever reason, there was also something else there. Something she would need to figure out if she wanted to win.

"Did you put the amulet where you need it?" Jolene asked the moment they stepped outside the locker room.

Alecto nodded. "Blaze will have the worst game of his fucking life, and he won't even know what hit him."

"That motherfucker is due some good old humbling if you ask me," Jolene teased, bumping Alecto's shoulder as they left the building and walked onto the rockey field. "I just hope he doesn't find out it was you."

Alecto didn't answer. She couldn't tell Jolene that Alecto would do everything in her power so that Blaze knew it was her who fucked with his performance tonight. How else will he know not to mess with her?

Alecto and Jolene walked over to the bleachers on the left side of the field. Most of the benches were already occupied, the whole student body gathered to watch the game.

Finally, at the very top, they found two seats empty. A few feet away from the bleachers, Venefica's coach stood by the team's benches.

A few familiar faces already lingered around the rockey boards, and Alecto noticed a few more faces of students who were not on the team last year. Finally, Andro and Blaze appeared from the building, striding towards their boards.

When Blaze reached the benches, the coach leaned over and whispered something. Blaze only gave a curt nod before walking over to his board at the very end of the line.

One by one, the team stepped on their boards, securing their feet with leather straps, and then Blaze glided through the air towards the middle of the field, where another team was already waiting. Barely a moment later, the referee's whistle pierced the air, and a round white ball rose up, Blaze and another skinny guy gliding towards it.

Under any other circumstances, at any other rockey game, Blaze would have surely caught the ball and be gliding away towards their opponents' gates, passing the ball to Andro so he could score mere moments after the game started.

But today wasn't a usual day.

Blaze whizzed through the air, pushing his opponent away with his shoulder. But the moment the ball reached his fingertips, Blaze lost it, letting it fall to the grass beneath their feet.

Alecto couldn't hold the smile in at the look of utter confusion on Blaze's face or the way his eyebrows scrunched when Andro glided over to him. Blaze only shrugged, rushing away towards their opponents.

"Oh, he's going to kill you if he finds out," Jolene said, laughing.

Alecto flashed her a devious smile. "Let him try."

I t was almost hard watching Blaze losing the ball over and over again.
Almost.

He deserved it. He more than deserved it for purposely getting Alecto detention. He deserved it for all those times he played with Alecto, teasing her in order to humiliate her. He deserved it for making her come so hard she could see fucking stars.

Yeah, he got what was coming to him.

After each game, there was a party hosted in the field next to the rockey field, with the whole faculty and all of the students celebrating the win. Well, tonight, the party was still on, but it celebrated anything but a win.

Alecto rolled her glass of bubbly wine between her fingers as she stood by Val's and Jolene's sides, completely ignoring the conversation as her eyes searched the field.

She was looking for him. Alecto needed to see his face, the battled look of defeat. Her heart was hammering hard with anticipation and fear. Fear of what would happen when Blaze realized it was her who fucked up his game.

Finally, Blaze emerged at the corner of the crowd, his hair still wet from the shower, falling messily over his forehead. He strolled towards them, both hands stuffed in the pockets of his black jeans.

If it weren't for the lines settled in the corners of his mouth, you wouldn't even think he was upset. He looked as charming as ever, the devil in disguise.

"Have you seen Andro?" Blaze asked, raking a hand through his wet hair.

Alecto pointed to her right, where Andro sat with Gael under one of the willow trees at the end of the field.

"What the fuck was that all about, *Blazy*?" Val chirped, hooking her arm around his waist, pulling him closer to her.

A sudden, sharp pain went through Alecto's chest, something so unfamiliar and foreign she shifted her gaze away from them, pretending to casually look around the field.

"Mercury in retrograde or some shit" was all he said, waving a hand for a server with drinks.

Blaze pulled away from Val and snatched two drinks from the tray, tipping one glass all the way back as he drained it in one gulp.

"Well, someone's thirsty," Jolene noted, arching a brow.

"Always." Blaze tipped the other glass up as his eyes locked with Alecto's. A shiver ran down her back.

If Alecto was stupid, she would have looked for a deeper meaning behind Blaze's words, one to match the scorching fire in his gaze.

But Alecto wasn't stupid.

"Where's Rogue?" she asked.

"Oh, he's busy carrying out my orders," Val said, her mouth curving up as she jerked her chin to their left, where most of the student body was gathering.

Alecto followed the direction to find Rogue leaning against the tall bar table, a charming smile on his face as he casually chatted with Galia Rathone.

"Galia?" Alecto's jaw dropped. "You seriously think she's going to fall for him?"

"The bitch already has." There was no mistaking the malicious flicker in Val's gaze as she sucked on her teeth.

Alecto shook her head. "Unbelievable. That was super-fast."

"Well, we designed him this way, remember?" Val cocked a brow. "He's nothing but a walking seduction machine. And now that they've all seen him with me at the party at the Tigers', they also want a piece of that ass."

Val's plan was in motion. Alecto could only applaud how smooth everything was going.

"If you manage to pit Rats against Tigers, it's going to be a scandal of the fucking century," Jolene drawled.

"You better fucking believe it will be," Val agreed. "The Rats do owe us for stealing our win last year."

Seemingly out of nowhere, Galliermo approached their little group, clasping a large palm over Blaze's neck.

"Good evening, Snakes," he greeted them. "Blaze, I will have a word with you before I go."

"Sure," Blaze murmured, turning to walk away with his father, Galliermo's hand still clasped over his neck.

Alecto followed them, not missing the way Blaze's shoulders squared or the way his head ducked down as they stopped further away from the crowd and his father leaned in to whisper something.

It wasn't a scene or even a conversation that would seem wrong to most people.

But Alecto knew the small signs well enough to recognize the way his father's mouth moved, tight and reserved. The way Blaze's face fell, eyes going blank.

And something inside Alecto twisted because she was too familiar with the touch of a parent you dreaded more than anything else.

She pushed the sorrow away, shoving it deep inside her. There was no place for mercy. Not for Blaze.

So, as Blaze's gaze turned to her, their eyes locking, Alecto didn't look away.

Instead, she allowed herself to smirk just before she lifted the glass to her lips, taking a long sip. There was no mistaking the realization that hit Blaze as his eyes widened, lips parting.

Yeah, he deserved everything that was coming his way.

20

Blaze swallowed a growl as he cut the piece of rare beef on his plate and put it in his mouth, chewing hard.

Like every other Sunday of the month, Blaze sat at the dinner table at his parents' house, Val by his side, and had the dreaded family dinner.

He wanted to be anywhere else but here, especially after the game last night. His father's anger seeped from him as he silently chewed on his own piece of beef at the other end of the long table.

Blaze couldn't be angry with Alecto, could he?

He was the one who took their innocent bickering and games and turned them into a serious pissing match. He shouldn't have been surprised that she got back at him for the detention.

But somehow, he found himself surprised and confused, which he absolutely didn't appreciate. At the same time, though, he loved the fact that Alecto retaliated.

The possibilities were endless for how Blaze would be able to even their score, how much more exciting it was when Alecto responded to him.

He just wished she had picked some other way of getting back at him.

Fuck me.

He wanted her suffering.

He dreamed of her in his bed, moaning and whimpering, at his mercy.

Maybe if Alecto was dead, Blaze wouldn't think about her anymore...

Well, that's something.

There was chatter going on around the table. The guests, mostly Blaze's father's business partners, were all having heated conversations, cutlery clinking as they dug into their dishes.

You'd think the noise would be enough to draw Blaze out of his own head, but it wasn't. He was too deep into this shit.

"You're brooding," Val whispered in his ear. "I understand you're upset about the game, but maybe don't make it so obvious for everyone? Your misery is *miserable*."

Blaze threw her a sideways glance, reaching a hand to pick up his glass of wine. He tipped the glass, draining it, and then waved at the server.

"Well, if I'm making you so miserable, you shouldn't have come here tonight," he shot back, holding a glass out for the server to refill. He only stopped the Crahen when the glass was filled to the brim, golden liquid almost spilling over.

Val's sigh was the only sign of her annoyance. "No need to be rude about it, *Blazy*. If it weren't for me keeping your mother busy tonight and assuring her that you're just upset about the game, she would be all up your ass about your foul mood. How about a little bit of gratitude?"

Blaze scoffed and drowned in his wineglass.

Maybe he had made a mistake by sleeping with Val the other night, looking for a distraction.

Before, he was quite good at balancing their agreement and relationship at the House, but now he sensed danger.

Val already had been acting territorial, and the last thing he needed was for her to sink her teeth and claws into him deeper.

Fuck me.

Blaze glanced at his mother, sitting by his father's side, wearing an elaborate ivory gown that accentuated her lean shoulders and long neck.

No doubt the dress was made to order by their tailor in the city, making sure that she would be shining bright dangling from his father's hand, like the sweet accessory that she was.

Blaze's chest burned with hatred at the way Auburn tipped her head back, cheeks flushed from the wine as she laughed at someone else's joke.

She was the walking embodiment of everything Blaze hated, so weak and fragile she could shatter at any time.

There was nothing worse than a spineless woman.

A woman who fought with her teeth and nails, on the other hand…

Once the dinner was over, the whole crowd transferred to the official lounge in the Leveau penthouse, with the windows opening to a view of Avalon Hills at night. The massive glass door to the roof terrace was wide open, and those who were not bothered with chilly September nights were spilling over to the terrace.

The sky was already pitch dark, only a crimson moon hanging heavily, surrounded by a multitude of stars, all shining in many colors. Blaze leaned his elbows on the iron railing, enjoying the noise coming up from the streets below and the city lights stretching as far as your eyes could see.

He missed the city when he was at Venefica.

Blaze preferred his room in the brownstone back in Darly over his room here. But he missed being surrounded by the noise and the lights, the frantic energy always swirling in the air.

He turned, leaning on the railing, and found Val standing in a circle with a few older men and women, deep in conversation.

Val knew how to work the room. She knew how to come in and demand attention, even from those who hated her, and part of Blaze envied her for it.

Val might not have come from a privileged background, but that gave her the advantage amongst them.

She wasn't plagued with the dread of not belonging.

Whenever Val didn't fit in, she molded the world around her to fit her.

Blaze swirled the golden liquid in his glass as he narrowed his eyes on Val, so focused and lost in his thoughts that he didn't notice his father approaching.

"You've been drinking quite heavily tonight," Galliermo noted, his black eyes plastered to the glass in Blaze's hand.

Blaze shrugged, tipping the glass to take another massive sip.

"It's been a long week, Father," he said, swallowing hard.

His father's eyes narrowed. "Why don't you join me in my study."

It wasn't a question.

And Galliermo didn't wait for Blaze's answer as he turned and made his way through the crowd towards the corridor that led to his private study.

Blaze followed a few feet back. He finished his drink and managed to grab another from the tray, finishing it in a few gulps.

As Blaze was about to leave the room, he caught his mother's gaze. Worry had settled in her soft features as she glanced between him and his father.

Auburn knew what was about to happen.

Yet, there was nothing she could do.

Would do.

So, the worry and the dread that graced her soft features only made Blaze's blood boil with anger, and he didn't miss an opportunity to sneer at her right before he left the lounge.

"Close the door," his father said as Blaze entered the study after him, striding towards his large oak desk in the middle.

Galliermo didn't sit in his chair though.

Once he reached the desk, he whirled, his black eyes drilling a hole in Blaze's skull.

There was nothing but pure hatred rooted in that sinister glance, but Blaze had gotten used to it throughout the years.

It was familiar.

"You're a total disappointment," his father spat. "Losing the first game of the season and showing up here to empty my bar?"

Blaze slid his hands into his pockets. "What can I say? I'm thirsty tonight."

Galliermo crossed the room in a flash. His fist gripped Blaze's black shirt at the front, dragging him closer to his fuming face.

"Don't you talk back to me, you piece of shit," he hissed.

Blaze let him have at it, not moving nor trying to get away from his grip.

There was no use anyway.

"When are you going to learn your lesson?" Galliermo continued, anger so strong in him that a vein in his forehead popped. "It might seem you have forgotten yourself. Maybe it's been too long since I last showed you what happens when you disappoint me."

Blaze flashed him a crooked smile.

A fist connected with his side, and Blaze grunted at the pain. His father's grip loosened, but before Blaze could step away, another punch came at him, right in his kidneys.

Blaze fell forwards on his knees.

Galliermo circled him. "If you lose one more game this season, you're going to find yourself in a very unfortunate situation. Do you hear me?"

Blaze didn't answer.

Another punch to his ribs came, sending Blaze to the ground as he swallowed the pain.

"I have scouts from professional teams coming to watch you play," Galliermo said. "There is big money involved, and if you don't perform, then I'm going to be embarrassed in front of all of my business partners. I won't have that."

Blaze managed to scramble back to his knees, his body trembling as he tried not to vomit out his dinner and all the alcohol.

But before he could rise to his feet, the black tip of the shoe glittered in the dim light before connecting with Blaze's ribs once more, sending him sprawling on his back again.

This time Blaze wheezed, biting hard on his lip as he tried to ride out the wave of pain.

"Remember this when you decide to fuck up next time," Galliermo warned, panting heavily.

Blaze lay on the floor for a long moment, looking at the dark wood panels on the ceiling, forming a herringbone pattern.

He was lucky he drank enough tonight because soon the pain drifted away, leaving him in floating space, as if he were not in his own body anymore.

Galliermo was smart. He never hit him where others would spot the marks.

But he always made sure the wounds were serious enough that Blaze would remember it for a long time.

And Galliermo had made sure Blaze would never fight back.

Not unless Blaze wanted to share the fate of his older brother.

After a while, he finally mustered enough strength to climb back onto his feet. He caught his reflection in the mirror hanging above the fireplace.

With his hair ruffled, bruises still healing from the incident with Gabe and his lackey, Blaze looked like Hel.

He slowly strode to the door, his ribs aching with each step he took.

If it weren't for *her*, he wouldn't have lost the game.

If it weren't for *her*, he wouldn't have been made a fool in front of the whole school.

If it weren't for *her*, he wouldn't have suffered.
Blaze had to make Alecto pay.

21

On Monday morning, Blaze was slowly dozing off, his head swinging forwards as Professor Namiad's voice floated further and further away.

Before Blaze could fully doze off, someone shoved him in the shoulder, and he jerked awake. Andro's bitter-coffee eyes were staring at him with an amused shimmer.

"What the fuck?" Blaze growled, clearing his throat.

"Are we going to talk about it?"

"Talk about what?" Blaze rubbed his palms over his face, desperately needing to wake the fuck up.

"About you going all *hero* and literally smashing Matias's face the other day?"

Ah.

Blaze glanced at the professor, now diving deep into a conversation with a redhead student at the very front of the classroom.

"What is there to talk about? You were there. You know what went down."

Andro rolled his eyes. "Give me a fucking break. You know damn well what I mean."

"No. I really don't."

Maybe if Blaze pretended Andro would let it go.

He really didn't want to think about what happened that day.

But Andro wasn't the one to let go, that mouthy little piece of shit.

"You've fucked with her since she started at Venefica," Andro whispered. *Loudly.* Val, sitting on Blaze's other side, stirred. "One would assume you'd be glad others were fucking with her too?"

Blaze rubbed his jaw, tipping his head to the side to steal a glance at Alecto sitting a few rows down, scribbling one of her illustrations in her notebook.

It was always the same scrawny-looking girl with an oversized head and large doe eyes that were hollow and empty. The only thing that changed was her outfits and poses.

Fucking weird.

"She's mine to fuck with," Blaze finally answered, bringing his gaze back to Andro, "and I don't like others messing with what's mine."

Andro chuckled, shaking his head as he leaned back in his chair. "We all are fucked up, but you are on another fucking level."

Blaze flashed him a half grin and returned his attention to Professor Namiad at the front of the auditorium, now speaking to the whole classroom.

"Anyone care to answer?" she asked, glancing from one student to the next.

Blaze didn't even know what they were talking about in today's Forbidden Arts lecture. When her gaze landed on him, she very wisely moved on.

"I don't know whether I should be glad that none of you pay attention in my class. At least it means none of you are interested enough to dabble in the forbidden magic," she said, crossing her arms. "Or maybe I should be worried because if one day you encounter a witch who practices Fanhy, you'd be dead in an instant. And all because you didn't pay attention when you should have."

Blaze exchanged glances with Andro and rolled his eyes.

The dramatics.

Professors at Venefica seemed to be out of touch with reality.

Yes, witches were cruel and savage. It was in their blood.

But they were not running around attacking each other like the old times anymore. They were civilized now.

That's why they had things like the Game, to get it all out of their systems in a proper manner instead of going mad and burning the whole world down around them.

"Miss Black," the professor said. Alecto's platinum blond head snapped up, hand frozen mid-drawing. "Care to answer my question? Should I repeat it, or have you been taking notes all this time your nose has been shoved in your notebook?"

"Aether magic draws the energy from the space in between the realms of Inathis, Hel, and the mortal world," Alecto answered.

Alecto seemed to always be ready to answer any questions that came her way from professors.

Blaze never thought about it before, but could provocative Alecto Black be a...*bookworm*?

The possibility of that girl being a teacher's pet was unsettling. And highly amusing.

"And why is that forbidden?" Professor Namiad prompted.

"Because disturbing the energy between the realms threatens to alter reality, which can cause drastic events in one or all of the three realms," Alecto explained, putting the pen down and closing her notebook. "If too many witches practice Aether magic at the same time, it can tip off balance."

Professor Namiad smiled, pleased at Alecto's answer.

"Thank you, Miss Black," the professor said, walking back to her desk. "I'm glad to see that at least someone is doing their reading."

A few mocking chuckles came from the left of the auditorium, but Alecto didn't seem to care, not even sparing a glance to a group of students whispering to each other.

"Half-breed teacher's pet," someone hissed, and more laughs went around the auditorium.

The professor didn't seem to hear the remark. Or maybe she just pretended not to.

Something inside Blaze's chest tightened, but he ignored the feeling, watching Alecto's reaction instead.

To his surprise, Alecto didn't react.

Instead, she leaned back in her chair, shoulders relaxed as she swiped her long hair over her shoulder, dropping one long leg over the other.

It was immaculate, watching Alecto ignore the hate coming her way like it was nothing.

Like it didn't touch her, sharp words didn't sink into her skin, her flesh, the marrow of her bones.

Alecto Black might have only had *half* of what made witches superior, but it seemed that she had all the right things in her blood.

How fascinating.

"You might be onto the right path here," Val whispered to Blaze.

When Blaze glanced at her, he found her attention on Alecto.

"What do you mean?"

Val smirked and caught Blaze's gaze, eyes flickering with something dark. Mischief? A touch of amusement? With Val, Blaze could never tell.

"Sometimes a witch needs a little nudge to start moving in the right direction," Val mused. Blaze frowned, lost at the meaning behind her words. "Surprisingly, you were the little push we needed."

Val's mouth bloomed into a full smile. Blaze was about to ask what the fuck Val was talking about, but he didn't get the chance.

"I know, it's absolutely heart-wrenching—"

Professor Namiad was cut off by the door opening and Miss Bellthrove strutting in, a file in her hands.

"I'm sorry to disturb your class, Professor Namiad," Miss Bellthrove chirped, adjusting her thick round glasses. "I just wanted to ask you to excuse Mr. Leveau, Mr. Weir, and Miss Black from the lecture. I need them to come with me."

Immediately, Andro tensed at Blaze's side.

"I thought you did damage control," Blaze whispered to his friend.

Andro swallowed hard, nodding as he watched Blaze with wide eyes. "I fucking did."

Blaze rolled his eyes, rising to his feet. "Well, apparently, not well enough."

22

Their parents weren't in the Dean's office, so Blaze considered that as a good sign.

If the Dean didn't want to bother the Alumni with their children's poor behavior, it meant that they weren't in any real trouble.

Yet, Andro's knee bounced like crazy as three of them sat on the sofa, waiting for the Dean to call them in.

"Will you fucking stop?" Blaze pinched the bridge of his nose as his palm landed on Andro's bouncing knee.

"I don't know how *you* can be so fucking calm," Andro hissed. "I've talked with everyone who was there. I made sure that nobody will speak or they're going to regret it."

The bouncing eased, so Blaze removed his hand, tucking it under his armpit.

"Well, that's so sweet of you, Andro," Alecto teased, a smirk gracing her calm face. She didn't look bothered by being called into the Dean's office either. "Sweet conversations definitely always work."

Andro shot her a glance. "At least I didn't try strangling people."

"What are you talking about?" Blaze blinked.

Alecto inspected her crimson nails as she said, "There was a small incident with Rebecca Moon. Nothing me and Val couldn't handle."

Now Blaze was interested.

How come he hadn't heard about it from Val?

"Or maybe you're here because Rebecca actually went to the Dean, *bitch*," Andro scoffed, the bouncing back on.

"She definitely didn't."

Blaze didn't think she could be more beautiful, but with that satisfied, sinister look, Alecto looked like the fucking goddess of his dreams.

"You're evil," Blaze teased.

Alecto rolled her eyes.

Before Blaze even had the chance to catch her gaze, her eyes darted to the floor, cheeks suddenly flushed. Alecto shifted in her seat, crossing her legs, and Blaze barely held a laugh back.

Ah, this was too sweet.

She felt uncomfortable in his presence, probably remembering him kneeling in front of her, her thigh draped over his shoulder as he feasted on her.

Sparks of pleasure went through Blaze, and he shifted in his seat himself, dropping one ankle over his leg as the vivid memories brought a stronger reaction out of him than he expected.

Right then, the door to the Dean's office opened, and Gabe appeared, Matias trailing right after him.

There was no mistaking the smug expression on Gabe's face.

"Please come on in," the Dean said.

Alecto rose first, padding into the office like she was walking a fucking runway, hips swaying.

Blaze went in after her, his eyes not so subtly on her ass, and Andro was right behind them, closing the door as he entered the office.

They took a seat in three chairs in front of the Dean's massive dark wood desk.

"Well, you probably know why I asked you here today?" the Dean inquired, lacing his fingers together, resting his elbows on the arms of his chair.

Andro was about to open his mouth, but Blaze cut in, "Not a clue, Mr. Gondalez."

The Dean searched Blaze's face, which clearly held the marks of what had happened, as his bruises were still visible on the jaw and his cheek.

"It was brought to my attention that there was a physical fight between the members of two Houses," he explained. "Does that ring any bells, Mr. Leveau?"

Blaze pouted, rubbing his chin. "That's rather vague, Mr. Gondalez. There were many fights I witnessed over the weekend. Isn't that right, Andro?"

"Mm-hmm, definitely. Many fights, Mr. Gondalez," Andro agreed, nodding.

"You'll have to be more specific." Blaze laced his fingers together, mimicking the Dean's posture.

Gondalez's eyes flashed for a moment, but his face remained still—a carefully engineered mask of blank calmness surely honed by years of dealing with little privileged shits.

"Do not play me, Mr. Leveau," the Dean warned, his voice even. "I know all about the fight. Who attacked who first, and how it all ended. The marks on your face are testament enough."

Blaze didn't like being disturbed for such nonsense. The Tigers were really trying hard to get on his nerves this year.

"You know that while the Game allows many types of different activities, such offences as fighting are taken very seriously at Venefica. We don't condone violence amongst students outside the Game. And this instance will need to be answered for."

"Do you also know about the cause of the fight, Mr. Gondalez?" Alecto asked. "Did those two man-children who came here crying about being beaten tell you why they got what they got?"

"I'm aware that it was due to jealousy over a girl between the boys from rival Houses," Gondalez said, carefully articulating each word. "That girl is you, Miss Black. That is why you're also here in my office."

Alecto shifted in her seat, leaning forwards as she rested her elbows on her thighs.

"You see, Mr. Gondalez, this is where you're wrong," she said. "The only reason why there was any sort of conflict happening was that your students—members of the House of Tigers—sealed a very intimate moment involving Matias and me in a memory orb with the intention of using it to blackmail me and the Snakes. Knowing my family's status, I'm sure you can understand why the House of Snakes couldn't let that happen."

The Dean stared at her for a moment.

"Now, considering that the Tigers acquired the blackmail material for the purposes of using it against the Snakes to probably bargain for our Book, I think we can all agree that whatever had transpired amongst us was, indeed, part of the Game." She looked so hot right now, all-powerful and calm, dangerously calm. Blaze couldn't take his eyes off her. "Which means that you can't really punish us for breaking any academy laws."

Fuck yeah.

"Miss Black," the Dean said slowly. He eyed her carefully, sweat gathering over his graying eyebrows. "If the administration were to believe that to be true, we would still need to conduct a proper investigation to determine that there is, in fact, a memory orb the Tigers intended to use for blackmail—"

Now it was Blaze's moment to shine.

He leaned forwards and said, "Mr. Gondalez, with all due respect, I'm sure we can settle this matter with no further investigations."

"Mr. Leveau—"

Blaze snapped his fingers, and with a silent *whoosh*, a piece of ivory paper folded and sealed with a wax stamp appeared in his hand.

Casually, he threw the piece of paper on the desk in front of the Dean.

"I'm sure you'll be interested in this, Dean Gondalez."

Gondalez glanced at Blaze, then at the paper before picking it up and unfolding it.

Blaze really tried to avoid abusing his power for such things.

Well, he tried as much as possible.

But sometimes, you just had to do what you gotta do to get things done.

And sometimes, it involved good old blackmail.

After a moment, the Dean snapped the paper shut, his lips pressed into a tight line. He tossed the paper on the desk, and before it hit the polished wood, it disappeared into thin air.

The Dean rose to his feet, a hand sliding over his belly to hook a button of his suit jacket into place.

"We have an agreement, Mr. Leveau," he said, his face once more blank. "For your own sake, I would avoid getting into any more physical fights in the middle of the campus. At least wait until the end of the day when other people are not around."

And with that, they were free.

They quickly rose and left the Dean's office, Blaze strolling in the front.

"What the fuck was that?" Andro asked when they were outside.

Blaze shrugged, placing a cigarette between his lips. "Just something from my father's files."

"Well, good job, team." Andro grinned. "That was hot."

Alecto crossed her arms, clicking her tongue. "Does your father have a file on everyone?"

Blaze inhaled the smoke, tilting his head backwards as he let it escape his lips in an easy stream. "Maybe. I don't know."

That was a lie.

Galliermo had a file on everyone he encountered in Inathis and beyond.

And Blaze was familiar with all of it.

23

On a chilly Thursday afternoon, Alecto met Jolene downstairs. Her friend wore a long burgundy coat over her outfit as the weather was finally cold enough.

"Ready?" Jolene chirped, and Alecto offered her a smile and a nod. "Great. Val should be with us in a moment, once she's done scolding poor first years."

Alecto snorted. "What did they do?"

"Probably breathed too loud."

They both chuckled. That was indeed how much it took for most people to piss Val off.

And after the shit that the Tigers tried to pull off with the memory orb, Val had been *exceptionally* pissy. Not that Alecto could blame her. Alecto didn't remember the last time she had been so angry. All the time.

"Ready, bitches," Val said as she walked from the kitchen, a black coat wrapped tightly around her tiny body. "I hope whatever it is you're going to show us today is gonna be worth it, Jolene. We have a locator spell to perform, the sooner the better."

Jolene snorted, and they left the House into the cold air. Alecto could see her own breath even in the daytime now, and she was pretty sure that if she caught the reflection of herself right now, the very tip of her nose would be red.

"So, where are we going again?" Alecto asked Jolene as they left their street behind.

"It's a surprise."

Alecto didn't like surprises. But she trusted Jolene as much as she was able to trust anyone at Venefica. So, Alecto didn't question her anymore and followed her friend through the park towards the Old Darly.

They walked in silence, only the sound of the damp gravel of the wide pathway crunching around them. Alecto pulled her black coat tighter around her as the chilly wind swooped over them, sending gusts of gold and red leaves rolling through the park.

Soon, the old iron gate appeared, one side crooked, barely held by the rims cemented in the stone fence. As they walked through the gate, Alecto inspected the mossy stones, so different from the ones they had on their side of town.

Not many witches stepped foot in this part of Darly anymore. This was obvious as they strolled down the narrow street, passing old buildings with windows barricaded with wide wooden planks or simply left with the glass broken.

Each building had stories to tell, and a shiver went down Alecto's back, hair at the back of her neck prickling as the wind blew once more. For a moment, she thought she heard voices carried within the breeze.

"This place gives me the creeps," Val said.

Alecto could only nod in agreement.

The Old Darly was creepy and haunted, just like most of the town's legends claimed.

"Are we trying to find a spirit to haunt the Tigers until they give up their Book willingly?" Alecto asked as they turned into a narrow alley with a wall blocking the very end of it.

Val laughed, which flooded Alecto with satisfaction.

Jolene said, "I would never dare disturb the dead for a prank."

Alecto exchanged a glance with Val, whose lips were still curled into an amused little smirk.

Finally, they reached the dead end of the alley and came to a stop. On the left, in a tall redbrick wall, there was an old metal gate door. Alecto hadn't noticed it until they were right in front of it.

Jolene fished for something in her pockets, checking a few before finally, she came up with a chain. There was a key on the chain, and to Alecto's surprise, Jolene used the key to unlock the metal gate door, opening the entrance to what seemed to be a small private garden.

Once they were inside, Jolene closed and locked the gate again, putting the chain over her neck so that the key hung between her round breasts.

"What's that?" Alecto asked, looking around the garden contained between the buildings, where you would never guess a small paradise, even if abandoned, lay.

The golden vines wrapped tightly around the brick walls, a bunch of fire-birds roaming around, darting in and out of the thickness of the leaves. On the far end of the garden stood a wrought iron table and three chairs. One was missing a leg, another its back. A whole bunch of red clay planters littered the surface of the table, young ivies spilling over the sides.

"It's the Old Church," Jolene replied, waving a hand at one of the walls with colored-glass windows stretching tall.

Jolene rushed towards another door, used the same key to unlock it, and then led them inside.

"Oh, shit." All Alecto could do was whisper as she took in the vaulted glass ceiling, stretching for several feet over their heads, and the elaborate paintings covering every available space on all the surrounding walls.

"How—" Alecto's words died in her throat as she strolled between rows of stools carved out of ivory bone, most of them damaged beyond repair either by witches from the past or by time itself. "How the fuck? I thought it was hidden centuries ago."

"You bitch." Val's voice echoed around them, but she didn't sound upset. In fact, she sounded ecstatic. "Frones were the ones who hid the church, right? That's how you have the key!"

Alecto turned to where Val and Jolene stood, Jolene twirling a string of her thick hair between her fingers, pouting.

"My grandmother was *one* of the four students who hid the church all those decades ago, yes," she admitted with a sigh. "Before you complain why I didn't tell you before, I just got the key from my aunties as a gift for starting my third year at Venefica."

"Why would they give it to you now?" Alecto frowned.

"I don't know. My aunties like to do things however they please. Maybe they thought that surviving two years at Venefica was a big enough deal to whip out an old family secret as a present."

Val eyed Jolene for a long moment. Her eyes narrowed.

"So, why did you bring us here today?" Alecto asked, turning back to the abandoned altar with a statue in the middle.

Figures of the Gods—the Mother and the Father—were carved out of cream-colored bone. They both had their backs to each other, their fingers linked together as both of their faces looked at the sky. It was just like the one that stood in the middle of Darly Park they passed on their way here.

The face of the Father was broken off, shattered by its feet. But other than that, the statue was quite intact for something that was probably centuries old.

"To be honest, I was curious to see how casting a spell would work in here compared with at campus," Jolene admitted, walking up to Alecto. "I thought it might be more effective."

Alecto cocked a brow in question, but Val was the one who explained. "They hid the church for a reason, you know? It's said that one of the Mother's bones is buried beneath the Old Church, fueling the rituals performed here with Her magic."

"Yeah, once it was the main point for all students of Venefica to cast spells. My grandmother used to tell stories of wild revels held in the Old Church before important rituals," Jolene said, rolling her eyes.

"You don't believe it?" Alecto asked.

Jolene shrugged, eyeing the altar. "I believe everything unless you give me a reason not to."

She sent a wink to Alecto and chuckled, bumping a shoulder into hers.

"Let's clean up the place," Jolene said, pushing the broken bone away from the altar, a cloud of dust rising in the air. Alecto sneezed. "Oh, sorry, babe. I forgot."

Alecto took a few steps away, waving her hand. She sneezed a few more times, which only made Jolene and Val laugh.

"It's kinda cute, don't you think?" Val asked, leaning a hip on the altar.

"There are lots of things that are cute about Alecto Black."

"Ain't that the truth. Especially when she's all mean and ready to get down to business."

Alecto's cheeks heated, but she didn't avert her eyes. The girl stalked towards Alecto. When she finally came to a stop, she was so close Alecto could smell her spicy perfume.

"Blaze told me all about the meeting with the Dean," Val said, lips curling. She tilted her head to the side and Alecto's heart picked up its pace. "You handled yourself very well. I'm pleased, Black."

Neither do they have it in them to be cruel or merciless.

Val didn't think Alecto had it in her, but from the way she looked at Alecto now, it was clear that Alecto managed to change her mind. Satisfaction flooded her, but she didn't get to reply as the door to the church swung open and a tall frame walked in.

"How the fuck did you know where to find us?" Jolene asked, eyes wide as she stared at Rogue.

Val rolled her eyes. "I got him to follow us."

"You what? For what?"

"For my own gains, duh."

Rogue took a few moments to glance around the church, taking in the ceilings and the paintings. And then, his amber eyes were on Alecto. His lips curled into a smile.

"I've got something for you."

His long finger elegantly unbuttoned his gray coat, and he slipped a hand inside. Out of the inner pocket Rogue fished something out. And when he opened his palm in front of Alecto, there was a clear glass orb sitting there.

"You retrieved the thing that could have cost us a win this year?" Val asked. Alecto took the orb, rolling it between her fingers without looking at either of them. "Good job, Black. And good job to you too, Rogue. That's the type of loyalty I wanna see. From everyone."

Val strolled off towards the statue of the Gods to help Jolene clean it up, leaving Alecto and Rogue alone.

Finally, Alecto lifted her eyes to his. Rogue's amber gaze was steady, his face solemn.

"Did you enjoy the view?" It was easier to will her words to be venomous than to give in to the embarrassment.

He pursed his lips and shook his head. "I didn't watch it, Black. If I do choose to watch, I'd rather do it live."

Alecto's heart jumped to her throat, heat rising all over her body, and she had to clear her throat before she could speak again.

"Thank you for doing this."

Rogue winked. "Anything for you."

24

"I thought it's only going to be us?" Andro asked the moment they set foot in the Old Church. Blaze didn't miss Rogue sitting next to Alecto on one of the benches carved out of bone.

Today Alecto wore her hair up, tied with that old clip she seemed to love so much, a few strands of hair escaping and waving around her heart-shaped face, framing it perfectly.

She was a beauty; Blaze couldn't deny it.

A cruel beauty.

Val rolled her eyes and waved her hand in a dismissive gesture as she made her way towards the altar.

The floor around the altar was covered in white chalk lines, curving into different symbols for the locator spell they were going to perform on the Tigers' Book.

A whole heap of white wax candles was burning atop the altar. Whenever the wax warmed, it turned black, dripping down the length of the candle, leaving a dark trail behind.

It hit Blaze then that it looked as if the candles were crying.

"I don't think it's smart to have Rogue participate in all of our meetings and spells," Andro said.

Blaze rolled his eyes at his best friend. It was as if Andro just waited for a chance to start an argument with Val.

"Rogue *is* going to participate in the Inner Circle meetings every week," Val argued, crossing her arms.

Andro shook his head, standing his ground. "He's *not*. He might be the perfect tool for our plans, but it doesn't mean that he should be in the Inner Circle meetings. It looks bad in front of the rest of the House."

Rogue looked nothing more than bored when he chimed in, "I'm right here, you know?"

"*Shut up*," Andro and Val both snapped at him.

Then Val turned to Andro and pointed a finger. "I don't give a fuck what the rest of the Snakes think of him attending our meetings or helping us with Inner Circle business. He needs to know the strategy, and I'm not about to repeat myself every single time. Besides he has been more useful than some of you."

Blaze arched a brow, crossing his arms. "Really? How?"

Alecto was the one to answer this time. "He got the orb back from the Tigers."

An icy blue gaze met Blaze's and for a moment they just stared at each other. Alecto seemed to be determined to stand with Val with this one. On Rogue's side.

Blaze glanced at the demon, who gave him a smug smile.

And for the very first time Blaze had the urge to go over there and push that bastard as far from Alecto as possible.

Confused at his own reaction, Blaze blinked and averted his eyes back to Andro and Val.

Andro was opening his mouth to argue some more, but Val shut him down. "I'm the High Priestess, Andro. Don't forget that. My word *is* the last."

"And here I thought we had democracy," Blaze mused, lighting up a cigarette.

Jolene snorted. "Yeah, sure."

Andro apparently wasn't done arguing. "We don't even know why the fuck Rogue is here instead of a fucking Guardian. Have any of you ever stopped to think about it? To figure out what the fuck went wrong?"

Blaze had to agree with Andro on that one.

In the past weeks, he had been so preoccupied with Alecto and their mind games that Blaze completely forgot all about it.

"Listen, we've already figured it out," Val assured him, rolling her eyes.

Then, she snapped her fingers, and their Book, lying on the altar, swung open.

Not so gently, Val flipped the pages and then waved for Andro to come closer. With an arched brow and a challenge in her eyes, Val stabbed a finger at the page.

"You see, here is the spell for the Guardian," she said. Andro inspected the page. Once he was done, Val flicked through a few more pages to another spell. "And this one is a spell for calling a demon. Apparently, Jolene was right when she pointed out first that it was due to the use of blood magic that we summoned the demon instead of a Guardian."

"I fucking knew it!" Andro bellowed, his eye twitching as he stared at Val. "And you said you didn't do it on purpose."

"I didn't," Val scoffed, rolling her eyes. She snapped the Book shut. "It was my mistake. I didn't read both spells beforehand, so I didn't know."

Andro was ready to say something more, Blaze could see it written on his fucking face, but somehow, his friend managed to swallow it down as he stalked away from Val.

Val never was one to admit to her mistakes. And she was not one who made them often either.

Blaze wasn't so sure it was an accident after all.

Val was too prepared for such accidents to happen.

"Now that we have this matter settled, how about we get to the damn locator spell?" Val said.

"Right, let's get to it," Blaze agreed.

They all took their places around the altar, standing in the formation of a pentagram, even if the star wasn't painted on the floor. Rogue stayed behind on the bench, watching them from afar.

"Should we, like, use sex magic for the spell?" Andro asked. He looked like a child contemplating getting in trouble. "Make it unforgettable. It's our specialty after all."

"Over my dead body," Alecto murmured, and that made everyone laugh.

"Prude," Andro teased.

"I'm offended, Alecto," Jolene countered, still chuckling.

"What, we're not good enough for you?" Blaze drawled.

To Blaze's surprise, Val on Alecto's left didn't tease. Instead, she jerked her chin, her athame in her hand. "How about a kiss then?"

Alecto sucked on her teeth, the others quietly waiting for her answer.

Blaze hated to admit it, but the prospect of using a little bit of sex magic excited him.

"*Fine*," Alecto finally said, not forgetting a roll of her eyes for dramatic effect. "A kiss."

Andro and Jolene howled, tilting their heads up, and Val barked a laugh, clapping and hollering.

Blaze watched Alecto intently. It was a surprise—another one of many recently—for Alecto to agree.

As if feeling his gaze, Alecto turned, and their eyes locked. Blaze's eyes dropped to her mouth. Right then, Alecto licked her lips, and heat surged up Blaze's spine.

Oh, dear Gods.

This girl was doing things to Blaze.

Things he didn't like.

"Jolene, will you do the honors?" Val asked, pressing the tip of the knife to her finger.

"Fuck yeah," Jolene replied with a large grin. Her eyes fluttered shut, and she took a deep inhale of air before starting the chant. "*Locarccio prioti.*"

Andro and Blaze joined her while Val pricked her finger, blood seeping through a small puncture in her skin. She brought the finger to her lips, smearing the blood over them, and then she left her spot, moving towards Alecto.

Val stopped right in front of Alecto, her black eyes intense. Blaze's magic awakened, buzzing under his skin and making his heart thrash against his ribs.

Slowly, Val's hand cupped Alecto's cheek. She smiled faintly before rising on her toes to press her lips to Alecto's.

At first, they just stood there with their lips touching, but then Val's tongue brushed the seam of Alecto's lips.

Blaze's jeans were suddenly too tight, and he licked his lips, unable to look away.

He found himself wishing he was in Val's place.

When Val finally moved away from Alecto, both were breathing hard.

Val winked before returning to her spot, and then it was Blaze's turn.

While Blaze waited for Alecto to come to him, he glanced to his side, back to where Rogue sat. The demon's attention was all on Alecto, his eyes intense.

He was feeling a certain type of way. Without even looking, Blaze's hands found their way to Alecto's hips. A breath hitched in her throat and right that moment, Rogue's gaze shifted to Blaze.

Blaze held his stare for a long moment, feeling the heat from Alecto's body next to him, his thumbs moving in circles over her flesh.

Rogue had to understand that he better keep his hands off Alecto.

If he wanted to keep them.

Finally, Blaze dragged his attention to the girl in front of him.

Alecto licked her lips and planted a hand over Blaze's chest. Then, she slowly leaned forwards for a kiss.

Blaze couldn't move, mesmerized by her and the feel of his magic under his skin at the same time.

Alecto brushed her lips past his without giving in fully, and Blaze mimicked her.

They were once again playing the game that only the two of them were aware of.

Just like that night at the Ceremony.

Blaze's hand came to cup the back of her neck. He pulled Alecto in with no space to escape and claimed her mouth like it belonged to him.

Magic swirled inside Blaze's chest, crackling like lightning, zipping through his muscles. And when Alecto finally pushed away from him, Blaze's head was swimming.

Hesitantly, Alecto took a step back and then another. Blaze's eyes didn't leave her until she was back in her spot.

Next, Blaze kissed Andro, both snickering once they peeled away from each other.

Lastly, Andro kissed Jolene, taking more time than was necessary, knowing he was more into Blaze than Jolene.

Once all five of them were chanting, their magic swirling inside their bodies and around them, heavy and thick, the wind rose out of nowhere.

They all gasped as the gust went through them, making the candles flicker for a moment.

Blaze didn't think there had ever been so much magic in one place, and it was hard not getting lost in it completely.

Suddenly, Blaze realized why the Old Church was hidden all those years ago. Why nobody would want students of Venefica to know where this precious gem was.

That sort of power was dangerous in the wrong hands.

Hands like *theirs*.

"Focus your attention on the House of Tigers," Val's voice boomed. "Channel the energy from our Book to conjure an image of theirs."

It took Blaze a few moments to concentrate, but he did it. He focused on their Book lying on the altar, next to the bronze bowl where the flame sparked to life right that moment.

A column of black smoke rose to the ceiling and soon the fog parted, revealing the image of the Tigers' House.

"Of course," Andro said, rolling his eyes. "Of course they'd keep it in their House."

Blaze arched an eyebrow but didn't say anything.

The Snakes kept their Book in their House, under the strongest protection spell that money could buy.

But it was rare that other Houses did the same. It would be the first place others would look.

And if you didn't have elaborate wards, it would be easy to steal.

Val broke the spell by stepping away from her spot, the wind around them dying down immediately.

"Do you think they got better wards this year?" Jolene asked.

"Could be," Val agreed, her eyes focused on something in the distance. "We'll need to either find a way to break them to get in—"

"*Or* we could draw them out," Alecto interrupted. She had settled on the altar at the base of the statue, her feet hovering good few inches over the floor.

Val's gaze snapped to her, her eyebrows hiking all the way to her hairline.

"You've got something on your mind, Black?"

Alecto took them all in, her lips blooming into a mischievous smirk.

Nobody expected to hear the next words coming out of *her* mouth.

"How do we feel about burning the House of Tigers down?" Alecto asked, voice light. "That will surely cause enough havoc to give us an opportunity to swoop in and steal the Book."

The silence in the church was deafening. And then, Andro and Jolene burst into laughter.

"You're fucking crazy," Andro almost screamed. "You're out of your fucking mind. I love it."

"Sign me the fuck up," Jolene said, lifting an arm.

Val glared at Alecto for a moment, her face unreadable. Then she nodded. "Bitch, I think I might be in love."

Alecto barked a laugh, her blue eyes filled with genuine…*joy*.

Blaze was too stunned to muster a response.

"Next week, after the game, the party is at the Rats' House. Everyone will be there. We come in while everyone's distracted, light the fucking House on fire, and go to the party."

"This is not going to be as easy," Andro warned Alecto. "They'll know about the fire almost immediately."

"That is why we create astral projections of ourselves and let them attend the party for everyone to see."

Blaze blinked, still taken aback.

Alecto really had thought it all through already.

"Smart." Jolene nodded. "The only issue is that it's a fourth-year spell and none of us has attempted it before."

"We've got the Book. What, suddenly we can't fucking read?"

"And we have a few bookworms on our hands. This is wonderful," Val said, grinning. "Demon boy, you will ensure that people are focused on you next weekend while we destroy the Tigers."

Rogue glanced at them all before shrugging his shoulders. "Sounds like a plan."

Blaze wasn't sure why he had bothered answering. It was not like Val gave him another option anyway.

Jolene flipped through their Book. "We'll need smoke quartz for the spell."

"I'm going to get us something better than smoke quartz, don't worry about it," Val said.

Jolene laughed. "Oh, this is going to be priceless."

"Yeah. The Tigers are going to lose their Book and accommodation," Alecto said. "We'll see how those arrogant fuckers feel about public showers with regular students when they have to live in the common housing."

That drew a burst of laughter from them all.

Blaze couldn't help but marvel at how perfectly cruel and calculated Alecto's plan was. It made the hairs on the back of his neck rise.

"You're truly evil," he muttered, coming closer to where she sat. Blaze pinched her thigh, just hard enough to draw her attention to him.

"And what if I am?" Alecto's eyes were full of dark excitement, challenge burning brighter than the stars in the night's sky.

He didn't think a half witch could be so...*witchy*. Rumor had it that their mortality fucked up their sense of what it was to carry their power.

But it seemed that not every half witch was mortal *enough*.

"I think that's hot," Blaze teased, his voice low enough so only Alecto could hear him.

25

Blaze wasn't used to *this* part of Avalon Hills, the filthy, bustling Upper West Side where he and Val now made their way towards a huge warehouse looming in the distance.

They passed multiple shops and cafés, most of them filled with large, bold men and their tattooed bodies. Even Blaze felt uncomfortable.

"Are you sure we're in the right part of the city?" he asked Val as they crossed the street.

"Of course," Val answered. "Helsgate is right there. I'm pretty sure it's impossible to mistake the location of the only black market in Avalon Hills."

From the way Val strode through the streets without fear or a second thought, Blaze was sure Val knew her way around this part of the city well.

All of them were aware that Val grew up basically on the streets, with two parents more involved in nursing their addictions than their child. But Val never got into details of what she did to survive or how she even made it out alive and in one piece.

Most importantly, how she managed to make her way to Venefica.

Finally, they reached the warehouse, walking through the broken gate, and two large satyrs greeted them by the entrance.

The fur lining their legs was shiny black, hooves polished and pristine as if all they did all day was lounge around and let someone tend to their every wish.

Even their naked chests looked like they were carved out of marble, every muscle chiseled to perfection, gleaming in the dim light of the streetlights.

"Why are you here?" one of the satyrs asked. His bright amber eyes were anything but kind as he glared down at them.

"We're here to see the Imp Queen," Val answered, her voice light as a feather.

Blaze straightened his back, blinking. "We are?"

Val threw him a glare, and that shut him up real quick. He turned to the satyrs, nodding.

The second satyr, with one of his black horns broken, snorted.

"The Imp Queen is busy," he sneered. "She doesn't have the time to take meetings with witches and warlocks who haven't even graduated Venefica."

Blaze wasn't sure why Val brought him here with her when Rogue would have been a much more useful ally in a place like this.

But when she turned to him with an eyebrow cocked, Blaze knew *exactly* what he had to do.

He slipped a hand in the inner pocket of his leather jacket, fishing out his wallet. With a heavy sigh, Blaze took a bunch of bills out and glared at the satyrs through his eyelashes.

They perked up real quick at the sight of money.

Blaze held out a hundred for each. "Is the Imp Queen still too busy to see us poor students of the best witchcraft academy in Inathis?" The satyrs exchanged a glance, so Blaze counted two more hundreds. "How about now?"

Broken Horn reached out a hand, and Blaze passed him the bills. "You'll find her somewhere on the floor. If you reach her before someone kills you, *witchlings*."

Val strode through the door first, Blaze following in her wake, and a wall of smoke hit them right in the face.

Inside, the warehouse was packed with stalls where traders had a variety of products set out, most of them rare and stolen.

As they made their way through the outer ring, trading stalls changed into gambling tables, where poor witches gambled their money, souls, and lives away as greenish goblins dressed in fancy black suits shuffled the cards.

"Do you even know what the Imp Queen looks like?" Blaze asked Val, leaning in closer to her.

Blaze knew *of* the Imp Queen, one of the few creatures of Hel who took up residence in Inathis, ruling this side of the city and, most importantly, the only black market in Avalon state.

He was sure his father had crossed paths with the woman before. Galliermo owned half the fucking city after all.

But even Galliermo never spoke of the Queen out loud.

"I do," Val said, glancing at Blaze. "Haven't you seen the illustration in the Demonology texts?"

"That's your source for what the Imp Queen looks like?" Blaze raised his eyebrows, but Val only laughed.

Most of the illustrations of creatures of their realms were accurate. Satyrs, goblins, sprites, and fairies, amongst many other creatures, all looked exactly as illustrated.

But the Imp Queen was no average creature.

And her illustration was the reason why Blaze had nightmares, like so many other students, after their first Demonology class.

Blaze glanced around, expecting to find a woman who stood out in a crowd, but there were none that fit his criteria.

But amid goblin dealers, faceless Crahen, and witches walking the edge of the blade, nobody stood out.

After they did a full lap around the warehouse, Blaze was sure the Imp Queen wasn't here.

"Well, what do we do now?" Blaze asked. "Should we just go check the stalls for the crystal?"

Val shook her head. "We won't find black quartz at one of the stalls. Heavy-duty shit like that is where you go to see the Queen herself."

Suddenly, a heavy hand landed on Blaze's shoulder, whirling him around. A pair of forest-green eyes stared at him, one slashed with a nasty scar right in the middle.

"You come with us," the Redcap announced, voice rough, and he pushed Blaze forwards, his hand still wrapped tightly around his shoulder.

Blaze glanced at Val, who didn't look alarmed by two murderous Redcaps escorting them to the corridor on the side of the main warehouse hall.

They walked in silence for a long time, the corridor leading them deeper into the warehouse, where windows were becoming scarcer. When they finally reached metal stairs, they climbed, Redcaps hurrying them forwards.

Blaze wasn't sure they'd survive a fight against the Redcaps.

One they might be able to take down *if* they were clever enough with their spells.

But two were impossible.

The thought raised Blaze's heart rate, but then they reached the door at the top of the stairs. One of the Redcaps knocked on it.

"Come in."

The door opened on its own. The Redcaps shoved them inside before slamming the door shut behind them.

Blaze and Val stood in front of the large slab of crimson stone serving as a desk, a tall, slender woman sitting behind it.

When she lifted her eyes from the papers scattered in front of her, Blaze's blood froze in his veins, that striking amber gaze locking him in place.

The Imp Queen who sat in front of him was nothing like the illustration in their textbooks.

She was worse.

With deep wine-colored hair flowing down her shoulders, creamy skin, and sharp, delicate features, she looked inhumanly beautiful.

But it wasn't the kind of beauty that made Blaze's blood boil with wicked desires.

It was the kind of beauty that was painful to look at. The kind that made him want to turn and run as far as his feet could take him.

"*Valeria*. It's been a while," the Imp Queen addressed Val and Blaze was sure that his jaw was on the fucking floor.

They know each other?

"Yes, Moren. It's been a while." Val smiled. "How have you been?"

"Busy," Moren replied, her face hard as a stone. Then, her eyes shifted to Blaze, and she cocked a brow. "Mr. Leveau. Does your father know you're here to see me?"

Blaze blinked but didn't let his surprise show. "He has no clue, my Queen. I don't ask about his affairs, and he doesn't ask about mine."

There was a tug at one corner of her perfect lips, and Blaze sensed it was as close to a smile as the Imp Queen ever got.

"I see you have his looks, but he doesn't have your charm," she said and then waved her hand to the chairs in front of her desk. "What is the reason for this interruption, Valeria?"

They obediently sat down, and Val said, "We need black quartz."

Moren's eyes narrowed on Val, but then she looked away as she opened the drawer and took out a silver cigarette holder.

Her elegant fingers popped it open, drawing a slim black cigarette and placing it between her sultry crimson lips.

Blaze was on his feet in a fluid movement, leaning over the desk as he flicked his lighter and held it for her. "Allow me."

The Imp Queen watched him intently for a moment; it seemed as if the air in the office was sucked out. Then she leaned forwards and let him light her cigarette.

"Black quartz is illegal," Moren said as the stream of smoke escaped her lips.

"Yes." Val nodded. "That is precisely why we're in the black market."

"Why are students of Venefica in need of a black quartz?"

"For a very special spell," Blaze said.

He wasn't sure how much Moren knew, how much Val was willing to give, and frankly, whether the Imp Queen even cared about the Game.

"And smoky quartz is not enough?" Moren arched a brow. "That's some spell."

"We need something stronger than smoky quartz," Val explained. "And don't worry, it's not going to be a favor this time, Moren. We're going to pay for your trouble."

Pointedly, Val glanced at Blaze, and so did Moren.

You'd think Val would at least try to hide the fact that Blaze was her walking bag of cash.

"Oh, there will still be a favor involved," Moren said, looking back at Val. She snapped her fingers, and a cluster of black quartz appeared on her desk. "It'll be three thousand garders and a promise from the Leveau boy."

Blaze's hand froze midway into the pocket of his jacket. He blinked. "Excuse me?"

"I do not repeat myself, Mr. Leveau."

"What kind of promise?" Blaze asked, taking out his wallet. He counted the bills and placed them on the desk between them, keeping an eye on the Imp Queen as he awaited her answer.

Deals with creatures of Hel were never good for witches.

"A promise that you'll come to me when I call you," Moren explained. "It'll happen only once. But when it does, you promise to answer my call."

Blaze furrowed his brows. "And what will I have to do once I come to you?"

"Nothing you're not willing to do, Mr. Leveau."

That sounded like a fool's bargain, a promise that's vague and filled with trickery.

"Deal."

26

The smell of bacon and eggs was making Blaze's stomach growl. He sighed heavily, watching Romeo work multiple pans on the stove at the same time, whistling a tune.

"Drilling a hole in the back of my skull won't make me cook faster, kid," Romeo threw over his shoulder.

Blaze rolled his eyes. "At least I tried."

Romeo's large body shook with laughter, and then Andro came into the kitchen, dark red eyeshadow on his eyelids, lips painted a color Blaze didn't know the name of.

"What's so funny?" Andro asked, plopping into the chair next to Blaze.

"Blaze is hungry, and Romeo doesn't give the boy what he wants," Romeo said. "It's probably a first for this one."

Andro barked a laugh, which only intensified when Blaze threw him a sideways glance.

Today Andro wore the academy uniform jacket, but instead of the pants, he wore the pleated skirt with white socks going all the way to his knees.

"Nice legs."

"What's between them is even nicer," Andro teased, winking. "Wanna see?"

"I'll show you mine if you show me yours."

"Get a fucking room," Jolene chimed in, rolling her eyes as she entered the kitchen, settling on the stool on the other side of Blaze.

Blaze turned to face her, just about to open his mouth, but Jolene slapped her palm over his lips to stop him. "Don't bother, pretty boy. I don't play for your team. And let me just say, thank the fucking Gods."

When her palm slipped away, Blaze pouted. "You hurt my heart, Jolene."

"You have to have one first."

Blaze laughed, draping his arm over Jolene's shoulders and dragging her closer so he could ruffle her hair. She squeaked and giggled, pushing him away.

"*Bastard.*"

"And you love it."

Romeo finally turned to them, a plate full of bacon in his one hand, a plate full of scrambled eggs in the other. He placed them on the island and then turned to get the potatoes and the maple syrup.

Blaze reached a hand towards the bacon, but Romeo slapped it away.

"Hands off, kid," the chef scolded. "The potatoes are not done."

"Romeo, I might die if you take this long."

When Andro reached a hand to grab a piece of bacon, Romeo didn't stop him. Blaze glared at Andro, who only smirked. "Maybe try being nicer."

"I don't think it's *biologically* possible," Alecto snorted, coming into the kitchen looking like a fucking snack.

Blaze glanced up and down her body before she disappeared behind the island, going over to the coffeepot.

Her pleated uniform skirt was rather short, and Blaze wondered whether it was on purpose. If she were to just hunch over a bit, you could see the contour of her ass.

A nice, perky ass Blaze would have loved to sink his claws in.

And that skirt right now carried rather naughty memories.

Fucking Hel. Get it together, Leveau.

Alecto placed a coffeepot on the stove, turning up the gas. Her coffee was always black, never with creamer, milk, or sugar.

While she waited, she turned to them, crossing her arms.

The door to the kitchen flew open, and Val rushed in, Rogue trailing after her. She plopped the notebook she carried on the island in front of them, barely missing the plates of food.

"We're *so* fucking ready for next Saturday," she breathed out, all excited. "Rogue just fetched me the last of the ingredients we need for astral projections."

"Should we maybe do it this Saturday then?" Andro asked. "After the rockey game?"

Val's lips curled into a wicked smile. "I like the way you're thinking—"

"No," Blaze cut Val off.

Everyone glanced his way, but nobody said anything.

This Saturday they had a big game. A game for which Blaze had to prepare.

There was no space for anything else in his mind.

Alecto leaned over the counter, glancing at the notebook. Blaze didn't miss the way Rogue found a spot right by her side. Her eyebrows shot up. "Where the fuck did you get black quartz from?"

"I've got my sources," Val said.

"Fucking Hel," Andro breathed out. "Can you imagine if we manage to pull this off and win the Game halfway through the first trimester?"

"That's gotta be a fucking record," Jolene said.

Val glanced at each of them. "Let's not get ahead of ourselves just yet."

Alecto's coffeepot started whistling and she turned away to the stove. Romeo passed her a cup, and she poured her coffee into it.

When she took the first sip, she didn't even blink at the bitterness of coffee.

A psychopath.

Blaze couldn't handle the taste of coffee unless it was packed with sweet syrup and creamer.

Lots and lots of creamer.

Sadly, Alecto didn't get to enjoy another sip of her morning coffee as Romeo shoved a plate with eggs and bacon into her hands. "Eat."

Reluctantly, Alecto placed it down on the island in front of her. Romeo pushed the maple syrup to her, whistling and completely ignoring their conversation.

"If this goes well," Val said, eyeing Alecto with such intensity, Blaze got worried for a moment. "We might burn all the other Houses this year just because we can."

"Can someone call the psychiatry ward?" Andro asked, dramatically looking around. "We have a crazy bitch on the loose."

"Someone's got to be the crazy bitch." She paused, bringing the cup of black tea Romeo placed in front of her to her lips. "Ruin them before they ruin you."

"Ruin them before they ruin you," Jolene murmured, lifting her cup in salute.

Romeo placed the potatoes on the island as well, and immediately Blaze grabbed the plate, filling it up his own. The others followed, digging in.

"Oh, my Gods," Jolene moaned, her mouth full. "Romeo, I could fucking marry you for your cooking skills."

"I'm going to need to get permission from my husband first," Romeo answered, leaning on his elbows. "I'm sure he'll be flattered I'm still in demand, kid."

Jolene and Alecto chuckled, so Romeo sent them both a playful wink before heading over to the sink.

Romeo *was* the best cook ever.

And Blaze should know—he had quite a few personal chefs growing up and none of them ever cooked food that was so delicious and heartwarming.

It was as if Romeo had put a piece of his heart into every meal he made.

Blaze finished his plate first, pushing it aside as he leaned back in his chair. "That was divine."

"How the fuck do you keep your lean physique eating like a fucking elephant?" Andro scoffed. "I have to play rockey *and* swim professionally. How's that fair?"

"What can I tell you, Andro?" Blaze shrugged. "Lots of fucking."

Romeo grinned at that, taking away Blaze's empty plate before throwing a sideways glance towards Alecto.

She played with her food more than she ate, nibbling on one piece of bacon and a tiny bit of egg. When she caught Blaze glaring at her, she put the fork down, pushing the plate to the side.

That was weird, wasn't it?

Blaze never paid attention to it before, but now that he thought about it, he had never seen Alecto eat a full meal.

In fact, he rarely saw her eat at all.

Rogue leaned closer—closer than Blaze liked—and stole a piece of bacon, biting down on it as he sent her a wink.

Alecto glared up at him through her lashes. Yet a small smirk appeared on her pretty lips as they stared at each other.

Blaze ground his teeth. He squeezed his thigh hard enough to make himself wince.

What the fuck did Rogue want with Alecto?

And most importantly, why the Hel did it look like Alecto was suddenly in on the joke with the guy?

Andro finished his breakfast and got to his feet. "Thank you, Romeo. I'll see you fuckers in class."

Rogue glanced at Andro and then at Blaze.

The bastard had the audacity to wink at Blaze, sending him aflame with anger before the demon leaned in to whisper something in Alecto's ear.

27

B laze hated academic lessons.

He never seemed to be able to concentrate enough to understand shit.

Or if he did, he would soon lose his train of thought.

Blaze blamed it on the pretty girls in his class, who were so much more interesting than the lessons anyway.

And it's not as if he needed the education to get a job.

He was a Leveau.

"Pair up," Professor Gabetown instructed. "You're going to work with your pair for the rest of the year to grow this garden, so choose wisely. It's going to be your main project, and I want to see some actual cooperation."

Nice.

Jolene was a perfect choice, of course, but Blaze knew better than to ask her to be his partner for this assignment.

So, Blaze had to find someone else…

To his luck, Alecto sat alone at her desk, chin resting in her palm. She didn't look as if she was trying to find a partner.

Blaze grinned to himself and immediately made his way towards her.

"How do you do, partner?" He dropped his book on the desk, making her jump.

Apparently Miss Black was lost in her thoughts.

She blinked. "No."

Blaze cocked a brow. "I'm afraid you've lost the moment, and I'm your only option left, baby."

Alecto glanced around the classroom.

It was so satisfying watching her face fall when she realized that everyone else was already paired.

Blaze pushed his chair closer to her, straddling it as he sat down.

Opportunities seemed to drop in his lap wherever he went. It was as if the Gods were giving Blaze their blessing to mess with this girl.

Blaze should fail Alecto in Herbalism for that little trick she pulled on him that made him lose the first game of the season.

He'd been nice to her recently. But that didn't mean he forgot.

Alecto would hurt as much as he did.

If not more.

"So, where do we start?" he asked.

Alecto glared at Blaze for a moment as if she were trying to drill a hole in his skull. "I'm not going to do all the work for you, motherfucker," she hissed. "And I'm not going to fail this class because you're incapable of anything more than fucking shit up."

Oh, it was delightful to hear how highly she thought of him.

Why the fuck did he even care about Alecto Black's opinion anyway?

"Let's make a deal, *partner*. What do you say?" Blaze leaned forwards into Alecto's personal space, cocking a brow.

Alecto sucked on her teeth. "I'm listening."

"You take the lead on this project, and I'll be your most willing servant, doing everything you need me to do so we ace this garden *thingy*. How does that sound?"

Alecto arched her eyebrow, clearly in disbelief. "And why would you be so kind?"

Before he answered her, Blaze slipped a finger in the pocket of his uniform jacket, taking out a small piece of black lace.

It dangled on the tip of his finger as Blaze cocked his head. "Well, you see, I've grown quite fond of you recently. And nothing would bring me more pleasure than making *you* happy."

The look on Alecto's face as she recognized her underwear from their little affair back in that classroom was priceless.

Blaze had to bite the inside of his cheek to not laugh.

Alecto's cheeks flushed a deep pink, eyes going wide as her pretty lips parted.

It took her good few moments to glance back at Blaze and hiss, "You're —you've got to stop this. *Now.* Put it away."

Alecto tried grabbing for his hand to hide the underwear, but Blaze was faster, moving his hand away from her reach.

"Ah, don't tell me you regret what happened?" Blaze taunted. "That hurts my feelings, I truly thought that we had something. Our dirty little secret."

Alecto growled as she finally gave up, falling back in her seat. She crossed her arms, her cheeks still glowing red as she shook her head.

"We have nothing," Alecto said. "You can go fuck yourself."

Blaze was *really* good at pissing Alecto off.

"Mr. Leveau is that a piece of underwear in your hand?" Professor Gabetown's voice came from their side, and Alecto went still.

Blaze turned towards the professor. "Yes, sir."

"Do you need it for your garden?"

The classroom erupted with laughter.

Blaze smirked, and Alecto looked as pissed off as ever. "Not really, Professor."

"Then why do you have it with you in my class? Were you looking to show off your personal underwear collection to your fellow students?"

Blaze spun the underwear on his finger, glancing around the greenhouse.

"I was actually just trying to find out what underwear Alecto liked," Blaze answered, glancing at her. "We couldn't agree on which color suits her better—black or red. Do you have any thoughts, Professor?"

A few whistles went around the greenhouse, a few inappropriate shouts following.

"I'm sure you can solve that personal issue on your *personal* time and not in my class," the professor said, walking away. "Get to work, Leveau."

"Yes, sir." Blaze stuffed the underwear back into his pocket, turning to Alecto, who still sat facing away from him.

Alecto was going to kill him.

"Did I tell you how fucking hot you looked back in the Dean's office?" he whispered, leaning closer to her. "All mean and sassy. With an attitude—"

Alecto slammed her book shut. "Fuck off." But he didn't miss the way she clasped her thighs, pressing her knees together. "I'm seriously going to turn you into a fucking plant right in front of the whole class."

Blaze only chuckled, grabbing her chair and pulling it closer to him. He didn't even care what other students would think anymore.

"Why do you fight it, Black?" Blaze sneered, cocking his head as his hand moved her hair away from her face. "Just give in and have fun. I know you enjoyed me just as much as I enjoyed you."

Alecto's jaw clenched so hard the muscle flared.

Mind games were the best type of foreplay. Blaze's heart hammered, his whole body on fire.

Why was Alecto Black getting him so heated?

Alecto grabbed her books and satchel and rose to her feet.

"Excuse me, Professor? I need to use the library for research," she said.

Professor Gabetown nodded.

Blaze smirked.

Did she really think she was going to escape him?

28

Next evening, Blaze made his way to the library on the campus. It was poorly lit and quiet when Blaze walked in, pushing the heavy door with his shoulder.

He strode forwards, trying to spot Alecto.

They had agreed to work on their Herbalism project tonight, and Blaze was looking forwards to some more quality time trying to rile Alecto up.

Finally, he spotted her sitting at one of the tables at the very back of the library, a stack of textbooks already by her side.

"Good of you to show up," Alecto said skeptically and arched a brow.

"I would never miss a chance to spend more time with you, Black," Blaze drawled, and Alecto rolled her eyes. "And of course, I promised to be your most willing servant in this project of ours. So, I'm here for whatever you need."

"For fuck's sake, does this really work for you, like, ever?"

He shrugged, his smirk deepening.

"I don't know, you tell me. Do the sweet words work on you, baby?" Blaze took a spot behind her, leaning down to whisper to her ear. "Do my words make you tremble, your soft thighs clenching at the promises they make?" Alecto's shoulders stiffened, and Blaze chucked, his breath tickling her neck as he continued, "Do they make you want to scream? Do they make you want to give in and forget?"

Alecto didn't answer, her breathing suddenly shallow. Blaze pulled away and strolled over to the corner where a massive brown leather armchair sat, one corner of it flush against the bookshelf.

He hummed a tune under his breath as he settled on it, his legs spread wide. He rested his head on the back of it, eyeing Alecto from afar.

A long, heavy silence stretched between them, but Blaze didn't rush to shatter it.

He let it sink its claws in them, building the tension that surely promised to lead them somewhere tonight.

He wasn't sure where, but he had a feeling it was going to be worth it.

There was something in Alecto's face, the way her sharp and usually cold features were unraveling in front of his eyes, the way her gaze changed from icy to warm to scorching.

"Why did you choose to study here?" Blaze asked, playing with his lighter, flicking it on and off.

"Because it's peaceful and quiet."

"Plenty of privacy, right? Not something you get back at the House."

Blaze dragged his bottom lip through his teeth. Alecto's eyes narrowed, lips pressed into a tight line.

And then, suddenly, Alecto straightened her back, her eyes widening as if she had just realized something.

Blaze was about to ask her all about it, but words died in his throat as Alecto rose to her feet, her intense gaze locked with his.

"You know what I just realized?" she asked, rounding the desk to stand in front of Blaze.

"Do tell me, Black."

"I could use a good fuck," Alecto confessed, licking her lips. Heat surged through Blaze. "And how convenient it is that you're right here, right now."

Out of everything that Alecto could have said, these words were the last ones Blaze expected to hear.

But the thing that truly worried him was the way his heart hammered behind his ribs, the way his cock twitched in his pants.

The anticipation of what those words promised was the thing Blaze was most surprised by.

Slowly, Alecto's hand reached for her breasts, squeezing one lightly before she let it slide down her waist, lower to her belly.

Lower, to her—

Blaze couldn't look away as Alecto lifted her skirt with one hand, letting the other glide between her legs. A moan escaped those pretty lips, and it did things to Blaze it shouldn't have.

He blinked, heat surging to his groin, and his cock swelled in his pants.

Alecto's hand moved over her length, stopping to press over her clit, and she spread her thighs wider as she gasped.

Blaze was speechless, his lighter still in his hand, the top open as he watched Alecto's hand, her body, and then her face.

He wasn't sure whether he wanted her to stop or whether he wanted her in his lap, riding his dick until she was trembling, the wetness of her wrapped around his hardness.

"Come here." Blaze's voice was low and husky when he spoke.

Immediately, Alecto's fingers stopped making circles between her thighs, her gaze snapping to his. She stood there still for a moment before she lowered herself on her knees.

What the fuck is she—

Blaze's breath hitched in his throat as Alecto started crawling towards him, lips parted and wet.

Blaze shifted in his seat, but Alecto's palm landed on his thigh, and he stilled, waiting.

Alecto crawled closer, sitting on her heels as she glanced up at him from between his legs.

Everything about that moment made Blaze's heart race, his mind getting lost in the dizziness of savage desire.

"Is this how you imagined me crawling to you, begging to take me?" Alecto asked, her hand stroking his thigh up and down.

There was no malice or shame in her tone.

It was soaked with the wicked desire, the same one that coursed through Blaze's bloodstream.

When Alecto's eyes dropped to his crotch, to the visible bulge of his jeans, she bit her lower lip.

And when she lifted her eyes again, glaring at him through her lowered lashes, Blaze almost lost it.

If she wasn't going to come and sit in his lap right then and there, Blaze would force her to do it and make her scream.

But then Alecto cocked her head and said, "Yeah." Another lick of those lips. "I think this is *exactly* how you imagined taking me."

Blaze couldn't read the expression on her face, the strange glimmer in those icy eyes that were a scorching fire burning right through him.

Blaze swallowed hard. "What are you doing, Alecto?"

"Taking what I want." Alecto's eyes darkened, a cruel smirk curling her lips.

Her hand traveled to his zipper and lowered it. And he didn't stop her. She then worked the button open and tugged on his jeans.

Blaze was too frozen to do anything until she said, "Lift your hips for me, baby."

He had said something similar to her before.

Hadn't he?

Alecto tugged once more, and Blaze obeyed, lifting his hips up enough for her to slide the jeans and his underwear down, freeing his hard cock.

He almost melted at the way Alecto's eyes glittered at sight, the way her lips parted, rosy and wet, ready to take him in.

She lowered her head to his lap, one hand gripping his base, the other resting flat on his hip. She took the tip of his cock in her mouth.

Blaze's hips jerked, and he groaned as her mouth closed over him, those lips looking perfect around his cock.

Alecto took her time, her head bobbing up and down slowly, her tongue swirling around his cock as she sucked on it.

Blaze was lost in the ocean of pleasure.

He was also lost in the dark sea of torture.

Alecto retreated a bit, her breath tickling him as she asked, "Will you hold my hair back for me?"

Blaze blinked, taking a moment to process her request.

He still couldn't believe this was happening.

But then Blaze nodded, bringing his hand to her head and gathering her long hair in his fist, away from her face. Alecto smirked before she lowered herself on his cock once more.

Her hair was soft as silk in Blaze's palm, and he held it with such care, as if he was afraid if he handled it too rough, it would disappear into thin air.

She would disappear into thin air, and Blaze would open his eyes and find that it was just a dream.

One of so many he had plaguing his sleep.

Alecto dragged her tongue over his length, drawing a low growl from depths of his chest, and Blaze leaned his head back, eyes still on her.

Blaze couldn't look away even if he wanted to.

Alecto on her knees, perched between his legs, as her pretty mouth sucked on his cock, was doing weird things to him.

Things he couldn't fathom, his mind drifting deeper and deeper into the thick pleasure that had been building in his body.

Alecto sucked and licked, moving her mouth around him without a pause as if she was thirsty for him. It was wet and sloppy, completely driven by a primal need.

Blaze's thumb massaged her head as she sunk onto his cock, swallowing him whole, and when he hit the back of her throat, he moaned.

She rose again, drawing air into her lungs, her striking eyes wide and round.

"You don't even know the things your mouth is doing to me," Blaze said, his voice thick.

Alecto blinked, slow and lazy, sucking on his tip that was red and hot now and then launched herself forwards again, taking him in deep.

"*Fuck*," Blaze cursed as he went a step closer to the edge.

Alecto didn't linger long, drawing back, gasping for wet air, her eyes full of tears. Two escaped, rolling down her cheeks.

Those tears…

Blaze could barely think as he basked in that look on Alecto's face. The idea of her struggling, hurting under his touch as she pleasured him, was unsettling *and* thrilling all at the same time.

What the fuck was wrong with him?

Blaze's lips parted at the sight, and he brushed a thumb over her cheek, catching one of the tears. "Oh, baby."

Alecto blinked once more, her long eyelashes wet with unshed tears, and then moaned, sending sparks of pleasure through him.

Blaze's abs tensed, and she picked up the pace once more, sucking him hard until Blaze couldn't keep himself back.

Finally, Blaze growled as his seed spilled into her mouth, hand gripping her hair tight.

Slowly, Alecto retreated, his cock sliding out of her mouth, and Blaze looked at her as she opened her mouth wide and large for him to see before she swallowed it all.

She licked her lips, eyes still wet with tears, and that might have been the most beautiful view Blaze had seen in his life.

Maybe that was why Blaze leaned forwards, his hand holding her hair sliding to cup the back of her neck as he dragged her face forwards, and his lips collided with hers.

He forced Alecto's lips apart, demanding her whole, and Blaze kissed her like it was their last day on this realm.

Blaze *was* in trouble.

When he finally peeled away from the kiss, both panting heavily, Blaze brought his forehead to Alecto's and breathed out the words over her mouth, "Don't ever do this again."

29

B laze barely slept last night.

Anytime he closed his eyes, Alecto was there in front of him, her eyes wet, lips parted as she kneeled between his legs.

"Blaze, snap out of it!" Andro slammed his locker shut, and Blaze flinched at the rattling sound.

Blaze blinked a few times, looking at his friend.

"It's fucking Grimswater," Andro growled, his face mere inches away from Blaze's now. "Fucking *Grimswater*. Get your head out of your ass."

Blaze scoffed. As if he didn't know that it was Grimswater.

The first official game of this University League season just had to be against that wretched all-boys academy. There was a lot riding on tonight's game, on Blaze's ability to play.

Blaze needed to win this.

Not only for his father but for himself.

And Blaze was ready to rip them to shreds with his nails and teeth if he had to.

"Fucking Grimswater," he murmured, stepping away from Andro.

"I've got your back." Andro clasped a hand over his shoulder and squeezed it.

He always had Blaze's back. Like a *true* brother should.

"Come on, fuckers!" Blaze shouted, clapping his hands as he went to the center of the locker room. "Form a circle!"

Lockers slammed closed, there was shuffling and murmuring, and then the whole team stood in a circle, all dressed in their uniforms, ready for tonight's game.

It never struck him as weird that he was the one to make the inspirational speeches that were supposed to encourage the team.

He was the least inspiring person in the fucking room.

Blaze smiled to himself as his eyes scanned his teammates.

"Tonight, we play against the worst of the worst. You remember that." Of course they remembered last year. *And* the year before that. "Grimswater doesn't play by the rules. They play dirty every step of the way. It's the only way those monsters know how to get anything done in life. That's why *they* are at Grimswater and not us, ladies and gentlemen."

Laughs and shouts went around the circle, a few witches banging fists on the lockers as they howled.

Blaze's smirk deepened, adrenaline coursing through his veins. "But we also know how to play dirty. And tonight, you're going to have to play like your fucking lives depend on it. Like the demons from Hel are chasing you on that field because we are here to show those fuckers who are the true kings and queens of the University League."

More shouts, more hollering, and howling.

"Now, get your asses onto that field and crush them the only way you know how," Blaze continued. "And *after* we claim the win, we're meeting at the Sparkling Hoof. All drinks are on the Leveau tab tonight."

More cheers, and the team rushed through the doors, onto the field where the crowd was already waiting for them on bleachers.

Blaze waited until the last player left and then went after them. When the crisp air of the night hit his face, he inhaled deeply, walking over to the bench where the coach stood over the lined boards.

"Leveau, I wanna see you win tonight," the coach said, his facial expression hard as he glared down at him.

"Will do, Coach."

Coach gave a harsh pat on his shoulder as he passed.

Before walking over to his board at the end of the line, Blaze stopped in front of Francesca from the House of Goats. She immediately straightened her back, securing her helmet under her chin.

"You're new this year," Blaze said, eyeing her. She gave him a sharp nod. "Grimswater is an all-boys school, and they don't have girls on their team."

"I know that, Captain," Francesca answered.

Blaze had to bite down a smile at how seriously she was taking him.

"They'll likely go for the girls first because of that. They'll try taking out the weakest links, and in their tiny minds, it's the women."

Francesca blinked, her jaw tight.

"Now, that puts you and the rest of the witches on the team at an advantage. Let them think that you're an easy target, and they'll lose their sharpness, arrogance taking over. That's going to be the moment you strike. Got that?"

Blaze offered her a half smile, and Francesca returned it, nodding once more.

Finally, Blaze took his place at Andro's side, lowering his board to the grass.

The field was empty, illuminated by the six large glowing orbs stationed around the perimeter. And there, on the opposite side, stood eight large figures from Grimswater.

It didn't take long for Blaze to identify Dominic amongst the guys, standing proud and tall at the very front, his hands clasped as he glared at Blaze.

Once their eyes locked, Dominic's lips curled into a wicked smirk, and he nodded.

It was a promise.

A promise that tonight was not going to be easy for Blaze because Dominic was on a mission to destroy him.

Roll of the shoulders, crack of the neck, and Blaze's feet were on the board, secured, and he was flying to the field to meet his opponent.

"Hello there, *Blazy-boy*," Dominic called as they met in the middle, waiting for the referee to give the sign for the game to start.

"Dominic." Blaze willed his tone to stay neutral.

"Ah, growing so fast, baby boy," said Raven, wiggling his long fingers. "Look at you, almost as tall and big as your daddy."

Blaze clenched his jaw so hard he thought his teeth were going to crack.

"And look at you, Raven, still locked up away," Andro teased back, smirking. "Just like *your* daddy."

Raven's eyes narrowed.

"Say that again, pretty boy." A guy on Dominic's left glided closer, floating eye to eye with Andro. Blaze was pretty sure it was Valentine, the nicest of the fucking bunch, which really didn't say much.

"Nah, V, don't bother," Raven shot back with a cocky grin. "Actions speak louder than words after all. Am I right, boys?"

"Fuck yeah," Dominic agreed. "Let's see if these pussies can play as well as they talk."

"Same can be said about you," Blaze shot back, and for a moment, he thought Dominic might smash his fist into Blaze's face.

But the referee's whistle pierced the air, the ball flashed at the corner of Blaze's eye, and he glided away towards it.

Of course, Dominic was right on his heels, and before Blaze snatched the ball, Dominic slammed into his side, sending him sideways.

Blaze quickly straightened himself, cursing under his breath, and sped up after Dominic, Andro already gliding through the air on the other side of him.

They exchanged a glance, and Blaze nodded.

Andro sped up, tearing through the wind, and came in close to Dominic from the left as Blaze came in from the right.

They both slammed into Dominic. Dom dropped the ball, letting it fall to the grass beneath them.

Andro maneuvered away, dipping after the ball, and caught it right before it hit the ground. He swiftly moved up and towards the gate, way ahead of everyone else as Blaze stayed behind with Dom.

The crowd cheered, screams and shouts coming from all sides as Andro scored, throwing the ball into the gate before the gatekeeper could even fathom what was happening.

Dominic grunted, whirling around and gliding away, but not before he threw a mean glance at Blaze.

Blaze couldn't help but smile to himself as Andro glided to him, and they high-fived.

"We keep at it, and we might as well win," Andro said, panting.

Now, the ball was on Grimswater's side, so Blaze regrouped, following Valentine as he flew across the field like a bullet, dodging every single player trying to block him.

Soon, Dominic and Raven were on Blaze's back, sharing a laugh as they tried closing the distance, teasing Blaze.

Blaze swallowed hard, shutting out everything around him and only focusing on gliding through the air towards Valentine.

Valentine was the nicest guy.

And he was also the best player Grimswater had.

Out of nowhere, Francesca whizzed past Valentine, cutting him off, and for a moment, he wavered, having to turn his board to the side to avoid crashing into her.

That was enough for Blaze to press forwards and close the distance between them.

Blaze threw himself at Valentine, making him stumble further, and then the ball slipped, landing straight in Blaze's hands.

The crowd roared, and Blaze's heart hammered in his fucking ears as he did a sharp U-turn and whirled around to glide towards the opposite gate.

But of course, Dominic and Raven were both there, just waiting for another chance.

With a laugh, Raven charged at Blaze, making him change his course and glide to the side, where Dominic flew right at Blaze.

Blaze cursed, and dodged Dom just by a mere inch and was back on track, gliding towards the gate.

Andro appeared at the corner of his vision. Before Blaze could give a sign, Raven blocked the view, flying in between them with a wicked smile curling his lips.

"Missed me, pretty boy?"

"It seems like you missed me more," Blaze snapped back, leaning forwards as he increased his speed. "Can't stay away, can you?"

Someone came around Blaze from the other side. When he turned, Valentine's brown face was there, mere inches away. Raven, on the other side, also came closer, squeezing him between them.

There was movement under Blaze. Dominic was gliding right under him.

He winked.

Valentine and Raven both moved closer, but Blaze was faster.

He ducked, almost falling on his knees on his board, and flew right out from under them. Without hesitating, without even glancing to make sure that Andro was still there, Blaze passed the ball.

There was no time to check whether Andro caught the ball because

Blaze's board went sideways as Dominic slammed into him from underneath, Valentine and Raven following soon after.

Blaze lost his balance, whirling in the air, and his legs were suddenly over his head, or his head was under his feet. He couldn't tell.

It all happened so fast, and then Blaze was falling.

Right into the trees of the nearby forest, branches scratching his face and naked arms as he fell.

Blaze's bones rattled as something hard hit his chest and knocked the air out of him.

When Blaze opened his eyes, he found himself draped over a branch, head and legs swinging a good ten feet away from the mossy forest floor.

Blaze groaned, his head pounding.

Fucking Hel.

Dominic seemed to be determined to actually kill Blaze.

The crowd cheered again, and Blaze only hoped that it was Andro who scored another goal.

B laze's rib was broken.

But he was alive.

And they had won the game.

"Don't forget to come by tomorrow for a checkup," the healer said as she finished bandaging Blaze's chest.

Blaze nodded. "Thanks, Gillian."

Gillian murmured something under her breath, her crooked bony fingers scrambling to pack away her tools. "One day, Leveau, you're going to find yourself dead."

Blaze chuckled.

"Is it my fault that I get hurt during the games?"

Gillian's black pupilless eyes bore into him.

"It's your fault you have a filthy mouth that pisses other people off."

Andro laughed. "She's not wrong, Blazy."

Gillian was indeed not wrong at all.

"Great game, everyone." The coach's voice boomed as he entered the locker room, striding towards Blaze. "Good job, Leveau. This is what I want to see every fucking game, you hear me?"

Blaze nodded, a cigarette already resting between his lips.

Coach yanked it right out of his mouth before he could light it, crushing it in his palm.

"What did I tell you, Leveau?"

"You told me not to *drink*," Blaze pointed out, sighing. "You didn't say anything about smoking, Coach."

Coach's eyes narrowed as he grunted. "Don't make me kick your ass, Leveau."

And then he was gone, leaving the team to finish getting ready and dressing up for celebratory drinks.

"Told ya," Gillian threw over her shoulder on her way out.

"Let's go get fucking wasted," Blaze said, rising to his feet.

Andro helped him put on a T-shirt and then his leather jacket, and then they were outside, strolling through the field and campus towards the Sparkling Hoof.

Once they reached the end of the campus, Blaze saw the rest of their Inner Circle already standing in front of the bar.

Dominic, Valentine, and another guy whose name Blaze couldn't remember also stood amongst them.

No fucking way.

Andro and Blaze crossed the street faster than lightning, walking right in the middle of a conversation.

"And who the fuck do you think you are?" Alecto scoffed, giving Dominic the meanest of her looks.

Something inside Blaze's chest warmed, seeing her vicious.

Dominic only smirked, stepping closer to her. Blaze barely held himself from slamming fists into his chest and pushing him away from her.

But that wouldn't do them any good.

"I'm Dominic *fucking* Leveau," his brother said, cocking his head to the side. The silence that fell around them was deafening. Blaze stopped breathing. "And who the fuck are you?"

Blaze ground his teeth, his palms curling into fists at his sides. "*Dominic*," he warned.

His brother, of course, disregarded him.

Even if Alecto was shocked to find out Blaze had a brother, she didn't show it.

She tipped her glass to her lips and turned her attention away to the bar.

"One too many Leveau men on this fucking earth."

"Oh, she's got an attitude." Dominic grabbed her arm, yanking her closer to his chest. "How about I fix that for you, honey?"

Blaze was about to lose his shit. Fabian, another of Dominic's dogs, said, "Dominic, we're leaving. Another time."

Dominic glanced down on Alecto, his eyes searching her face. He wet his lips. "You better hope we don't cross paths ever again."

He brought his lips to her ear and whispered something.

And then he let her go, walking away with Valentine and Fabian towards the edge of the field where the rest of their team was waiting for them.

"Are you okay?" Andro asked Alecto.

"Yeah, I'm peachy. Here I thought we had the worst of the Leveau bloodline with us. But apparently, it can always be worse."

Always insults coming out of that pretty mouth when it came to him.

Or moans of pleasure.

Never anything in between.

"Consider yourself lucky."

"I didn't know you had a brother," Jolene mused, still eyeing the Grimswater pricks.

"Neither did I," Val agreed.

She was probably already calculating which brother would be more useful to her.

Blaze exchanged a glance with Andro, who was the only one who knew everything there was to know about Leveau family affairs.

Including his older brother, who was kept under lock by his father.

"There's a reason for it," Blaze said when he realized that they were still waiting for an explanation.

"A reason why he's at Grimswater, and we didn't know he even existed?" Jolene arched a brow.

"Exactly."

Venefica played rockey games against Grimswater once or twice a year to satiate the hunger for competition for those boys who attended that wretched academy.

To indulge them and remind them at the same time what they've lost and what they could have had if they hadn't fucked up.

It was also a reminder to Blaze, for which he was grateful.

If he didn't behave, sooner or later, he would join his brother.

Galliermo would make sure of it.

30

Next Saturday night, their basement had transformed from the entertainment area into something entirely else.

Alecto descended the stairs, her boots clunking on the old wood. To Alecto's surprise, Gael was on his knees, white chalk in his hand as he drew the lines of a circle connected with the pentagram in the middle.

Val stood over his shoulder, arms crossed over her chest as she intently watched his every move.

"Right on time, Black." Jolene's voice came from the large bookshelf that took up one whole wall of their basement. The Book was open in her arms. "Do you have the black candles?"

Alecto lifted the paper bag she was holding that held five black wax candles, sourced from the southern side of Inathis. The ones they needed for this spell. The one Alecto had suggested. Jolene nodded her approval.

"Where's Rogue?" Alecto asked.

"What? Missing him already, Black?" Blaze sneered.

Alecto pointedly ignored him and his sour mood, turning to Val and Gael. "Can I place the candles around the circle? Or are you not finished yet?"

Gael sat on his heels, his brown curls bouncing as he nodded. "I'm done."

Alecto walked around the circle, placing a pillar candle at each corner of

169

the five-pointed star. When she was done, Blaze walked over to her, flickering the cap of his lighter on and off.

They hadn't spoken about what had happened between them back at the library. Alecto wasn't sure what to say.

Don't ever do this again.

"I'll keep you company while Rogue's not here," Blaze whispered, his voice hoarse and low enough so only Alecto would hear him.

His words were sweet, but his eyes were scorching fire. Alecto wasn't sure what to make of it.

When she didn't answer, Blaze's eyes took her in, really taking their time as they inspected every inch of her outfit.

She had chosen a bloodred silk dress with an open back and thin straps. It had two small slits at each thigh. There was a lot of naked flesh showing, just the way she liked.

Because the dress had an open back, Alecto didn't bother with a bra. And when Blaze's gaze stopped at her chest, she regretted her decision because her nipples hardened.

Alecto tugged his chin up, so his eyes were on hers. "If you stray too close you might get burned with the Tigers."

Blaze's eyes flickered. "Is that the sort of thing you're into, Black? Violence and torture? If so, you've come to the right place."

Alecto rolled her eyes, letting her hand drop away from his chin. She pushed past him, walking over to Jolene and Andro, who were inspecting the Book.

What the fuck she and Blaze were doing, she wasn't sure anymore. They were supposed to hate each other. At least, Blaze had hated her more than anything since her first day at Venefica. But there was also something else there now.

Don't ever do this again.

Back at the library, it was intoxicating, watching Blaze succumb to her touch, his face dark with desire. But Alecto didn't miss the fear in his eyes.

She pushed those thoughts away, focusing all her attention on Andro and Jolene.

"What's the matter?" Alecto asked when Andro furrowed his brows at the Book.

"It says here that we need to use *blood* magic for this spell to work," he growled. Then, he turned to Val and spread his arms. "Does anyone in this fucking group ever read the spells before we decide to cast them?"

"I do," Jolene said. "We already talked with Val about it, and we don't see a reason why we can't use blood magic for this small spell. Nobody is going to know."

The look on Andro's face when he turned to Jolene was priceless. Alecto could have sworn Andro's eyebrow twitched.

"You're supposed to be the responsible one in the group," Andro said accusingly, and Jolene snapped the Book closed. "You think the Dean doesn't have spells in place that detect any usage of blood magic on campus?"

"He does," Val agreed. "But I tested it on the night we summoned Rogue, and on a few more occasions, the signal only triggers when a certain threshold of blood magic is channeled. And this spell won't go over that."

"And even if we do go over and trigger the signal," Blaze mused, smirking, "it's not like we will get in any real trouble. We're *legacy*, remember?"

Andro just glared at Blaze, his face stone cold.

"What is it? Afraid you'll get in trouble?" Blaze asked. "It's gotten even worse this year."

"Well, maybe because I actually do give a fuck about what my parents will think of me," Andro snapped. "I know it's your thing to see how far you can push to piss your father off, and that's your prerogative. But that's not my game, so back the fuck off."

A muscle in Blaze's jaw ticked.

"Okay, boys, get over yourselves." Val came to stand between them. "Blaze, light the tortollesc incense and candles. The rest of you, take your fucking places."

Without another word, Blaze went over to the first candle while the rest each stood at the corner of each point, the black candles burning at their feet. Soon, the earthy aroma of tortollesc filled the air around them. When Alecto inhaled it greedily, her mind relaxed.

Gael entered the circle, settling in the middle on his knees. He opened the Book and set it on the ground next to the bronze bowl.

"Gael, lead the spell," Val instructed when Blaze took the last place, and all of them were ready.

For a moment, Gael scanned the page and then nodded, rising to his feet. He took the bowl into his hands, moving towards Val. From one of his jean pockets, he fished out an athame with a sapphire-encrusted handle and opened it with a click. "Give me your palm."

Without any hesitation, Val placed her palm in Gael's hand, and he dragged the sharp tip over her skin, flesh parting and blood starting to drip.

Gael quickly fisted Val's hand, squeezing it as he held it over the bowl, droplets of blood dribbling inside.

Alecto's heart thundered, her muscles tensing at sight. *Shit*, she was so deep into this shit, there was no way to back out now.

When she came up with the plan to set the Tigers' House on fire, it wasn't only for the Game. Alecto was seeking vengeance for the memory orb. For the humiliation. For Matias thinking she was easy enough to use.

The Tigers probably thought Alecto was the weakest link.

Alecto wasn't sure how far she was willing to go. Did her ruthlessness have any limits anymore? Right now it felt as if there wasn't much she wasn't ready to sacrifice or do to prove that she was just as bad as they were.

If not worse.

Her mom wouldn't have been proud to meet this version of her daughter. Alecto wasn't sure of much, but she was sure of that.

Gael moved around the circle, slicing each and every one of them, drawing a tiny amount of blood that swirled inside the bronze bowl. When he reached Alecto, she didn't even wait for him to ask for her hand.

She held her palm out to him.

A corner of his lip curled at her eagerness, but he didn't comment, pushing the tip of his athame into her palm. Alecto bared her teeth at the sting of pain, watching as her blood dribbled with the others'.

Once Gael had enough, he returned to the middle, kneeling in front of the Book. He placed the bowl in front of himself and then lowered the cluster of black quartz inside the bowl, dipping it in their blood.

"Repeat after me. *Exteeo*," Gael instructed.

They chanted the words after Gael, their power buzzing in the electric air, and Alecto closed her eyes, savoring the tingles dancing over her skin.

She wasn't sure whether her heart raced because of the anticipation of what they were about to do or whether it was due to their magic. Or maybe it was both.

When she opened her eyes again, a familiar pair of icy blue eyes were in front of her, glaring maliciously.

Alecto gasped at how accurate her projection looked. It was as if she was staring in the mirror, but more defined and realistic.

"It's done," Gael announced, breathless.

"Yeah, *duh*," Blaze said.

Gael still kneeled in the middle of the circle, his hands on his thighs. And he had to remain there until they were done with their prank for tonight.

Val laughed, and Alecto wasn't sure whether it was Val or her projection.

"Do they have a mind of their own?" Alecto asked.

"Of course we do, you dumb bitch," her projection replied, stepping away.

"Apparently attitude as well."

Blaze chuckled at that, and Alecto threw him a glare. Though she wasn't sure to which Blaze, the real one or the projected one, because they looked identical.

"That's fucking creepy," Alecto said, shaking her head. "I would not want to have two of you at all times."

"Are you sure about that, Black? An extra pair of hands, an extra mouth, and an extra *somethin'* else could definitely be worth it. Don't you think?"

"Leave it for Blaze to suggest a threesome with...the other Blaze," Andro said, chuckling.

"How about we get moving?" Val asked. "Gael, you'll keep the projections in check. Jolene stays with you to make sure that everything is intact."

Gael and Jolene nodded.

"I'll send you a message once we're done," Val instructed. "Make sure that they don't do anything we wouldn't do."

"The list isn't very long," Jolene said. Or maybe Jolene's projection.

"Then it shouldn't be hard."

31

This time, they had overestimated themselves.

When the Inner Circle reached the old Victorian mansion at the outskirts of Darly, the light on the second-floor window was on.

Someone was home.

"Fuck," said Andro.

"Who the fuck skips a party on a Saturday?" Val asked, frowning.

They stood at the edge of the property, by the main gate. It was supposed to be an easy job. The only reason why they all had to come in tonight was to break the protection spell over the property.

But with someone still home, it was a risk.

"We can still try," Alecto insisted. "We remove the protection spell, get inside, and see whether someone is really inside or if they just left the lights on."

"Could be that someone just forgot," Blaze agreed.

"And what if someone *is* inside?" Andro asked. "What the fuck do we do then? Turn around and run?"

They all exchanged glances in silence. Andro's eyes widened. "Don't you even dare think about it. We're not burning the House down with someone inside."

"We never suggested it," Alecto said. "We would never."

The truth was, Alecto wasn't sure anymore whether they wouldn't.

But Alessandro didn't need to hear that right now.

"Relax, Andro," Blaze said. "We will put them to sleep and carry them outside. Then, we'll burn the House."

Val nodded.

"Do you think these types of conversations happen in other universities?" Andro asked, turning to Alecto.

She smirked, shrugging. "I doubt it."

"Get together, fuckers," Val hissed, spreading her arms.

Alecto grabbed her bones, clenching them in the same hand she took Andro's palm in. She almost recoiled when Blaze took her other palm, lacing their fingers together.

The fact that Blaze hadn't gotten back at Alecto for his losing the game hadn't slipped her attention. Blaze Leveau never forgave and forgot. Even if the two of them were engaging in rather reckless behavior recently.

"*Obliteus,*" Val started murmuring under her breath, and they all joined in.

Alecto conjured the image of a box inside her mind, locked without the key, and she focused all her energy on prying the lock open.

It was not coming easily this time. The House of Tigers had good security, just like all big four Houses. They'd probably even gotten one of the cheapest spells from Gill's to protect their House.

They continued chanting, Blaze's fingers twitching, then curling tighter around Alecto's hand, the sharp metal of his rings pressing into her flesh.

After a few more moments, Alecto sighed. The lock rattled before the box flew open. Electric current zipped through her, and when she opened her eyes, she managed to steal a glance at the shield evaporating around the property, orange streaks retreating rapidly.

"And we're in," Val announced.

"Promise we're not going to kill anyone tonight," Andro insisted before they opened the front gate.

"Promise," Val assured him.

Alessandro could be a real pain in the ass sometimes. It was as if he was denying himself the true nature of their kind, trying desperately to be *just*. For what reason, Alecto couldn't tell. Sometimes she envied Andro for that. It must have been nice not to worry about being seen as too weak and fickle because of your nature.

The gates creaked as Val pushed them open, and they entered the property, the gravel crunching under their feet. The path wasn't long, and soon they were standing at the front door.

Val checked the lock.

"Mistake," she snorted as the door opened, revealing a dark foyer.

Alecto looked around the familiar place, now quiet and empty, and they all stopped for a moment to listen for any sounds.

Nothing.

"Andro, check the first floor," Val instructed. "We three are going to check upstairs."

As the group split up, Alecto followed Val up the stairs, Blaze trailing behind them. Val stopped at the top of the stairs abruptly, and Alecto barely had the time to stop herself before walking into her friend.

She turned back to Blaze to find his gaze plastered on her ass, head cocked to the side. There was a side of Alecto that wanted to hiss, to slap his face.

But Alecto couldn't deny the satisfaction, that little sneaky feeling of being wanted, and it made her angry with herself.

"Alecto, check the east wing, Blaze go west," Val whispered.

"And what are you going to do?" Blaze came to the top of the narrow landing.

"Keep an eye here."

Alecto didn't argue. She took the corridor to the east wing and quickly checked the rooms, listening for any weird sounds. All she found was darkness and silence.

When she came back to Val, Blaze was not back from the west wing yet.

"What the fuck is he doing?"

Val waved her hand for Alecto to follow. They went down the corridor to the very end where the room with a light in the window was.

Blaze stood by the door, watching something through the small crack. When Alecto and Val approached, he lifted a finger and pressed it to his lips.

Quietly, Alecto moved to stand behind him, pushing onto her toes to peek over his shoulder.

Someone was indeed inside the room.

And that *someone* was not a student from Venefica.

A girl, no older than twelve or thirteen years old, lay on a twin bed, her knees pressed to her chest, long golden hair sprawled around her cream face.

"What the fuck?" Alecto hissed.

How the fuck did this girl get in here?

"It must be someone's sister," Blaze whispered, turning to them.

"That's a violation of the House rules," Val said. The corner of her lip curled up as she stared at the girl, clearly scheming.

"*Val*," Alecto warned.

For a moment, Val ignored her. But then she averted her gaze. "It seems as if the Gods are truly on our side tonight."

There were the sounds of rustling and feet shuffling behind them as Andro approached.

"Is there someone inside?" Andro whispered, pointing a finger at the door.

Alecto nodded.

He peeked inside, and his eyes widened before his eyebrows came together in confusion at the sight of the girl on the bed. "What the fuck?"

"A little gift for us," Val answered, a wicked smile gracing her beige face.

Andro blinked, and then he scrunched his nose.

"We're going to shoot two birds with one stone," Val said, glancing at each of them, her eyes flickering. "You follow me?"

It took Alecto a moment to catch up, but when she did, a smile broke over her face. "Genius."

"Oh, for fuck's sake," Andro growled, rolling his eyes. "You greedy bastards."

"You don't seem to complain when it's time to revel in the fruits of our labors," Val shot back, and that seemed to shut Andro up.

"We can't just dump the girl outside in the middle of the night, can we?" Blaze asked.

"We won't," Alecto assured him. "Boys, get the most comfortable armchair from the living room and place it as far from the House as possible. We're going to put a spell on her and settle her comfortable in the seat."

Val glanced at Blaze and Andro. "Move."

They didn't need to be told twice, and soon only Val and Alecto were left. The girl, still deep in her sleep, had no idea what was coming.

"How do you feel about putting on a little Sleeping Beauty action?" Val grinned.

"You mean cast a spell that needs breaking instead of a simple sleeping spell?"

"Is that a little bit too much for you, Black?" Val questioned, tilting her head to the side. "I can understand if your mortal side says it's too cruel, too dangerous."

Neither do they have it in them to be cruel or merciless.

Once again Alecto was reminded that Val didn't think she had it in her. That Alecto wasn't their equal, always someone beneath.

"Nothing like that," Alecto said, her voice firm. "I hope you have a spell on hand."

Val's smile turned predatory.

"I have just the spell."

The old floor cried out with each step they took, but the girl didn't break out of her sleep. Val settled on one side of the bed, while Alecto took the other.

Suddenly, the girl shifted, muttering something under her breath as she rolled on her back. They went still, not daring to even breathe for a moment, but the girl didn't wake.

Alecto glanced at Val and a black bag of bones resting in her palm. Ready. From the way Val's eyes flickered, it was clear she was enjoying herself. Alecto arched a brow, determined not to let it show how hard her heart was hammering against her chest right now.

"*Deleresco ignatios,*" Val started the chant, and Alecto joined her.

After a moment, the girl shifted again, her nose scrunching. A warm wave rolled off Alecto, shielding the girl in an invisible white blanket. After a few more moments, the girl went completely still.

Not even her chest rose as she breathed.

Val's lips curled. "Get that, motherfuckers."

Alecto chuckled, shoving her bones back into her boot. Her magic was gone, but the excitement still buzzed underneath her skin, making the whole world feel more alive.

Val went over to the desk perched by the window and checked the drawers. From the first one, she took a notepad, fishing out a pen from the third one, and then Val hunched over the desk, scribbling something on the paper.

After a moment, she turned to Alecto, holding the paper up with a rough sketch of a crown. It wasn't the best indication as to what kind of spell had been cast on the girl, but it was a clue.

"Let's take her," Alecto said and went around the bed to grab the girl by her arms.

Val took her ankles, and they scurried out of the room. When they reached the bottom of the stairs, Blaze and Andro were just coming inside from the garden.

To Alecto's surprise, Blaze took the girl into his arms. They let him carry her outside.

The leather armchair was perched at the very end of the property, right by the main gate, and he sat the girl in the armchair, folding her carefully in the leather. Val hurried over, folding the paper as she walked. She shoved it in the girl's small palm before returning to the House.

"Well, now let's get to the fun part, shall we?" she asked, her smile growing. "Hands together."

They obeyed her, forming a circle in the middle of the foyer and weaving their fingers together.

"Alecto, will you do the honors?" Val asked.

Alecto smirked. "Abso-fucking-lutely. *Inferereo.*"

She said the words loud and clear, the rest joining in, their voices filled with the same anticipation and mischief.

Alecto conjured the flame in her mind, letting it burn through her until her palms were warming up. She released her friends' hands. When she opened her palms, flame bloomed. She couldn't hold back the chuckle.

"Come on, bitches," Val shrieked. "Let's burn these motherfuckers to the ground."

Without a word, Val broke into a run and disappeared behind the stairs at the back of the House. Andro laughed, ducking inside the living room on their left.

With a smile, Alecto caught Blaze's dark gaze and hurried up the stairs.

Alecto went into one room after another, slamming the door open and sprinkling the flame after her, watching it cling to the curtains, furniture, and bedding. It was getting hotter with each room catching fire, but Alecto ignored the heat caressing her cheeks and made her way through the rooms towards the one room she wanted to see burn the most.

She didn't think it would feel this good to be reckless. To be cruel. But it was as if she was standing at the top of the fucking mountain, the whole world lay under her feet.

When she reached Matias's bedroom, the door was already open. Blaze stood in the middle, casually glancing around.

"So, is that what you like?" he asked, slowly turning to her. "Alpha-male bullshit with a touch of debauchery?"

Alecto smiled. "Last time I checked, debauchery was *your* forte. So you can't really judge."

A small smirk appeared. "Yeah. Then I'm at least half your type."

Something inside Alecto's chest swirled—heat, not from the flames devouring the House, building in her belly, pooling between her thighs.

Her heart was beating a thousand miles per minute, threatening to escape her rib cage.

Blaze took a step closer, and then another one, bringing them so close together Alecto could *feel* his presence. His head dipped, lips coming close to hers, and despite herself, Alecto lifted her face towards him, meeting him halfway.

It was the adrenaline to blame.

Definitely the adrenaline.

Blaze's lips brushed hers, his warm breath making the hairs at the back of her neck rise. "Let's burn this fucker down. What do you say, Black?"

Alecto smiled and took a step away. Still keeping Blaze's gaze, she threw the rest of her flame onto the dresser.

Blaze mimicked her, throwing his onto the desk perched by the opposite wall.

His eyes burned just as bright as the flames rapidly growing around them. Alecto blinked, and he was right in front of her. Another blink, and his mouth closed over hers, devouring her whole.

Alecto wrapped her hands around his neck, pulling him closer as she hooked a leg over his. Without hesitation, he cupped her ass with his palms, lifting her up, and then they were on the move.

A gasp escaped Alecto when her back hit a wall, but she didn't let his lips slide. She kissed harder, harsher, biting on his lower lip so hard the taste of copper filled their mouths.

That only seemed to draw a growl from Blaze, and he pushed his hips into her, grinding his hard-on into her core.

Alecto was going to melt. She was burning from the inside, her blood molten lava, and the heat was threatening to overcome her from the outside—

She gasped as a heatwave hit them, and their kiss broke. They both turned to the side, to the corridor where they came from, which was all engulfed in a flame.

No escape route.

"Oh, shit," Alecto whispered.

Blaze slowly released her, waiting for her to find her footing before he let her go.

Looking at him was painful, with his black hair ruffled, lips red and swollen from their kiss. But Alecto pushed past him, walking inside Matias's room, which was also aflame.

"Fuck," she cursed, her heart thundering for a completely different reason now.

She gasped when Blaze's hand wrapped around hers, and he dragged her outside the room, to the other side of the corridor. At the very end, there was a window, the only one with curtains that hadn't caught fire yet.

Blaze pushed it open, peeking his head outside. He then started climbing out, but Alecto grabbed for his hand.

"Are you crazy?" she hissed. "We're on the second floor. We can't jump."

"No. But we can climb. Do you trust me, Black?"

"Not even one bit."

"*Smart.*"

And then he was gone. Alecto didn't wait, shoving her head outside to find him perched on a small landing, one hand holding the drain. He offered his free hand for her.

"Come on."

Alecto sighed, glancing at the grass so far from where they were, but climbed out the window, ignoring his hand. Only when she was outside, Alecto took his offering, and Blaze immediately pulled her closer to him.

"Now would be the perfect time to push me," he said into her hair as he mounted the pipe, drawing her closer to his chest.

Alecto chuckled. *This motherfucker.*

"I might still," Alecto replied as they started the climb down.

Alecto felt the strength of his chest pressing into her back, warm and assuring, despite the fact it was Blaze Leveau.

They slowly climbed down the wall, Alecto holding on to the pipe, carefully placing her feet after Blaze. Blaze was carrying most of their weight and doing most of the work, but Alecto focused on not making a wrong move that would send them to the ground.

But then Alecto's feet slipped on the wet brick, and she lost her footing, falling. Before Alecto could catch herself, the pipe wasn't there, and the wall was moving further from her.

Her bones rattled as her back hit the hard ground, her lungs heaving as the wind was knocked out of her. Behind her, Blaze groaned.

Oh shit, she fell *on* him.

She scrambled onto her side, rolling on the wet grass, and turned her head to see Blaze lying on his back, eyes closed.

She grabbed his shirt, rattling him *hard*. "Are you okay?!"

For a moment, Blaze didn't respond. But then the same stupid smirk appeared, and he opened his eyes just a bit to catch her gaze.

"You're a dangerous woman."

Alecto sighed and slammed her palm into his chest, but then she laughed.

"You're a fucking moron."

"I think you wanted to say, 'Thank you, Blaze, for saving my perky ass.'"

32

Blaze rubbed his palms over his face, growling into the silence of the night, only the chirping sounds of cicadas coming from the outside through his open windows.

It's not as if it was Blaze's first time ruining a girl.

No, he was an expert at this point, and Genevieve last year was his best work so far.

But *this* was something completely different—so much more thrilling and exciting, it was hard for Blaze to get calm enough to sleep at night.

Anytime his eyes closed, Alecto's face appeared in front of him. He could hear her soft whimpers and gasps, he could still taste her in his mouth. It was driving him mad.

Alecto said she had never had an orgasm with another person before, but it was hard to believe that, given how willing she was to surrender to his touch.

Maybe Blaze could go even further with his plan.

Tease her, seduce her, ruin her.

Or maybe, Blaze could tease her, seduce her, *enjoy* her, and ruin her.

Maybe his cock was an issue.

Blaze threw a scorching glance at the bulge pressing into his jeans.

As if that would help.

"Fuck," he growled, a fist landing on the desk so hard his typewriter and the bottle of whiskey shuddered.

No. He had to put a stop to this nonsense.

There was nothing for him with Alecto, just a pure need for him to put her in her place.

Alecto was a half breed, someone who shouldn't even be a part of the most powerful House at Venefica.

She needed a reminder of how things were supposed to work in Inathis. And Blaze was willing to be the one to remind her.

With a heavy sigh, Blaze rubbed his eyes. He knew what he needed to do next.

Blaze grabbed the pack of cigarettes from the desk, popped one between his lips, and lit it. As he inhaled, the smoke burned his tongue, and he leaned back in his chair.

An unfinished draft sat in his typewriter, looking at him accusingly. He hadn't been able to write anything for months now.

And the longer he sat in front of the typewriter, the longer he wondered whether it was even worth trying anymore. It wasn't as if he'd ever be able to do anything with his words anyway.

Galliermo would never entertain the idea of Blaze being anything else than a professional rockey player and then the heir to the Leveau empire.

Blaze might try to drink himself stupid most weekends, but he was never going to stand up to his father about it.

Not unless he wanted to end up at Grimswater with his brother, losing all the privileges he had.

Nah, Blaze wasn't that stupid.

He tapped his fingers on the desk, one knee bouncing as the cigarette burned between his lips. He couldn't write, but he couldn't quit either.

A black raven flew through the open window and landed on the windowsill. There was a white envelope in its mouth.

Blaze rose from his desk and walked towards the raven, its black eyes watching Blaze's every step. He snatched the envelope and tore it open to find a note from Killer.

"Sweet," Blaze muttered to himself.

There were no more questions about whether Blaze should or shouldn't wait before he made Alecto pay for what she had pulled to mess with his game.

Everything was ready.

Swiftly, Blaze went over to his closet and grabbed his leather jacket before he crushed the butt of his cigarette into an ashtray on the windowsill.

The House was quiet as he left his bedroom.

Of course, it was well past midnight on a weekday, and most students, even the Snakes, were sleeping or pulling all-nighters in the library.

Blaze left the House, going down the street towards the campus. Killer's note said to meet him at the back of the library, and it was about a ten-minute walk.

The air was already cold; it was nearing the end of September. Blaze could see his breath as he crossed Main Street and took the path leading down to the library at the corner of the campus.

The campus was eerily quiet; soon the large wooden doors emerged in front of Blaze. Instead of entering, Blaze took the path on the left, rounding the building.

As he passed the large windows opening to the inside of the room with tall bookshelves and tables with lights, something drew his eye.

In the very corner, at the long table, sat Alecto and Jolene, both laughing at something Jolene was saying.

Not far away from them was the goddamn leather armchair, only the small corner of it visible from his vantage point.

What are you doing, Alecto? Blaze had asked her that night.

Taking what I want.

The image of her kneeling in front of him, eyes wet with tears as her sultry mouth took him in, was ingrained deep into Blaze's mind.

The pressure inside his chest built, and for a moment, Blaze thought he might lose the fight against himself.

He slowed his steps, stopping as he watched them, so different from what he was used to seeing in the House.

None of those in the Inner Circle were the nicest people. None of them treated each other or people outside of the Inner Circle *decently*.

And it never bothered Blaze before. It was their way of communicating, and it worked well.

But seeing Alecto so happy and carefree at that moment, still in her uniform surrounded by textbooks, was doing something to him.

Right now, the girls didn't look like Snakes.

They looked like normal students who were simply attending the school of their dreams, seeing their friends every day, and deciding what time was the best to go to the common showers.

No legacies. No Houses. No Games.

Blaze blinked, suddenly remembering himself, and left before they noticed him staring through the window.

When Blaze reached the back of the library, Killer was already there, leaning against the wall with his hands shoved inside his pockets. He had a hood pulled over his head, and when Blaze approached, he glanced around.

"Nobody's here," Blaze assured him.

"You can never be too sure," Killer said, pushing himself off the wall. "I wouldn't want to be seen with you in the middle of the night."

"Do you have what I need?"

Killer inspected Blaze for a moment as if evaluating whether he was worth the effort. Then he nodded and pulled a small bag out of his pocket, pinching it between his two fingers.

"Money first, Leveau."

From his inner pocket, Blaze grabbed his wallet and took out a couple of notes. He snatched the bag out of Killer's hand, bringing it closer to check the pink powder inside.

"I trust you're not trying to sell spiked shit to me," Blaze teased, stuffing the bag in his pocket.

Killer flashed him a smile. "I'm gonna be honest, I thought about poisoning you. But then I changed my mind. I owe you one."

"It's a good thing you remember."

Behind them, the voices carried over from the Dean's building, and when Blaze glanced in that direction, there were three dark figures walking through the campus.

Killer cursed, and without a word, whirled and strode off.

Blaze had to bite down the laugh. Sometimes Houses took their rivalries *too* seriously.

When three dark figures finally reached the path illuminated by light orbs, Blaze recognized Jack Riverblood accompanied by his two dads.

Neither of their faces were happy or calm.

In fact, one of Jack's dads was fuming, his angular face red as he scolded Jack. "This was irresponsible. Bringing her with you for a weekend and then leaving her alone while you go get wasted."

"What if whoever burned the House would have done that with her still inside?" the other dad chimed in. His face was less angry and more concerned.

Blaze pressed his back to the stone wall, hiding in the shadow as they neared the library.

"And now not only have you fucked up your Game," the first dad continued, "but there is also no way the Tigers will be able to recover from the fire quickly enough. And you're also suspended for a month, which leaves your House vulnerable. Do you understand how bad this is, Jack?"

Jack's face was grim. "I understand, Father."

They passed Blaze and disappeared around the corner of the library, so he couldn't catch the rest of the conversation.

But what he'd heard was more than enough.

The Snakes had scored a jackpot with Alecto's idea to burn the House down. With Jack suspended, they had the path towards the Tigers' Book free.

The Tigers are so fucking done.

Pleased, Blaze whirled on his heel and walked away.

As he took the same path home, he once again stopped to look inside the library window at Alecto and Jolene, now both studying their books.

Alecto's hair was pulled back with that cute clip, a few strands wild and free around her face. Blaze loved the way she looked like this the most.

After next Saturday and what Blaze had planned for her, Alecto would never look at him again.

So he stood there for a few more moments, soaking in the view of her before he fucked shit up once more.

33

The House of Dragons was an old Victorian mansion said to be haunted. It stood where Darly ended and the Cursed Forest began. Dragons loved to show off how fearless they were, but Alecto wasn't fooled.

Their mansion wasn't haunted. And Dragons did not ever step foot in that forest behind their House, despite rumors of their secret rituals.

Those fuckers were all bark and no bite, even if being in the presence of their High Priest Norse Fox sent chills down Alecto's back. And *not* in a pleasant way.

Alecto was the last one to show up to the party, it seemed. As she walked through the old gate and passed people outside, already tipsy and enjoying themselves, she glanced around looking for her friends.

Alecto often got whispers and mean looks as she walked through campus. But, somehow, during the parties, most witches managed to forget what their problem with her was.

Not today, it seemed.

As Alecto entered the House and made her way through the living room and dining room, many eyes were on her. And neither of them were kind or friendly. She snorted. Guess people really suspected the Snakes for the Tigers' House burning down last week.

Finally, a familiar face popped up in the crowd. Sadly, it wasn't the face of someone Alecto wanted to see.

But it was too late because Blaze noticed her. He extended a hand with a glass of vodka, neat.

"Here you are, Black." Alecto took the glass and downed the drink in one gulp. He whistled. "That's the spirit."

"Where are the others?"

Blaze casually looked around. "Val's with her new boys, Andro is probably with *his* new boy, and Jolene is somewhere, probably talking with a plant or somethin'."

"Don't be a fucking dick."

Blaze smirked but didn't say anything else as he refilled her drink.

"I guess it's only you and me."

"And a couple more dozens of people as well," she replied, walking away from him.

Alecto wasn't going to spend the night with Blaze fucking Leveau.

Nah-ah.

She didn't need any temptations or any more reckless shit happening. They were bad for each other, and the further away Alecto was from Blaze, the better.

Apparently, Blaze had missed the memo because a hand wrapped around Alecto's forearm, yanking her back.

"Not so fast," he said. "Why don't you have a drink with me?"

Alecto yanked her arm away from him, both standing in the middle of a crowd in the dining room with tall ceilings and an old dark wood dining table covered with alcohol.

"I already have a drink," Alecto sneered, lifting the glass he gave her.

Blaze bit his bottom lip. "Oh, come on. One night. Give me one night, and maybe I'll surprise you."

Alecto stilled.

Maybe she was fucking crazy, but there was something inside her that wanted to indulge Blaze. After all, Alecto was always craving an adventure, and Blaze was nothing if not an adventure.

One with massive consequences, but to Hel with it.

"One night."

Blaze's face lit up. Before Alecto could say anything more, he swooped her into his embrace and led her through the dining room into the kitchen and into the back garden.

The cool night air greeted them. None of the partygoers were in the back garden; half of it bled into the Cursed Forest. It was creepy out here and gave Alecto chills, seeing the mist from the forest lingering around the perimeter of the Dragons' territory as if testing the limits of how far it was allowed to go.

Blaze walked them over to the old swing at the very edge of the property and guided Alecto's hips into one swing, plopping onto the other one next to her.

For whatever reason, Alecto's heart was hammering like crazy. As if she was going to throw up.

Ignoring the weird feelings in her stomach and chest, she brought the glass to her lips, eyeing Blaze as he lit a cigarette, letting it hang between his lips as the stream of smoke escaped.

He tilted his head backwards, inhaling the smoke, and closed his eyes for a moment, letting it out with an exhale.

Alecto's throat went dry at sight. Blaze was beautiful, and whenever he looked at Alecto with those black eyes, her heart skipped a beat, whether she wanted it to or not. It was a reaction most girls had around him.

It was a given.

But like that, so relaxed and calm, in the darkness of the night, Blaze looked more than in his element. Alecto could almost believe he could be somewhat decent. And maybe even real.

If that was even possible.

"So, you're not jealous of Val being with other boys?" Alecto asked after a long moment of silence.

Blaze turned his head to the side, glancing at her through heavy-lidded eyes. "Why would I be jealous? She's not mine."

Not his. Val *wasn't* his.

Alecto ignored the way her heart jumped at those words.

They sat in silence for a long moment, Blaze not looking even one bit disturbed. As if sitting together and being quiet was a thing they were used to doing.

Alecto shifted in her seat, curling her fingers around the swing chains as she glanced at her feet.

Everything was getting more and more confusing as the days went past.

None of what Blaze said or did made sense to Alecto. He hated her, but did he really?

Why would he do to Alecto what he did back in that classroom if he hated her? At first, she thought it was just to prove a point, to deny the rumors. But after their *exchange* at the library and that kiss back at the House of Tigers, she wasn't so sure anymore.

Fucking bastard.

"So, did you bring me here to sit in silence?" Alecto said, glancing at Blaze. He leaned his head on the chain, but his eyes were already on her, face solemn. "The party is back there, *Blazy.*"

"Does silence make you uncomfortable?" he asked. "I feel like there is so much more you can learn about a person from the way they're silent than when they're talking."

What?

Alecto glared at him.

"When someone's talking, they think about what they're saying, how they're saying it. They consider whether something is going to make them sound stupid or smart, better than everyone else or smaller," he explained. "It's all calculated. It's all a show, no matter how much someone claims they're honest. We all do it."

Alecto blinked. What a weird choice of topic.

Blaze pinched a cigarette between his three fingers and brought it to his lips, sucking so hard the ember burned bright red, glowing in the darkness.

"Now, when someone's silent, it's a whole other deal." Smoke streamed out of Blaze's mouth as he spoke. "If you look close enough, you'll get to see the things that are happening in their mind, without them even knowing."

Alecto stilled. Somehow, it was as if he'd placed her under a magnifying glass.

"Are they nervous because they fidget mindlessly and bite their lip? Are they looking for something or someone, their eyes darting around the room?" Blaze mused, his eyes sliding down her body and then back up again. "Are they uncomfortable when it's only them and their own mind and no other noise around?"

Alecto licked her lips, and Blaze's gaze dropped to them.

Alecto found herself wishing he would kiss her again.

He made Alecto's heart beat faster. He made her alert and scared, which should have been a bad thing. But it was the thing that made her feel alive like nothing else… And it was addicting.

A lazy grin spread on Blaze's face, and he lifted his gaze back to hers. Slowly, he drew his hand out of his pocket, bringing it to his lips.

Before Alecto knew what was happening, a cloud of pink dust hit her face, and she coughed, something burning her eyes and her nostrils like a bitch.

She opened her mouth to scream or to say something, but her throat burned, and she wheezed, the burning reaching her lungs.

The last thing Alecto saw before passing out was the grass moving closer to her.

Or was it the other way around?

34

Alecto's eyes were burning.

Lungs on fire.

Her throat refused to work as she tried to swallow.

Finally, she managed to peel her eyes open, sniffling.

The world was upside down.

"What the fuck," Alecto croaked.

She tried to move, but she couldn't. Her legs were tied, hands hanging above her head. Or, rather, down her head.

Alecto shifted, testing the restraints holding her, but it was no use. The earth beneath her was too far as she hung in the air.

"Ah, wonderful. You're awake," Blaze's voice came from behind her, and soon, his tall figure emerged in front of Alecto.

Blaze stopped a few feet away from her, one hand in his jeans pocket, the other holding a burning cigarette.

"What the fuck is this, Blaze?" Alecto demanded.

They were at the party, on the swing by the forest, and then—

The cloud, the burning…

Blaze *drugged* her.

"You motherfucker," Alecto screamed, thrashing.

That only made him laugh.

"Ah, yes," Blaze said, chuckling. "You're going to hate me for this."

"I already fucking do," Alecto sneered.

How fucking stupid.

How fucking stupid could she have been, going anywhere with him, ever thinking he could be a decent fucking person.

"What the fuck do you want?" Alecto asked once she'd calmed herself down. She wasn't getting out of that rope, no matter how much she tried. "Where am I?"

"You know where you are."

Alecto growled, looking around. They were in the middle of the forest, trees as far as the eyes could see. Nobody was around, the sounds of the party nowhere to be heard.

White mist covered the ground, and the hairs on the back of Alecto's neck rose.

They were in the Cursed Forest.

"Blaze, I don't know what fucked up joke you think you're—"

"It's not a joke, Black," Blaze said. "It's a warning."

A warning? What the—

Ah, of course.

Alecto should have known that sooner or later, he would try to get back at her, even if it wasn't fair. It wasn't Alecto's fault she had to get back at him for detention. But of course, Blaze wouldn't see things that way.

For him, everything was a game. And he always had to win.

"You thought that you could fuck up my rockey game and walk away?" Blaze asked, coming closer.

Alecto snapped her mouth shut, glaring at him.

He shook his head, tsking. "I'm actually surprised it was as easy to get to you as it was. But I guess I shouldn't be surprised, knowing how easily swayed you are with a little bit of attention. Isn't that right?"

Rage surged through her, and she swung her arm, trying to catch Blaze's jacket or his arm, but he stepped away just in time, laughing hard.

"Don't be too mad about it, now. I didn't lie when I said that I enjoyed myself with you. It's always fun when she's trying to pretend like she hates it. But you didn't hate it, did you?"

Alecto pressed her lips into a tight line, refusing to speak. Her heart was hammering so hard she thought it might leap out of her throat, and her cheeks were burning with heat.

Chuckling, Blaze lowered himself to squat in front of her, their eyes on the same level.

"The moment I showed you a little bit of attention, you were ready to jump me and do whatever I wanted you to do, isn't that right?" Blaze asked, cocking his head to the side. "All of that tough-girl act is just a facade. You're a *half breed* after all. You're beneath us all, no matter who your father is or which House you belong to."

Needles prickled Alecto's throat. She couldn't swallow.

It wasn't something new, being punished for not being a pure-blooded witch in the world of ruthless witches. There was not a single day in her life when she didn't have to fight to prove her own worth. To belong in a world that didn't want her.

But the Snakes had become the one place where Alecto didn't have to worry about it. She belonged because it was her birthright. She more than earned her spot in the Inner Circle.

Apparently, all that was in her head. She didn't belong. She'd never be equal in their eyes.

"Let me make it very clear for you," Blaze said with a sigh. "You dare fuck with me one more time, and I'll end you. Consider this a *friendly* warning."

"Fuck you," Alecto spat. "If you fuck with me, I'll fight back."

"Yes, and that's all fun and shit. Our little bickering back and forth. But know your fucking place, Black. There are certain things you half breeds are good for. I can't deny it. Stick with that, why don't you? It's what you know best after all."

Alecto growled, thrashing once more, trying to reach for Blaze.

She was going to rip his fucking throat out.

But Blaze jumped back on his feet, whistling a tune as he turned and strode away. After a moment, he stopped and lifted his hand, a cloth bag in his palm.

"Good luck getting home tonight," Blaze threw over his shoulder and walked away.

Alecto's chest burned with anger so bright it was hard to breathe. But she was grateful for it because anger meant there was no place for other emotions.

The forest was dark and gloomy, and Alecto had an uneasy feeling.

There was a reason why this forest was forbidden and no students were permitted to enter it. There were things here that were better left alone.

Especially at night.

She closed her eyes, taking deep breaths as she tried to come up with an idea of how the fuck she would escape. She wasn't strong enough to pull herself up and untie her legs, and right now, she wished she was part of the swimming team or something.

Blaze took her bones, so there was no chance for her to use her magic. Not unless she wanted to draw from herself, but she knew better than to do that.

A few more breaths, and Alecto opened her eyes. She glanced around, checking for any threats, but she couldn't see very far in pitch blackness. She lifted her arms to her hips, checking her pockets for something, anything. To her surprise, there was a pocketknife in her back pocket.

Alecto brought it to her face, inspecting the black blade. It wasn't hers. She never carried knives with her. She didn't even own one, apart from her athame that she only used for the spells. Did Blaze—

Something on her left rattled, and Alecto went still. She slowly turned her head to the side where the sound came from.

Six pairs of red eyes glowed in the darkness. The same rattling sound echoed in the night again, and Alecto barely held the whimper inside her as she recognized the sound.

Hollowa spiders made that rattling sound right before attacking their prey.

Panic rushed through her. She didn't have time. She needed to act now. The large body moved forwards, long hairy legs inching towards her as the creature approached.

Fuck. Fuck. FUCK.

Alecto drew in a breath, glancing at the knife. She wasn't going to fight the fucking spiders with it. They'd end her before she even got to stab them.

Think, think.

There was only one way out of this.

The creature moved in closer to her once more, emerging from the thick darkness, and Alecto recoiled at the sight of the spider.

Without another thought, Alecto opened the knife and slammed it into her palm, letting the blood pour out of her wound.

It took everything in Alecto to not scream at the pain that took her breath away. Her stomach twisted; she was going to throw up, but she just bit her lip hard.

"*Isolentus mixortis*," Alecto whispered, her voice shaky, and she closed her eyes.

In her mind, she conjured the red silk blanket wrapping around her. She chanted the words as a prayer.

She was afraid to stop, afraid to open her eyes to see whether the spell worked.

There was a hissing sound, and Alecto's eyes snapped open to see the red tendrils wrapped around her in a circle.

Forgetting the pain in her hand and her fear of the spiders, Alecto smiled and cried out.

Fuck me.

More spiders emerged from the darkness, crawling closer to her. She needed to get the fuck out of there before her shield dropped.

She didn't know how long it would hold or what would disturb it.

Suddenly, the branch she was tied to dipped, and Alecto glanced up to find one large spider climbing it, nearing the rope. The creature swiped at the rope with one claw, and Alecto fell, barely having time to cover her head before she hit the ground.

One creature advanced forwards, but it hissed and jumped back as it hit the shield. The smell of burning flesh filled the air.

Alecto sat up, keeping the bleeding hand against her chest, the knife still wedged in her flesh as she tried to pray the rope from her feet. After a few moments of fumbling, finally, the rope gave in, and her feet were free.

Her legs trembling, whether from the fear or adrenaline or both, Alecto jumped to her feet and ran for the bushes where no spider was blocking her way.

She ran without looking back, hearing the branches snap behind her as the spiders advanced towards her.

The good news was that Hollowa spiders were big and slow and Alecto could outrun them.

The bad news was that Alecto was out of shape, had barely eaten, and had been drugged, which meant she wasn't going to be running for long before she passed out.

With her heart hammering in her chest, throat, *and* ears, she almost missed the blaring music.

She stopped, bending over and leaning one palm on her thigh as she panted heavily. Lights appeared in the distance. She wasn't far from the House of Dragons.

Without a glance back, Alecto sprang forwards, ignoring the way her lungs burned and the stinging pain in her side, the pain of the knife still stuck in her palm.

After a few more torturous moments, Alecto ran out of the forest into the back garden of the House of Dragons. Only when she saw Jolene and Rogue walking out of the House did she stop running.

Exhausted, Alecto fell onto her knees, panting. Her mouth was filled with the taste of blood.

"Alecto," Jolene gasped, running up to her. Rogue was right behind her. "Are you okay? What the fuck happened?"

Alecto took Jolene's hand, but she could barely keep her head up.

"You're hurt," Jolene said. "Let me get Val and the rest and take you—"

"No," Alecto croaked, shaking her head. "Not Val. No others. Please."

Without waiting to hear Jolene's answer, Alecto let herself drift into the blackness that had been waiting to consume her.

W hen Alecto opened her eyes this time, she sighed with relief. She was comfortable, warm, and staring at the black ceiling of her bedroom at the House.

"Thank fucking Gods," Jolene said with a heavy sigh. "I thought you'd died or something."

Alecto turned her head to find her friend kneeling by her bed, tending to her bloodied palm. The knife was out.

"Did you tell the others?" Alecto asked, her voice hoarse. She cleared her throat.

Jolene caught her gaze, stopping what she was doing, but it was Rogue's voice that came from the other side of the bed. "No. Nobody knows."

Alecto turned her head to where Rogue sat near her desk. "Thank you."

For a long moment, he looked at her, a line wedged between his eyebrows in worry and concern. It was the last thing she expected from a demon.

They stayed silent for a moment, Jolene finishing wrapping the bandage over the wound and Alecto just letting herself breathe.

She thought she knew how cruel Blaze was. After everything she saw him do to others, after everything she *helped* him do, somehow, she thought that she knew what he was capable of.

This night proved that she knew nothing.

And not only did she know nothing about Blaze and how far was he willing to go to ruin her, but she also couldn't even trust the rest of her House because she didn't know how they felt about her anymore.

You're beneath us all.

Alecto swallowed the lump in her throat, her eyes starting to burn.

"Alecto," Jolene said gently. "Do you want to tell us what happened?"

Needles in Alecto's throat didn't let her speak. She slowly shook her head.

Jolene dropped her eyes, hesitant.

"Do you want to tell us why you didn't want Val or the others to know?" Rogue asked, his voice soft.

Again, Alecto only gave them a shake of her head. She met Rogue's amber eyes and he nodded, as if to say that he understood.

Even demon from Hel could be kinder than Blaze fucking Leveau.

Jolene sighed. "Okay then. When you're ready, I'm here. We're here."

Rogue added, "We're going to get back at whoever did this to you. Whenever you're ready, Black."

"You know that, right?" Jolene asked.

Alecto didn't know. Not anymore.

III. SOULLESS NIGHTS

35

That was exactly what Blaze wanted—to make Alecto suffer.

So why the fuck did he feel *worse* than before?

He pinched the cigarette between three fingers and brought it to his lips. What a fucking shit show the last week has been.

He hadn't seen Alecto at the House. Clearly, she'd been avoiding him. But nobody else from the Inner Circle seemed to know what happened between them, which meant that she hadn't talked.

Which was a surprise.

From the wound in her palm, Blaze realized Alecto had used blood magic to get herself home. Blood magic *over* nature magic.

That spoke volumes.

Blaze was impressed.

"Hey, fucker," Andro whispered into Blaze's ear, and he jerked in surprise.

"Right about fucking time," Blaze said, flicking off the ash of the cigarette. "I thought you stood me up."

"I would never."

Of course, Andro would never. Andro had his flaws, but he was as loyal as they ever got.

They fell into step, walking swiftly through the campus towards the rockey field. The sun was just starting to rise, half the sky still covered in the dark blanket of the night.

When they reached the field, most of the team was already there, some stretching, some barely able to open their eyes, clearly still half asleep.

"Get in line. Two by two," Blaze instructed, clapping his hands as he jogged to the front of the line. Andro was right beside him.

Blaze waited for the team to get into the formation. "Five laps. Then, stretch. After we practice the formation for Saturday's game."

Blaze started to jog. Andro yawned as he caught up.

"They look at you like a bunch of obedient puppies," Andro commented. "It's either impressive or pathetic. I can't decide."

"They do what they know they need to do to win," Blaze replied. The crisp air of the morning was burning his lungs.

"Yeah, sure. But still, they look at you like you're the only fucking star in their night's sky."

Blaze couldn't hold a mocking laugh back.

"They want to be you. But because they can't, they at least hope to be *with* you. Haven't you noticed how even the coach looks at you as if you're his most prized possession?"

Oh, Blaze had noticed.

He knew exactly how people looked at him and *why*.

Blaze didn't reply, so Andro didn't say anything else, and they ran another lap in silence.

Of course, who wouldn't want to be Blaze Leveau? He had it all—the status, the money, the future.

Except for Blaze Leveau himself, but even then, only on some days. On most days, he was more than content with all the privileges that came with his name.

After the laps, Blaze and Andro went to the middle of the field, leading stretches in front of the rest of the team.

Even Gabe and Matias stayed silent, biting their tongues as they stretched their large bodies.

Of course, with their High Priest suspended and away, even those dumb fucks knew the Tigers were vulnerable.

"Has Val briefed you about our new course of action?" Blaze asked, glancing at Andro as he bent his leg and brought his left foot to his right thigh.

Andro nodded, panting. "Sure did. She literally screamed the new strategy over the dinner last night to the whole House. You're lucky you missed it."

Blaze smirked. He could only imagine how fun it was to sit through dinner when Val was in one of her foul moods.

"Imma gonna need your help," Andro singsonged. "Val tasked me with going to get the blood moss for a ritual and she told me to take you with me."

Blaze quirked a brow. Andro leaned back on his arms, lounging.

"You need me, long legs? Me and nobody else?"

Andro rolled his eyes. "Suck my dick. You know it. I'm not going to repeat myself."

Blaze chuckled. He rose to his feet and came to stand behind Andro as he grabbed his forearm, dragging him up to his feet.

"Stretch, lazy pants."

"Fuck you. Who are you calling *lazy*? I'm the one who has swimming practice after this. And what are you gonna do?"

"I also have swimming practice," Blaze shot back, "of sorts."

"You're such a whore."

Blaze turned to the team, clapping his hands. "Get into your positions."

As the team spread out on the field, everyone taking their stances, Blaze brushed a hand over his hair. "So, what time and where do I need to be?"

A wide smile spread across Andro's face. "Tonight, after sunset. I'll pick you up."

R ight after eight o'clock, there was a knock on Blaze's door.
"Come in."

The door opened, and Andro walked in, dressed in classic black pants and a matching turtleneck. His shoes were polished to perfection, and the buckle of his black leather belt had not a single scratch, despite the daily wear and tear.

"Since when do you knock?" Blaze asked, crushing the butt of his cigarette in the ashtray.

Andro stuffed his hands in his pockets and looked around.

"Since you started fucking Val, that's the last thing I want to walk in on."

Blaze froze midway to his closet, surprised how the Hel Andro knew about that when Blaze was sure he told nobody.

"Who told you?"

Andro walked to his desk, plopping his ass in the chair. "Nobody had to. I have eyes."

Ah, sure. Mm-hmm, of course.

Blaze grabbed a black ripped T-shirt from his closet and pulled it over his head. Then, he slid into the leather jacket and turned to Andro, spreading his arms.

"How do I look?"

Andro eyed him for a moment, clearly trying to hide a smile. "Like expensive, junkie trash."

Blaze smirked. "Perfect. Exactly what I was aiming for."

His friend chuckled, shaking his head.

They left the House, and Andro led them towards the campus. Once they reached the main path, instead of going straight towards the cafeteria, Andro turned left, walking straight through the grass towards the right edge of the campus.

Blaze followed him without question, his hands shoved in his pockets.

Once they crossed half of the field, Blaze realized they were headed towards the Cursed Forest. Blaze stole a glance at Andro, whose face was calm, lips pressed into a tight line.

"Feeling dangerous tonight?"

Andro glanced at Blaze, a corner of his lips curling. "Always when I'm with you."

Blaze chuckled.

When they reached the edge of the campus where the Cursed Forest started, someone was already there, waiting for them.

"What the fuck are you doing here?" Blaze asked Rogue, who was leaning on the trunk of a tree.

"He's here to help," Andro answered. "You didn't think I would be going into the forest without some backup?"

Blaze placed a hand over his heart, wounded. "I thought *I* was your backup."

Andro rolled his eyes. "You know what I mean. It's the Cursed Forest we're entering. Having a demon to watch our backs is smart."

Of course it was smart.

And Andro *was* the smartest of them all.

But Blaze wasn't going to admit it.

"Pussies," Blaze said and strode forwards. After a few steps, he stopped, turning back. "Where do we find the blood moss?"

Andro caught up with him. Rogue trailed right after him, hands stuffed in his pockets.

There was a paper in Andro's hands, and he frowned as he tried to read it in the dark. "We need a Banshee's blood to soak the moss from the Cursed Forest. There is also an incantation to use but I can't—"

Blaze cocked a brow. "Fuck, Andro."

"What? Not feeling up for some Banshee hunting, *Blazy*?"

"Who doesn't want to spend a lovely Tuesday night chasing death?"

Andro strolled forwards with his chin held high.

"Do you know how to catch a Banshee?" Blaze asked after a few moments.

The further they went into the forest, the thicker the mist on the ground was, and soon they would lose track of where they came from and where they were going.

It was the way the Cursed Forest worked.

"They should be close to the edge of the Blood Lake," Andro said, gesturing to their left where the crimson lake was supposed to be. "Let's go see if we can find them."

"Don't we need, like, bait or something?" Blaze asked, following Andro.

He smirked, throwing a glance at Blaze. "That's why I brought *you* here."

Ah, well, that's just great.

"Thank you, Andro. I'm flattered that you planned on using me as bait without even telling me."

"I was gonna."

"When? When the Banshee was already halfway down my throat?"

"Exactly."

"Bitch."

Andro bumped his shoulder into Blaze's.

They walked through the forest, Blaze occasionally glancing back to where they came from to check if they were still able to see the edge of the forest.

He also stole glances at Rogue, who was silent as they made their way, his shoulders relaxed as if he was on a casual stroll in a park.

Maybe Val was onto something.

Having a demon to watch your back did make things easier for them, it seemed.

Should have thought of it sooner.

Soon, they reached the edge where the forest started going down the hill, which meant that they were getting closer to the crimson lake. The slope was barely there, but Andro stopped, looking around.

There was not a single sound in the forest, no birds, no bugs, not even a single branch moved, despite it being windy when they left the House.

It was as if they had entered a whole new world the moment they stepped foot in the forest.

Since starting at Venefica, Blaze would often find himself wandering here. It wasn't his first time. But he always came prepared, and somehow, tonight, he felt anything but.

Andro continued his stroll, and they walked in silence, only the branches snapping under their feet, moss crunching.

"So," Andro said, clearing his throat. "Did you see the wound in Alecto's palm?"

Blaze could feel his friend's eyes on him now, but he didn't turn. "Mm-hmm."

"That's some nasty cut, and she refuses to tell anyone how it happened," Andro continued. "Jolene guessed it was one of the other Houses, probably trying to pull a prank using her, because some still believe she's the weak link of our House."

"Oh, why is that?"

"You know why."

Oh, yes, Blaze knew.

Because Alecto was a half breed, some believed that made her weaker.

Blaze believed it too up until recently.

Now, he was *certain* that Alecto was as vicious as any of them.

Believing she was weak was dangerous.

"I didn't tell Jolene that I don't think it's someone from the other Houses," Andro mused.

"No? You sound so sure." Blaze's pulse picked up the pace.

"You see, Jolene gave me the knife that she found in Alecto's palm the night of the incident." Andro paused, and there was a click as the knife snapped open. "Doesn't this look familiar to you?"

Finally, Blaze turned his eyes to his friend, a black pocketknife resting in his palm.

His pocketknife.

The one Blaze slipped into Alecto's pocket the night he brought her to this forest to teach her a lesson.

Also, the *one* that Andro gifted him for their ten-year friendship anniversary because Andro was sentimental like that.

It was one of a kind, another little gift from the mortal world.

Blaze sighed. There was no point in denying anything to Andro.

"What do you want me to say?"

Andro tossed the knife at Blaze, coming to a stop. His eyes were shooting fire.

Rogue also stopped, keeping a few feet away from them. Watching, Blaze had no doubt.

"I don't even fucking know why, but I at least expected some kind of remorse from you."

"Why the dramatics, Andro?"

"*Dramatics?*" Andro took a step closer, fuming now. "I told you to leave her the fuck alone the last time. What the fuck did you do now?"

Blaze shrugged, refusing to feel guilty.

Why the fuck was he feeling guilty while his friend scolded him?

Like Blaze was a damn child or something.

"Nothing you have to worry about," Blaze said. "She's alive and well, isn't she?"

Andro's nostrils flared. "What the fuck is wrong with you?"

"Many things. You know that."

The bitter coffee brown of Andro's eyes warmed for a moment, but not enough for him to back off. "You're either going to fuck up our Game, or you're going to get yourself *and* us expelled with this nonsense. Is that what you want?"

"No."

"Then leave her the fuck alone. What did Alecto ever do to you that you have to behave this way?"

She was there.

Always. Fucking. There.

Alecto had things Blaze didn't.

And she made him *feel* things he didn't want.

But Blaze couldn't say it.

Not even to Andro.

"I can't" was all Blaze said, turning to continue walking. "I won't."

A sharp pain pierced Blaze's face as a fist connected with his jaw.

"What the fuck?" he spat, turning to Andro.

"I know you, Blaze. Did you forget?" Andro growled, closing the distance between them. "I *know* the language you speak."

Blaze smirked, heat surging down his neck and arms, his chest squeezing briefly at the words that cut him deep.

Just like Andro intended.

But when Andro advanced on him once more, this time Blaze was ready to dodge the punch coming his way and swing one himself.

Andro grunted as Blaze's fist connected with his side, but he just swung another fist, and this time it got to Blaze, sparks of pain spreading along the other side of his face.

Blaze squeezed his eyes shut, trying to ride out the wave of pain, but Andro didn't give him a chance to breathe.

Andro pushed Blaze, sending him to his knees, and then was on top of him, straddling him as he punched his sides.

Blaze tensed his core muscles and swung his fist forwards, connecting with Andro's jaw.

Copper filled Blaze's mouth, but his blood was on fire, heart racing. He rolled over, pressing Andro to the mossy ground as he spread out on top of him, every inch of their bodies touching.

"I thought it was supposed to be bros *over* hoes," Blaze whispered in Andro's ear.

Andro struggled beneath him, throwing his head back, trying to headbutt Blaze, but Blaze dodged it just in time.

"Fuck you," Andro hissed. "It's not about that, and you fucking know it. We're *Inner Circle*. We're building a family here, you dick."

Blaze scoffed.

A family?

Andro was fucking delusional.

"Guys," Rogue's voice came from behind them.

"We're busy. Don't you see?" Blaze turned his head to glance at Rogue behind his shoulder.

He then turned back, struggling to keep hold of Andro.

"I leave you to your thing, and you should do the same with me," Blaze said through clenched teeth. "It's always worked great for us."

"I'm not going to watch you ruin everything we've built," Andro warned, his struggle dying down. "I'm not going to watch you ruin yourself."

For a moment, Blaze was still as a statue.

He wasn't sure whether he wanted to lash out and strangle Andro…or whether he wanted something else.

Slowly, Blaze released Andro, climbed off him, and sat on the moss.

His lip was split, jaw aching. Surely tomorrow there would be a bruise or two.

They sat in silence for a long moment, just staring at each other.

Maybe Andro was right about them.

Maybe he wasn't.

But it did feel as if Blaze was losing it. He was losing his fucking mind.

And while Blaze was fine with that, he wasn't fine with losing his best friend.

Andro sighed as if he could read Blaze's mind, see straight through his soul. His eyes were warm and calm once again.

"*Guys*," Rogue repeated, this time his voice deeper, full of warnings.

Blaze followed Rogue's gaze to somewhere in the distance, and the hairs on his neck rose.

There, between the trees, a lone white figure loomed. Her black hair hovered around her head like a lion's mane, pale face devious in the shadow of the night.

Andro got on his feet, dragging a stunned Blaze with him.

"You see, I knew you're going to come in useful," Andro whispered. And while his voice was filled with amusement, his rapid, shallow breathing betrayed his fear. "Okay, so here's the plan. Blaze, get the Banshee's attention. And keep it. Rogue, I'll need you to catch her and hold her for me while I perform the spell. Are we clear?"

Wordlessly, Rogue and Blaze nodded. The Banshee moved forwards, her feet barely touching the mossy floor of the forest as she came closer to them.

Her black eyes were bottomless, and they were settled on Blaze. Hungry.

It was the blood. The violence that drew her. Or maybe she could taste Blaze's rotten soul, and she wanted it.

At least someone did. Blaze snorted and took a step forwards.

"Blaze," Andro warned. "Don't make sudden movements. Rogue needs to be able to get a hold of her before she devours you."

Blaze gave a curt nod, eyeing Rogue. He was supposed to trust their demon to stop the Banshee before she killed Blaze.

That was a lot of faith to put in someone.

Rogue seemed to read Blaze's hesitation. "Don't worry about it, Leveau. I've got you."

"You better."

Blaze took a few steps away from Andro, closer to the creature.

"Want a piece of that, honey?" Blaze asked, wiping the blood from his lip and extending his hand towards her. The Banshee shot forwards, hissing. "Then come and get some."

The creature jumped, and Blaze's heart skipped a beat as her long fingers turned into sharp claws, reaching for his throat.

But before the Banshee could reach Blaze, something flashed in the air, getting hold of her lean body and slamming her down to the damp forest moss. Rogue straddled the creature, caging her in with his body while she thrashed and hissed.

Blaze pressed a finger to his ear, massaging it. Even with a fraction of its scream, the ringing was still present.

"Great," Andro chirped, all cheery. He went over to them, falling on his knees next to the Banshee.

He fished out his athame, a golden blade with a handle made of solid onyx, identical to Blaze's. Banshee snapped her teeth at Andro when he brought the dagger closer and his best friend jerked backwards.

"Pussy," Blaze said.

Andro turned back. "Why don't you do it then, huh? Let's see how you feel about the prospect of losing a hand."

Blaze only chuckled.

Blaze's eyes widened when Rogue's fingers turned into blackened claws right in front of their eyes.

The demon brushed a claw through Banshee's hand. The creature wailed, thrashed again, and its clear blood poured out of the open wound.

It smelled like death and Blaze gagged once the scent hit his nose.

Andro murmured something under his breath, a chant, surely. The moss underneath the Banshee's hand turned from dark green to deep crimson.

"Excellent," Andro murmured, picking up the moss and stuffing it into the cloth bag.

With a happy grin, Andro got on his feet and turned to Blaze.

Blaze arched a brow. "And how do you suggest we escape the Banshee now?"

Andro's face lost all its amusement.

"Oh."

Both glanced at Rogue still pinning the creature on the ground. The demon took in their expectant looks and rolled his eyes.

"Go. I'll take care of it."

Having a demon on their side should really be a permanent thing.

36

If Blaze hadn't known Alecto's family since he was a child, he would have been surprised to find the Black residence so warm and airy from only knowing Alecto at Venefica.

The moment the door to his carriage opened, the salty, cool air greeted his nostrils, the ocean wrapping itself around him.

He made his way inside, walking the rounded white stone path that reminded him of the stony beaches he used to visit with his mom when he was a child. The Blacks' residence stood on the edge of a cliff overlooking the ocean, and it was all warm shades of beige and earthy brown.

Totally different from Alecto's room at the House with all black walls and ceilings and dark wood furniture that dated back to when neither of them was alive.

Following the stream of people down the airy corridor, Blaze strolled into their ballroom at the end of the house, with huge windows opening the view to the ocean down the cliff.

Thousands of firebirds were trapped in glass jars floating around the ceiling, thick green and rust ivy vines wrapped around the tall columns holding up the ceiling, trailing around the edges of windows, and a massive white oak fireplace was in the center of the main wall.

Blaze inhaled, tasting the cozy atmosphere on his tongue.

It was a delightful place, where nothing bad seemed to happen. Where the kids were safe and taken care of and had a happy space to come back to.

Nothing like Blaze's home.

Blaze's eyes locked with his father's on the other side of the room, his weakling of a mother hanging prettily off his arm, dressed in an airy white gown that once again accentuated her lean shoulders.

Blaze's stomach twisted, and he turned away, stopping a passing Crahen with a tray to grab a drink. He lifted the glass to inspect the black liquid inside, a large strawberry sitting on the rim.

"What the fuck is this shit?" he muttered.

"It's tonight's special drink, Blazy," a voice drawled from behind. "As black as your soul. I thought you might like it."

Blaze whirled to find Andro standing there, a wide grin plastered on his brown face. Tonight, he wore a bright red suit over his black turtleneck, and his long dreadlocks were neatly pushed back.

"I never thought I would have to say it," Blaze said. "But I'm actually glad to see you here."

"Suck my dick." Andro lifted his glass to Blaze's, clinking them together before he took a sip of the black liquid. "Where is your sidekick?"

"Val?" Blaze asked, glancing around the room casually. "For the first time, she had more important matters than attending a party with me."

"*Oh?*" Andro cocked a brow.

Blaze nodded. He was just as surprised as Alessandro because Val did not miss a chance to mingle with influential people.

Not ever.

"The question is, what the fuck are you doing here?" Blaze asked, tilting his chin towards Andro. "You hardly come to my parties, but you come to Alecto's?"

Andro rolled his eyes. "First of all, it's not *your* parties, it's your *father's*, and it's not *Alecto's* party, but *her* father's. And second, I wouldn't be here if my father had been able to go with my mother. I didn't want to leave her without a plus-one."

"Mm-hmm, I wouldn't want to leave Octavia alone either," Blaze murmured with a smirk, looking around the room for the most gorgeous woman that was Andro's mother.

"Exactly the reason," Andro said.

That only made Blaze grin wider. "I would have taken care of your mother, you know that."

When Andro's jaw clenched tight, Blaze had to bite down a laugh.

"Keep talking, and I'll add a few more bruises to your pretty face."

It was all a joke, of course. Blaze would have never done such thing as try to seduce his best friend's mother.

Mostly because Octavia Weir only had eyes for one man—her husband.

Andro and Blaze strolled through the crowd towards the windows and found a comfortable nook where they had a perfect view of the whole ball-room and all the people still streaming inside from the corridor.

Blaze mindlessly hummed a tune under his breath, trying to come up with an excuse to leave the party early. There was really nothing for him here, and the drinks weren't good enough for him to stay.

He once again lifted his glass up, trying to determine whether he liked the scorching sweet liquid or hated it.

It was hard to say.

Maybe, if he had more of them...

"Look at that," Andro whispered, jerking his chin towards the door.

Blaze followed his gaze to see Lyra and Reverie Frone walk in. Lyra was sporting an expensive black suit decorated with mother-of-pearls all around, and Reverie's curves were draped in a black silk gown with matching pearls lining the silky material.

"No fucking way." Blaze almost choked on his drink.

Frones *never* attended Leveau parties, no matter the occasion or importance.

But apparently, they were more than welcome at the Blacks' residence as Alecto's father strode towards them, grinning wide and planting kisses on both of their cheeks.

"I didn't know Frones mixed with the Blacks," Blaze murmured, eyeing the elegant women as they made their way to the bar, Alatar walking ahead of them.

Andro chuckled. "It's the old money, babe. They stick together no matter what. Maybe that's why Jolene seems to like Alecto the most out of all of us."

Old money, right.

Blaze tended to forget that the Leveaus' wealth was new money, his father being a self-made billionaire, just like Andro's parents. While the

Frones and Blacks had generations of prominent witches and warlocks at the very top of their society.

"I thought it didn't matter anymore," Blaze noted, glancing at Andro. "We're the next generation. We don't give a shit about old money, new money..."

Andro cocked a brow.

"As long as it's money."

"I guess we'll see when we graduate."

Andro swiped two more glasses of tonight's special from the passing Crahen, planting them on their tall table. Blaze bit into his strawberry. It was ripe and juicy, like the ones they got during the peak of strawberry season.

Blaze glanced around the room, looking. For what, he wasn't sure.

Or, rather, he didn't want to admit it to himself.

But his heart still picked up its pace the moment the silky white-blond hair came into view.

Blaze smirked, concealing it with his glass so nobody else could notice the tilt of his lips.

Apparently, Miss Black either didn't get the memo on the dress code for tonight's party, or she simply didn't care.

Knowing her, it was the latter.

It was a black-tie event, where warlocks wore their most expensive tailor-made suits, and witches showed off the most elaborate, elegant gowns that each told a story.

Alecto Black made her way through the crowd, towards *their* table, in a backless lace dress that showed the black underwear she wore underneath as well as her small, rounded breasts that were very prominently *not* covered with a bra.

Blaze had to bite the inside of his cheek to get his mind and body under control because when she stopped by their table and her round cherry-colored lips moved, he had urges surfacing that had no business being inside him.

Not after what he did to her.

"What happened to your face?" she asked, reaching her hand to Andro's jaw where a bruise rested.

Andro grinned, jerking his chin towards Blaze. "You should see the other guy."

To Blaze's surprise, Alecto glanced his way, eyeing his bruised-up face with blank, bottomless eyes.

He wasn't sure what reaction he expected after the incident in the forest.

But the coldness and lack of any emotions in that gaze were not it.

It was like a bucket of cold icy water washed over him.

Alecto turned back to Andro. "It's nice to see you here tonight. I didn't think any of you would come."

"Honestly, you have to thank my father for me being here," Andro said, lifting a glass in cheers. "If he didn't have to go out of town at the last minute, I wouldn't be here."

"I'll be sure to remember to send him a thank-you note."

"So, is there anything we might want to buy at tonight's auction?" Blaze asked casually.

She once again turned her attention to him, the same dead expression in her eyes. "Nothing that would be of interest to you, Leveau."

Blaze stole a glance at Andro. There was a warning in his eyes when their gazes locked though.

Something pinched at his chest, and he swallowed the rest of his drink in one gulp. His best friend was supposed to be on his side.

They were fucking brothers.

Why wasn't his best friend on his side anymore?

Before Blaze could say anything else, the light dimmed, letting the fireplace be the attention of the whole room.

Alatar Black stepped in front of the mantel, and when he spoke, the whole room echoed with his voice. "Welcome to the Black residence. As always, I'm very glad to have you here with us tonight for our annual Black Swan Inc. Foundation auction."

He paused, letting the crowd cheer. Blaze lazily clapped his hands twice before grabbing another drink from a passing tray.

"Tonight, we have an assortment of glorious treasures for you, witches and warlocks of Avalon Hills," Alatar continued. "Some pieces have come from the mortal world, and some were scavenged and brought from Hel itself."

That sent a few awed gasps and a sea of chatter over the crowd.

No better way to entice their kind than with some dangerous, rare piece of old junk rumored to be brought from the deepest pit of Hel.

The crowd parted as the first item was pushed on a golden trolley by a tall woman with ebony skin and eyes darker than the night. A roughed-up antique chest lay on the trolley.

"The first piece we have is the secret treasure box that's rumored to have belonged to the Imp Queen for centuries before disappearing. The legend says that it hasn't been opened in centuries, and it houses the secrets of the Imp Queen that would allow the bearer of those secrets to fully control her," Alatar announced, gesturing a hand over the old piece of trash. "Ten thousand garders is the starting price."

"Who the fuck buys into this shit?" Blaze downed his drink. "Only a fucking idiot would pay that much for a rusted piece of metal with a good PR team behind it."

Andro chuckled.

"Twenty," a deep voice came from the corner of the crowd. Blaze's father was the one holding the gold stick with the Leveau name on it for Alatar.

Blaze rolled his eyes as Alecto and Andro exchanged glances and shared a laugh.

"Apparently, a Leveau," Alecto teased.

Blaze threw her a glance, but instead of getting angry, he found himself relieved.

She spoke to him. Made a joke.

At his expense, granted.

But who cared?

It seemed as if his father was indeed the only fool in the crowd because nobody else countered his offer.

"Sold to Leveau," Alatar announced, and a round of applause went around the ballroom as the woman pushed the trolley away, another one already on its way.

"Oh, it's gonna be a long night." Andro fetched another drink.

Blaze lifted his glass and Andro brought his, smashing them together.

A fter the auction, Blaze finally was feeling tipsy.

And he liked the special drink for tonight's party, he decided after all.

He had wandered outside, standing on the deck overlooking the back garden with a lone tall willow three hanging heavily over the cliff's edge and a pool.

Even with the cool air of autumn, the illuminated water swirling over the white rocks that lined the floor of the pool looked inviting.

As he drew another deep breath, inhaling the smoke, Blaze's eyes wandered back to the ballroom. From outside the windows, he had a better view of everyone because no one could see that he was watching.

The Frones were surrounded by multiple people, all surely trying to appeal to the sisters who ruled over the fortune bigger than everyone in this house combined.

Blaze tipped his head to the side, eyeing the gracious woman who looked just like Jolene, but at the same nothing like the wild girl with books always in her lap and plants everywhere she went.

The rest of them flaunted their wealth, left and right. It was the only way they knew after all.

Even Alecto.

But Jolene wasn't like them. If you didn't know her last name, then you would have never guessed she was the sole heir of one of the oldest families in Inathis.

Blaze flicked the butt of the cigarette, already taking out another one when Alecto once more came into his view.

She stood at the edge of the ballroom, almost hidden behind the tall columns as her father towered over her, his lips moving as he said something in her ear.

Her face didn't reveal much as she stared somewhere in front of her, but the muscle in her cheek jumped as she ground her teeth.

Blaze's hand slipped from his lips, cigarette falling on the stone beneath his feet as he eyed the exchange.

Something in it looked vaguely familiar.

The way her jaw clenched, the way she didn't look into her father's eyes even though his face was pleasant and focused all on her.

Blaze knew that so well.

Too well.

Alecto's back straightened, her whole body stiff as her father planted a hand over her naked back, moving away from her path, and she let him lead her out of the ballroom.

Without another thought, Blaze opened the glass door, slipping inside and striding after them to the corridor and then into the other one, leading to the east wing.

The noise of the party stayed behind them as Blaze followed Alecto and her father in the darkness.

He wasn't sure what it was, whether it was his curiosity or whether it was that weird pinching feeling in his chest that brought him there, to the double door of a dining room, opposite where Alecto's father led her to.

It was a study, a home office of some sort.

Blaze leaned against the jamb, keeping himself hidden in the shadows as he watched Alecto come to the middle of the room, then turn to face the door.

Alatar hovered in the entrance, his back to Blaze so he couldn't see his face. But when he spoke, there was something not quite right in his tone. "You're not to walk around dressed like that. I won't allow it. Do you hear me, my sweet? You're not for others to see—"

The sentence cut off as Alatar closed the door behind them.

But right before the door shut, Alecto's eyes met Blaze's, and there was nothing but emptiness in them.

He wasn't sure whether she saw him, or maybe it was just a coincidence she glanced his way, and her eyes landed on him in the darkness.

As Blaze made his way back to the ballroom, his stomach felt like a bag of rocks.

37

Alecto didn't cry. Not anymore.

She had long lost all ability to feel sorry for herself.

It was only pain and disgust. Shame mixed with hatred that she needed to stop.

Her skin was red from all the scrubbing, but Alecto's hands didn't stop as she continued making circles with the sponge, the scalding shower beating at her back.

This pain was better than the other pain.

Finally, when she couldn't feel anything else other than burning on her skin, she managed to get out of the shower and wrap a towel around herself before returning to her room.

Unlike her bedroom at Venefica, her bedroom in her family home was light and airy, matching the interior of the rest of the estate with light wood panels stretching over the ceiling, white windows opening to the ocean.

It was the same as her mother had designed it when Alecto was a little girl. Alecto hadn't bothered updating it, even as her mother left her behind, even as she aged and grew into the woman she was today.

Alecto hated the decor. She hated the white furniture and light curtains.

But it was all right because she wanted to hate her bedroom.

It was all just as she wanted it to be. Never a comfortable moment, so she would never forget.

Slowly, she picked up the black lace dress she wore before at the auction and shoved it into the bin, together with the rest of her ensemble.

From her closet, she picked out black straight pants with a skintight turtleneck and slowly dressed. Then she grabbed her black high-heeled boots from the floor.

When she glanced at herself in the mirror, a stranger was looking at her. Her eyes were rimmed with red, making the dark circles more prominent.

It took her a few long moments to turn her eyes away from the sight in the mirror. She could have put concealer on, the whole layer of foundation that would make her flawless.

But there was this weird urge to wear her pain openly. Because of it, Alecto grabbed her cherry lipstick, smearing it over her dry lips with a trembling hand.

Instead of going back to the ballroom, where the party was now in full swing, with laughter and cheerful chatter coming all the way to the front of the house, Alecto turned towards the kitchen.

She grabbed a coat hanging on a hook by the door leading outside, and then went into the pantry, shoving the packs of cereal to the side and pushing the wooden panel behind to reveal a hole in the wall.

Alecto fished out an old, crumpled pack of cigarettes. To her relief, there were still eight cigarettes left, just like the last time, so she shoved them in the pocket of the coat and headed outside to the chilly night.

The back garden was dark, only the dim light orbs illuminating the white gravel path around the house.

Alecto reached the end of the estate, coming right to the edge of the cliff. The ocean was dark, almost black, and the waves seemed to be angry today as they crashed into the shore.

Alecto lowered herself over the edge, letting her legs dangle, and only then did she let out a long breath.

For a moment, she just sat there, staring at the ocean, drinking in the familiar smell of salt and water. It used to be a smell that carried so many good memories. It used to be a smell that made her heart sing with happiness.

Now, it was a smell that tugged at the corners of her heart, ruthlessly bringing up memories Alecto wanted buried deep inside.

She fished the pack of cigarettes out of her pocket, pushing one between her lips. Then, she reached in her pocket for the lighter, but it wasn't there.

She closed her eyes, trying to calm the sudden urge to snap at or break something.

When Alecto opened her eyes again, a flame waited for her, inches away from her face.

She could have said no, but she didn't have it in her to fight anymore.

Not tonight.

She leaned in, letting the flame light her cigarette. When the smoke hit her lungs, she almost moaned.

"I didn't know Miss Black smoked," he said after a moment, plopping right next to her.

There was no mockery or amusement in his voice. He sat there, still as a statue, his face without a mask, black eyes boring into her as if he were trying to read her soul.

"You don't know many things about me."

He cocked his head, his eyes searching her face for a moment. "Indeed."

Alecto brought the cigarette back to her lips.

Why the fuck he was here right now? Just a week ago, he drugged her and dragged her into the Cursed Forest to die. He made it very clear that she was nothing but trash beneath his shoe.

She tried to pretend she wasn't hurt. But she couldn't kill those feelings that had been suffocating her the whole week.

Him being here was confusing yet comforting at the same time.

"Thinking of pushing me off the cliff?" Blaze asked, lighting a cigarette. He tipped his head back, revealing a long neck as his throat bobbed, and then he glanced at her from the corner of his eye.

"Maybe."

"It would be just," he said, a smirk pulling one corner of his lips. "Do it if it's gonna make you feel better."

"Since when do you care how I feel?"

Blaze sighed heavily but didn't say anything. They sat in silence for a long moment, both sucking on their cigarettes, watching the horizon.

Then, Blaze lifted a bottle he'd been holding, offering it to her. She eyed it for a moment before taking it and swinging it back, the whiskey burning her throat as she downed a few large gulps.

"That's the spirit," Blaze said when she returned the bottle and wiped her mouth with the back of her palm.

"What can I say? I'm thirsty," Alecto said, already fishing out another cigarette.

She wasn't allowed to smoke. Her father didn't think it was appropriate for a lady like her. Mostly, he just didn't like the taste of it on her.

A shiver passed through her.

"Why do you hate me?" The words came out of her mouth before she could think better of it. But maybe it was for the better.

Maybe tonight, Alecto was ready to finally stop playing and just get everything off her chest.

Didn't she deserve at least that much?

For a moment, she thought Blaze wouldn't answer. He sat there, watching the ocean for what seemed like forever.

"I don't hate you," he admitted. "Not anymore."

"When did you stop hating me? When you got me detention or when you left me in the forest to die?"

"Somewhere in between."

Her hand was up from her side, crossing the air between them and connecting with his cheek.

It was a hard blow and it stung her palm, but Blaze merely flinched, his smirk turning into a grin now.

"Harder next time. I *like* it rough."

Alecto obliged him, serving another blow, this time harder. Blaze's head swung to the side, but the grin on his face didn't waver.

"Is that all you got, baby? I would think someone as vicious as Alecto Black would hit harder than that."

Heat surged through her body, warming up her face. Alecto didn't stop, slapping him once more, leaning her whole body into it as she slapped him again without waiting for him to recover.

Before the fourth slap, Blaze caught her wrists. She panted heavily, angry and confused, wanting to claw his eyes out or rip his throat. She wasn't sure.

"We wouldn't want to fall off the cliff now, would we?" He tugged her onto himself as he rolled them further away from the edge.

He was sprawled under her, her legs on either side of him, and then he released her hands, letting his fall next to his head.

Alecto hesitated for a moment, blinking as she glared down at him. One cheek was already red where she had hit him.

His lips curled again. "What? That's it? Come on, baby. You can do better than that."

That was enough for Alecto's anger to surge to the surface once more, and she growled as she slapped him again, this time on the cheek that hadn't suffered yet.

And she continued at it, sending one slap after another, scratching at his neck, leaving red marks behind.

He deserved it.

For every single time he let her feel like she was lesser.

For the time when he got her in trouble.

For the time when he pleasured her, making her feel things for the very first time she wasn't supposed to feel with someone like Blaze Leveau.

And then, she hit him because *she* was hurting.

Alecto slammed her fist into his chest, breathing hard as more and more anger surfaced, and it was getting difficult to breathe.

She curled her fists into his white shirt, wishing she could rattle his body and his bones, growling at him.

But Blaze just lay there, his hands beside his head, and took every single punch and slap with a calm expression settled on his beautiful face.

Not once did he flinch, not once did he try to stop her.

Alecto slapped and pushed, tugged and scratched, hurting him the way she hurt inside until there was nothing left but serene emptiness.

When she was spent, she let go of his shirt, sitting back as she panted, her heart fluttering in her chest like a wild bird in a cage.

Slowly, Alecto crawled off him and sat on the cold ground next to him. Blaze didn't rise, fishing out a pack of cigarettes and offering one to her.

Without a word, she took the offering and let him light her cigarette before he lit his own.

They sat there in the dark night, not talking for a long while, with only the sounds of burning cigarettes and the ocean crashing to the shore.

Alecto had never felt more at peace.

38

It took Blaze exactly three seconds to know that something was not quite right at tonight's dinner party at the Leveaus'.

He never knew every name of every person attending.

But he always recognized the faces.

Tonight, there was not a single face he recognized sitting around the dining table.

Also, his mother wasn't around.

Galliermo had ensured it was because she went away for the weekend, to some retreat in suburbia.

But Blaze knew better than to trust what his father said.

Something was weird, but he couldn't figure it out.

At least Val didn't seem to pick up on the difference. She was chatting away as per usual, her face pleasant and voice sweet.

Blaze glanced around the room, and when he found the Crahen, he waved it over, letting the server refill his wineglass.

If it weren't for his father, he would have asked for the whole carafe of wine to be left by his side. He was determined to drink it all.

But Blaze didn't want to piss his father off tonight.

Some part of him was flattered that his father offered him smiles and encouraging words in front of other people. He wasn't ignoring him tonight, proudly parading Blaze like a puppy, telling his associates about his win at the last rockey game.

Of course he would be happy Blaze won against Dominic.

At least one son was less of a disappointment than the other.

"The crowd is definitely colorful tonight," Val murmured to Blaze, and that snapped him out of his own head.

So, she had noticed after all.

"What do you mean?" Blaze asked, his voice low.

Val glanced around the room for a moment. "Half of the Upper West Side is here tonight. Not the usual crowd your father runs with."

That was something worth the attention.

Why would Blaze's father invite people from the side of town where he didn't do business?

"Any ideas why?" Val asked.

Blaze blinked a few times, rubbing his chin. "Have no idea. You know more about my father's business than I do."

Which was a thought that made Blaze feel a certain type of way.

He just wasn't sure how yet.

Suddenly, the chairs shuffled, and the guests were rising to their feet, getting ready to move to the lounge for dessert and cocktails.

Blaze strolled towards the double door leading to the lounge, Val's arm looped in his.

"I know someone who knows someone," a tall woman with sickly pale skin said to Galliermo as they passed.

Blaze's spine stiffened. Val's hand tightened around his, but they didn't stop moving, drifting with the crowd.

"You heard that, right?" Val asked once they were settled on one of the leather couches, right where they could see everything going on around them.

Blaze nodded, bringing his glass to his lips as he eyed the woman who spoke before, still chatting with his father in the corner of the room.

"Do you think he invited the Imp Queen tonight?" Blaze asked Val. "And she didn't show?"

Val's lips curled as she shook her head.

"He wouldn't dare to invite her when he has her chest."

Now, Blaze's curiosity was piqued.

"How do you know about the chest?" he asked. "You weren't at the auction."

"I have my sources, Blazy."

Indeed. After all, Val was close and intimate with the Imp Queen herself.

"So, does it mean that the legends are true?" He didn't like the picture forming in his mind.

Val didn't answer, her gaze scanning the crowd while her palm rested on his thigh.

"You are using me," Blaze mused, and his words drew Val's attention away. He tipped his head back, glaring at her down his nose. "I don't mind, not at all. I let you use me willingly."

"Poor little Leveau boy."

"But entertain me, at least a little bit," he continued, nudging her gently with his shoulder. "I'm just so fucking bored."

Val regarded him as if she was considering something, weighing the options.

When she spoke, it was so quiet, Blaze had to lean in to hear the words.

"Everything you hear is true," she whispered. "Demons have many abilities. They're capable of things our kind doesn't even dream of. And while they're the perfect tricksters, they can't lie."

"How fascinating."

"It is when you think about all the stories and lore about them, and you know that none of them could have been forged."

Blaze looked down at her for a moment, considering what that meant for them.

What was his father doing with such things? Surely, business came with risks, but risking pissing off the Imp Queen herself to buy another piece of this city seemed to be rather dangerous.

Even for Galliermo Leveau.

"Shall we go explore?" Val asked.

Blaze glanced around the room, unsure whether it was a smart move to sneak out. Surely, his father would notice and come looking for them.

"Oh, come on," Val insisted, rising to her feet.

Blaze regarded her outreached palm for a moment before lacing their fingers together.

They had the perfect excuse to sneak out.

An excuse that none would dare object to.

So, Blaze let Val lead him out of the lounge, letting the wondering guests read into their laced fingers however they wished.

When Blaze's eyes met his father's, his gaze dropped to their hands before coming back up, and there was a smirk on his face that made Blaze's stomach drop.

They left the party behind, walking down the corridor to the dark foyer.

"Where do you think he keeps it?" she asked once they stopped by the stairs to the second level.

In his father's study, Blaze was sure.

It was the only place his father kept anything worth anything.

He would have rather poked his own eyes out and waited for the healer to grow them back without any painkillers than go to his father's study.

But he couldn't let Val know.

So, now he was leading the way down the other corridor to his father's study, which was, to their surprise, unlocked.

Blaze pushed the door forwards, and they both slipped into the dark room only illuminated by the burning fireplace.

Val crossed the room to the large glass cage, which was now standing by one of the walls. She planted a hand over the glass and hissed, bringing it back to cradle it against her chest.

"Of course it's warded," she muttered.

All Blaze could focus on right now was standing in this wretched room that only brought pain and suffering for him since he was a child.

Never did his father invite him to his study to talk, to have a drink on one of the leather couches, like he did with so many of his business associates.

Never did he invite Blaze to come and admire his collection of rare and expensive daggers that lined the whole wall, like he did with everyone new who would come by their home.

No, Blaze only came through those heavy double doors when it was time for punishment.

When Blaze brought his wineglass to his lips again, his hand was trembling.

"Well, that's not going to give us much," Val said, still inspecting the chest locked under the glass dome. "These wards are as old as the fucking Inathis."

"I bet. What, did you expect to steal it tonight?"

"What am I? Twelve?"

"Let's go. I'm really bored."

He turned and slipped back into the corridor. Val followed him out.

Then, her hand was on his chest, and she pushed him against a wall.

Blaze *let* her push him against the wall.

She glared at him, a whole head and then some shorter than him, her eyes filled with hunger and promises of a good time.

Slowly, her tongue peeked through her lips, and she let it slide over her bottom lip.

"I know something that surely would help with boredom," she whispered, her hot breath hovering over his lips.

Blaze blinked.

Val took his silence as a yes and lowered herself on her knees, her hands already eagerly working his belt.

And then it hit him, out of the blue. The want, the *need* to see someone else kneeling in front of him instead of Val.

His throat went dry, and he averted his eyes, his hand gripping Val's wrists before she could unbutton his pants.

"I'm not in the mood," he said. "Not for that."

"Not in the mood?" Val was on her feet in a heartbeat. "Since when is Blaze Leveau not in the mood for sex?"

Ah, of course, Val's temperament wouldn't make this easy.

There were very few things a girl like Val hated more than rejection.

Blaze forced his hands on her shoulders, his thumbs moving in circles over her soft, delicate skin.

"I already had my dick sucked right before we came here," he said. Val's lips pressed into a tight line. He brushed a thumb over her cheek. "Next time."

Val lingered for a moment, her eyes narrowed as she searched his face.

And then she whirled on her heel and strolled away, back into the party, leaving Blaze leaning against the wall in the dark corridor.

He sighed, tipping his head back to the wall as he buckled his belt.

She was already ruining his fucking life.

And for the very first time, Blaze didn't know what to do to stop it.

Worse—he wasn't sure he wanted to stop it.

39

On a Wednesday night, the sound of a nail tapping at the glass woke Alecto up.

She opened her eyes to find her room dark, the clock on her bedside table showing a mere three o'clock.

The witching hour.

It was silent. Alecto sighed, rubbing her eyes. She hated waking up in the middle of the night for no reason.

After a few more moments of listening to the night and not hearing any more weird sounds, Alecto turned on her side, and the blood in her veins froze.

Just outside her window, a creature lurked. The moment their eyes locked, it cocked its skeletal owl head to the side and lifted one of its limbs to her window. A claw, long and sharp, landed on the glass.

Alecto had to cover her ears at the screeching sound the claw made as it dragged along the glass. Her insides recoiled.

She sat up, throwing her legs over the side of her bed as she narrowed her eyes and inspected the creature. It was a Hellbate, one of the many deadly creatures roaming the Cursed Forest.

Alecto blinked, her heart racing. No creatures wandered away from the Cursed Forest on their own, so what the Hel was this monster doing at her window?

A long claw tapped on her window again, and Alecto's muscles seized. But then she remembered.

The protection wards.

Their whole House was secured. No chance in Hel this thing was getting inside.

She was going to kill Blaze. It probably followed her here all the way from the forest, tracking her smell when he left her there.

Fucker.

Just as Alecto was about to get back into her bed, ignoring the creepy thing watching her, a scream pierced the night, coming from somewhere inside the House.

She was on her feet and out into the corridor. One by one, all the doors opened, and witches and warlocks streamed down the corridor, terrified.

Alecto glanced around, swallowing the panic as she threw herself into the closest room. There were two Hellbates at the window, staring through the glass with their bloodshot eyes.

One flickered its black tongue, licking the glass and leaving a nasty streak of saliva behind.

"They can't get inside!" Alecto shouted, returning to the corridor. "Calm the fuck down."

Another scream came from downstairs, and Alecto ran to the top of the stairs at the same time that Val and Blaze appeared.

"What the fuck—"

"They're inside!" Gael's voice, from the first floor. "Move away from the windows! Move away!"

No. They couldn't have been…

But then there was a roar, low and deadly, sending shivers down Alecto's spine. It came from downstairs, followed by a sea of screams and cries.

"Fuck." Alecto breathed out the words, looking between Val and Blaze.

"There's like a dozen Hellbates outside our windows," Jolene said, rushing from her room. Andro was right behind her.

Another wave of screams came from the first floor.

"Yeah, and from the sound of it seems like there's a dozen of them inside," Val snapped. "Blaze, Andro, go check on the protection wards. Pull them back up. Take Rogue if you need to."

Blaze nodded, and he and Andro ran up to the third floor.

"Jolene, what is it that Hellbates don't like?" Val asked. "Fire and…?"

"Light, not fire, any sort of light," Jolene said, her breathing shallow. "They're the night's creatures, so they can't stand the light. But it won't kill them."

Alecto ran back to her room, grabbed her bones from the nightstand, and returned to the girls. Without waiting, she closed her eyes, chanting as she conjured a ball of daylight in her mind.

"Good, Alecto," Val said. When Alecto opened her eyes, a ball of light warmed her palm. "Keep that going. Well, what the fuck is going to kill them?"

Jolene bit her lower lip, frowning.

"Think faster, Jols!" Val insisted, and Alecto slapped her shoulder.

"Pressure is not going to help."

"Smoke of the burning Girther!" Jolene blurted out, her hands moving frantically over her body and hair. "Yes, yes, the smoke is deadly to them."

"Do we have it?" Val asked, glancing down the stairs.

Jolene was already on her way to her bedroom. "I'll get it. But I'll need some time."

"Jolene, get the shit and meet us downstairs. Alecto, with me. We need to get everyone into the basement where there are no windows."

Alecto followed Val downstairs, keeping the light in her palm going.

"I'm not going to let a single fucking witch die tonight," Val hissed through her clenched teeth as she rushed to the living room.

Three witches were pressing against the wall as two Hellbates crawled inside through a broken window.

Alecto jumped into the space between the creatures and the students, transferring light into her free palm as she held it against the creatures. They both stopped, screeching and hissing.

"Move, fucking move!" Val snapped behind Alecto, and when she glanced back, she saw Val gesturing for the witches to move to the corridor.

Alecto glared back at the Hellbates, all of their attention clearly focused on her now. All thoughts left her mind as she stared at them.

"Alecto, leave it, come here," Val said, pulling at Alecto's pajama shirt.

Without turning her back to the creatures, Alecto let Val lead her to the corridor.

"Move to the basement, close the door, and stay there. Got it?" Val said to the witches, and they obeyed.

Alecto rushed into the meeting room on the opposite side of their corridor to find another bunch of witches trying to shoo three Hellbates, already inside, by throwing random items at them.

"Stop that!" Val snapped, and Gael's hand froze. "You're just going to make them angrier, you dumb fuck!"

Gael glared at her, then back at the creatures. "Well then, what am I supposed to do?"

"Conjure light!" Val said and ducked as one Hellbate went for her.

Alecto threw one ball of light. When it hit the creature, it screamed in agony and retreated. The others stayed back.

Another few light balls appeared in the room, and the creatures retreated to the furthest corner.

"Go, now go to the fucking basement and stay there," Val instructed, waving her hands to the corridor. "Light keeps them at bay, but it doesn't kill them!"

Once the room was cleared, they moved back to the corridor and into the kitchen at the back of the House.

There were three more Hellbates, their sharp claws sunk into the body of a bleeding student.

"Fuck," Val hissed. "Shit."

Alecto split the last remaining ball of light into two and threw one at the creatures, sending them scattering around the kitchen to hide in the shadows.

Val rushed to the witch lying on her belly, tears streaming down her face.

"Can you walk?" Val asked, and the girl nodded, sobbing.

Alecto kept an eye on the creatures, keeping herself as the barrier between them and Val with the girl as they both stumbled out of the kitchen.

Val helped the girl downstairs, and then came back, shutting the door.

"Is that all?" Alecto asked, her eyes scanning the doorways.

"Yes, all are there and safe," Val said, panting. "Just one is hurt, so that's good news, I suppose."

One for now, but Alecto didn't say that out loud.

Another low growl shattered the silence. Two pairs of claws curled around the doorway from the living room, another set appearing on the doorway out of the meeting room.

They were coming for them.

"Get up the stairs," Val instructed in a whisper.

Alecto walked towards the stairs, keeping the remaining ball of light between them and the Hellbates were crawling into the corridor now, their eyes hungry.

"It would be a great time to conjure some more light," Alecto said over her shoulder.

"I left my bones in my room," Val answered, holding on to Alecto's shirt as they climbed the stairs to the second floor.

Great, just fucking fantastic.

Just when they were almost at the top of the stairs, the Hellbates advanced, coming up after them. But none were quite brave to attack with Alecto holding the light.

She stumbled as her heel hit the last stair, and for a moment, the light wavered, but Val straightened her. They were now on the second floor.

"Strengthen the light," Val instructed.

Alecto chanted the spell as she grabbed for the bones. The ball in her palm grew, and Hellbates backtracked on the stairs, hissing.

"I'm going to run grab my bones," Val said, breathless. "Hold them here. Don't move, not unless you have to."

Alecto's throat was too dry to say anything, so she just nodded, following Val's back as she went up to the third floor.

For a long moment, Alecto just stood there, on the top of the stairs, glaring at the Hellbates sprawled at the bottom as she waited for Val or Jolene or someone else to come back.

She could hear feet shuffling upstairs, probably Andro and Blaze trying to reinforce the wards, but it seemed like it was taking forever.

Before she heard the growl, she *felt* it. All hairs on the back of her neck rose, her stomach dropping.

Alecto stole a glance behind her shoulder to find two more Hellbates crawling towards her through the corridor. More must have made their way through the windows on the second floor.

Fuck.

She stepped away from the stairs, rounding the railing, and advanced backwards, further away from the creatures crawling at her.

Her heart raced so fast it was hard to catch her breath, and her thoughts were racing just as fast.

Alecto glanced behind her, stealing a couple more steps as the Hellbates moved in closer to her, despite the light.

Maybe they were smarter than they knew. Maybe they could taste her fear, and that was enough to overcome their discomfort with the light.

Alecto's back hit the wall in the corner of the corridor. Two more growls came from the room next to her.

She was backed up in the corner with Gods know how many fucking killer creatures all coming for her.

Alecto closed her eyes and took a deep breath. When she exhaled through her nose, she opened her eyes and split the light off, throwing one globe of it at the creatures in the room next to her.

They hissed and retreated, but just for a moment.

Then, they seemed to come in angrier, hungrier, and Alecto couldn't hold in the scream of agony as one claw dug into her forearm.

It was as if her whole hand was on fire, muscles burning with a pain she had never experienced before. She backed away out of the corner and pushed against another wall.

With trembling hands, she threw the light at the creatures sprawled in front of her. They all retreated, burned by the massive light ball.

Alecto used that moment to run back down the corridor, hoping to make it up the stairs to the third floor, but there were more Hellbates waiting for her there.

"Oh, for fuck's sake," Alecto growled and then hissed as the pain in her hand intensified.

She tried flexing her fingers, but they weren't cooperating anymore. She whimpered, fear freezing her muscles. Or was it something in the claw that made her muscles refuse to function?

The burning rose further up her arm, getting closer to her shoulder.

Tears sprung to Alecto's eyes, and she couldn't stop taking in sharp and shallow breaths as she imagined whatever poison taking over her whole body, leaving her helpless.

She was left alone to face the horrid creatures all crawling towards her, and she soon wouldn't be able to protect herself.

Of course. Of course they would leave me to fend for myself.
The half breed.

Anger surged to the surface. Exactly what she needed.

She backed away from the stairs, moving towards her room, not turning her back on from the creatures. Her bathroom didn't have a window. She could hide there, buy herself some time.

Her shoulder burned, numbness creeping up the side of her neck when she finally reached the door.

Alecto couldn't turn her head to check whether the room was empty, so she just ducked inside, hoping for the best.

Once in her room, she moved to the bathroom. When she opened the door, a wave of dread washed over her at the sight of two Hellbates already inside her bathtub.

"Fuck."

Alecto whirled, slamming the door shut. Two more were already in her doorway.

Fisting her bones, Alecto murmured the spell to conjure more light, but with her other hand completely numb, she couldn't wield power.

She swallowed hard, part of her throat refusing to work already, and then it dawned on her.

When her throat muscles locked, she wouldn't be able to swallow.

She'd fucking choke on her own saliva.

Hissing and screeching sounds came from the corridor, light bouncing off the walls into Alecto's dark room. Then, there were a few screams that didn't sound natural, and then a ball of light flew at the backs of the Hellbates in her doorway.

They pounced forwards, hissing as Blaze stepped into her room, eyes wild, a ball of light in both his palms.

When his gaze landed on her, Alecto could have sworn a shadow of relief passed through his face, and he moved towards her, Jolene in his wake.

She held a thick bundle of herbs in her hand, the other one holding a lighter to keep the flame going. The room filled with thick, sweet smoke, and Alecto's eyes started burning.

And then the creatures started screaming, thrashing around as if they were in agony.

Blaze stopped right in front of Alecto, light evaporating in his palms as he inspected her. "Are you all right?"

She opened her mouth to answer, but nothing came out as her throat refused to work.

Her eyes widened, and she grabbed for her throat as if that could help.

"Jolene," Blaze called. "Jolene!"

Alecto could only breathe through her nose as she tried to keep herself from swallowing and choking. Blaze's hand wrapped around her waist, dragging her away from the wall.

Jolene's eyes widened with worry.

"What the fuck?" she whispered, eyes darting from Alecto's face to her arm. "They got their claws into her. Venom. They're venomous."

"I can see that," Blaze snapped as he led Alecto to her bed. His palms guided her hips to sit, but he didn't move away, kneeling beside her. "What do we do? You have an antidote or something?"

Jolene shook her head, coming to her other side. She poked Alecto's numb arm, then her fingers traveled to her neck.

Only when her soft fingers probed her cheek did Alecto feel something.

"I don't," Jolene admitted, her breathing shallow. "I haven't learned the antidotes yet."

Blaze cursed under his breath. "We need Gillian."

Andro and Val came into the room. Andro held an identical bundle of herbs. "We cleared the first floor. What—"

"Get to Gillian," Blaze said over his shoulder. "Alecto's poisoned."

"I'm on it," Andro said, handing the bundle to Val. "Give me ten minutes!"

"I don't know if we have that long," Jolene whispered. Alecto tried to swallow as her eyes widened, but she just choked.

A tear escaped down her cheek. Blaze cupped her face in his palms, turning it to meet his.

"Hey, relax, baby," he muttered softly. "He's going to be here soon with help, and we're going to get the venom out of you, all right?"

Alecto blinked, her panic leaving space for another type of feeling.

She didn't think Blaze had ever been so gentle, so caring with her before.

There was nothing but worry in his dark gaze as it held hers, his soft expression making his face even more beautiful.

She tried breathing through her nose, but her chest was going numb, and she struggled to get the air in.

"Jolene," Blaze said. "She can't breathe."

Jolene cursed.

Alecto blinked, trying to relax, trying to just not feel and not freak out over the sudden need for air when she couldn't have any. Her eyes fluttered closed as her lungs burned, and soon her head was swimming.

"Let's freeze her. For fuck's sake, take my hand."

It was Blaze's voice, or maybe Jolene's. Alecto couldn't tell as she drifted in and out of the blackness.

When her lungs finally stopped burning, she could take in a breath and let herself float away.

It was nice.

40

Alecto looked fucking dead.

Lying on her bed with her snow-white hair draped around the pillow, Alecto looked like a corpse.

Blaze could hardly bear seeing her like this.

He would have rather not lived at all than live in a world where she wasn't around.

What a weird little thought.

Unsettling.

Instead of letting himself wallow in it, Blaze decided to channel his anger into something better.

"Why the fuck did you leave her alone?" he snapped at Val.

Val's eyes widened. "She was doing great before I left! I forgot my bones, and I went to fetch them just for a moment!"

Blaze narrowed his eyes. "You left her for longer than that."

"Yeah, because I went to help you fuckers reinforce the fucking wards. She was alone for less than ten minutes."

"Well, that was more than enough," Jolene chimed in, crossing her arms as they all stood over Alecto's bed. "You should have fucking known, Val."

"Oh, don't fucking blame this on me," Val snapped back. "Alecto is more than capable of taking care of herself. She basically saved everyone downstairs!"

"Yeah," Blaze said. "It should have been you, our leader, to make sure that every witch is safe and sound. But of course, your protection doesn't extend to Alecto, does it?"

"Careful, Blaze. You really don't want to mess with me."

It was a warning.

Oh, that's a first.

Blaze was about to snap back at her, but then Andro and Rogue appeared in the doorway, Gillian right behind them.

"Are we too late?" Andro ran up to the bed, almost screaming.

"We froze her to stop the venom from spreading," Jolene said, grabbing Andro's arm. "She's going to be fine."

"Move away." Gillian came around the bed.

Blaze forced himself to give her space, stepping aside and leaning on the wall with his arms crossed.

Gillian placed her little satchel on the nightstand and opened it. There were a dozen different glass vials and bottles with herbs and weird-looking mixtures inside.

She twirled a finger over them as if unsure which one to pick, and Blaze's heart lurched, but he didn't let it show.

Val's eyes were already on him, watching every move and reaction intently. He didn't need her reading his mind.

Not when it came to Alecto Black.

Gillian picked out two vials, one with bright amber liquid and another with a spring-green powder. Slowly, she poured the powder into the liquid, and it bubbled, a sour scent filling the room.

Jolene stood over Gillian's shoulder, inspecting what the healer was doing.

"This is going to release the venom?" she asked.

"Yes. And it will remove the freezing spell, so she'll be awake immediately." Gillian leaned over Alecto, one hand pulling her jaw down, parting Alecto's lips. "But it's not going to be pretty."

"What do you mean?" Andro asked.

"Hellbate poisoning is a bitch," Gillian said with a heavy sigh as she poured the antidote into Alecto's mouth. "She's going to be sick until it's fully out of her body. So, one or two of you should keep an eye on her."

They all exchanged glances.

"So she doesn't die during the detox," Gillian added.

Blaze ground his teeth, his fingers curling into fists. He hid them by crossing his arms tighter over his chest.

Just as quickly as Gillian came in, she left. Val instructed her to check the basement and another witch, also apparently hurt by the Hellbates.

Then, they waited.

Alecto didn't wake for a good ten minutes.

But when she did, all Hel broke loose.

Her whole body spasmed, her back arching as she bared her teeth to keep the screams of agony inside.

"Fuck," she hissed, a vein in her neck bulging. Her forehead was already slick with sweat, eyes unfocused as she scanned the room. "That hurts like a bitch."

Jolene managed a chuckle, even if it was a nervous one, as she pushed Alecto's hair away from her face and secured it with a clip. "But you're a tough bitch."

Alecto managed a half smile before her body was sent into another wave of pain, her palms fisting the sheets underneath her.

"I'm going to get some water," Andro said and left the room.

Val paced at the foot of the bed, her eyebrows drawn together.

"Can you help me keep her still?" Jolene asked. "She can sprain her fucking neck when her muscles are spasming."

Rogue was the first to spring into action, stepping closer to the bed to help Jolene.

Before Blaze even knew what he was doing, he surged forwards, coming face-to-face with Rogue. He planted a hand on his chest. "I don't fucking think so."

Rogue arched a brow.

"*Blaze*." Val's voice was full of warning.

"I'm not the enemy, Leveau. It wasn't me who left her to die in the forest, was it?"

Ignoring the sting, Blaze went over to the bed. Jolene lifted Alecto, letting him slide under her with his back to the leather headboard.

Alecto's head lolled on his chest, and Blaze ignored the weird feelings rising to the surface as he wrapped his arms around her to keep her in place for when another wave of pain came in.

"Don't you have something to make this easier?" Blaze asked, looking at Jolene sitting at the end of the bed.

She shook her head.

Alecto's muscles trembled, her whole body burning. When Blaze felt her start shaking, he tightened his grip, holding her head to his chest with his palm.

Her teeth were chattering, breathing uneven, but she didn't scream.

No, Alecto held it all inside, her eyes shut closed as she rode one wave of agony after another.

Andro came back into the room with a carafe of water and a glass. He placed it on the nightstand, filled the glass, and held it to Alecto's mouth.

She shook her head. "No."

"You need to drink," Jolene said, patting her leg. "It's going to help remove the venom faster."

"Not yet."

Jolene nodded to Andro, and he returned the glass to the nightstand.

"We need to talk about what happened tonight," Val said, finally stopping at the end of the bed.

"Someone fucking got to us," Alecto croaked.

Blaze hadn't had the time to process events from tonight.

What the attack of the Hellbates meant.

Someone had managed to come for their Book. And they hadn't even seen it coming.

Worse, someone broke through their elaborate protection spells.

"We had the highest tier protection wards from Gill's," Andro said, settling on the desk in the corner. "There is no way a simple student, even a fourth year, could break through those."

"Are you suggesting they had help from a powerful witch or a warlock?" Jolene asked.

Andro spread his arms.

"We have help this year," Val said, waving a hand at Rogue. "If we thought of that, it means that the others could too."

"You forget," Alecto chimed in. She stopped, swallowing hard before continuing. "Not many Houses are as reckless as we are. And not many have Blaze Leveau and his stash of blackmail material to get them out of trouble."

They chuckled, even Blaze, which eased the tension.

But not for long.

"Or it could be an inside job," Val suggested.

"Fuck," Jolene breathed out the words. "Who? Almost everyone here is legacy."

"And even legacy could betray. If the price is high enough, every witch is on their own. It's in our blood, don't forget that."

"Is the Book safe?" Alecto asked. Her trembling seemed to have lessened, at least for the moment.

"You almost died and that's what you're worried about? We created a little monster."

Slowly, Alecto lifted her arm, fist curling into an obscene gesture, aimed at Val.

Val smirked.

"Drink," Jolene insisted.

This time, Alecto didn't argue when Andro brought the glass to her lips.

She downed the whole glass, clearly parched, and then leaned her head back on Blaze's chest. Her eyes fluttered closed, her breathing finally even.

"Well, that wasn't so bad," Andro said.

But it wasn't the end. Not yet.

Alecto lurched forwards, thrashing against Blaze's hold as she bent over the side of the bed and hurled the contents of her stomach. Black tar-like liquid came out of her, filled with tiny bones and tattered feathers.

"What the—" Jolene muttered, a hand coming to cover her mouth.

Alecto coughed, gasping for air, and Blaze jumped to his feet. He lifted Alecto from the bed, hooking one hand over her knees and the other over her back, and carried her to the bathroom.

"Breathe," he muttered softly as he lowered her into the bathtub. "Breathe."

Alecto nodded frantically. Her nails dug into his arms, piercing the flesh, but he ignored it.

"It's going to be a long night," Val sighed, leaning on the jamb with her arms crossed.

"Karma is a bitch, I suppose," Alecto muttered through clattering teeth.

Witches didn't believe in Karma. It was a mortal thing.

If they did, they would never get a decent night's sleep.

.   .   .

N one of them got much sleep, all staying with Alecto until the dawn. At least she got the venom out of her system and was looking healthy today.

For someone who was poisoned and almost died.

"Well, get your asses outside," Val snapped, yawning, a cup of coffee in her hand as she walked through the back door in the kitchen outside.

Blaze dragged his ass after her. They came to stand in their back rose garden.

In the middle of the round stone pathway, a hill of black bodies had been stacked together. While the Inner Circle watched over Alecto, the rest of the House was busy cleaning up from those monstrous creatures.

Their dead bodies reeked worse than when they were alive.

Blaze scrunched his nose as he turned away from the pile.

They needed to burn this shit immediately, or the stench would be permanently lodged in their surroundings.

"You're sure about this, Val?" Andro asked, glancing up at their brownstone.

"It's the only way. We have to reinforce the protection wards with our blood, or someone can fucking break in anytime."

"And if we cross the threshold?" Jolene asked. "The Dean won't let it slide. Even if it's to protect ourselves."

"The Dean can fucking suck it," Alecto muttered, crossing her arms. "Val, you know how to monitor the levels so that the blood spell doesn't trigger the Dean's spell?"

"Mm-hmm." Val glanced at Blaze. "And we always have you, pretty boy. If something goes wrong, I'm sure there won't be much that Daddy's money or blackmail won't buy, right?"

Blaze cocked a brow but didn't argue.

Val wasn't wrong.

Even if it annoyed the fuck out of him that Val always seemed to turn to him when she needed…

Not him, really.

His status.

"Well then, let's do this," Alecto said.

Blaze came to stand on her left, Andro on the right. They all weaved their hands together.

Consciously or unconsciously, Blaze circled his thumb over the inside of

Alecto's palm; to his surprise, she didn't jerk her hand away.

Val closed her eyes and started chanting, "*Renoeum.*"

They all followed, and the air around them stilled.

Not a sound of a bird. Not a breath of air.

Blaze scrunched his nose when pain prickled his chest. When he glanced down, he found a thin line, like a delicate cut of a knife right in the middle of his pecs.

Blood trickled in a tiny line, and then a large drop floated away to the middle of the circle.

It joined with the blood of the others, and the moment their blood collided and merged, an electric current zipped through Blaze's body.

They continued chanting, their blood molding in the air, swirling together with each word.

Blaze's eyes widened when the blood orb floated over their heads, moving over to the brownstone.

It collided with the wall, and the magic of their protective wards rippled, tendrils of magic turning red as it merged with their blood.

For a moment, Blaze's hands trembled as he felt the wards draw strength from his blood, but then it was gone as if nothing happened. The birds chirped once more, a cool breeze ruffling his hair.

"Done," Val said, clapping her hands. "Now, if anyone tries to mess with the wards, we'll be able to feel it."

"Did we trigger the Dean's spell?" Andro asked.

"I don't know. I guess we'll find out." When his face dropped, Val laughed. "I'm joking, you idiot. It wasn't triggered. We're clear."

"If it did trigger, you know I'll blame it on you," Andro said, walking past her.

Val only laughed harder. "*Pussy.*"

"All bark and no bite," Blaze teased, draping an arm over Andro's shoulder.

41

I t's been a long time since Alecto was exhausted.
     Tired even.

Thanks to her witchy side, Alecto never got sick or tired or even felt under the weather.

But getting clawed by a Hellbate and having to detox its venom was taxing even for a witch.

Sadly, there was no rest for the wicked; the Snakes had things to do. Houses to ruin. And tonight, they were making their final move on the Tigers.

When Alecto climbed the stairs down into their basement, only Val was there. She sat at the corner of the pool table, a fresh blunt burning between her fingers. The Book lay open on her legs and Val was hunched over it, reading something intently.

Val was so focused on the Book she didn't even hear Alecto approach. When Alecto spoke, Val jumped, almost losing the blunt from her grip.

"What are you reading?"

"I've been double-checking the spell for tonight," she said. "Don't want any more mistakes and surprises."

Alecto sat next to Val on the pool table. "You think we're going to find what we're looking for tonight?"

"The Tigers' Book you mean?" Val put the blunt between her lips, inhaling the smoke. "It's still in their House, even after the fire."

"Don't you ever think we crossed a line?"

Alecto wasn't sure where the question came from. Or why it came out right now. But it was too late to take it back. So, she waited for Val's answer with a racing heart.

Val's lips curled into that dark, predatory grin. The one—Alecto only now realized—she wore as her armor.

"Tell me something, Black. Do you like our House? Do you like the luxury surrounding you, the infinite resources and opportunities that are guaranteed to a Snake?" Val paused, taking another puff. "Do you like the taste of power, when even the Dean himself can't do shit to you?" Val leaned in closer, her breath hovering over Alecto's lips. "Do you like the feeling of *safety*?"

A chill ran down Alecto's spine. She didn't know what safety meant. Not anymore. Alecto imagined it would remind her of the feeling she would get as a child when her mother wrapped her in her arms and the blanket of her black rose perfume.

Or it would feel like the relief Alecto would get anytime there was a Housebogg hiding in her closet or underneath her bed during the night and her mom would be the one to shoo it away by lighting sunset orbs around Alecto's room.

It'd been a long time since Alecto experienced safety. Yet, she didn't even have to think hard for the answer to all those questions.

"Yes."

Val looked pleased. "Then there are no lines not worth crossing."

Alecto didn't know what else to say. She decided it was smarter to focus on the task ahead of them while she took the time to figure out what Val's words meant for her. What the reaction of her body, the tingling excitement rising inside, meant.

She took hold of the Book and pulled it into her lap, scanning the page with the spell for breaking blood protection spells. The Snakes used it to ward their Book, so they assumed the Tigers would have used this type of magic to protect theirs as well.

When Alecto lifted the Book, something slipped from the pages. It wasn't a piece of paper but a small Polaroid picture.

"That's weird. I've never seen a Polaroid camera in Inathis—"

The words died in her throat when she recognized the blue eyes of the woman in the picture. Alecto's eyes.

It was her mother, standing in a familiar ballroom. Her long dress was made out of pink satin, flowing down her frame like a spring river. The corset hugged her curves in all the right places, making her waist unnaturally small.

And there was a hand resting on her waist. A hand that belonged to a tall man with inky black hair and dark as night eyes that flickered with the familiar cruelness looking straight into the camera.

Galliermo.

"What the fuck is this?" Alecto finally found her voice, turning to Val.

Neither Val's eyes nor smile was kind when she spoke. "Oh, you didn't know?"

"Didn't know what?"

"Once upon a time, Galliermo Leveau, a young second-year student and a member of the House of Snakes, fell in love with a fellow mortal student, Demitria Hollander. I'm sure you know the gal."

Alecto stopped breathing.

"Demitria seemed to return Galliermo's feelings. I mean, he wasn't the bachelor that Blaze is today because back then, Galliermo didn't have anything yet. He was a simple warlock who had nothing but his love to offer," Val continued. "They were great together though. The couple of the motherfucking century. Galliermo and Demitria were chosen to be the King and Queen of prom back in 1954. I think this picture was taken that night."

Val tapped a sharp black nail on the picture in Alecto's hand.

Alecto ground her teeth so hard her jaw ached. "How the fuck do you know this?"

"Now, as you know already, there was no happy ending for Galliermo and dear Demitria. Because Galliermo's best friend, Alatar Black, swooped in and stole his bride. I mean, Demitria went willingly, of course, because, unlike Galliermo, Black was a man of status already."

This couldn't be true. Val had to be lying. No way in Hel was Alecto's mother in a relationship with Galliermo when she attended Venefica. She was sweet and soft. Nice. Mortal. She'd never leave one man to be with another just because of *money.*

"Some people believe that Galliermo was the one who actually killed your mother," Val added. She seemed to be enjoying herself. "If you ask me—"

Val didn't get to finish the sentence, because the door to the basement opened and the rest of the Inner Circle climbed down the stairs, talking over each other.

Alecto was grateful for the interruption. She quickly closed the Book, stuffed the Polaroid into her boot, and hopped off the pool table.

"Well, are we ready?" Andro asked.

Val eyed Alecto for another moment, her smile growing.

"Yeah," she said. "Let's go win the Game."

The sickly sweet stench of old fire hung heavy in the air when the Snakes got to the Tigers' House. At night, the blackened skeleton of what once was one of the most beautiful architectural pieces in Darly stood abandoned.

Goose bumps rose all over Alecto's body, and not from the chilly air. She wrapped her coat tighter around herself, painfully aware of the others behind her.

"Lovely," Jolene observed. "You really did a number on their House. No wonder the Tigers have been skulking around."

"Who knew all it took for them to lose their wits was taking away the comforts?" Val's words were dripping with arrogant satisfaction. When Alecto glanced her way, she winked.

Alecto immediately looked away, willing herself to focus on the House. She hated Val. She knew more than she was letting on, all this time.

"That's one of the first things you do when torturing people," Rogue mused. The silence stretched between them until Rogue huffed a laugh. "Forgot I'm not native to Inathis?"

Alecto frowned, turning away. She didn't think it would be possible to ever forget Rogue was a demon. But strangely, Alecto had become used to him. To the intense gaze of those amber eyes.

We're going to get back at whoever did this to you.

Rogue had been kind when some others were anything but.

Alecto stole a sideways glance at Blaze standing a bit further away from her. A cigarette was resting between his lips as he tilted his head back. His eyes were half-closed to avoid the streaming smoke.

Things had been weird. Alecto couldn't forget the way he cared for her after Hellbates attack. Blaze was the one who held her all night and stood by her side while she sweated and retched the venom out of her system.

They hadn't spoken since then. She wasn't sure what was there to say. Her pride didn't let her say *thank you.*

As if sensing her eyes on him, Blaze glanced sideways, and their eyes locked. Alecto averted her gaze. She didn't know how to feel about the recent revelation about their parents.

Did Blaze know? Was that why he hated her so much?

"There are no wards around the perimeter," Andro said, appearing from around the corner.

"Yeah." Jolene came around the other side of the fence. "Even the House itself isn't warded."

Val nodded. "Their Book should be in the basement."

She opened the gate and led them to the back of the House, where a wooden door was cemented into the foundation. Most of the townhouses in Darly had entrances to the basements from the outside.

The Snakes had cemented theirs off to avoid having to guard another entrance point to their brownstone. When Val wrenched the double door open with one spell only and a flight of stone stairs appeared, it was obvious that the Tigers didn't share the same worries.

"Are they really that stupid?" Blaze asked.

"Apparently," Andro mused.

Val said nothing as she stared at the dark basement for a long moment. She jerked her chin at Jolene.

"Have the tracker, Frone?"

Jolene lifted a long, thick needle hung on a red thread.

Val nodded and her attention shifted to Rogue. "Why don't you make your way downstairs and check if there are any traps?"

Rogue smirked, something flashing in his eyes so quickly Alecto couldn't catch the meaning of it. But he didn't argue and descended the stairs into the basement. They waited in silence. For a few long moments there was nothing, not even the sound of his boots on the floor.

But then, the light illuminated the dark basement and Rogue called, "Safe. There's nothing there."

Alecto didn't think he meant it literally.

When the Inner Circle reached the bottom of the stairs, they were met with a blank room. No furniture, no boxes. Not even a single web beneath the stairs leading up to the inside of the House or a crack in the polished concrete walls.

Alecto couldn't smell or feel the magic around them, yet the needle Jolene was holding was swinging in circles like crazy.

"The Book is here." Val's grin grew as she stared at the needle. "It's probably hidden somewhere in the walls or the floor."

Jolene didn't waste any time. With the tracker in hand, she hurried to the far end of the room, holding the needle close to the walls, near the stairs. It spun and spun but didn't stop at any location.

"Nothing," Jolene said, her shoulders slumping.

"It has to be here," Val said, a weird edge to her voice. "Come here. Give it to me."

As Jolene crossed the floor between them, the needle finally stopped. Alecto drew a breath as they all stared at the straight needle pointing at the floor beneath Jolene's feet.

Right at the center of the basement.

"Rogue, draw a circle," Val commanded. "Jolene, set up the candles. Blaze, light the incense and you two." Val glared at Alecto and Andro. "Prepare the bowl."

They didn't need to be told twice. The group prepared the circle for the ritual. Alecto got on her knees as she took out the bronze bowl out of cloth tote. Andro placed the blood moss, tears of Sea Monster, and a bunch of other herbs Alecto didn't remember into the bowl.

Once Rogue was done with the chalk, Andro brought the bowl into the middle of the circle. Val didn't need to command them to get into the formation for the spell.

When Alecto's fingers linked with Jolene's and Blaze's, her heart skipped a beat. They were so close to victory.

"*Obliteus sangioni*," Val recited, and they all joined in.

Rogue stood on the outside of their circle, his face unreadable. There was a small frown between his eyebrows, eyes intently watching the bowl in the middle.

Alecto closed her eyes and imagined a massive knot of the red string in her mind. Soon the air around them was vibrating with their power, chants gliding over their skin with a gentle caress.

Carefully, Alecto untied the knot in her mind, the strings moving together fluidly until there was nothing left but one long piece of the red string. Electric currents zipped through their hands, and when she opened her eyes, the bowl was vibrating.

"Hidden safe," Val said, smiling. "Smart."

Alecto flinched when the bowl flew into the air and smashed into the wall next to them. Their circle wavered as they all took a step back away from the hole opening in the floor.

What appeared out of the hole was not the Tigers' Book.

A scream tore out of Jolene's throat when a swarm of spirits wrenched free from the vault in the floor. The temperature around them dropped; Alecto could see her breath. She wanted to scream, but nothing came from her parted lips.

"Get outside!" Val screamed. Before Alecto knew it, someone was dragging her away by her forearm.

Now that they were out, Alecto could count that there were three spirits. From their outfits, it was clear they were not freshly passed, and from the halfway melted flesh of their faces, it was clear that they hadn't been buried right after their passing.

They all scurried up the stairs, Rogue leading the way. But when they reached the top of the stairs, the door to the outside had slammed shut. They stopped abruptly, and Alecto realized that Blaze was the one who carried her all this way.

"What's the matter?" Blaze asked Rogue.

Rogue's amber eyes were wide. "It doesn't open."

"Are you fucking serious?" Blaze snapped. He let go of Alecto and shoved Rogue aside, pushing the door to the basement up with his shoulder.

It didn't budge.

It didn't even rattle as Blaze pushed harder.

The door to the outside was sealed. With the Snakes inside.

Andro's eyes widened, lips parting. It seemed as if he had forgotten to breathe. "They knew we were coming."

"They were prepared." Val's voice was as hard as the expression on her face.

Val whirled and ran back down the stairs. They all followed. The spirits sneered at the sight of them, and Val stopped.

"If I had to guess, the door to the House is also sealed," she muttered.

Alecto came to her side. She was about to speak, but there was no time as the spirits advanced towards them, hissing.

"Rogue, protect!" Val screamed.

The demon appeared in front of them out of nowhere, his forearms black. In the place of his fingers, there were black claws now. At the sight of the demon, the spirits bristled, but didn't stop. Rogue slashed the air between them, making them stumble backwards with a hiss.

"Need a spell to banish the spirits," Alecto said, her heart beating in her throat. She turned to Jolene. "You know one?"

Jolene bit her lip. The spirits scattered, moving in on them from different directions.

Clearly, they were smart enough to know their options going against the demon. But Rogue couldn't counter them all if they attacked from different sides. It was Alecto's first time coming across malicious ghosts.

She hoped it was her last.

"I don't know what holds them to this realm," Jolene finally said. "If it's something strong, then it might not be enough for a simple banishing spell to work."

Shit.

"What if we use blood magic?" Blaze asked.

Jolene blinked. One of the spirits was closing in on them from the left. Alecto shifted closer to the group, eyeing the ghost closely.

"Nothing is guaranteed," Jolene said after the pause.

"I'm willing to risk it." Blaze's eyes narrowed at Rogue's back in front of them. "Get ready, Frone."

Blaze slipped a hand in his pocket and fished out the pocketknife, the same one Alecto used to stab herself in the palm that night in the Cursed Forest. Blaze moved forwards, pressing close to Rogue's back.

"I hope you don't mind. I'm about to borrow something of yours," Blaze said into his ear. Without waiting for an answer, he brushed the sharp tip of his knife over the back of Rogue's neck, drawing blood.

Rogue stilled, and so did they.

"The chant, Jolene," Blaze snapped.

"*Exission lustro,*" Jolene called.

Alecto picked up the chant and so did the rest. The blood dripped down Rogue's neck in a trickle, dropping on the floor and sinking right into the concrete, leaving black marks behind.

None of them stopped chanting, even as Alecto felt her magic surge through her, the electric current making her muscles tremble. It was like nothing Alecto had ever experienced. It roamed inside her before finally making its way out.

The beam of light exploded around them, and the spirits shrieked in agony. Alecto closed her eyes because she couldn't bear to keep them open at the intensity of the light.

When the shrieks died down and she felt her magic retreating, she opened her eyes to find the basement empty. Just them and Rogue, all panting heavily.

"Fucking Hel, that was close," Andro said, and then huffed a laugh.

"The Tigers have a death wish this year, so it seems," Val muttered, brushing her hand through her ruffled hair.

Alecto eyed her for a moment, the adrenaline from what just happened surging through her, making her muscles tremble.

"Then we shall deliver." Her voice was low.

Blaze glanced at her, his smile deepening.

Alecto had gathered that there was something in Blaze that always awakened in the time of cruelty, especially when Alecto was the one being cruel.

She didn't want to admit it to herself, but she kind of liked it.

That fire in his eyes made her heart beat faster, the air she breathed in feel fresher, and it seemed as if the whole world was more divine in the face of their wicked madness.

To be admired for her cruelty, for the darkness that stained her half-mortal soul, was even better than feeling desired.

"Let's get out of here. I'm pretty sure this little spell won't go unnoticed by the Dean."

And someone was going to have to pay for it.

42

"Alecto Black as Carmen," Madame Raquel read out loud from the book in her hand as Alecto sat in her acting class the next afternoon.

There were a few claps in the audience, but mostly only whispers between her classmates.

Alecto couldn't hear anything specific, but she didn't have to. She already knew what the other students were saying.

Fucking half breed, if it weren't for her name, she wouldn't be here.

Of course a Snake would get the main role. I bet they fucked all night for her to land that role with a bit of magic.

Half breed.

Half blood.

Mortal trash.

Alecto had heard it all already.

It didn't matter that it was her very first time landing the main role. It didn't matter that she did nothing but practice her craft, polishing her skills all summer instead of going on trips around Inathis or drinking herself stupid on the beach.

None of that was ever important.

She brushed a hand over her skirt, straightening it. She ignored the glances her way as Madame Raquel finished assigning the roles.

"I want to congratulate you all," Madame said, scanning the crowd in the auditorium.

There was no way she could make out the faces of students with the lights glaring, but when her intense gaze landed on Alecto, it seemed as if she could see right into her soul.

"Today, I want you to find your partner, the one you'll be practicing with for the rest of the year," Madame Raquel said. "You'll need to work together to actually make the best out of this play. As some of you might know, there will be scouts coming to see the opening night. I really don't need to remind you how easily it would be for dreams to come true if you just nail your performances, right?"

Alecto recoiled at the thought of pairing with Norse, who was assigned to play Seville.

When their eyes locked, the feeling seemed to be mutual.

Even without the official announcement, most of the students knew the Snakes were behind the fire at the Tigers' House.

Well, fuck me.

She'd have to play nice because she needed to be the star of the show. She was going to prove that even a half breed could play Carmen.

Madame Raquel clapped her hands, indicating that they should pair up, but Alecto didn't rise from her seat.

Norse was the one who came over and sat on the chair next to her, his cold gaze sliding down her body, stopping on her legs, right where the skirt ended.

"Are you going to cause me trouble, Black?"

"I would never." A small smirk pulled her lips despite her efforts to stay neutral. Norse arched a brow.

"You know, you really should come with a warning sign," he mused, tracing a long finger over his sharp jaw. "You walk around like the love goddess, luring poor warlocks to your embrace. But Gods save the souls of those who dare to lay their hands on you."

Alecto scoffed, crossing her legs.

As if it were her fault that Gabe and Matias got what they deserved?

The rules were simple at Venefica. Kill or be killed.

"So *tragically* poetic," she said, her words clipped. "So *fucking* dramatic." Norse's lips pulled up, just slightly.

"Believe it or not, Alecto, I'm your friend," he said. That was the last thing she expected to hear. "All I'm saying is that I wish I had you in my House."

With a wink, he turned away, shuffling through the pages they were supposed to memorize and practice.

Alecto sighed, shoving his weird words to the very back of her head, and opened her own script.

First, she needed to learn the lines.

Then, she would need to perfect the performance.

And once that was done, she'd need to figure out how to turn herself into Carmen and not a starving Victorian orphan version of one of the greatest women in their history.

Alecto was jolted from her thoughts as the door to the auditorium opened and the Dean's secretary walked in, the same pleasant smile plastered on her face. She adjusted her glasses, scanning the crowd, and Alecto didn't even need to hear her say it.

She already knew who she was going to call.

"Oh, for fuck's sake," Alecto murmured. Norse chuckled.

"Madame Raquel, I'll need to ask you to excuse Miss Black from the rest of the lecture," Miss Bellthrove said, chipper as fucking always. Madame nodded, waving her hand. "Miss Black, please come with me."

Alecto gathered her stuff, shoved it into her bag, and rose to her feet. They weren't even in the middle of the first trimester.

It's going to be a long year…

As Alecto passed Norse, he murmured the words that were meant only for her: "No Queen rules forever. Don't forget that, Black."

Well, at least this time, the Snakes weren't the only ones getting called into the Dean's office.

Every fucking House was crowded together in the reception, members throwing mean glances at each other. Alecto barely held herself back from laughing. It would be pathetic if it weren't so funny.

She plopped on the empty seat between Andro and Val. "Where's Blaze and Jolene?"

"They're calling us in in pairs," Val said, looking bored as ever. "Unlikely pairs to interrogate. You know, so that the Dean's sure we haven't had the time to practice the story."

Alecto chuckled. As if that would really help. They had their story straight the moment they returned home last night.

"Norse wasn't called in with me," Alecto noted.

"It's because some of the Houses were already questioned and dismissed," Andro said, not lifting his head from the textbook in his lap. "Have you had the time to prepare for Herbalism check-in next week? I don't fucking understand shit about gardening. My Tenefor plant hasn't sprouted yet."

Alecto glanced at the book, then at Andro. "I don't fucking know. Ask Jolene for a chant or something. We haven't even started on our garden."

Andro lifted his gaze and chuckled. Alecto punched him in the shoulder.

The door to the Dean's office flew open. Jolene appeared in the doorway with Blaze following her.

Alecto straightened her spine, glaring at them both, but there weren't any signs of worry on either of their faces. Did Blaze pull his blackmail card once more?

The Dean's expression was hard as stone, so she couldn't tell.

"Miss Black, Miss Lang, and Mr. Weir, please come in," the Dean said, ducking back into his office.

Jolene gave Alecto a playful wink as they passed each other, and Alecto tried not to look at Blaze, even though his shoulder brushed hers as she went into the office.

She was the last to walk in and close the door.

"I'm not going to waste any time here," Dean Gondalez said, lacing his fingers as he glared at all three of them sitting opposite him. "Last night, someone broke into the House of Tigers, attempting to acquire their Book, which was left behind after they had to move due to the fire. Apparently, it either went wrong, or it was intended to be reckless and go against the laws of the academy."

"How so?" Val inquired, her voice sweet as honey. "What laws were broken, sir?"

Alecto had to bite the inside of her cheek to stop herself from smiling.

"Practicing of blood magic," the Dean replied. "And what's even more concerning is that the blood that the witches or warlocks used was not even of this realm. They used the blood of a demon for the spell. Which is another unforgivable crime that doesn't exempt even students who are *legacy*."

At the last word, the Dean glared between Alecto and Andro. Both remained still. Andro even managed to keep his knee from bouncing.

Why wasn't Andro nervous though?

The last time they were in the Dean's office, for an offence that was way smaller than this, Andro was about to lose his shit. And yet, today, he sat there cool as a fucking cucumber.

"So, I'm going to need to ask you where you were last night," the Dean continued. "And I'm also going to need to check your blood for recent traces of magic."

Even though Alecto knew the Dean wouldn't find anything, she still stiffened. She quickly went over every single spell she performed in the last twenty-four hours, even though they had drained their blood, clearing out any residues of the magic spells they performed last night.

"I can go first," Andro suggested, reaching his arm towards the Dean.

Dean Gondalez didn't waver. He walked around the desk and took Andro's hand. He took out the pin off the lapel of his jacket and nicked the tip of Andro's finger, drawing blood.

Without a word, he brushed a finger over the wound and rubbed the blood between two fingers, murmuring chants Alecto wasn't familiar with.

Her heart was drumming like crazy as they waited. But if Blaze and Jolene were all right, then it had to mean that they also would be fine.

Alecto swallowed hard, feeling her palms get sweaty.

"Thank you, Mr. Weir," the Dean finally said, moving on to Val.

She gave him her hand without hesitation. And her results also came out negative. Then, it was Alecto's turn.

"All right," the Dean said with a sigh, "you're all clear to go. None of you were practicing magic last night."

"Don't look so disappointed, Mr. Gondalez," Val teased as they rose from their seats.

The Dean threw her a curious glance, arching a brow.

"You might still get a chance to catch us in a *compromising* position," Val said. She winked and then strode towards the door.

There was something in the Dean's face, the way his eyes flickered as he watched Val walk out of his office, that left an uneasy feeling deep inside Alecto's stomach.

She wasn't sure whether it was lust or hate or something in between. But whatever that was, it couldn't mean anything good for Val or the Snakes.

43

On a rainy Monday morning, Alecto sat at the very back of the History of the Sexuality of Witches class, Rogue dozing off by her side as Professor Fallo read an excerpt from the *Diaries of Hell Galliano*.

Alecto had already finished the book.

In fact, she had read it twice, the first time for the class and the second time highlighting and annotating it for her own personal use. Surely, there were tons of secrets to learn from the woman so powerful and influential in the bedroom that she managed to cause a war.

As the professor's calm voice recited the words from the page, Alecto found her mind wandering off to places it shouldn't have.

Like Blaze a few desks ahead of her.

He leaned back in his chair, long legs sprawled in front of him, head slightly tilted backwards. Val sat very, very close to him, her knee pressed into his thigh.

There was a sudden pressure building in Alecto's chest, the feeling of dread and something else clawing its way out, but she couldn't look away.

She watched as Val leaned into Blaze, whispering something in his ear, her lips brushing his skin. He then turned his head to her, and Alecto had a view of half his face, his smile as his eyes jumped from Val's eyes to her lips.

His eyelashes were so long they brushed his cheeks when he gazed down, and the way his lips curled, soft yet cruel at the same time, should have been fucking illegal.

Alecto had to swallow bitter fire rising in her throat as Val slipped a hand under their desk, casually planting it over his thigh.

Blaze didn't react, letting her have her way, Val's hand moving up and down, clearly on a mission to do something rather inappropriate.

Alecto gripped her pen harder, anger surfacing, yet she couldn't figure out why. What did she care if Val and Blaze did whatever the fuck they did?

It was not news, she knew about their affairs last year, and she knew it at the start of this year. Yet now it hit rather close to home.

Alecto cursed herself.

She was stupid enough to let herself think that whatever game they were playing, it was just between them. That having Blaze succumb to her touch the way he did back in the library meant something more.

Don't ever do this again.

Many women misunderstood the true meaning of blow jobs. They viewed it as something degrading, something that would only please the man whose cock they had between their lips.

But that was not true.

Sometimes, surrendering your power made you more powerful. Sometimes, submitting to someone else physically meant dominating their heart.

After that night, Alecto convinced herself that there was something in Blaze that wanted her.

Hel, even after he dragged her to the forest and left her to die, she was still convinced that maybe the reason he always seemed to find ways to hurt her was because he couldn't deal with his own desires.

She was a fucking fool. Witches couldn't feel anything except cruel satisfaction when they tortured others.

Blaze glanced back over his shoulder, as if feeling Alecto's gaze, and for a moment, their eyes met. Alecto turned her attention to the professor, who had stopped reading.

"So, can someone tell me what Galliano meant with this quote: 'Our souls didn't care for the obstacles built in their way. They're meant to wander through time and space, knowing their direction altogether, never having to stop and doubt their way'?" she asked, scanning the class.

As per usual, no hands rose.

Alecto lowered her head, glaring at the pen clenched between her fingers so hard it hurt.

"Nobody?" Professor Fallo asked. "Miss Black, how about you? Have any thoughts?"

A few heads turned to her. Alecto didn't even need to look up to see the faces. She could feel them. Somehow, it never went further than glances and a few chuckles.

Maybe it was the fact that the class was small and intimate, and the professor couldn't pretend to not hear the bullying, or maybe Professor Fallo was liked or feared enough.

"Galliano meant that love doesn't depend on the realms we live in, on the Gods we believe in, or the species we belong to," Alecto said finally.

"And what prompted her to speculate in such a way?"

"She had changed her mind briefly about the nature of love after she went to the mortal world and fell in love with a mortal."

From the way the professor arched her brow, Alecto realized a short answer wasn't going to cut it.

"Mortals believe in the concept of a soul mate, that there is one perfect person for you, and once you find them, the love is infinite. Witches, Galliano included, don't believe in such things, being more generous with their love and never believing in the need to settle for one partner."

"But witches have the sanguilian bond," Professor Fallo countered. "Wouldn't that be similar to what mortals call soul mates?"

"Galliano didn't believe it was the same because a sanguilian bond doesn't have to be romantic. Whereas the soul mate concept is always about romantic love. When she became infatuated with a mortal, Galliano believed that maybe witches' beliefs about love are all wrong, and there is the one perfect person for everyone."

"Yes, indeed. And this is the ultimate question within all three realms— what truly is romantic love, and how many people can one love without compromising on the quality of it?"

"Well, at the House of Snakes, we believe in the power of sharing," Val drawled, pointedly caressing Blaze's cheek. The whole classroom burst into laughter.

"So we've heard," Garcia muttered.

Alecto narrowed her eyes, about ready to jump the bitch, but then the bell rang, indicating the end of class, and everyone was on their feet.

"Finish chapters forty-four and forty-five for the next lecture," the professor said. "We're going to write an essay at the end of this trimester on soul mates and the sanguilian bond, so please prepare."

Alecto gathered her stuff and rushed out of the class, angry and agitated. Chocolate was always the way to lift her mood, and today she might need a whole fucking pound of it to help her out.

On her way out of the building, she stopped by the snack stand, where a tiny water sprite was tidying up the three branches with tons of different snacks, inside a massive glass dome. Her deep blue wings flapped, scattering the salty smell of the ocean all around.

Alecto dropped the coin into the slot on the side, and the sprite whirled around, snatched the coin, and tossed it into the moss lining the floor of the dome.

"I'll have a chocolate skull," Alecto said.

The water sprite hurried away, and the branch slowly unwrapped, letting the chocolate skull fall in the fairy's tiny hands. The sprite rushed to the hole in the floor of the glass container, dropping it there for Alecto to take.

"Thank you."

But just when Alecto was about to open the glass door to fetch her chocolate, Blaze's shoulder slammed against the glass dome, blocking her way.

"Do you mind?" Alecto glared at him.

Blaze glanced at the chocolate skull. "Craving something sweet, Black?"

When she didn't answer him, he leaned in closer, the smell of smoke and fire overwhelming her senses.

"I think I can help you with that."

Alecto whirled on her heel and strode off to the door leading outside, forgetting her chocolate.

She would never have peace, not if he was around. And she would never be the one in control because Blaze wasn't to be tamed. It was never equal between them, even when she thought that she had evened the score between them, it was an illusion.

Apparently, storming off wasn't enough of a hint for Blaze to back off. A moment later, he was behind her, yanking her towards him.

Blaze Leveau was the plague, the fucking curse, and there was no way Alecto could get rid of him.

But she still tried.

Her palm stung when it hit Blaze's cheek, sending his head to the side. His jaw clenched tight, muscle flaring.

"It's becoming a rather annoying habit of yours," he bit out, voice low, "slapping me every chance you get."

"Fuck you."

Alecto channeled all the anger she could muster to not let the tears burn her eyes. She turned, almost slipping on the wet pavement, and walked away.

But of course, Alecto only made it to the edge of the campus when Blaze's fingers wrapped around her forearm, yanking her back again.

"You don't fucking walk away from me," he warned.

The rain was pouring down on them, and his black hair hung over his forehead, sharp tips hovering over his eyes. Even his thick eyelashes were soaked with raindrops as he tried to blink them away.

She winced as his grip tightened and tried to jerk away from him, but his fingers just dug deeper into her flesh. Tomorrow there would be a bruise.

A mark of him.

"Get off me," Alecto growled, glaring right back at him.

Blaze didn't budge.

She tried to yank her arm away once more, pushing on his chest. But it was useless. He let her thrash against him, still as a statue.

When she was panting heavily, having spent her energy, Blaze arched a brow.

"Are you done?"

"Fuck you," Alecto repeated, breathless. But she didn't fight him anymore. "I'm not in the mood to deal with you today, Leveau."

"And why is that?"

Alecto wished she could just make him disappear. If he wasn't there, she wouldn't have to think about him.

"I thought we were all right." Blaze sounded serious and firm, and those words and his tone threw Alecto off for a moment. "I know I *technically* tried to kill you, but I thought we'd moved past it."

The fucking audacity of this man.

"What the fuck do you want from me, Blaze?"

Blaze frowned. For a moment, he seemed lost in thought. His hold on her arm loosened just a bit, and Alecto used that opportunity to pull her arm away, taking a few steps backwards.

"What the fuck do you want, hmm?" she asked again, determined to get to the bottom of it. No more games, no more power plays. She was tired. "You hate me, you tease me, you *pleasure* me, and for what? You clearly have your hands *full* of choices, so why the fuck can't you just leave me the fuck alone?"

He tried to blink the rain away, his gaze burning, but he still couldn't find words to speak.

With a growl, Alecto turned and crossed the street. The rain was getting harder, thunder rumbling somewhere in the distance, and she was soaked right through her underwear already.

Right before she turned into their street, a hand wrapped around her waist, yanking her backwards.

"Can you fucking wait? For fuck's sake," Blaze said into her ear. His warm breath sent shivers down her back. "You can't ask me a question and not give me a moment to fucking think."

Alecto whipped around, pushing at his chest. To her surprise, he let her go. Thunder rumbled somewhere closer, the lightning piercing the sky.

"Oh, I'm sorry, *Blazy*, I thought your smart ass could come up with shit to say on a whim," Alecto mocked. "Maybe the bag of tricks is really empty, huh?"

"The meaner you are to me, the more I like you, you know?"

The way he said those words, the way that scorching gaze caressed her body... It was intoxicating.

"I hate you," she hissed. And she did. But then something hit her. A realization. "Oh, I know what it is. You said it to me that night in the forest, but I didn't listen. You think I'm easy, isn't that it? The half breed only good for one thing, right?"

All humor was gone from his face in an instant, his jaw tight.

"You should pay attention to my actions *rather* than my words," he said, and it almost sounded like a warning.

Alecto laughed, her body shaking with anger and the cold.

"I'm not going to be here to entertain you," she snapped, backing away from him towards their House. "I'm not here to be your little plaything when Val or the others are not enough to satiate your fucking needs."

Alecto whirled and walked away once more, this time proud that she said what she wanted to say and walked away from him.

Well, it wasn't truly what she wished to say to Blaze, but it was the *right* thing to say.

This time, he didn't grab her. Instead, he walked across her path, blocking her way just when she was a mere few steps away from the House.

Alecto clenched her jaw to stop her teeth from chattering as she glared up at him.

"Can you just let me fucking say something?" Blaze's voice was frustrated, eyebrows drawn together. "I *can't* leave you alone. I *can't* let you go and live out my days like you don't exist."

Alecto's back straightened, her heart skipping a beat at his words. She didn't want to hear what else he had to say, but she also craved nothing more.

"Why?" Her voice was so weak, the words almost got lost in the madness of the full-on storm now raging around them.

Blaze took a deep breath. "Because it's *physically* impossible. Wherever I go, I always look for you in a crowd, even if I don't want to. Whenever you're not around, I find myself imagining you were there because otherwise, everything is so fucking dull."

Alecto was pretty sure her jaw was on the fucking floor, which made Blaze smirk, the weird heaviness evaporating from his face, even if it still lingered in his gaze.

"You're a fucking curse on my poor immortal soul, Black."

At that, Alecto couldn't hold the laugh back. Blaze's smirk deepened, and he used the moment to slip his hand into hers.

Then he was dragging her into the House. Alecto didn't stop him.

44

Alecto's back hit the wall next to Blaze's bedroom door, and his strong body pressed into her. She was grateful for it because she wasn't sure she would have been able to stand on her own.

Both were soaking wet, raindrops falling on the hardwood floors as they glared at each other, breathing heavily.

Blaze blinked, breaking out of the haze they seemed to be lost in for a moment. "You're cold. And soaked."

Alecto snorted. "Yeah, asshole, so are you."

Blaze chuckled, backing off a few inches, his hands still around her waist. "Undress."

With that, he left her, disappearing into his bathroom. A moment later, the sound of water running came, and then Blaze appeared again, his shirt already gone.

Alecto inhaled a sharp breath at the sight of his naked chest, the broad shoulders and the defined abs, the carved-out V-line pointing at something hidden in his black jeans, which she already knew was worth fantasizing about—

Blaze cleared his throat, and that snapped Alecto out of her thoughts. He was standing right in front of her, with a smirk and an eyebrow cocked, clearly reading her thoughts on her face.

"I see you're waiting for me to undress you," Blaze said. "Fine, I'll do it myself then."

On an instinct, Alecto tried backing away, but there was nowhere to go. The wall was right behind her.

Blaze peeled her soaked coat and school jacket off, letting them drop on the floor. Then, his wicked fingers unbuttoned the white shirt sticking to Alecto's body. As he let it open, his fingers trailed over her shoulders and arms, sending shivers through her.

Alecto had to bite her lower lip to stop herself from jumping him right there. Somehow, she still didn't want him to know just how much of an effect his hands had on her. As if she would be more vulnerable and naked than she was right now, standing just in her underwear in his room.

Blaze's eyes flickered hot as coal, lips parted as his eyes roamed her body, taking in the black lace bra and the matching underwear. His fingers trailed the curve of the side of her breast, her waist, stopping at her hips, and Alecto let her head fall back, savoring the sensation.

"Come here." His voice was a whisper, and she didn't argue.

She let him lead her into his bathroom, where a clawfoot bathtub waited already filled with steaming hot water. Blaze guided her to the bath, letting her go for a moment as he shed his pants and underwear.

Alecto almost whimpered at the sight of his long, beautiful cock, already hard.

Blaze caught her glance, tilting his chin. It was her turn to get naked.

Slowly, Alecto unhooked her bra. The straps slid down her shoulders, freeing her breasts, which were already sensitive.

When his heavy eyes landed on her nipple piercings, Alecto arched her back slightly, she slipped fingers underneath her panties and pulled them down.

She had never experienced the sight of someone as hungry for her as Blaze was right that moment. In fact, it wasn't just this moment.

When they first met, when Alecto came into the House of Snakes for the first time, and he backed her against the wall in the corridor, his black eyes seemed intense and even scary.

But now she knew Blaze well enough to recognize that same hunger in his eyes. The same hunger he had that day on the stage during the ritual. In that classroom. At the library.

It was seeing that hunger that prompted Alecto to climb into the bathtub, settling between Blaze's legs, leaning back against his hard chest.

"That feels nice," she said with a sigh as the hot water worked its magic on her stiff muscles.

The water was steaming and smelled like a mix of lemongrass, eucalyptus, and peppermint. Blaze had added some essential oils to the bath, and the thought made Alecto smile.

They lay in the bath in silence for what seemed like forever, only the sound of rain and thunder outside. While their naked skin touched, sending delicate sparks of pleasure through Alecto's body, it wasn't needy or even sexual.

It felt much more than that. Deeper.

Alecto's eyes followed Blaze's thumb resting on her thigh, making lazy circles and lines as if he were writing poetry on her skin. The kind that was invisible and could only be read by heart.

His other hand reached for the ashtray on the windowsill, and he brought a half-smoked joint to his lips.

"You're warm?" Blaze asked as he lit the blunt, smoke streaming through his parted lips.

She didn't answer, watching his lips and his throat move. Instead, she just gave him a nod and then turned her head away to look through the window at the storm raging outside.

It was weird, this feeling. Feeling safe in the hands of someone who tried to hurt her.

His hand appeared in front of her, offering the joint. Alecto wrapped her lips around the base of it, sucking in a long drag, and then pulled away, letting the smoke burn her lungs.

When she released it, letting it stream through her lips, her head was light once more, muscles relaxing. Alecto sighed, her cheek falling against his chest. Blaze's heart drummed against her ear, just as fast as hers.

"I truly never believed you to be the soft kind," Alecto said.

"Is that so?"

She looked up at him. "You can't blame me for imagining you as cruel and rough. You certainly look the part."

His eyebrow cocked. "You've been *imagining* me?"

It was fitting for Blaze to cling to that word. Alecto might as well indulge him.

"I have."

His tongue peeked out, wetting his lips, and for a moment, memories of it all over her came back to her.

She brought her thighs together, and Blaze didn't miss it, a wicked smirk curving his lips.

"Do tell me all about it, baby."

"Well, usually, I would imagine you barging into my room in the middle of the night," she said. When he didn't say anything, she continued, "I would be hot and bothered, unable to sleep as I lay there naked in my bed. And you would come in every time as if knowing what it was I was hungry for."

His eyes were the scorching, bottomless pit of Hel that Alecto was glad to get lost in.

"Yeah?" Smoke escaped his lips. "And what did I do to you?"

"You would prowl towards the bed, looking dangerous and predatory," Alecto admitted. "Sometimes, you would throw me over on my belly, pull my hair and take what you craved until I was trembling and unable to even remember my own name."

"*Mm-hmm*. What else?"

The hand that had been resting on her thigh slowly inched closer to her core, fingers trailing a path up and down her inner thigh.

"Sometimes, you would crawl on top of me, press me against the bed. You'd leave a trail of kisses against my jaw, neck, nibbling at my shoulders as you reached the valley between my breasts." Alecto's breath hitched in her throat as his fingers slipped over her length, thumb stopping to caress the bundle of nerves.

"I'm listening," he whispered. "Continue, *please*."

"You'd kiss my breasts, nibble on my nipples." His fingers slipped between her folds. She had to focus very hard to keep her words making sense. "Then, you would bite me."

One finger slipped inside her, and Alecto's hips bucked backwards, pressing against his hard cock. He let out a moan.

"*Bite* you?" he asked, the chuckle caressing Alecto's neck. "You'd want me to bite you?"

Alecto's words were breathless when she answered, "*Yes*. You'd bite my breasts, leaving blue marks behind. Then, you would bite my neck, my shoulder, my thighs—"

She hissed as his teeth sunk into the sensitive flesh of her neck, his mouth kissing and sucking as he slid another finger inside her, caressing her from the inside.

"Oh, *Gods*," Alecto whispered, grinding her hips against him as sparks of pleasure and pain moved through her; it was hard to tell them apart anymore.

When Blaze's mouth let go of her neck, he whispered, "Go on. What else?"

It took a moment for Alecto to gather her thoughts and resume talking. "Some days, you would force my legs apart and kiss me down there until I was sick of it."

Blaze's thumb moved over her clit in slow, torturous circles, and Alecto's hips rolled, chasing after the sensation.

"*Force* you?" His lips caressed her ear, his voice husky. "Is that what you like, baby?"

Alecto shook her head, whimpering.

"No," she admitted, trying to catch her breath as his wicked fingers worked on her, bringing her very close to the edge. She could feel the sweet orgasm building inside her belly. "But I wanted *you* to."

The admission made her cheeks burn, and Alecto bit her lower lip.

"I see." Blaze's voice was gentle. "Well, in that case, I want you to remember something."

Alecto opened her eyes, turning to look at him.

"What?"

Blaze licked his lips as his fingers stopped whatever magic they were doing. Alecto whimpered. She was so close to her orgasm it almost hurt to stop now.

"Mercy," he whispered over her lips. "Say the word, and I'll stop."

A safe word.

Blaze was giving her a way out of her own fantasy, willing to indulge her, and that sent a hot wave over her body.

Alecto inched closer to capture his bottom lip between her teeth.

Blaze chuckled as she nibbled on it. "So hungry. So eager."

His fingers started moving again, and this time, they were not slow or teasing. No, they were ruthless and determined, his other palm holding her hip tight and pressing it to him as his hips ground against her.

Alecto moaned, letting her eyes shutter closed, and she moved against him, her nails digging into his thighs on either side of her.

"You like to hurt me, don't you, baby?" His hot breath was against her neck again. "With your nails, teeth, your soft little hands?"

And her words. Her sharp glances. Her tongue.

Alecto nodded frantically because the tension building inside her was about to erupt.

"So cruel." He chuckled, his breathing ragged now. "It's a good thing I love it."

Alecto shattered, her muscles going taut as the pleasure spread from her core, through her thighs, to the very tip of her toes.

Her nails dug deeper, and Blaze also moaned, going still behind her as his release found him.

Alecto fell deeper into his embrace, both breathing heavily, bodies still recovering from the intensity of their shared pleasure.

Yeah, Alecto didn't want this to end.

Ever.

45

It was the first time he'd woken up to someone else by his side.

And somehow, despite everything that went down between them and everything that was still on the horizon, Blaze didn't think there was a more perfect person to find in his bed.

He blinked a few times, unsure whether what he was seeing was real.

Whether Alecto *fucking* Black really was in his bed, her palms neatly tucked under her cheek, plump lips parted as she slept.

Blaze was afraid to move, to even breathe so he wouldn't wake her or disturb the spell that surrounded them in their little bubble, the rest of the world far, far away.

But as his eyes scanned her naked flesh, taking in the bruises his teeth left on her neck, another on her shoulder, and even her waist, even though they hadn't done anything yet...

They didn't *do* anything.

What the fuck?

Blaze frowned at the idea that he had allowed someone to sleep in his bed, yet they hadn't fucked.

Not really.

Something pinched in his chest, and he turned away, glaring at his ceiling.

Blaze had hurt her, scared her. There was no mistaking the fear and later hatred in her eyes when he left her alone in that forest.

Did the moment they shared at her house change things?

He thought that it did.

Worse, he kind of hoped that it did.

Judging from the fact that Alecto was lying next to him, naked, it meant that it did.

There are certain things you fucking half breeds are good for. I can't deny it. Stick with that, why don't you? It's what you know best after all.

Blaze regretted those words the moment they left his lips, not an ounce of truth in them.

They were only intended to hurt her, humiliate her. At that moment, it felt good.

Powerful.

Blaze should say something to her, make her understand. But he didn't know what.

An apology wouldn't be fair because no matter the regret in his chest, the urge to hurt her, to see her kneel in front of him was also still there.

He wasn't sure it would ever go away.

This was dangerous.

More than Blaze realized, and yet he was stupid enough to allow it.

No matter what he might be feeling, no matter how good it felt to have her around with him, either angry or happy, disturbed or desperate, there was no happy ending for them.

He was a Leveau, and she was a Black.

And while Blaze never understood why his father hated Alecto, knowing that her father was his best friend *and* a business partner, he was sure that whatever wants or needs Blaze felt for this girl, it could never happen.

Either Blaze hurt now, breaking the spell before it took root deeper in his heart, or he hurt later when his father surely would find a way to destroy yet another thing Blaze cared about.

Blaze swung his legs over the end of the bed, snatched his cigarettes from the nightstand, and stalked over to his nook by the window.

He opened the latch, letting the cool morning air in, and lit a cigarette while he watched the sun rise over the park.

From a distance, it always looked sinister but serene. You would have never guessed it was the only thing separating the Old Darly with its dark mysteries from them.

With a cigarette smoldering between his lips, Blaze went over to the pile of clothes that he had dried last night.

As he tugged his black jeans on, letting them sit low on his hips, the black underwear caught his attention.

Blaze hooked the panties over his finger, lifting them as he glared at the lace that belonged to Alecto. Memories of her wearing them right before she went into the bath came rushing to him. He growled, annoyed as his cock twitched in response.

He dropped the lace and returned to the windowsill, taking an aggressive drag before crushing the cigarette in an ashtray.

Against his will, his eyes wandered to the girl lying tangled between his black silk sheets.

His eyes traced the curve of her shoulder, the slope down her narrow waist before the delicate curve of her hip emerged, the sweet little dimple perched right in the middle.

He rested his head against the wooden panel inside the windowsill, nibbling on his lower lip as he watched Alecto sleep.

She was so sweet and calm when she was lost in her dreams. The complete opposite from when she was wide awake, always wearing a smoldering yet cruel look on that angelic face.

Blaze would never admit it to her face, but he was as much terrified of her as he was enamored of her.

Val he could read; he could understand the primal needs that drove her forwards, that made her the ruthless, calculating leader she was.

Jolene was also easy to understand because, in a way, he could relate to her. She was an heir, with tons of responsibilities on her shoulders that she never spoke off, but he knew they were there.

Most of the other girls on campus would also be easy to read, as most of them had clear intentions from the start.

But with Alecto, Blaze could never tell.

She walked like she owned the place, despite the bullying and taunting. She used her looks and her body however she liked, clearly knowing her own worth. She knew where she was going, but Blaze didn't know where that was.

Alecto Black was a mystery to him.

Blaze *was* in trouble.

He knew it the moment he realized he couldn't break her, no matter what he did.

He wasn't sure whether she wouldn't break him though.

Suddenly, Alecto stirred, brushing a hand through the sheets where Blaze lay before, before turning on her back.

As she stretched her muscles, eyes still half-closed and sleepy, she arched her back, her small breasts poking out and stirring up a storm inside him.

When she turned her head to the window and found him sitting there watching her, she went very still.

Surely, all the memories of last night came rushing back to her and were playing in front of her eyes right now.

"Morning," he said.

Alecto rose to lean her back against his headboard. "Morning."

Blaze was grateful he had put some distance between them when he woke up because if he was in that bed near her right now, he would make sure they never left.

He almost groaned with the need to have her whole, to sink his teeth again into her flesh as his dick sank into her at the same time.

But he shouldn't.

They shouldn't.

Blaze cleared his throat, jerking his head towards the pile of clothing as he lit another cigarette. "Your clothes are dry."

Alecto rose from the bed, letting the sheet slide away from her naked body, and strolled towards the pile.

Blaze almost choked on the smoke.

With tears burning his eyes, Blaze moved the cigarette away from his face, unable to take his eyes from Alecto getting dressed.

Her uniform was back on, and the final reminder of last night was gone.

She should leave. He should tell her to leave.

But what he'd told her last night, the admission of a fraction of his confusing feelings, was true.

When she wasn't around, everything was so fucking dull.

So, he might as well let himself indulge. Just this once.

He liked pain anyway. So what if it'll hurt more later?

It was why he said, voice husky, "Come here."

At first, Alecto stayed by the fireplace, her eyes narrowed at him. But then, she padded over to Blaze, plopping on the windowsill opposite him.

She seemed to share his hesitation, even if it was clear that she craved his company.

Oh, he knew she craved his company.

Blaze extended the pack of cigarettes to her, and she took one, letting him light it.

As they stared at each other, smoking, Blaze waited. Expecting.

Would she ask him what last night meant? Would she ask him to be exclusive with her?

Would he say *yes*?

But instead, Alecto said, "Last night was fun."

Blaze blinked.

"Clearly, there was some tension that needed to be released," she continued, and it made him smile.

"Certainly. Tons of tension."

But the words that came out of her lips next were nothing if not surprising. "But we got it out of our systems, right?" She paused for a moment as Blaze's face dropped. "I mean, we had our fun, and we can move on to everything being as it was. It's going to be better for everyone, the House, I mean."

Blaze resisted the urge to close his eyes and pinch his nose.

This woman.

This *fucking* woman.

Mercy?

He should have picked something as *Crush My Immortal Soul, Stomp on My Balls while You're at It, and Break My Fucking Ego on Your Way Out* as her safe word.

Un-fucking-believable.

He let her sleep in his bed.

He gave up a piece of himself, and in return, she made him just another boy she had fun with before moving on to the next one.

Of course, Blaze didn't say what he was thinking.

Instead, he willed his lips to curl into a smirk once more. "Of course, baby."

Alecto nodded, crushing the butt of the cigarette in the ashtray before rising to her feet.

Just before she slipped through the door though, Blaze added, "I hope your fantasies are going to be enough to satisfy you." Alecto stopped, her gaze snapping to his as her back stiffened. Blaze smiled lazily and then landed the killing blow: "But if not, I'll make time in my *busy* schedule for you. Don't worry."

The door slammed shut.

Back to *exactly* how it used to be, indeed.

46

People could only speculate that the Snakes were the ones to blame for the burning of the House of Tigers. There was no evidence. Yet, with each passing day, more and more students at Venefica were convinced that it was the Snakes' fault.

And now Alecto had to face the rest of the Houses in the Liaison meeting. It'd already been more than a week since the prank, but no one was looking rather happy when Alecto walked through the door and took her seat at the table.

"Alecto," Garcia said.

"Garcia," Alecto replied, crossing one leg over another.

"So," Garcia announced, straightening her back as she scanned the Liaisons at the round table. "Samhain is in two weeks' time, and the Dean wanted to make sure that each House is ready for the celebration."

"We're always ready, sweets," Killer said, winking. A few chuckles went around the table.

"Well, apparently not, because if my memory serves me well, it was your naked ass found in the park when the spell was broken last year," Garcia shot back, and that wiped the cocky grin off Killer's face real fast.

"Back to this year's Samhain," Garcia said. "The Dean passed me an official list of responsibilities that each House will have to take."

She snapped her fingers, and a bundle of papers floated around to land in front of each student. Alecto glared down at the list that seemed to drag on forever.

Wouldn't there be a fairy of some sort running around to organize events? Did they really have to do all that?

"You can see the things the Dean requires from each House, so you can bring the list back to your leaders and get to fucking work. Any questions?"

"Can we change the theme?" Mariana asked, and a wave of moans went around the table, quite a few witches rolling their eyes.

"You and your fucking themes," said Helion, from the House of Dragons.

"Well, I'm sorry if I want something more interesting this year," Mariana snapped back, her glasses sliding down her nose. "I feel we've done enough dressing up as our Houses, haven't we?"

Mariana glared at Alecto as she said the words. Alecto wasn't sure what her problem was now.

"Suck my dick, Mariana," said Alecto. "Besides, you look great dressed as a piggy with your sweet little pigtails."

The girl bristled, squaring her shoulders, but Garcia intervened before the argument could go any further.

"Okay," she said, slamming the gavel on the table, unnecessarily. "Maybe Mariana has a point. We could change the theme of the masquerade into something fresh. Any ideas?"

A few ideas went around the table.

Holly Hills celebrities, Helion suggested, clearly hoping to see most girls dressed as Marilyn Monroe so he could drool all night long.

Night in Hel, Drake, from the House of Dogs, suggested because he clearly had a hard-on for demons, which was a little bit creepy, even for witches.

Creatures of the Cursed Forest.

Spirits of the dead.

So on and so forth; at some point, Alecto stopped listening.

"How about *Fairy Tales*?" Mariana asked.

That seemed to draw everyone's attention.

"Dressing like someone from your favorite fairy tale for one night could be fun," Mariana pushed.

"That doesn't sound half bad," Killer agreed, grinning. He jerked his chin at Drake. "You can dress like a swamp gremlin from *Magical Henry's*

Adventures." He then jerked to Helion and added mockingly, "And you can dress like the goblin from *Sleeping Boggler*. You sure as Hel have the nose for it."

"And you, Killer, will be able to dress like that kid who fell in love with his own reflection in the lake and didn't see the mermaid come in time to avoid getting eaten," Alecto chimed in, her voice light as a feather. She then covered her mouth with a hand, gasping. "Sounds like something you'd get yourself into."

Killer's eyes narrowed, his jaw clenching as another wave of laughter went around, this time at his expense.

Alecto sent him an air kiss before Garcia announced the meeting over, and they were up from their seats.

A lecto came back to the House right in time for the weekly House meeting taking place at their meeting room.

Twelve pairs of eyes turned to her as she entered the room and came to a stop.

"Right on time, bitch," Val said. "We were just about to start, so we can get right to what there is to know from the Liaisons."

Alecto cleared her throat, fishing the paper out of her bag.

"Well, for the next two weeks, we're only going to be living and breathing preparations for Samhain," she said.

Val snapped the paper out of her hand, burying her nose as she scanned the information.

"The Dean gave each House a number of tasks because apparently we don't have the funds for an event planner."

Jolene and Andro snickered. "Oh, dear, soon we won't have fresh bagels every morning!"

"Well, that's great," Val said as she finished reading. She glanced up, scanning the room. "The first years will have a moment to shine and get to know our traditions better."

Alecto almost felt sorry for the two first years who would probably have to do most of the heavy lifting.

Almost.

"So, what are we responsible for this year?" Goose bumps erupted over Alecto's skin, her stomach twisting at the sound of that voice. His voice.

Alecto glanced at Blaze, sitting in the leather chair in the corner of the room. When their eyes locked, she had to try very hard not to let herself get lost in those dark holes that were staring at her as if she was the only person in the room.

"Well," she said, willing her voice to sound bored as ever, "we're actually responsible for clearing out the ruins in the Blessed Forest." She took the paper from Val, scanning it. "Yeah, all of it relates to making sure that it's clean, ready, and safe."

"That's gonna be a nasty job," Andro mused, inspecting his black painted nails. "It's been raining the whole past week. There's literally going to be mud and all that shit."

He grimaced, and Alecto had to bite the inside of her cheek so she wouldn't laugh. Andro was such a fucking princess.

"Okay, listen up," Val said, clapping her hands. "First years will do the initial sweep, making sure there's no trash and shit. I'm sure there is a spell for that, but don't be lazy to also use your fucking hands." Val glared at the two unfortunate souls, nodding frantically.

Then she turned her attention to the next group. "Second years, I want you to work on reinforcing what's left of the ruins. Each year we need to make sure that they're protected from whatever fun the witches will have as they must be still standing by the time the morning comes. Got that?"

"Are you going to give us a spell for that?" Bea, one of the second years, asked, and her cobalt eyebrows shot all the way up to her matching cobalt hairline.

"I'm sure you know how to use the Book by now, Bea," Val snapped, and the girl clapped her mouth shut. Val scanned the crowd and then continued, "Now, third years will work on clearing and securing the tower, and the fourth years will have to scan the perimeter and enforce the protection wards, just in case someone decides to have some fun and lure Hellbates or other fucking abominations as a way to spice things up."

"Actually, that would be something we would do," Blaze mused, a long finger trailing the line of his sharp jaw, his eyes still settled on Alecto.

She had the sudden urge to fidget, to clamp her legs together at the intensity of his gaze. The memories of their last night together were still very much fresh in her mind.

Sleeping had become a true fucking burden for the past week as well.

Anytime Alecto closed her eyes, lying tangled in her sheets, she could hear his voice in her head.

You'd want me to bite you?

She could still feel his gentle whispers over her skin.

Say the word, and I'll stop.

The bruises on her body were quickly fading, but she could still feel his mouth on her skin, those wicked fingers sinking into her flesh.

Now that she was thinking about it, why did she tell him that they shouldn't do it again—

"Alecto?" A voice snapped her out of her thoughts. Alecto blinked at Val, who stared at her expectantly.

"What was that again?"

"I was saying that Gael will lead the first years, and you'll have to lead the second years as a member of the Inner Circle. But if you're not capable of concentrating for longer than ten seconds, then maybe we need someone else to take charge?"

Alecto smirked, flashing her the middle finger. "I'll manage."

Val smirked back, returning her attention to the group. "Blaze, lead the third years, and I'll join the fourth years because nobody out of your bunch is capable of doing so."

A few snorts and eye rolls went around the group, but no one said anything.

Of course, even their old High Priestess, Cassandra, who ruled the House and Venefica until Val showed up, knew to keep her mouth shut and take Val's insults like a big girl.

Sometimes, Alecto wondered whether their little group took things too far.

But then she would remember that the only way to survive at Venefica was to destroy the others before they destroyed you.

And Alecto was a survivor.

47

The Blessed Forest lay on the other side of Darly and the House of Snakes, just down south of Venefica.

It dragged on for miles even beyond their town, and most of it was unexplored as far as Alecto knew, housing many more creatures she only learned about in Inathis's lore. But unlike the Cursed Forest, the students were allowed into the woods.

Right on the edge of the forest, just a few minutes' walk from 3rd Avenue, lay the ruins of the old psychiatric ward said to hold the most dangerous witches under lock before Kelthazane, the unbreakable prison, was built.

Not much was left from the once-grand building anymore, just a single tower stretching all the way over the tops of pine trees and two pairs of tall stone walls that were overgrown with moss and red ivies.

Alecto approached the ruins, Bea and the other second year, Cadre, trailing after her. The Book was shoved in her leather satchel, weighting her shoulder down.

"Bea, why don't you go and inspect the walls and what's left of the ruins and see if there are any weak spots we might need to pay extra attention to?" Alecto instructed, setting her bag on the trunk of the fallen tree.

The witch obeyed without a word, shuffling towards the crumbling walls.

"What do you want me to do?" Cadre asked, setting the bag with tools they would need for the spell on the mossy ground.

"Help me set up the altar for the spell," Alecto said. There was nothing around that could be used as a place for their tools, so they'd have to use the ground. "This seems to be a good enough place."

Alecto walked a few steps towards the flat surface, where moss didn't grow, leaving the earth underneath exposed. It has been used for something before because it was a shape of a perfect circle, and the moss still hadn't grown back.

Alecto worked on drawing a circle in the damp sand with her athame. Then, she stepped in the middle, drawing the five symbols inside, making sure that the lines were connecting where they were supposed to.

Then she let Cadre carry the candles and set them around, marking the spots they each would have to take. He lit them with a spell instead of a lighter.

Show-off.

Just when they were almost finished with the circle, voices came from around them, and Alecto turned to find Val and the rest of the fourth years walking over their way. She had her hands linked with Rogue, who seemed casually bored, as per usual.

They came to a stop when they noticed Alecto.

"Good job, kids," Val said, grinning as she eyed the circle. "Of course, it would be Alecto Black who's the first one to take on the task."

It was a compliment. But it wasn't.

Alecto ignored the fire in Val's eyes, the malice in her smile.

"I've got places to be later," Alecto drawled. "Might as well finish earlier."

"Do you need help with the spell?" Blaze asked.

Apparently, Alecto somehow managed to piss Val and Blaze off at the same time, now having to deal with two of them acting like total assholes. And all because one thought she was sleeping with the other, while the other…probably had his ego hurt?

Alecto wasn't even sure what Blaze's fucking problem was now.

"I think we'll manage," Alecto said, each word clipped. Blaze narrowed his eyes. "But I'll make sure to come to you for help if any issues arise."

Blaze licked his lips before they all moved again. As he passed her, he murmured, "My schedule is rather busy. I wouldn't wait too long if I were you."

Alecto ground her teeth, clenching her jaw so tight it hurt.

That fucking bastard really was trying for something here with his double meanings. *He's busy?*

Of course, he was *busy* with Val and all the other fucking whores ready to climb him the moment he lifted a finger or even glanced their way.

Alecto flexed her palms, taking deep breaths and counting to ten. She didn't have the right to be angry about it.

She was the one who told him that they shouldn't be doing anything anymore. It was her choice, her decision to keep him at bay because she wasn't sure she could handle whatever the fuck they were doing.

Sleeping with boys who couldn't give her what she craved was easy enough. There would always be space for disappointment, which would stop other feelings from coming in.

Things weren't as simple when mind-blowing orgasms were involved. Sadly.

"Done," Bea's voice came from behind Alecto. "The walls seem to be intact, for the most part. The enchants from last year are still lingering in some places."

"Good," Alecto said, nodding. "Let's do this quickly and get it over with."

She led the spell. It didn't take them long to finish placing a strong protective barrier over the old ruins. If someone decided to cause some damage or get into a brawl, the historical monument would stay unscathed.

After they cleaned up their circle, Alecto sent the rest of the Snakes home, staying behind to walk around the ruins and make sure that they hadn't missed anything.

She had to wait for Jolene to finish anyway, as they agreed to go shopping this evening for their costumes for Samhain next week.

As she strolled around the perimeter, the dry leaves rustled under her boots, and she savored every moment of it.

It was easy to miss the delicate change of the seasons when summer bleeds into golden autumn because it always seemed to come out of nowhere.

One minute you were on the beach, sun hot and high in the sky, and the next, you were cuddled in your favorite sweater, warming your hands with a cup of hot chocolate because the sun couldn't be bothered to stay up long enough.

As Alecto finished off her walk and prepared to go look for Jolene, Rogue approached her.

"Black, you're busy?" he asked.

"What's up, Smolder?" she asked, jerking her chin.

He dropped his eyes and scratched the back of his neck as if he was suddenly shy, unsure of himself.

"I have a question."

Alecto arched both of her eyebrows. "Spill it."

"I was wondering if you already have a partner for the party next week?"

The question took a couple of moments to process. It was the last thing she expected to hear from Rogue.

"I don't. Why?"

"Well, I was wondering if you would like to go with me?"

Another pause. Alecto blinked. Sure, Rogue had been useful and kind to her when she least expected it. But somehow, she didn't think he would be…into her.

"You're asking me on a date, Smolder?"

"Yeah," he said with a shrug. "I'm asking you to go with me, Alecto. No hidden agenda or dinner or a quick little fuck behind the tree in the forest."

"Smooth, Smolder. Real smooth."

"Comes easily for my kind," he replied, eyes flickering.

Alecto considered whether it was worth going with Rogue or if she should just stick with the usual and go alone like she always did.

But then, Blaze and Val drew Alecto's attention from behind Rogue's shoulder as they both walked out of the tower. Val was clinging to Blaze. And Blaze seemed to be consumed by whatever Val was saying, his eyes on her, watching intently.

Alecto wasn't sure what was rising in her chest, burning bright like a flame, but she turned her attention back to Rogue. "Sure, I'll go with you."

The best way to get *over* someone is by getting *under* someone, right?

The sun was setting sooner and sooner these days. As Jolene and Alecto walked out onto Main Avenue just after six o'clock, it was already dark outside.

"So, what happened with your pen pal?" Alecto asked as they passed bars and restaurants on their way, all decorated for the upcoming holiday.

"Oh, nothing," Jolene said, glancing at the windows of a shop they reached. "She's good, and we're still in contact."

"Are you going to be meeting her, finally?" Alecto asked, stopping and inspecting the clothes dancing on invisible people to demonstrate how good they would look if you were wearing them. Cheap tactics.

But Alecto couldn't argue that they weren't indeed effective as she spotted a hooded cape made from red silk and matching lace.

"Let's go inside," she said, dragging Jolene into the shop.

"I'm going to meet her," Jolene answered hesitantly, and Alecto turned to look at her friend. She arched a brow in question, and Jolene rolled her eyes. "Well, it's not that simple. She's a journalist. She knows all the elite families of Inathis."

"So?"

"So, she hasn't seen me yet, and she doesn't know I'm a Frone," Jolene said, exasperated. "Once she sees me, she'll know who I am, and then…"

She'd either wouldn't want to be with Jolene at all, or she'd want to be with Jolene due to her status and name.

Jolene didn't have to explain it.

"Well," Alecto said, sighing. "How about if you get her to come here for Samhain? It's going to be a masquerade party. Everyone's wearing masks. You won't have to show her your face, and it can be kind of cool and mysterious meeting this way. *Kinky.*"

Jolene chuckled, bumping into Alecto's shoulder.

"You know," she said after a while, "maybe that's not a bad idea at all."

Alecto rolled her eyes.

Jolene wandered away towards the wall lined with elaborate masks, and Alecto strolled towards the red cloak that drew her to this shop in the first place.

The silk was soft to the touch, melting under her fingers as she dragged her hand over the length of it. The red lace lining was carefully crafted, perfectly blending in with the rest of the cloak.

Alecto didn't know who she was dressing up as for Samhain. It had been a long time since she read any fairy tales. But she knew that she had to have this cloak, and the rest would fall into place.

"Oh, that's so hot," Jolene commented from behind her.

Alecto turned, grinning. "I know, right?" She glanced at the blue and silver mask in Jolene's hand. "You found something?"

"Yes. I feel like this one matches my soul, you know?" Jolene mused, bringing the mask over her face.

"Sure does."

"I came over to say that I've found one that matches *your* soul. And it will fit the cloak, I think." She tipped her head to the side as she inspected the cloak. "Are you going to be like a Red Riding Hood?"

Alecto's eyebrows shot up. "I hadn't thought of it, but I might. Do you think I'd be suited to dress as a girl clad in red, running from a wolf?"

Jolene only snorted, draping an arm over Alecto's shoulder and dragging her towards the masks.

"I assure you if you wear that at the party, you'll definitely be running from plenty of hungry wolves."

48

Two weeks came and went, and Blaze found himself walking through the Blessed Forest, deep into the old ruins.

Samhain was indeed his favorite celebration.

He didn't know what it was, but his heart beat faster as he made his way through the masked crowd gathering in the forest tonight.

Maybe it was the masks and the ability to hide for one night.

Or maybe it was the night's air filled with magic and promise.

Whatever it was, Blaze was alive, his skin prickling with excitement as the warmth from the massive bonfire in the middle of the ruins touched him.

He pinched the blunt between his three fingers and brought it to his lips.

Tonight was all about getting intoxicated, dancing in the grace of the Gods, praying to the ancestors, and hoping for another fruitful year.

Usually, Blaze was great at it.

Get wasted and don't waste time on fuckery.

Yet, this time, Alecto had done a number on him, and for the past two weeks, Blaze was a brooding bastard.

A hand clasped over his shoulder. Blaze turned to find Andro in his long silver gown and a matching silver mask covering the left side of his face.

Gael, his latest fucktoy, stood by his side, wearing a bright golden suit and a matching gold mask hanging to the side.

Blaze had to bite down a laugh.

Andro was always too invested in his fucktoys. Too much sentiment, too many feelings way too soon, always ended in a tragedy.

"You're late," Andro said, stealing the blunt from Blaze's hand and bringing it to his red-painted lips.

"Not according to my time."

"I see you're still a rather big pain in the ass," Andro commented, returning the blunt.

Blaze didn't say anything, taking a hit as Andro brought his lips to Gael's, blowing a stream of smoke into his mouth.

"Oh, by the way," Andro said. "If you see Jolene tonight, don't mention her surname or her status or say anything about her family."

"What's that about?"

Andro glanced around, looping his arm with Gael's. "Well, she's on a date. And that date doesn't know she's a Frone, and she *can't* know that Jolene is a Frone."

What a weird thing.

But whatever. Blaze wasn't planning on seeing Jolene tonight anyway.

The whole faculty was gathered around in the old ruins, some already dancing around the massive bonfire, while the others simply mingled around.

A few of the Rats were gathering under the large pine tree with low-hanging branches, memory orbs hanging from them.

Each orb carried a memory of someone Venefica had lost in the years, the ancestors who were invited each Samhain to join the living as they celebrated the one night when the line between all realms was barely there.

Some of the Tigers, Gabe and Matias included, sat around on the opposite side from the Rats, using overgrown pumpkins as their seating.

Next to them, a few witches accidentally knocked off black pillar candles, and Blaze had to bite down on a laugh when Gabe pointedly stiffened at the sight of the flame devouring dried pine needles on the floor of the forest.

Lined up against one of the remaining walls was a group of girls from Venefica, who didn't seem to belong to any of the Houses, or at least they were new enough that Blaze didn't know which House they belonged to yet.

They noticed Blaze looking at them, so they exchanged words between each other and giggled.

Potential prey.

Despite himself, he knew who particularly he was looking to find in the crowd.

"I'm heading to the bar to start getting wasted," Blaze announced, turning to Andro and Gael. "You down?"

"Always, Blazy."

How Andro still dealt with Blaze when he was in the worst of his moods was beyond him.

On days like these, Blaze didn't even like being with himself.

They made their way through the crowd to the other side of the ruins, where a long banquet table stood, together with a floating bar where three fire sprites tended the witches.

As every year, the table was lavish and crowded with all sorts of fall harvestables—apples, dark berries, all sorts of nuts, and root vegetables.

Tall white, black, and orange pillar candles were scattered amongst the feast of fruits and vegetables, the only source of light.

Going around the table and the crowd gathered there, the guys finally reached the bar. Blaze ordered a round of drinks, and before they even downed them, he ordered another round.

"Look at that bitch." Andro whistled. Blaze followed his gaze to where Alecto stood on the opposite side of the table, hanging off Rogue's arm.

Fucking Rogue's arm.

Blaze turned his whole body towards her, greedily taking in the tight red dress hugging every line of her body.

It was a rather conservative dress, considering it was Alecto wearing it, without a naked back, or provocative décolletage, ending way below her knees, so even her long legs were covered.

Her shoulders were hidden beneath a long, red cloak, the hood dropped over her hair, only the thin red mask covering her eyes peeking through.

When their eyes locked, there was a flicker of some sort, and then she turned her attention back to Rogue, smiling wide at something he said.

"I thought Val's dating Rogue," Gael commented.

Blaze threw him a dark glance, and Andro chuckled, shaking his head.

"Val's not dating anyone," Andro explained. "Val's kinda dating *everyone*."

That was the most accurate way to put it.

"Miss Black is a busy gal," Andro teased. When Blaze glanced at him, he found Andro's eyes already watching him with an expression Blaze couldn't quite read. "Who would blame all the boys for falling at the feet of such beauty?"

Gael grinned, nodding.

Blaze scoffed into his glass. "There are plenty of hot girls around the campus. Beauty is not something that's rare amongst witches."

"Oh, Blazy, are you just mad that Alecto seems to be the only girl on campus not falling for your *irresistible* charms?" Andro mused, grinning.

Blaze emptied the glass, already waiting for the fire sprite to bring him a refill.

Andro was a loyal friend. A brother.

But he could also be a true pain in the ass. Most of the time, right at the time when Blaze needed it *least*.

"I couldn't care less about Alecto Black," Blaze said, willing his voice to sound bored.

But, *oh*, that was a lie.

And from the way Andro swallowed a laugh, it was obvious that his best friend knew it was, indeed, a lie.

Blaze sighed, grabbing his new drink and pushing himself off from the bar. "I'll catch you later. Time for a hunt."

Andro's laughter followed Blaze until he slipped in the crowd, blending in but keeping his eyes focused on Alecto.

His feet seemed to be moving of their own accord because soon he found himself stalking towards her, now alone as Rogue seemed to have gone off somewhere.

"That's a rather conservative outfit for you," he whispered over her shoulder.

Alecto only turned her head slightly to the side, so he could see the tilt of her lips. "As if that's any of your business, Leveau."

Blaze's feet stalked around her, coming to stand in front of her as he glowered down at her.

"Rogue? *Really?* You've moved on from warlocks to demons now?"

"Suck it," she snapped. "Why don't you go off and be *busy* somewhere else?"

Blaze narrowed his eyes, his knuckles going white from how hard he fisted the glass in his palm.

He had spent hours going over their encounters in his head.

Fucking hours.

What went wrong at what moment that made her suddenly so cold and distant?

Even almost getting her killed hadn't deterred her from seeking him out.

And then, when Blaze *actually* acted decently and told her he wanted her, she whirled and denied him.

What the fu—

Ah, and then it hit Blaze. The realization.

"Tell me. What is it that bothers you about me the most?"

Blaze let his thumb brush over Alecto's lower lip, and she immediately smacked his hand away.

But he didn't miss the shiver, the way her body tensed at his touch. There was something in her mind stopping her from giving in.

"Is it your issue with sharing?" Blaze mused. Alecto's jaw tightened, lips pressing into a thin line. "Is that it? You want me all for yourself, right? But because you can't, you would rather not have me at all?"

"It's bold of you to assume I want you at all. There is nothing you can offer me that I can't find elsewhere. And without all the debauchery, might I add."

Blaze chuckled, walking around her again. He leaned in to whisper in her ear, "Oh, but I do. It looks that your body only responds to me."

Satisfaction flooded him as Alecto's shoulders squared.

"How unfortunate, isn't it?"

Without waiting for an answer, Blaze turned and slipped into the crowd, leaving her alone to ponder his words.

The girl who was eyeing Blaze before stood alone by the wall now. Blaze floated over, clinking his glass to hers.

"Cheers," he said.

The girl's cheeks flushed as she batted her eyelashes.

Young. Soft. Inexperienced, probably.

It didn't matter.

Blaze only needed her for a little bit of play.

He placed a hand on the wall next to her head, leaning into her. She immediately responded, lifting her chin.

Blaze chuckled at how eager she was. His lips brushed hers, teasing, coaxing, and a gasp escaped her lips as she fisted the front of his shirt in her palm.

It wasn't for nothing, all this effort.

So, before Blaze dove into her mouth, he tipped his head to the side, finding Alecto standing right where she was before.

As expected, Alecto's eyes were on him, burning. And Blaze kept her gaze as he lowered his lips, melting with the girl underneath him.

He continued keeping her gaze as he parted the girl's lips with his tongue, diving deeper, claiming her.

Alecto didn't look away.

Finally, Blaze turned his gaze from her at the same time as he moved away from the girl.

"It's been a pleasure," Blaze said, tipping his head and leaving the girl by the wall alone, panting and probably confused *and* elated that Blaze Leveau just graced her with his mouth.

As he walked through the crowd, he once again locked eyes with Alecto.

Blaze was going to make her come to him, groveling and begging for his touch, for his mouth on her again.

Or he might as well drag her out of the party, away from people, and force her to be his, just like she wished.

Somehow, Blaze was sure she wouldn't beg for *mercy*.

But then Rogue returned to her side.

Alecto's palm landed on his chest, and then her lips were on his, and Rogue's hands wrapped around her waist, pulling her closer.

Blaze could barely breathe.

At first, Rogue was hesitant, stiff, as if he wasn't sure whether he should respond to her kiss or not. But then, his fingers dug into the flesh of her hips as his whole body leaned into her.

It wasn't the first time Blaze had seen Alecto with another guy.

But somehow, this time, it was different. Something deep inside him was…not quite right. And he had a desperate urge to fix that uncomfortable feeling, get rid of it at any cost.

He should have looked away. Blaze should have turned and walked away, finding something better to do.

But he didn't.

He *couldn't*.

Blaze made his way through the crowd, ignoring how roughly he pushed people to the side. He stopped by Alecto and Rogue, their lips still pressed together, and cleared his throat.

After a few more moments, Rogue pushed himself away from Alecto.

His lips were swollen from the kiss, haze glazing his bright amber eyes. "Blaze, good to see you here tonight."

Blaze didn't even spare the demon a glance. "Can't say the same about you. Alecto, I need to have a word with you."

"I don't think so," Alecto replied, straightening her dress.

Without giving her a chance to protest, Blaze yanked her forearm, pulling her into his embrace, and dragged her through the crowd.

The demon shouted something in their wake, but Blaze didn't give a fuck, and Rogue had enough common sense not to follow them.

Alecto thrashed against his grip, but it was no use. When they reached the tower, further away from the party, only then did Blaze let her go.

When her palm connected with his cheek this time, Blaze was prepared.

"What do you think you're doing?" Alecto demanded, trying to adjust her cape. "You've been acting like a fucking asshole. I mean, like an even *bigger* asshole than you usually are—"

Blaze didn't let her finish her sentence. He pushed her back against the stone wall of the tower, his hand wrapping around her throat.

Alecto gasped, her eyes widening, but it wasn't from the intensity of his grip.

No, Blaze didn't tighten his grip enough to cut off her air supply.

Only having his hand resting against her throat was enough to send her heart thundering.

Part of it was probably fear.

But another part, and not so little he believed, was excitement and desire.

Blaze brought his mouth over hers and whispered, "I'm tired of waiting."

"Tired of waiting," Alecto breathed out the words, "for what?"

"For you."

"Then you're free to fuck right off."

Blaze slammed a fist on the wall next to her head, bringing their foreheads together.

"You misunderstand me," he said. "I'm tired of waiting for *you* to come to your senses and give me what I want."

A breath hitched in her throat, her pulse hammering under his fingers.

"So, I'm going to take it myself."

Without giving her a moment to say anything, Blaze dragged her to the door to the tower.

They stopped. Two pairs of forest-green eyes lazily opened, and then the mouth in the door croaked, "It starts with *S* and ends with *N*, and most who meet her won't get to live to tell the tale."

"A siren," Blaze answered.

With a chuckle, the door swung open, and Blaze swooped inside, dragging Alecto after him.

Before taking the long spiral staircase up to the very top of the tower, Blaze pulled Alecto into his embrace, and carried her up the stairs.

To his surprise—or not really—she stayed silent until he reached the top of the stairs, where a small room was, narrow windows perched on all four walls overlooking the forest and the town stretching in all directions.

Blaze walked Alecto over to the only chaise by one of the four walls, laying her down on her back.

He remained standing over her. "Are you going to beg for mercy?"

Alecto shook her head, staring at him defiantly.

Blaze inhaled a sharp breath, relieved and satisfied at the same time.

He had been waiting for this moment for so long, it was hard to believe he was standing here with her.

His fingers found the clasp of the cloak under her chin, opening it and letting the cape slide away from her, leaving her in the daring red dress.

As his fingers trailed the line of her shoulders, Alecto suddenly sat up.

"This doesn't mean anything you think it does," she said, lifting her chin.

Blaze moved his hand to caress her jaw, his thumb brushing those lips that drove him mad for so many different reasons.

"What do you think I think this means?"

Blaze lowered himself on the chaise, sitting next to her long legs, letting his fingers roam free.

"You think that you hold some sort of power over me," Alecto said, her voice coming out almost in a whisper. Blaze slipped his hand under her dress, higher up her soft thigh. "You think that this is a game, and you're winning."

"You couldn't be more wrong even if you tried."

Alecto's eyes narrowed, but she didn't move away. She allowed his hands to explore her. Through the thin material, Blaze could see her nipples, already hard.

He pushed her down on the chaise, straddling her. His fingers slid under the straps of the dress, pulling them down her shoulders.

"Once upon a time, it was a game," Blaze admitted, his voice quiet and even. He dragged the material down to reveal her beautiful breasts and pebbled nipples. "It was a game of who could be smarter. Crueler. More twisted."

A gasp escaped her lips as he brushed a finger over one of her nipples, another hand exploring the soft skin of her breast, teasing.

Alecto arched her back, leaning into his touch, asking for more of it, and Blaze smirked.

"But then I realized I couldn't break you, no matter what I did," he continued softly. Their eyes locked for a moment before he let his gaze drop down to her breasts. He pinched her nipples between his fingers, slowly rolling them back and forth. "I realized that if I can't break you, then I can't win. And I don't like to play if I can't win."

Alecto moaned as Blaze played with her nipples, the soft skin hot under his touch.

Slowly, he lowered his head, nibbling on her neck, leaving a trail of light kisses as he moved down her throat, the valley between her breasts.

When he took one of her nipples in his mouth, Alecto whimpered. He licked and sucked, watching her body wither under his touch.

It pleased him more than most things in life to see her like this underneath him.

Blaze moved down, leaving kisses over her stomach, dragging her dress down each step until she was out of it and left only with a cheeky little thong that could barely count as underwear.

His mouth went dry at the sight of it. "How naughty."

Alecto chuckled, rubbing her thighs together.

Blaze gripped her flesh, making sure his fingers dug hard enough to leave marks, and pried her thighs apart.

When his finger slipped underneath the triangle of the material, he already found her wet and warm, hungry for him.

Blaze pushed the underwear aside and leaned in to plant a kiss over her clit. Alecto's hips bucked, back arching, so Blaze dove in for more.

When Alecto's hands slipped into his hair, her hips grinding into his mouth, moans and whimpers filling the air around them, Blaze retreated, getting up to undress.

His muscles were trembling, his whole body vibrating with the need to be inside her, to claim her and take her until she was screaming his name.

It was a feeling so primal and intense, Blaze had to blink a few times to get himself under control enough to not get it over with too soon.

At the same time, he also wanted to savor this, to make it last as long as possible.

It always was sweetest when you waited longer, worked harder for something.

And this was one of those things.

Blaze positioned himself at her entrance, keeping himself up with one hand as he let the other caress Alecto's face.

She bit her lower lip, whimpering as her hands pushed his hips into hers, begging for him to finally give her what she wanted.

With a smirk, Blaze indulged her, sliding inside her, slowly, inch by inch, filling her whole.

Alecto threw her head back, moaning so loud it sent shivers down Blaze's spine.

Just as slowly as he entered her, Blaze retreated, and it took him every ounce of his strength not to lose control.

Being inside her felt just as good as he imagined, if not better.

Alecto's legs wrapped around him, locking him in place, and they moved together, their bodies molded to fit.

"Oh, *fuck*," Alecto gasped as Blaze leaned down and sunk his teeth into her neck. "Harder."

Blaze chuckled before biting harder at the same time as he slammed harder inside her.

Alecto moaned in response, her nails digging into his shoulders.

His lips moved over her throat, kissing and licking.

Once he reached the contour of her breast, Blaze once again sunk his teeth into her soft flesh, and he had to groan as she gripped him tighter inside her.

"Don't you dare do *that*," Blaze warned once he pulled away, panting.

Alecto smirked, glancing down at him. "What? Are you talking about this?"

She did it once more, sending sparks of pleasure through him. With a growl, Blaze pulled out, turning them over so that he was on his back now, and she was straddling him.

Before he could lead her hips, Alecto gripped his arms, pinning them over his head with one hand as she positioned herself over him.

It wasn't enough to keep him in place, and she knew that. But Blaze let her take the lead, curious to see how wild this beautiful witch could be.

Alecto lowered herself onto him, throwing her head back, and then started rolling her hips, one palm braced on his chest for support.

She was beautiful, and she was wicked.

Blaze wanted nothing more than to lose himself in her because when Alecto was around, the world was colorful once more.

After another moment, her grip on his hand slipped away as she braced another palm over his chest, her sharp nails digging into his flesh.

She was moving more frantic, needy, and Blaze cupped her hips, pushing her into him so she could reach even deeper inside her.

"Fuck, yes," Alecto moaned, "just like that. *Ah—*"

Blaze held her in place, his cock buried deep inside her as her orgasm washed over her, making her muscles tremble.

He ignored the stinging as her nails broke the surface of the skin on his chest. A few more thrusts was all it took for him to come undone, spilling inside her.

Alecto stayed sitting on top of him for a few long moments, trying to catch her breath. There was sweat beading on top of her eyebrow and between her breasts, even though the air between them was chilly.

Blaze's thumbs made circles over her thighs, his eyelids heavy as he took in the view in front of him.

It was all too sweet, too intoxicating.

That was the dangerous thing about getting what you want—once you've had a taste, you never want to stop.

Finally, Alecto cleared her throat. "We should get back to the party."

Blaze smirked. "Did you really think that was all?"

49

The last time Alecto opened her eyes in the morning to find herself in Blaze's bedroom, she was alone in the bed.

This time, there was a hard body pressed into her back, and a hand wrapped tightly around her waist.

No fucking way.

Who would have thought Blaze fucking Leveau was a *cuddler*?

She stayed still for another moment, letting herself enjoy the weirdly comfortable embrace of someone she used to hate not too long ago.

They left the party after that steamy exchange in the tower, and Alecto spent the night in his bed, tangled between his sheets and his limbs. It was nothing if not divine.

Blaze sighed heavily, his warm breath ruffling her hair, and then he groaned, rolling on his back, and his hand slipped away from her waist.

Alecto glanced over her shoulder, her muscles going taut as if she were waiting for the moment when the spell would be gone and Blaze wouldn't be here with her.

He knew how to be mean, better than anyone else. And while most of the time Alecto could take it, she wasn't sure if she could right now.

Fortunately, when those dark eyes opened, taking her in next to him, all he did was roll back on his side and nuzzle his nose into her neck, breathing in her smell.

"Morning," he murmured, his voice husky.

Alecto didn't push him away, allowing his hands to wrap around her once more and pull her closer to his hard body.

"Good morning," she replied. She let the butterflies inside her belly to fly around freely for once.

"So, are you going to tell me once more how fun it was, but we shouldn't do this again?" Blaze asked, his face still buried in her neck.

"It almost sounds as if you were deeply wounded by it."

Blaze lifted his head, glaring at her through lowered lashes.

"It wounded me so deeply. I'm still trying to recover," he said seriously, but there was a smile at the corner of his mouth. His gaze dropped to her lips, eyebrow arching. "And I think there must be some sort of *payback* for the damage your words had done to my poor soul."

Alecto giggled as Blaze dived back into her neck, his lips tickling her skin, teeth nibbling gently.

She tried wiggling away, but his grip around her waist tightened, his mouth working her neck and sending sparks of pleasure down her belly to her core.

Blaze crawled on top of her, pressing her to the mattress. Alecto felt how eager he already was, his hard-on pressing against her belly.

She let her eyes roam his face, still softened by the traces of sleep. It was scary how attracted Alecto was to this cruel boy looking down at her.

Goose bumps rose over her skin whenever his fingers explored her body. Blaze had seen her at her worst... *No*, he himself was responsible for bringing out the worst in her. And yet, those obsidian eyes were still flickering with want and need, despite all the ugliness.

What a strange thing it was. And how comforting.

"What's the matter?" Blaze asked, his eyebrows drawn together.

Alecto met his gaze once more, letting her hands run down his back, feeling the marks her nails had left last night.

"I thought we've got the unfinished business of payback..." Alecto mused.

Blaze wiggled himself between her legs at the same time one of his hands gathered both of hers and pinned them over her head.

"Oh, so you're eager to pay up?" he teased, brushing the tip of his nose over hers.

"Why are you so sure I'm the one who's going to pay up?"

Blaze released a sound somewhat between a growl and a moan as his hand moved away from keeping her wrists pinned, long fingers wrapping around her throat.

"You're a real piece of work, you know that, Black?" Blaze muttered, almost exasperated. And if it weren't for the gleam of desire in his gaze, Alecto could almost believe it bothered him.

She leaned into him to catch his lower lip between her teeth, nibbling on it and sucking it into her mouth. That was enough for Blaze to dive in, his grip around her throat tightening a tad as he claimed her mouth.

Alecto melted under his touch, arching her back so that her chest brushed over his, that skin-on-skin contact driving her mad with overwhelming sensations.

When Blaze peeled his lips away, both panting heavily, Alecto whimpered her dissatisfaction with the loss of his lips on hers.

"So needy," he whispered. "So demanding. Now that I think about it, maybe I should let you suffer without the release as a payback. What do you think?"

Alecto wanted to argue against the prospect of it while at the same time her body tingled with the excitement of letting him do whatever he pleased. Even if it meant denying her the sweet, sweet pleasure she craved.

"Maybe," Blaze continued, "I should make good on my promise and drive you close to the edge so many times that you end up *begging* for me to give you what you want."

Alecto's body heated at the memory of those wicked promises he had made that day in the classroom when his head was between her thighs.

There were many things Alecto wished Blaze would do to her. Many weird, wicked things she only had allowed herself to ever imagine in her head, never having the bravery to say them out loud to anyone.

"Yeah," Blaze concluded. "I think that's exactly what I'm going to do."

Alecto gasped as he moved his hips into her, his hard cock sliding over her length, over her core, never slipping inside even though that was precisely what she ached for.

The muscles of his back under Alecto's fingertips were taut, shifting with each movement, and Alecto wrapped her legs around his waist, pulling him closer.

Blaze chuckled, his hips grinding into her harder. "Oh, don't think that it'll help."

Alecto rolled her head to the side as his mouth closed over her left nipple, licking and sucking the sensitive flesh, his tongue toying with the metal, sending intense sparks all the way down to her core.

She moaned, digging her nails into his shoulder, feeling the heat building deep inside her, ready to burst at any moment now—

Blaze retreated, putting just enough distance between their hips so that he wasn't touching her anymore, and the intense wave retreated, leaving Alecto hot and bothered.

She exhaled a heavy breath. "That's just fucking rude."

Blaze chuckled, more amused than she liked.

"So was saying it was *fun*," he muttered, planting a kiss on her throat. "So was saying it was just a *whim*." His lips traveled lower, kissing the skin between her breasts. "So was implying we got it out of our systems, when clearly…" His gaze found hers as he planted a kiss right above her navel. "Clearly, we have not."

Alecto's breath was uneven, her heart hammering so hard it was hard to follow his train of thought as his mouth hovered over her core.

"It was very rude of you to think that it could never happen again," he continued, planting one kiss on her left thigh, then moving to do the same on the right one. "Just so fucking rude."

Blaze leaned down to flick her clit with his tongue, and Alecto's hips bucked. She gasped, her whole body hypersensitive to every touch, every kiss, every breath on it.

His hands massaged her thighs, and then he dove into her, his mouth closing over the sensitive bundle of nerves and doing terrible things to her. Her toes curled, thighs falling wide open as she arched into him, once again chasing her pleasure.

She bit her lip when he slipped first one finger, then two, inside her. Then, he groaned over her, and Alecto cried out at the intense vibrations tipping her even closer to the edge.

"Oh, please," she whispered, her fingers gripping his hair. "Please—"

Blaze pulled away, his lips glittering with her slickness. "Oh, we're already begging? Go on, baby."

Alecto scoffed, but it wasn't very effective knowing how desperate she was, and Blaze knew it.

"I won't do that again," she offered. "I won't walk away. I won't wound your poor immortal soul *ever* again."

"Liar."

Alecto tried to stifle a smile by biting on her lip, but it was futile. She loved torturing Blaze just as much as he did, and she'd do it any chance she got.

And Blaze knew it.

He tsked, shaking his head, and then returned his mouth to her, making her squirm and gasp.

Just when she was about to come, Blaze pulled away, allowing the wave of pleasure to retreat once more.

Alecto fisted the sheets by her side, only able to muster a whimper and a growl of frustration. Blaze climbed back up, kissing her neck again.

"There, there," he soothed, his hands kneading the flesh of her thighs on either side of him. "I'm almost done with you, I promise."

He caught her lip between his teeth, and Alecto wrapped her arms around his neck, pulling him closer to her. She wanted to devour him whole. She wanted him to devour her in return.

Blaze seemed to feel it too because soon the kiss turned demanding, impatient even, as if he wanted more of her and he couldn't wait for it anymore.

When his mouth closed over her neck, his teeth sinking into her flesh, Blaze drove himself inside her deep. Alecto gasped with the intensity of the pain and the pleasure.

It didn't take long for the warmth to start building inside her again. Alecto was so wet, she could feel her own slickness everywhere, even on her thighs, and she eagerly moved her hips to meet his.

She let her head fall back, eyes shuttering closed.

"*Fuck*." The curse came from Blaze's lips now, making Alecto smile.

Suddenly, he slipped a hand between them, his thumb finding her swollen clit and pressing on it with each deep thrust of his hips.

Alecto gripped his back, bracing her nails into his flesh as the first heat wave surged through her, bringing her very close to the edge.

"Look at me," Blaze demanded.

Alecto opened her eyes. All of it felt too much, too intimate suddenly, and Alecto wanted to turn away, to close her eyes again.

"You are *mine*," he said. It was a warning and a promise. Something inside Alecto swirled, and she struggled to breathe. "Don't you forget that, baby."

With one last thrust, Alecto shattered, her body going taut at the pleasure so intense she could barely take it. Her mind went blank, swimming, and for a moment, she almost felt herself float away from her body.

Only when a few moments later, Blaze went still and cursed under his breath, did Alecto gather herself enough to open her eyes again and take a deep breath.

"Fucking Hel," she managed, brushing the strands of hair away from her face, slick with sweat.

Blaze chuckled into her neck before rolling away from her.

Alecto closed her eyes. She wanted to rest for a moment as the last strands of pleasure left her, but Blaze didn't give her that, dragging her out of bed into his arms.

"I don't think you've had the pleasure of seeing the inside of my shower yet," he said and winked before he carried her into his bathroom.

50

What made Blaze fucking Leveau such a good lover?

That was the question plaguing Alecto for the past week since Samhain night and the morning after.

More precisely, the thing that bothered Alecto was why could she orgasm with him, but not the other men she'd had sex with in the past.

Was it the fact that she kind of hated him, and he hated her? Was that her *kink*?

Her eye caught the sight of the leather chair where she sucked him off not that long ago, and she had to shift in her seat because of all the memories flooding back.

It must have been the sense of danger that did it for her. Or the fact that it was forbidden and had to stay a secret. Right?

She rubbed her temples; a headache was trying to make its way into her skull.

Maybe the thing that did it for her with Blaze was how exciting he was. He was cruel and bad but caring and soft, which still baffled her. How could one person be both?

A book slammed on the table in front of Alecto, scattering her thoughts and making her jump.

"Alecto, I've been looking for you," Val said. She pulled up a chair and plopped into it. "I need your help."

Alecto rolled her eyes, shoving away her notebook, which had nothing but her illustrations because she hadn't been studying.

"What do you want from me, Val?"

"Well, why wouldn't I want you? You've proved to be the most useful member of our House this year."

Yeah, there wasn't much that could top burning a fucking house down. Even if they hadn't gotten their hands on the Tigers' Book, it was still an impressive thing. All Alecto's idea.

"Am I going to be your new favorite pet now?" Alecto cocked a brow, her tone mocking. But her heart thrashed against her chest as she waited for Val's answer. She wasn't sure what she wanted to hear. "Or am I—a half breed—still not merciless and cruel enough?"

Val's smirk turned into a grin that was anything but friendly and warm.

"Look how sharp tongued you have become, Black. Quite an improvement from the start of the year. Keep it up and you might become my favorite pet."

Once again, from the way Val's eyes flickered, Alecto was sure she was challenging her. It was as if Val was curious to see how far Alecto was willing to go. How cruel she could truly be.

"Fascinating," Alecto replied. "Now, how can I help you?"

"I'm glad you asked. I have a little thing I need your help with."

"Yeah?"

"While we're focusing on the Tigers and their Book this year, it doesn't mean we can forget other Houses along the way," Val said. "Rogue hasn't been as useful as I'd like in getting the High Priests and Priestesses interested, so we need to get creative. It would be useful to break up the Dragon and Rat alliance."

Alecto frowned. "I don't follow. You said the Dragon and Tiger alliance was the problem for us?"

"It is and it isn't." *Val and her thousand and one games.* "Venefica's politics are a complicated thing, Black. Every alliance or the lack of one matters. Anyway, I have a plan to speed things up."

Alecto cocked a brow, crossing her arms. "Well, spill. I can't wait to hear all about it."

Val didn't let Alecto's sarcasm bother her as she leaned in, closing the gap between them before she spoke. "I want to steal something from the

House of Dragons. I wish it was something as important as their Book, but it's something else."

Alecto nodded. "So, what is it then?"

"Well, it's one of the heirlooms that Dragons pass down generation to generation." Val swirled her finger in the air, rolling her eyes. "It's a small chest filled with the Black Pearl treasure."

"And is it cursed?"

Val exhaled a long breath, falling back in her chair with crossed arms. "Everything is cursed if you think about it, really." When Alecto didn't reply, Val added, "You won't even have to touch it, so you don't have to worry about the curse making you bold or melting your pretty face away."

"And the curse won't transfer to the House if we keep it?" Alecto was still not convinced it was a smart idea.

Curses and jinxes were at the heart of witches' magic. There was no reason to play with something that might fuck them up without them even knowing.

"I won't keep it in the House," Val assured, growing impatient as she once more shifted in her seat. "Why are you being such a fucking pussy about it? Andro would have fussed less than you do now."

"A real nice way to convince me to help you, Val. What do you need me to do?"

Val pointedly glanced at the golden watch on her thin wrist.

"Well, I know that you have a line rehearsal with Norse later today, just before the Saturday game. I'll need you to distract him for me so I can slip in and steal the heirloom. Oh, and of course, I'll need you to help me get inside without being noticed."

"Norse is not stupid, you know that? He was the one who warned me that all Queens die or some shit like that."

"Yeah, well, he also happened to be the one who told you personally that he would like to see you in his House," Val retorted. Alecto couldn't hide her surprise. She didn't remember offering this piece of information to Val herself. "Norse doesn't throw statements like that around for anyone. We'll use it against him. Come on, Black."

"*Fine*," Alecto agreed with a heavy sigh. "Be there at 5:30 and not a minute later. I think we'll be in the library, so I'll make sure he's gone so I can let you in through the window."

Without another word, Val rose from her seat, beaming. "You're an asset, Black."

Despite herself, Alecto couldn't stop the feeling of satisfaction at Val's words.

51

Alecto was a smart girl. At least, she liked to think that she was.

That was why she chose a particular outfit for tonight, which she knew would suit Norse's taste. It wasn't her usual provocative and open ensemble, even if she knew that Norse appreciated seeing her in the least amount of clothing possible, just like all the other men.

But she had gathered in the last year and a bit that Norse had a particular taste in girls. He liked them with black-lined eyes, cozy dark sweaters over crisp white shirts, and short, pleated skirts.

So, that was the outfit Alecto wore for tonight.

She even added thick, over-the-knee socks that ended midthigh. Most of the clothing was from Jolene's closet, and she was lucky her friend was Norse's type.

Maybe Val should have asked Jolene to be the bait—

The door of the House opened and Norse's tall figure appeared in the doorway. Alecto took in the ruffled hair and the crisp white shirt that usually was pristine, now half-unbuttoned and untucked from his black pants.

"You're on time," he said.

He moved away to let her in.

"Was I supposed to be late?"

Norse walked around her, leading the way to the library at the back of the House.

"You're always late to the parties," he observed, opening the double door. Alecto took in the view of the tall walls lined with books, the spiral stairs going to the next floor, and the set of leather chairs in the center of the room, right under the massive chandelier hanging heavily from the ceiling.

"So?" Alecto asked as she walked past him, settling in one of the chairs without waiting for permission.

"So," he said, taking the seat opposite her and dropping an ankle of one leg over the knee of the other. "I just assumed you're late to everything else. My mistake."

Alecto didn't know what else to say, so she didn't say anything.

She fished out her script from her satchel. Then, she fixed Norse with a glare, which seemed to amuse him.

"*So*," she said, "shall we begin?"

"Straight to business? I thought we might have a lovely evening, have a drink and get to know each other before practicing."

Alecto tossed the script on the coffee table between them, crossing her legs. She made sure that he got a slight glimpse of her underwear as she moved one leg over the other.

"Well, nobody really offered me any drinks so far," Alecto said, letting her arms rest on the buttery arms of the chair. "So, I only assumed you wanted me in and out as quickly as possible."

Norse rose to his feet. "Right, that makes me a lousy host. What's your drink of choice?"

"I'm not drinking tonight, thanks." When Norse's eyebrow arched, she added with a small smile, "I don't like alcohol when I'm on my period. It makes me feel groggy and sick."

Norse's face hadn't changed at the mention of her period. "Well, then is there anything else I can offer you instead?"

"If you have chocolate, bring it all here," Alecto said, shrugging.

"I'll be right back."

The moment the door closed behind him, Alecto was on her feet, rushing towards the window at the back of the room. She opened the latch and swung it open to find Val crouching beneath.

"Give me your hand," Val instructed.

Alecto leaned over the windowsill and reached a hand to help Val in. Instead of taking her hand, Val pricked Alecto's finger with something, drawing blood. Alecto hissed, but Val ignored her, smearing Alecto's blood over the middle of her forehead.

"What the fuck are you doing?" Alecto asked when Val let go of her hand. She glanced behind her to check if Norse was coming back. "Get inside. *Now.*"

Val murmured something under her breath, then climbed through the window. When she was inside, she closed it and righted her outfit.

"Norse adjusted the wards to let you inside," Val explained in a low voice. "I'm not allowed, so I needed your blood so that the wards would recognize me as you. It won't work for long, so I have to work fast."

Alecto returned to her seat, glaring at Val inspecting the library.

"Well?" she urged. Norse could come back anytime.

"Relax, Black."

She checked a few more shelves and then came over to Alecto. At the same moment, the door swung open, and Norse returned with a tray in his hands.

Alecto turned to where Val stood before, but she had vanished, probably wearing an invisibility spell. Norse walked over to Alecto and set the tray on the coffee table. Then he returned to close the door and walked over to the bar to pour himself a drink.

There was a box of different, probably handmade, chocolates on the tray and a cup of steaming hot chocolate next to it.

"I wasn't sure which form of chocolate you'd prefer," Norse explained when he returned to his seat. "So I opted to go with both."

Alecto couldn't hide the surprised smile as she leaned in to grab one candy out of the box. She almost moaned when she popped it into her mouth and the chocolate melted on her tongue, subtle hints of mint spreading over her taste buds.

"Chocolate is *better* in Inathis," Alecto observed.

"Better than in the mortal realm? Isn't everything?"

Alecto brought the cup to her lips, shaking her head. When she took a sip, the hot liquid was thick and smooth over her tongue.

"Not everything," she answered.

"What isn't?"

For a moment, Alecto let herself go over everything she'd tried in both realms, comparing the tastes and sensations.

"Champagne," she said finally. Norse cocked a brow in surprise. "Yeah. The shit we have here can't compare to champagne in mortal world."

"What else?"

"Well, chips and gummy bears," Alecto said, nodding to herself. "It's all artificial, and it feels like you're eating pure chemicals, but man, does it taste divine."

That made Norse smirk. "I might need to visit the mortal realm one day just to see if you're right."

"There is really not much to see."

It was a lie because there was plenty to see, and Alecto wished she had seen it more before her mother passed away.

Yes, she could return anytime she wanted. Any of them could. But Alecto didn't like coming back alone as it was one of many things she used to do exclusively with her mother when she was still around.

Crossing the door to the mortal realm always would be a reminder Alecto didn't need.

"So," Alecto said and cleared her throat. "What is it specifically you would like to talk about, Norse? Are you here for a confession?"

"Confession from you or me?"

"Both, perhaps."

At that, Norse smirked, letting his fingers run through his messy hair.

"I don't see a point in confessions," he admitted after a moment of silence. "But I do believe in the power of a good proposition."

"Are you going to ask for my hand in marriage?" Alecto asked, bringing her hand to her mouth as if she was scandalized. "I think it's a bit early. We at least should meet each other's parents before we commit."

Her words almost won another smile from Norse, and it was then Alecto started to wonder whether Val's words had any truth to them.

"Marriage between a Dragon and a Snake?" Norse asked, shaking his head. "That would be the scandal of the century."

"Indeed."

Norse's face grew serious. "It's not too late for you, you know? Don't get me wrong, you're hated just as much as the rest of the Inner Circle. But you being half mortal earns you forgiveness points. Most witches think you're under the others' spell, just doing their bidding."

Alecto recoiled inside, ready to lash out. But she held herself together, only tipping her head to the side.

"And what do you think? Am I just a poor little pawn in their cruel game?"

Of course, leave it to witches to think a half blood was so different than them.

"I'm not stupid to think that," Norse replied. "I think you're more than capable of the worst behavior all on your own. And because people overlook you, it makes you even more dangerous. So, as I was saying, it's not too late for you."

"Too late for what?" Alecto asked, curiosity urging her forwards.

Norse's lips curled, but it wasn't a kind smile. "To choose the winning side. Having you would be my pleasure."

It was a warning.

Alecto's stomach flipped, uneasiness coming over her. It was as if she was missing something very vital, very important, but she couldn't figure out what it was.

"I'm already on the winning side," she teased.

Norse brought the glass to his lips, draining the liquid before placing it on the coffee table.

"Not for long."

IV. VANITY IN DEATH

52

Another family dinner to attend. Another evening of snide witches and warlocks to entertain.

At least, this time around, it seemed as if the usual crowd of the *crème de la crème* of Avalon Hills had returned to the Leveau penthouse, politicians, socialites, and even a few celebrities mingling around.

Galliermo's business dealings were the last thing Blaze gave a shit about, but there'd been something suspicious about his father since the auction.

And his mother still hadn't returned.

Blaze brought his glass to his lips, sipping on amber liquid as his eyes focused on the sunset in the distance.

"Listen, I think we need to lay low," Andro argued.

He never attended Blaze's father's dinner parties, but today he and his mother decided to grace them with their presence.

Blaze was grateful his best friend was here, occupying Val, because tonight Blaze's mind was further away than ever.

"Andro, sweetheart," Val said, her voice sweet as honey. "As someone who's *legacy* and is part of the most powerful House in history, you're a fucking pussy."

"Call me a pussy however many times you want. I call myself the only sane one amongst you psychopaths."

Blaze lifted a finger to say something, but Andro beat him to it: "You are probably the biggest psychopath. Some days I don't even think Val comes close to you."

Blaze shrugged. "You say it as if it's a bad thing."

He was sure Andro's eye twitched.

He clapped a hand over his shoulder, leaning closer to whisper something to further agitate him, but his father signaled for him from the other side of the room.

Blaze sighed. "Be right back."

He followed his father from the lounge into the corridor and into his study. Dread slowly settled in his bones.

To Blaze's surprise, his father strode around his desk and plopped heavily in his chair before turning his attention to Blaze.

He seemed to be in a rather good mood.

As good of a mood as Galliermo Leveau ever was.

"Tell me, how many girls are at Venefica?"

Blaze's mouth fell open at the unexpected question. His father raised his brows, waiting for the answer.

"I never counted," Blaze said slowly. "But I suppose plenty."

His father nodded. "That's right, Blaze. There are plenty of women in the academy. Knowing the name you carry, and that you indeed got your looks from me, I am sure most of them are more than willing to spread their legs for you whenever you wish."

Blaze brushed a thumb over the middle of his lip. "I've never checked, but you might be right."

Galliermo's face settled into a cold expression. "So why do you find yourself between the legs of a fucking *half breed*?"

His father never screamed. Never once did he raise his voice.

He never had to.

The sinister look and the way his voice filled with the darkness from the deepest pits of Hel was enough to send Blaze's body into freezing fear.

Fuck.

Blaze swallowed hard. "I don't know which half breed you're talking about."

As the fists slammed into the desk, rattling the pens and the papers stacked neatly around the edge, Blaze flinched.

"Don't fucking play me for a fool."

"Why does it matter to you who I sleep with? You don't seem to be worried about me fucking Val, and she's a 'breed-less street rat' to quote you."

His father rose to his feet and rounded the desk.

This was the part where Blaze was going to get the beating.

"Valeria has potential," he said, voice low. "She might not be the best choice to marry into the Leveau family, but she could be useful."

Blaze could only blame himself.

He had brought her with him, thinking her being from the streets would deter his father from trying to marry them.

Apparently, he was wrong.

"But you and *Alecto Black*," he spat her name as if it was a curse, and Blaze's fists curled in response, "shouldn't be getting close. Leveaus are above shagging with half breeds. Even being in the same House as her is a disgrace."

Blaze took a deep breath, his body trembling. "I will fuck who I wish."

His father was quick as he moved towards Blaze and threw a fist at his stomach.

"You'll do as I say," he growled. "If I hear that you even talk with that filth outside school, I'm going to make sure it's the last time you see her."

Blaze straightened his back.

"You don't have that kind of power. She's a *Black*."

Another punch, this one to his side, sent him to his knees.

"Yes, and what do you think her father will do when he finds out that his precious little angel has been fucking you?" His tone was mocking, and something in his words didn't sit right. "He's going to make sure that you never lay a finger on her again."

Blaze glanced at his father, confused at the triumphant expression that hid something cruel and sinister behind it.

"Get yourself together," his father spat, fastening the button of his suit jacket. "We have a party going on."

He walked around Blaze to the door. "Don't ever allow the Leveau name to mix with that half breed, or you won't see the end of my wrath."

And with that, Blaze was left alone.

He rose to his feet, catching a glimpse of himself in the mirror. It was someone else starting at him back, dark gaze and shadows settled in the hollows of cheeks that were supposed to belong to him.

He raked a hand through his hair before he went over to the bar behind the large desk, pouring himself a drink.

As the whisky hit his throat, burning all the way down to his stomach, Blaze whirled, glancing at the neat desk.

There was only one note out of place.

A paper he had recognized.

Blaze slowly lifted it, the expensive ivory paper marked with a black coiled snake in the corner.

In the middle of the note sat words written in handwriting Blaze knew well.

Your son is sleeping with Alecto Black.

Of course it was Val. Blaze should have known from the start.

He emptied the drink in one gulp, smashing the glass on the desk as he strode outside the study back into the lounge.

Val and Andro were standing right where he'd left them, and Val smiled as Blaze approached. "Hey there, handsome—"

Words died in her throat as Blaze sunk his fingers in her forearm, yanking her close to his chest. "We're going."

Without waiting for a response, Blaze dragged Val with him as he made his way to the elevator. Andro was right behind them.

The door opened, a faceless man greeted them, and Blaze guided Val inside. "Ground floor."

The door closed, and they started moving down. Blaze's rage choked him.

"Do you really have to be such a dick?" Val complained. "I was actually enjoying myself—"

"Shut the fuck up."

Blaze didn't look at either of his friends. His eyes focused on the elevator doors. Once they opened, he strode through the massive foyer, ignoring the receptionist, and went outside.

The Crahen at the parking lot immediately whistled for their transportation, and a moment later, a round carriage with red and black branches flew over, stopping right in front of them as the door swung open.

Blaze shoved Val inside. Andro climbed in, closed the door, and settled on the seat in front of them.

The moment the carriage moved through the air, Blaze let go of Val's hand, his fingers gripping her neck instead.

She didn't even gasp.

"You fucking crossed the line, Val," he hissed right in her face.

Val's face remained still for a moment before her lips twitched. Blaze tightened his grip, but her grin only grew.

"I did what I had to do to ensure that our House doesn't burn."

Blaze slammed her into the wall behind her back. "You did what you felt was good for you. Don't fucking pretend that you did it for the House."

"Can someone explain what the fuck happened?" Andro asked.

Val kept Blaze's gaze when she spoke to Andro. "Oh, didn't you know? Blaze and Alecto fucked, both finally not clearly pretending to hate each other."

"*Oh.*"

"It's none of your fucking business," Blaze warned. "You should have kept your mouth shut about it. If I hear about you spying on me for my father one more time, I'm going to—"

"You're going to do what, *Blazy*?" Val challenged him. "You're going to beat me like your father beats your mother, huh?"

Blaze was *nothing* like his father.

"You're going to punish me by getting me in trouble at school? Maybe getting me expelled by blackmailing the Dean into giving in to your whim?"

Blaze blinked, his chest heaving for a moment.

He moved away, pulling his hand off Val's throat.

"Or are you going to drag me to the fucking forest and leave me as a meal for the spiders, hoping I won't survive?"

Stop. Fuck.

With his heart hammering, Blaze turned to the window, watching the distant lights of night city being left behind as the carriage flew over the thick forest.

He fucked up.

What was inside him was no better than what his father was. You can't offer anything good to those around you when all you've ever known was darkness.

"You don't know shit about me," Blaze said, raking a hand through his hair.

Val remained silent.

"I'm not going to hurt you. I'm going to take the one thing you value more than anything else in life instead."

"Blazy—" Val started, but he didn't let her finish.

Blaze turned his cold, hollow eyes on her then as he warned, "I'm going to ruin you, Val. Mark my words."

Maybe Blaze was more like his father than he'd ever allowed himself to believe.

53

Blaze sucked on the blunt between his lips so hard, his lungs burned. He ignored the pain, the urgent need to gasp for air as he held the smoke in. After a moment, he released it in a low, steady stream, watching as the gray tendrils danced with each other—lean bodies, thick bodies, unnaturally long bodies whirling together before disappearing into thin air.

A light cough rattled his chest, and then he brought the blunt right back between his lips.

Blaze liked it when it hurt.

In fact, he *loved* it when it hurt.

His eyes fluttered closed, and he leaned his head back against the cold tub, allowing his muscles to relax, wrapped in the warm rose water as the drug worked him from the inside.

There was this urge inside him, trying to claw its way out, for violence.

If he let it go, it would wreak havoc around them, hurting everyone the beast encountered on its way to self-destruction.

Blaze wasn't sure why he tried to subdue it.

Maybe letting everyone burn around him for once would be the right thing to do.

A shadow appeared in the corner of his vision, and Blaze looked around to find Alecto leaning against the jamb.

Her face was blank. She wore that perfectly crafted mask of obliviousness Blaze found extremely beautiful.

If he were honest with himself, she was always beautiful.

When her eyes rolled whenever she was snarky, she was stunning.

When her eyes narrowed due to silent rage, she was breathtaking.

When her eyes widened, face falling still whenever she was surprised, she was a fucking *vision*.

Blaze blinked, slowly catching her intense gaze.

She tipped her head to the side. "I suppose my invitation got lost in the mail."

Words died in his throat as Blaze stared at her, his mind going blank.

There was only one thing left to do.

Slowly, with the blunt loosely wedged between his lips, he stood from the bathtub and grabbed for the towel.

Alecto's gaze slid from his face down his chest and belly to his groin, and it took Blaze all his strength not to react as he wrapped himself in the towel.

He should have spread his arms towards her, calling her to his embrace.

He should have wrapped his arms around her tight and burrowed his face in her neck as he greedily inhaled her smell.

He should have brought her to his bed and lost himself in her body, allowing himself to lie next to her after they were exhausted and enjoyed the silence between them that said more than words ever could.

Instead, Blaze stepped closer to Alecto and said, "Or maybe your invitation never went out."

The familiar warmth in her eyes evaporated.

It was as if Blaze had stabbed himself right in the chest, but he couldn't figure out that feeling.

"Is that so?" she asked, cocking a brow. "Are you having one of your moments, *Blazy*?"

There was no kindness in her words, and Blaze was grateful for it.

It made everything so much easier.

His lip twitched as he cocked his head to the side. "Actually, I think I'm *done* having one of my moments. It's been fun, though, baby."

"Excuse me?"

Blaze wet his lips. "You heard me, Alecto. I'm rather bored with you now. It was fun playing around, the whole back and forth between us. But now that I've *conquered* my goal, things are looking rather dull."

Anger flashed in her eyes, her cheeks flushed with the raw emotion he was sure was burning her chest right now.

"You've *conquered* nothing. Let me assure you of that," she said, her voice low.

Blaze laughed, hollow and mocking, which only seemed to brighten her hate.

"Oh, sweet Alecto. I played you better than you even know."

Alecto held his stare, unflinching as his next words came at her. "I've hurt you, humiliated you, literally left you to die out in the woods. And what do you do?"

He laughed once more, the cruelty in it shaking his whole body.

Did it feel as painful to her as it did to him?

"You fucking come crawling on your knees at me, dying for that sweet little touch," Blaze continued. He lifted a hand to caress her cheek, and she allowed it. "You're pathetic, Alecto. Did you know that? You act all tough and cold, the heartless bitch, but deep down, you're just a little girl jumping from one asshole onto the next one, desperately trying to find your own worth in men who want you for nothing more than your body."

He dropped his hand from the silky soft skin of her cheek, his lips curling into a snarl.

To his utter surprise and relief, Alecto searched his face for a moment, calm and collected.

Alecto Black was unbreakable.

Ah, Blaze never wished for that to be true more than right that moment.

When her eyes found his again, one corner of her lips curled. "Damn, Leveau, you should pick up psychology classes next trimester. You're really good at reading people."

With one last smirk, she left Blaze's room, leaving her scent lingering after her.

It was better this way.

They were always supposed to be enemies.

Whatever this game was, whatever Blaze thought he felt for a moment, it was out of hand.

He had more important matters to focus on than playing with Alecto Black.

But then why did the sharp pain linger in his chest?

"Do you have the Book?" Val asked the moment Blaze stepped foot outside his room.

"No. I've got better things to do."

Better things being going to get completely wasted in one of the local bars, preferably in the company of multiple women.

Preferably *not* blondes.

Val grabbed his arm, digging in her nails. "I'm serious, Blaze. Forget your fucking little tirade on our way home. This is not something you should mess with."

Blaze twisted his arm out of her grip. "I'm not fucking messing with anything, Val. I couldn't give less fucks about your Book or anything else right now."

The sudden flash of worry on Val's face was the thing that made Blaze stop in his tracks.

Val never showed any other emotion that she would consider a weakness. Just the fact that she showed this much was *alarming*.

"Could the others from the Inner Circle have it?" Blaze asked, but Val was already moving down the stairs.

Blaze cursed, rushing after her.

Without knocking, Val burst into Alecto's room to find her sitting on her windowsill, a script of *Carmen* resting on her knees.

Alecto removed the earbuds, surely ones she got from the mortal world, and asked, "Do you mind?"

"Did you take the Book?"

"No, I did not."

"Son of a bitch," Val cursed.

Alecto let her legs down. "What the fuck is going on?"

Blaze didn't miss the fact that she hadn't glanced his way, as if he once again didn't even exist.

He couldn't be mad about it. This was what he wanted.

But it still stung.

"The Book is gone," Val hissed, brushing a hand over her hair. "It's not in the basement anymore, and I can't find it anywhere in the House."

"Maybe Andro or Jolene?" Alecto asked.

"No, I've asked them. I've also performed a locator spell, and nothing is showing up in the House."

Blaze rubbed his face. "Someone got past our protection enchants."

Oh, fuck.

"We're going to have to call a meeting with the rest of the House," Val announced after a moment. "Meet me in the living room in ten. Blaze, get Andro and Jolene."

With that, she was out of the room.

Blaze didn't linger, following her without a glance at Alecto.

He rushed down the corridor and swung open the door to Jolene's room to find her lying on the floor, writing.

Before she could ask a question, Blaze blurted out, "Someone stole the fucking Book. Meeting in ten."

"Wait—" Jolene called after him, but Blaze didn't stop rushing down the corridor to Andro's room.

He found his best friend straddling Gael in his bed.

"Do you mind?" Andro asked.

"Our Book is gone," Blaze snapped. "You'll have time to fuck around when we find it. Meeting in ten."

Andro immediately jumped off his bed.

"It's impossible," he said. "I didn't feel anything trying to mess with our wards. Did you?"

Blaze raked a hand through his hair, then shook his head. "Let's move," he urged, and then he was rushing down the stairs to the first floor, where the rest of the House was already gathering.

Once the Inner Circle were all there, they waited for a few more moments for the rest of the House to come.

Twelve heads were sitting in the room, all their eyes wide with fear and worry.

Someone was missing though.

"Val…" Blaze said, scanning the room.

"I know," Val gritted through clenched teeth. Blaze's heart sunk. "Rogue is gone."

54

They were fucked.

Royally.

"When was the last time any of you saw Rogue?" Val demanded.

Nobody had seen him since yesterday morning.

"Fantastic," Alecto murmured. "Fucking phenomenal."

"Have any of you been approached by other Houses?" Blaze asked.

With his arms crossed over his chest, he looked intimidating, black eyes shooting daggers. The real Blaze had shown up, finally.

Alecto scanned the students. Nobody wanted to admit to anything.

It was unlikely that other Houses tried to recruit the Snakes. Most of their politics depended on the House's legacy, so there was no point in betrayal.

They should have known it would be the fucking demon who was fucking them over. The only question was *why*?

Demons couldn't lie. Rogue said that he was bound to them, that he couldn't hurt them. Something wasn't making sense.

"Okay, listen the fuck up," Val snapped. "I want every single one of you working on the protection of our assets. I don't care how you divide, but I want at least five people watching the wards at all times so that nothing comes through, or nothing more disappears. You hear me?"

There were nods of acknowledgment, and then the Snakes rose to their feet.

"Inner Circle, the basement, now." Val didn't wait for them to say anything, rushing through the archway, down to the basement.

Alecto and the rest followed. Once they were downstairs, all Hel broke loose.

"I fucking told you summoning a demon would come to bite us in the ass," Andro snapped at Val, his color deepening.

"I never summoned a fucking demon!" Val screamed back at him. "And don't you fucking blame everything on me, Alessandro! You were involved every step of the way. It's not like you didn't have a choice or a fucking voice!"

Andro growled, but Jolene beat him to it.

"Yes, we do have voices, and we're free to give you our opinions," she spat, "but nothing means shit because it's not a fucking democracy. You've said it yourself, time and time again—your word is the last, so you know, this is your fucking fault, Val. Because you bit off more than you could chew!"

Val's shoulders squared as she gritted her teeth.

"And where the fuck do you think you would be if it weren't for me and my plans?" Val responded, fury barely controlled within her voice. "Would you be in the Inner Circle, you think? Would you be at the fucking top of the food chain if it weren't for me and my wicked, horrible plans? I don't think so. Despite the name you carry, you're fucking spineless."

They all fell silent for a moment, breathing heavily.

Alecto cleared her throat before speaking. "Listen. Andro and Jolene are right." Four pairs of eyes snapped to her. "Val is a fucking dictator. No point in denying it."

"Thanks so much," Val snorted.

Alecto shot her a glare. "But she's also right. Because if she wasn't the one to force us to be who we are, however fucked up that might be, we wouldn't be where we are. At the top of the fucking food chain."

They all stood in silence once more, considering Alecto's words.

"We've made enemies," Alecto added after a moment. "If we fight, they will win."

"She's right," Blaze chimed in, but Alecto refused to look his way. "Someone has our Book. If they find a way to open it, they'll have centuries of spells and secrets of the Snakes that will easily help them destroy the House once and for all."

"Who would have been able to pull off something like that?" Jolene asked, spreading her arms. "Rogue clearly wasn't working alone, right?"

Val paced back and forth, a joint already perched between her fingers, burning.

"Who do demons work for?" Blaze mused. "The Imp Queen."

Val stopped. "It was not the Imp Queen."

"How can you be so sure?" Andro asked. "If the Imp Queen is behind this, we might as well just give up."

"It was *not* the Imp Queen," Val snapped before returning to pacing once more. "She has no interest in seeing the House of Snakes fall."

"How do you know that?" Alecto asked.

"Val knows the Imp Queen intimately," Blaze supplied.

Alecto, Jolene, and Andro stared at Val, waiting for an explanation. But Val didn't offer them one, ignoring them for another heartbeat.

"Someone's probably fucked with the guardian spell," Val said suddenly. She whirled, her eyes wild. "We called for a Guardian. A demon showed up. I thought it was just because we used blood magic to summon a creature, and the spell for calling a demon and a Guardian is very similar. But—"

"You think someone interfered with the spell and that they were the ones pulling the strings all this time?" Alecto interrupted.

The thought alone was terrifying. But it was a smart move, the only way to infiltrate another House.

"Fucking Hel," Jolene breathed out the words. She rubbed her temples. "Fucking Hel, we're fucking idiots."

Alecto snorted a laugh.

"I warned you not to have him in all the meetings," Andro said, crossing his arms. Val glared at him, and that seemed to shut him up from saying anything else on the topic of *I told you so*.

"We need to find him," Val said suddenly. "Once we find him, hopefully we can get the information out of him."

"How? By asking nicely?" Jolene asked.

"By torturing it out of him."

Alecto's mouth fell open. She wasn't going to ask how Val was planning on doing that.

One step at a time.

"Prepare the circle," Val instructed. "We're going to perform the locator spell."

"You have his blood?" Blaze asked as he walked around to the cupboard.

Val shoved a hand down her oversized shirt and dragged up a chain up with a small vial attached to it. There was something black inside.

"I have his blood, his nails, his hair, and even his fucking tooth," Val said.

"Alarming," Andro mused, helping Jolene draw the chalk circle on the floor. "But I suppose I'm grateful that you're a psychopath at times like these."

Alecto rolled her eyes as she took the bronze bowl from Blaze's hands, still avoiding looking at him, and placed it in the middle of the almost finished circle.

She plucked the herbs and dropped them inside, then added the black salt and the feather of a Hellbate as well. Then, she extended a hand towards Val. Val dropped the vial in her palm, and Alecto poured the blood over the other ingredients.

Alecto took her place around the circle, linking her fingers with Jolene and Blaze on either side of her.

"*Locarccio prioti*," they all chanted in unison, and Alecto closed her eyes.

She conjured Rogue's face in her mind, tracing the lines of his body, his outfit as accurately as she could remember.

When the smell of burning weeds reached her nose, Alecto opened her eyes to see the flame in the bowl. After a moment, it died down, expelling a gulp of smoke into the air. In the ball of smoke, an image of Rogue walking through the woods appeared.

He was rushing, looking around him nervously, and the Book was tucked neatly underneath his armpit. At first, Alecto couldn't recognize the forest around him, but then the old ruins emerged.

"He's meeting someone at the ruins," Jolene observed.

The smoke swirled. Rogue's figure stayed clear while everything else blurred.

"What the fuck…" Blaze trailed off as the smoke parted, and now Rogue was moving through the long corridor in the Dean's building.

Val cursed under her breath.

The smoke shifted once more, revealing Rogue striding down the hill to the Blood Lake, their Book tucked under his arm.

"Motherfucker," Alecto scoffed. "He knew we would perform the locator spell. They want us to split up."

"We can't do that," Andro blurted out. "We split up, and we're going to be fucked."

They exchanged glances, letting their hands fall to their sides.

"We go together and swipe every location," Val said. "One by one."

They were going to lose time this way. It might be too late if they got unlucky.

By the time they reached him, he might be gone. And the Book with him.

"Have you tried tracking the Book?" Alecto asked. "Maybe it will give a precise location."

"It doesn't show up at all," Val said, shaking her head. "I've tried."

Only one way to go then. "Okay, where do we start? I think the Blood Lake is the least possible location."

"I agree." Jolene nodded.

"First, we go to the ruins," Val said, "then we move to the Dean's building. If that doesn't work, we'll head to the Blood Lake and hope that the sirens got to Rogue before we did. For his own sake."

55

The moment they stepped foot in the Blessed Forest, the smell of magic hit Alecto's nostrils.

It was thick and sickly sweet, not the magic from the wards around the ruins that still lingered since the Equinox.

Silently, the five of them made their way through the dark forest, the dried leaves and forest moss crunching under their feet. Alecto found it hard to focus on anything with the thoughts swimming in her head.

The moment she had a grasp on one thought, it slipped away, melting with the rest of the chaos. It had been a hard night, one she hadn't anticipated.

And maybe it was her fault.

If she had listened to her gut about Rogue, if she had paid him more attention in the last three months, then maybe right now they would be in a very different place.

If she hadn't lowered her defenses, then maybe she wouldn't have had her soul shattered by the devil walking a few steps away from her.

Stupid, stupid bitch.

When the ruins emerged in front of them, the remnants of the last revel still lingering around the perimeter until next year, they came to a stop.

Alecto strained her ears for any sounds. And soon enough, there was a rustle of leaves. A movement flashed between the walls of the ruins, a laugh following.

"Here for your Book?" Rogue teased, appearing from behind the wall.

"Give it back nicely," Val warned, "or I'll get it from your dead hands."

"I greatly doubt that. None of you even know how to kill a demon." He laughed. "You don't know shit about demons at all. That's why it was so easy to trick you."

Val muttered a chant under her breath and threw her palm towards Rogue, but he slipped away back into the darkness and disappeared out of their sight.

"Get him!" Val shouted, taking off after him.

Blaze followed her. Jolene and Andro went to the left, rounding the ruins from that side, and Alecto moved to the right.

She ran around the walls, going over the spells that would help her deal with Rogue.

She could freeze him, trap him, turn him into stone…

A body emerged in front of her from out of nowhere, and Alecto couldn't stop herself from hitting the hard chest. Her first thought was that it was Rogue.

But the chest wasn't covered in a cotton T-shirt but rather a smooth, skin-like material.

And it reeked like death and…rotten flesh. Alecto gagged as she pushed herself away.

When she lifted her eyes up, she was met with white pupilless eyes that froze the blood in her veins.

56

Alecto's scream pierced the night.

Blaze came to a stop abruptly, his heart hammering so hard in his ears, at first he didn't hear Val shouting at him.

"Blaze, let's move!" Val screamed, a few steps ahead of him. "Rogue just went into the tower. We have to get the Book!"

"And leave her to whatever happened there?"

Val ran up to him, tugging on his hand as she dragged him forwards. "We don't have the time. If anyone can survive anything, it's Alecto fucking Black. The Book!"

Blaze wrenched his arm out of Val's grip just in time for Andro and Jolene to run up to them from the side.

"Alecto's not with you?" Blaze asked.

"We thought she went with you," Andro said. "Do you know where Rogue is?"

"Yes!" Val said, exasperated. "In the tower. We need to go."

"I'm not leaving Alecto behind!" Jolene snapped.

"Andro, go with Val to get the Book," Blaze said. "Jolene, we go find Alecto."

Blaze didn't wait for Val to bark orders at him. He jogged back towards the ruins, going around the side where he thought the scream came from.

When he rounded the wall, he stopped in his tracks, and Jolene walked in his back.

"What's…" Jolene trailed off as she walked around him and saw the three creatures backing Alecto into the corner. "What the fuck?"

Blaze shook his head. He didn't know in the dark. It could have been anyone, anything.

But whatever it was, it wasn't anything good.

Alecto looked at them, and blinked.

That was enough for the creatures to notice them as well. Their necks turned with loud cracks as if their bones were shifting.

"You know any good spells that would kill these motherfuckers?" Alecto asked, her voice trembling.

"*Grothics,*" Jolene whispered. Blaze threw her a glance. He didn't think that was a spell. "The creatures are Grothics, from the Cursed Forest. They —they feed on witches' souls."

Another creature lured from the Cursed Forest. It couldn't be a coincidence.

Someone was really trying to take out the Snakes.

The creatures craned their necks, sniffing the air, and then one took a step towards Blaze and Jolene.

"You know what will stop them?" Blaze asked, keeping his voice low.

Jolene nibbled on her lip. "Well, hmm…the only way to kill them is with a witch's athame doused in mortal blood."

Blaze pinched the bridge of his nose.

Just fucking great.

Another creature shifted towards them, coming closer.

"No sudden movements," Jolene warned, loud enough that Blaze hoped Alecto could hear. "It'll agitate them."

"They look agitated as it is to me," Alecto hissed.

"It can get worse," Jolene singsonged slowly.

They needed to do something.

"What weakens them?" Blaze asked again. "Light? Flames? *Anything?*"

Jolene's eyes locked with his, and he knew the answer before she even said it out loud.

"I don't know," she admitted. "I suggest we throw everything we have at them."

"And see if anything sticks. Fucking fantastic."

One of the creatures advanced on Blaze, its long legs moving so fast it only took one blink, and then it was towering over Blaze, opening its round mouth filled with sharp teeth.

Blaze stumbled backwards, putting distance between him and the creature, but it didn't help. The Grothic was on him.

"Don't look in its eyes!" Jolene's voice came just in time as Grothic brought its face to Blaze's.

He snapped his eyes shut, willing his breathing to be even, and slipped a hand in the pocket of his leather jacket for his bones.

The creature's face was so close that he had to fight the urge to move away, his insides recoiling at the stinking smell of blood and burned flesh.

Grothic released a low growl, and Blaze gripped the bones hard in his palm, muttering a chant under his breath. When he felt his palm warm, he shoved it over the creature's face, the smell of burning flesh intensifying.

The creature shrieked.

The cries of pain were enough to stir the other two Grothics into action, and they shrieked before attacking.

Blaze shoved the burned creature to the side, letting it hit the wall nearby. He caught a glimpse of one of the monsters going after Jolene, but right before its claws made it to her, Jolene muttered a spell and froze it.

Alecto cried out. When Blaze found her backed in the corner by the remaining beast, there was a slash in her forearm, bleeding heavily.

To Blaze's surprise, the Grothic hissed, retreating as it shook the long arm whose claw dug into Alecto.

Oh, fuck. Of course.

"Jolene, you have your athame with you by any chance?" Blaze asked.

Jolene lifted her pleated skirt to reveal the ritual blade sheathed to her thigh.

"Good girl," Blaze remarked, throwing a glance at the Grothic whose face he burned. It still wailed in pain, trying to scramble to its feet. "Here is what we'll do. I'll draw the attention of the last monster while you'll get to Alecto and rub her blood over the blade. You follow me?"

Jolene looked at him for a moment before realization flickered in her face. She nodded.

"Try to stab it before it steals my soul. Deal?" Blaze conjured the bolt of light in his palm.

"If you promise to be a good boy."

Blaze snorted and threw the ball of light at the creature, drawing its rage to himself.

"I'm always a good boy."

The Grothic growled and advanced towards him, baring its sharp teeth. Blaze barely managed to move away from its path.

He hit the wall, pushed off it, and whirled around to find the creature advancing towards him once more.

The back of his head hit the hard stone as the creature pushed him against the wall, and Blaze closed his eyes.

"Don't rush," he called. "Take your time, ladies. I'll just wait here."

The creature hissed again, but its grip loosened.

And then it was gone.

Blaze opened his eyes to find the creature slumped at his feet, a dagger with a ruby-encrusted handle stuck in its back.

As his gaze moved up, he met Alecto's eyes.

"You okay?" he asked.

She just nodded, pulling the dagger out of the creature.

"Should we finish the others?" she asked.

"Just to be safe," said Jolene.

They worked fast and in silence.

When all three bodies were dead and stacked together, they turned to get back to the tower where Val and Andro hopefully had Rogue cornered.

When they emerged from around the corner, they found Val and Andro both standing by the door to the tower, pacing.

"What's the matter?" Jolene asked.

Val whirled. "The fucking door won't open! The fucking riddle is impossible to solve. I've never heard of shit like that in my life!"

Blaze narrowed his gaze, walking up to the face in the door.

"Door, are you being rather sinister tonight?" he asked.

The door chuckled, its large lips curling into a grin.

"It starts with *T* and ends with *K*, and if you ever get in its way, you're off to meet a tragic end," it croaked, amused.

Blaze turned to the rest of the group.

"I have no fucking idea what this shit means," he said. "It must be something very old."

"Wouldn't there be a spell to make the door open without the riddle?" Val growled. "I bet you the Book has it!"

Jolene rolled her eyes. "Yeah, and the Book is on the other side of the door!"

Alecto walked up to the door, her wounded arm pressed to her chest. "A truck."

The door chuckled, and the latch opened, revealing the stone-carved corridor of the tower leading up to the round stairs.

"What?" Andro asked, his eyes wide. "What the fuck is a *truck*?"

Alecto glanced at them through her shoulder. "It's a mortal world thing."

They exchanged glances. How the Hel did the door come up with a mortal world riddle? But there was no time for details like that.

They made their way up the stairs, Val and Blaze at the front, the others close behind them. When they finally reached the overlook, Rogue was sprawled on the chaise, their Book resting in his lap.

Still closed.

"You're still alive," he observed, eyeing them with a closed-off expression. "Took you long enough though."

"You were the one who lured the Hellbates to the House?" Blaze asked.

Rogue's lips curled into a crooked smile, but he didn't say anything.

"No, he wasn't," Val answered for him. Her eyes were sharp as daggers as she glared at Rogue. "Who summoned you here?"

No answer.

Val took a step closer. "Who the fuck summoned you here?"

Rogue laughed, dropping an ankle over his knee.

"Oh, Valeria," he said, shaking his head. "I can't tell you that. It would ruin the surprise. If you were smarter, you'd figure that out for yourself."

Blaze's blood boiled.

"You are truly the worst House of all," Rogue mused. "And not because you're terrible and with no sense of shame or remorse, but also because you're completely blinded by your own arrogance."

"Fuck off," Andro said.

Rogue tossed the Book aside, leaning forwards as he braced his elbows on his knees, amber gaze flickering.

"I showed up on your doorstep, and all it took to convince you that I was on your side was my word," he said. "You haven't even considered that someone could have messed with your spell because who would dare mess with the House of Snakes, right?"

"Demons can't lie," Val gritted out.

"No, we can't," Rogue agreed. "But we can evade the truth and bend it to our will."

"Give us the damn Book."

"Why don't you come and get it?"

As if it was that easy.

Rogue was a demon, and he was right about one thing—none of them bothered to find out how to deal with a demon who *wasn't* on their side.

One wrong move and this would end bad.

"Yeah, thought so." Rogue chuckled. He leaned back against the chaise, spreading his arms over the length of it. "I'm not even sure I can say it was worth the trip all the way from Hel to sabotage your House. I was told you'd be a real challenge."

"Who told you that?" Alecto asked. "We will make sure they pay for your trouble."

"*You*," Rogue said, ignoring her words. He wet his lips, eyeing Alecto, and Blaze had a sudden urge to break his face. "How would you feel about immortality?"

"What?"

"Your half-mortal soul for eternal life. How's that sound?"

"Are you seriously making a bargain right now?" Alecto asked, her eyebrows rising. "I'm not going to sell my soul."

Rogue pouted. "What a shame. Half-mortal souls are rare. It would have been a sweet deal."

"Now's not the time to search for a bride, Rogue," Val drawled, taking another step closer. Rogue's attention landed on her again. "How about we make a deal instead?"

"I don't want your soul, Valeria. It's been already promised to someone else. And let me tell you, I have no interest in fighting her."

Blaze's heart hammered as the things clicked into place. That was how Val knew the Imp Queen. She had made a deal before.

He knew Val was crazy. They all did. But this was crazy even for her.

"My deal is simpler," Val continued. "You tell us who controls you, and I'll let you live."

"Try me, Valeria."

"Suit yourself," Val said and extended a hand towards Rogue, a black tourmaline resting on her palm, and then she chanted, "*Exission*."

Blaze's muscles seized.

But nothing happened.

Val's hand wavered, and words died in her throat as Rogue barked a laugh. "Nice try."

"I don't…" Val trailed off, and it was the first time Blaze, and probably all of them, had seen her confused. "It's supposed to banish you back to Hel!"

Rogue grinned once more.

If the spell didn't work, it was either because Val didn't have the right spell or—

"He's not here," Alecto snapped. "It's a fucking astral projection."

Alecto moved forwards, reaching towards Rogue, but he flickered in and out. And then he was gone, the Book with him.

"Motherfucker." Val headed towards the stairs. "He fucking wasted our time. Move!"

When they reached the bottom of the stairs, the door opened, and five dark silhouettes greeted them with low growls.

"Well, just fucking fantastic," Alecto said. "If we keep this up, I'll bleed out dry before the night even ends."

57

The Dean's building was dead quiet.

Only a few dimmed orbs floated around the ceiling, lighting up the corridor as they made their way deeper into the building.

Blaze reeked of blood and burned flesh. The smell was so potent it seemed as if it was lodged in his nostrils permanently.

"I smell like those fucking creatures," Jolene muttered, wrinkling her nose as she sniffed the arm of her sweater. "Rotten fish and lake mud. I'm going to need to burn my clothes."

"What?" Alecto asked. "They smell like death and rotten flesh to me."

"No, they reeked of rusted metal and something sickly acidic like vomit," Andro said. "What did it smell to you?" Andro asked, looking at Blaze.

"*Shut up*," Val snapped at them, and they fell silent.

They reached the end of the main corridor, where the path was divided into three.

"Where are we looking?" Andro peeked through the windows in the doors nearby.

"Everywhere," Val growled. She was clearly not happy about the prospect of having to scout the whole perimeter.

If Rogue was even here and not his astral projection, stalling them.

"We'll need to split up," Alecto said. She looked down the two corridors going to the east and west wings and then glared up to the stairs that led to the Dean's office. "We've already wasted tons of time."

"Yeah, and look what happened when we didn't stick together." Andro gestured at her wounded arm that Jolene had wrapped with a makeshift bandage.

Blaze's eyes lingered over the bloodied material. He didn't like the idea of going their separate ways.

He didn't like the idea of leaving Alecto, even if just for a moment.

He might have pushed her away, but he wasn't about to let her get hurt or worse.

Someone was out for their blood tonight, and witches never played nice.

"We split up then," Val said. "Blaze—"

"Andro, you go with Val and take the east wing," Blaze interrupted Val, not even sparing her a glance. "Jolene and Alecto with me, we take the west. Meet at the Dean's office after."

Val glared at Blaze, but nobody argued as they moved out in different directions.

Three of them checked every door to the teachers' offices and class-rooms, just in case there was something hidden under the spell.

But there didn't seem to be anything.

When they reached the end of the corridor, only one door was left, next to the massive glass shelf that housed all the trophies the students had won.

Alecto wandered off to the shelf, so Blaze went to check the last door. It was a utility closet with shelves lined with tools and cleaning supplies.

Blaze sighed, closing the door shut.

"Nothing," he said to the girls.

He could only hope that Val and Andro were luckier.

Blaze was about to walk back, but the girls didn't seem to have heard him. Alecto stared at something inside the glass shelving unit. Jolene stood beside her.

"What's the matter?" Blaze asked. "It's not the time to be checking out Venefica's history."

He stopped behind Alecto, following her gaze to the black-and-white memory orb of his father, about Blaze's age, and a girl next to him.

They both wore elaborate gowns, and there were matching crowns resting on their brows. It was probably taken at the Beltane Ball when his father was graduating.

He didn't recognize the woman pressed close to his father's side, and he'd never seen the relaxed and happy expression on Galliermo's face.

"What are you looking at?" he asked. "We don't have the time!"

"She was telling the truth," Alecto said. "That bitch wasn't lying."

"Alecto, who do you mean?" Jolene asked gently.

Alecto shook her head, squaring her shoulders.

"What are you talking about?" Blaze asked, looking back at the corridor where they came from. "You're interested in my father all of a sudden, Black?"

Alecto whirled on her heel. "Did you know about it?"

"For fuck's sake, I don't know what you are even talking about. What am I supposed to know?"

"This woman." Alecto pointed at the memory orb. Blaze eyed the blonde woman whose smile was wide and dazzling, long white hair waving down her shoulder like a waterfall. "This woman is my mother."

Alecto's mother was a mortal. There was no chance that Galliermo would be standing with her in that memory orb.

They looked intimate. Definitely intimate.

This couldn't be.

Galliermo hated mortals. He hated Alecto for being half-mortal—

"Son of a bitch," Blaze cursed.

"You didn't know your father dated my mother at Venefica back in the day?" Alecto asked, her voice filled with fury, but there was a line between her eyebrows as she eyed Blaze. "You know what, never mind. I don't care."

Before Blaze could say anything, Alecto whirled and walked away from them.

"Where the fuck are you going?" Blaze shouted, following her as she walked away from the main corridor. "We're not supposed to split up."

"I need to fucking pee," Alecto snapped back. "Are you going to follow me into the bathroom now? Why don't you fuck right off, Leveau!"

Blaze stopped abruptly, anger simmering in his chest.

Alecto flipped him off and pushed the door to the bathroom open with her shoulder.

"I don't know what's been going on between you two," Jolene said, coming to stand at Blaze's side. "But I'm pretty sure it's your fault."

He couldn't argue.

Minutes passed as Jolene and Blaze waited for Alecto, but she didn't come out.

"I'm gonna check on her," Jolene said, biting the inside of her cheek.

Blaze leaned against the wall as Jolene went into the bathroom. After a moment, the door swung open, Jolene's face pale.

She didn't need to say anything.

Alecto was gone.

A string of whistles came from the main hall, followed by a mocking laugh.

"Rogue's here," Blaze said, and then both were running back.

Blaze almost ran straight into Andro once they reached the main foyer.

"You heard that?" Andro asked. "Where did it come from? Where's Alecto?"

Blaze shook his head. "Gone."

"For fuck's sake, how can you lose a girl like that?" Val said. "You were supposed to stick together."

Blaze clenched his jaw so tight it hurt but didn't say anything.

Another laugh came, and their heads snapped to the stairs.

"He's in the Dean's office," Jolene said, and she didn't even wait for the rest of them, running up the stairs two at the time.

They followed her.

Nobody was in the Dean's reception, and the door to the office was wide open, dim light coming from inside.

Val took a step forwards, but Blaze yanked her back.

"You have a spell that can banish him?" he asked, keeping his voice low. Val nodded. "And he doesn't know it because it was a projection back in the tower. We have the upper hand then."

"Yes," Val breathed out. "But I don't want him banished. I want him chained in our basement. If we banish him, we don't find out who the fuck messed with us."

Blaze glared at her for a moment, wanting to argue that catching a demon was not smart.

But Val was right.

They needed to know who was after them.

When they entered the office, Rogue occupied the Dean's chair, his legs resting on the desk, crossed over the ankles.

Alecto wasn't with him.

"Wonderful," Rogue said, grinning. "Everything is going according to the plan, I see."

"Where did you take Alecto?" Blaze gritted out.

"I didn't lay a finger on Black."

Fucking bastard.

Someone else was there with them.

"Where's the Book?" Val asked.

Rogue opened a drawer, lifting their Book and tossing it on the desk.

"Where is Alecto then?" Andro asked.

"I'll give you your Book back," Rogue said. "Well, I'm not going to give it to you, but I'll tell you where it is."

Son of a bitch.

"This is another projection," Blaze said. "Fuck him, let's go to the Blood Lake."

Rogue didn't seem to be worried about them figuring out that detail. His smile didn't waver.

"Wait," Val said, gripping Blaze's forearm. She then jerked her chin at Rogue. "Where is the Book?"

"So, you want the Book more than you want your Liaison?"

Blaze clenched his jaw. Rogue chuckled.

"Answer me," he urged. "We don't have all night."

A beat of silence passed amongst them, and they exchanged a glance.

It was an impossible question to answer because they cared about both.

They had to.

But right about then, Blaze gave fewer and fewer fucks about the Book.

"Is that it?" Blaze challenged him. "Is that your game then? Making us choose so either way we lose?"

Rogue shrugged, amusement dancing in his eyes. "Life is always about choice. You always have to give something to gain something. Sacrifice something to win something. Your kind, out of all, should know better than anyone about the balance of nature. Everything has a cost."

"What do you want then?" Jolene asked. "No, not you. What do the people who summoned you want? At least if you're not gonna tell us who they are, tell us what they want."

"Isn't it clear already? They want the House of Snakes to be no more."

So, it wasn't just about the Game then.

It was about completely ruining their House, removing the Snakes once and for all.

"That's ambitious," Blaze observed.

Rogue cracked his neck. "Maybe it is. Maybe it isn't. I'm not here to judge." He glanced at the clock on the wall. "What will your decision be then? Alecto Black or the Book?"

"Both," Jolene snarled.

Rogue tsked. "One or the other. Tick, tock." When none of them answered, Rogue sighed. "All right then, I see you need a moment to think. I'll leave you to it."

Before they managed a reply, both Rogue and the Book evaporated.

Only a burned slice of paper remained, its edges still smoldering.

"Fuck," Blaze growled. "Motherfuckers. Which House has that many fucking resources?"

Val walked over to the desk, picking up the paper and killing the embers.

"It's two locations here," she said, eyes still on the paper in her hands. "The Book is hidden in the park, under the statue of the Gods where all five paths meet. There is even a spell here that will break the wards they placed on the Book."

"Okay," Andro said. "And where is Alecto?"

"She's at the Blood Lake. By the main pier."

"Who's gonna stop us from getting both?" Jolene asked. "We can get the Book and then Alecto, or get Alecto and then the Book."

Val met her gaze, her lips pressed into a thin line. "We only have thirty minutes."

"What?" Andro plucked the paper out of Val's hands, scanning the text. "Motherfuckers."

Half an hour.

Half an hour was not enough to get to the park and break the spells. But if they went for Alecto, they risked losing the Book and the legacy of their House.

The history, the spells, the secrets that could destroy families.

From the pained expressions on everyone's faces, Blaze knew the right thing to do. Which path any of them were expected to take.

Because the House was above everything.

Even its members.

Val's voice was a whisper. "You know what we have to do."

58

Before Alecto even opened her eyes, she knew there was something wrong.

Her head was splitting, part of her face in pain, lip throbbing. And then there was the smell of damp weed and water wedged—

Alecto's eyes opened to the dark night sky above her, stars hidden behind heavy clouds. Thunder rumbled in the distance.

She tried getting up, but her limbs weren't responding, lazy and heavy. *Restricted.*

"What the fuck?" she muttered, lifting her head just to lean it back because it was too damn hard.

"Rise and shine, bitch." A familiar voice came from somewhere close.

This time, Alecto managed to lift her head and keep it up long enough to see what was going on around her.

She was in a small boat, perched on the shore of the Blood Lake. Matias and Gabe stood at the foot of the boat.

"I was getting worried you were going to miss all the fun," Gabe said.

"Yeah," Matias muttered. "It would have been so upsetting if you'd died in your sleep. After all this trouble."

Bile rose up to her throat. Memories of being back in the Dean's building, walking into the bathroom…

She remembered going over to the sink, and then there was a hand over her mouth, and everything went black…

Fuck.

"What the fuck do you think you're doing?" Alecto croaked.

She tried to clear her throat, but it was too painful, and she started coughing.

"What does it look like we're doing, sweetheart?" Gabe cocked a brow. "It's time to teach the Snakes a lesson. They won't rule for much longer."

"You fucking idiots. Killing me is not going to ruin the Snakes."

Matias chuckled. "You're right. It's not. But it's just the start, and oh, you better believe we have things much worse than this planned for your House."

"Fuck you." She wiggled her arms and legs.

They tied her real good, she couldn't wrench free, and there was no chance to reach her bones. If she even still had them.

Panic was threatening to take over, so Alecto closed her eyes and breathed through her nose. She could find a way. She *would* find a way.

It was dangerous, but some part of her hoped that the Snakes would notice her missing and that they would come for her. She was sure they already knew. Jolene and Blaze must have realized she was gone when she didn't come back from the bathroom.

Would they come for her? Would they figure out where she was before the Tigers pulled whatever the fuck they had planned?

She needed to buy herself some time.

"You know," she said, managing to finally scramble into a sitting position, "it's against the rules of the Game to kill another member of a rival House in such an open way. You won't win the Game. You will simply win yourself another suspension."

Gabe and Matias exchanged glances, smirks cracking on their faces.

Right at that moment, Alecto was faced with the terrible truth of how poorly she'd chosen her lovers. Three men she'd had sex with had tried to kill her in one way or another. This was a real wake-up call.

Blaze was right.

"I wouldn't be so sure of that if I were you," Gabe said. "Did you really think last year's incident with the Rats was not carefully planned? They knew exactly what they were doing when they set those first years up to die.

No death on campus is ever a fucking accident. It's always just a well-calculated and planned execution that makes it look that way."

"She's a half breed, did you forget?" Matias crossed his arms over his chest, his jaw working a piece of gum. "She doesn't think the same way we do. Lacking the killer instinct and shit."

"Right. I keep forgetting with that tight ass and legs for days that she's only just a *half*." His eyes flashed on her, and Alecto recoiled inside. "At least you were lucky enough to get the good genes from the witch side of your family."

"Yeah, nothing worse than an ugly witch." Matias *literally* shivered.

What an arrogant prick.

Alecto glanced at the hill stretching behind their backs, stopping at the very top of it where the campus ground started. The Dean's building wasn't far.

Maybe they weren't coming after her.

"Don't look for your friends," Gabe said, glancing down at his watch. "If they'd chosen to come after you, they'd already be here."

"Chosen?"

"Yeah, we gave them a choice," Matias said, beaming. "They can either save you or the Book." He looked at Gabe's watch and tsked. "Guessing from the time, it's clear that your Inner Circle left you to die."

They both laughed as if it was the funniest thing in the world.

Alecto swallowed. Her throat prickled with needles. She had to bite her tongue to not let herself fall apart.

Of course they chose the Book. It was the smart thing to do. The clever choice. A witch could be replaced, even the one who was legacy.

The Book, however, could not.

"I say we end this sooner," Gabe said. "Clearly, they're not coming. We might make it in time to see them ripped into shreds by Grothics if we get rid of her now."

Fear rolled down her spine. She once again tried her restrains, the ropes chafing her naked skin.

Fuck, fuck, FUCK.

"Of you go, pretty witch," Gabe said. "You were a nice fuck; I'll give you that. Tight, pretty to look at. I'm almost sad we gotta get rid of you."

Matias laughed, and the boat shifted as Gabe pushed it into the lake.

A scream lodged in Alecto's throat, but she bit her lip. She wasn't going to give them the satisfaction of seeing her scream with fear and beg for her life.

She'd rather die.

Which she probably would.

Alecto's heart raced as the boat floated further from the coast. She stayed sitting in the middle of the floor, but it wouldn't help her once the creatures of Blood Lake smelled her blood.

And they would smell it. Soon.

Alecto bit her lip, a whimper escaping as the realization that this was the end hit her. The view of the coast became blurry, and she blinked hard, letting the tears fall.

For a moment, she just lolled on the water. Her mind was becoming heavier with each inch she floated further away from the coast.

There was a swish of water that snapped Alecto out of her trance, and she fought to keep her mind clear as she looked around. Another swish, the water moving a few feet away from where her boat was.

"Whooo," Gabe hollered. "Who do you think came first for you, Black? The sirens or the blood serpents?"

"If I were you, I'd hope it's the sirens," Matias called. "At least they'll make you imagine you were on the beach as they devoured you."

Their laughter filled the air.

Another swish of water, this time closer. Alecto strained her eyes to see which of the many horrible creatures living in the Blood Lake it was. But the water stayed silent.

She whirled her head to the other side, but something caught her eye at the foot of the boat. Slowly, with her heart hammering in her throat, Alecto turned to meet two pairs of lime-green eyes staring at her.

A breath hitched in her throat.

Out of all the creatures, it just had to be the Water Bride that came for Alecto first.

Alecto didn't dare even breathe as the creature rose from the water, its long white hair reaching all the way to its lean waist. The wet piece of ruined material that barely covered its ebony skin hung tightly around its curves.

Cold sweat broke over Alecto's skin as she let her eyes roam the creature's face. Recognition hit her.

"Genevieve," Alecto's voice was a whisper.

The Water Bride didn't bristle, didn't even react at the name she once carried as her own. Of course, once the witch was turned into a Water Bride, they had no memories of their life before death.

Alecto swallowed panic, together with all the other emotions that were not going to help her survive, and stared back at the girl in front of her.

This was her future if she didn't find a way to escape the fucking boat.

"Lucky you, half breed!" Matias called again. "It seems as if you'll be roaming the waters of the Blood Lake for the rest of eternity."

Another wave of laughter.

The creature's crimson-stained lips curled, revealing a row of black teeth. It hissed, climbing over the edge inside the boat.

Alecto wiggled, pushing herself as far away as possible as the Water Bride braced her palms on the deck, its slender body moving unnaturally fast inside.

There wasn't much space in the boat for Alecto alone. With the Water Bride on deck, there was barely space to breathe. Alecto curled her legs as close to her chest as possible, putting distance between them. But it wasn't much use.

The moment Alecto's back pressed to the front wall of the boat, something poked her in the ass. She scrambled a hand over the sharp object to find a piece of metal wedged in the wood.

Alecto stifled a breath of relief as she positioned her wrists against the sharp edge, hoping the friction was enough to cut through the rope in time.

The Water Bride regarded Alecto, her eyes inspecting every inch of her face, neck, chest, even her arms, and legs. Alecto didn't move anymore, hoping the creature would take its time and not attack her immediately.

When the rope loosened around Alecto's wrist, the creature advanced, bracing its palms over the sides of the boat and caging Alecto beneath it.

The smell of salty water and mud hit Alecto in the face, suffocating her, but she didn't budge.

Just a little bit more, and Alecto's hands would be free.

And what then?

She wasn't sure, but it was better to go down fighting than helpless.

The Water Bride leaned forwards, sniffing the air between them. Its black tongue peeked out, and it dragged it along Alecto's cheek, all the way down to her neck.

Alecto shivered, recoiling at the cool touch of the creature, but she kept her lips shut. The sharp metal cut into her skin as she worked on what she hoped were the last strands of the rope, and that drew the creature's attention.

It backed off, sniffing the air harder, and then cocked its head to the side, regarding Alecto. Its lips peeled back, revealing the sharp teeth, and it hissed into Alecto's face, the smell of mud and weeds so strong Alecto gagged.

Before the Water Bride could sink its teeth in, Alecto's arms were free. She braced her palms against the creature's chest. "*Infernotis.*"

The creature hissed, the smell of burning flesh surrounding them, and then it backed off, falling back into the water over the edge of the boat.

Panting heavily, Alecto whirled to position her legs against the sharp metal thing, which turned out to be a rusted nail sticking out from the wood. She worked quickly to cut through the rope.

Finally, when her legs were free, she got on her knees, looking back at the shore where Gabe and Matias still stood.

"When I get my hands on you both, you'll wish you were never born," she called.

"Good luck with that, sweetheart," Gabe called back.

Alecto sat back on her heels, looking around the calm water. She could jump into the water and swim back to the shore, but with how much blood she had already lost and how much energy she would need for a swim, the creatures could get to her.

And in the water, Alecto wouldn't be able to fight them off. Not when they had all the physical advantages.

She'd have to row the boat into the shore.

With a deep exhale, Alecto lifted her palms over the edges of the boat, hoping that the blood magic she would use for this to work wouldn't set off any of the Dean's alarms.

"*Drusttelio,*" Alecto whispered, her voice unsteady as she conjured an image of her hands turning into oars, slicing the water, and moving the boat forwards.

A moment later, the boat was moving slowly through the water towards the shore.

Closer and closer she was getting. And the moment she stepped foot on dry land, Matias and Gabe would learn once more what happened when you fucked with her.

One lesson was not enough, apparently.

A few feet away from the shore, the boat hit something, the bottom scraping through the obstacle, and then the boat stopped.

Matias and Gabe both laughed as Alecto's heart sank.

She leaned over the edge of the boat to see if she could determine what it was, and immediately froze.

Three pairs of black eyes were staring her from underneath the surface of the lake, pale faces hungry and eager.

"Fuck." Alecto reeled back and plopped on her ass. "*Fuck.*"

The sirens, of course, the fucking sirens. When she was so close.

The water swirled, making the boat rock slightly.

"It looks like you'll die tonight, Black," Matias called. He bumped a shoulder into Gabe's. "Lucky for us."

Witches were cruel and merciless, and if Alecto survived tonight, she'd have to work twice as hard to match them.

The boat rocked again, this time harder, and Alecto grabbed for the sides, hoping she could keep the balance enough for the boat to not tip.

When one of the sirens bashed its tail over the water, swinging it at the boat, Alecto cried out as there was now a hole in the boat, the crimson water pouring inside.

"*Crahsticio!*" A scream came from the shore, and the hole in the boat sealed shut.

Alecto's gaze snapped to the top of the hill, where three familiar figures appeared. She almost cried out of happiness as Blaze, Jolene, and Andro ran down the hill towards Gabe and Matias.

They had come for her in the end.

59

If they'd showed up thirty seconds later, it would have been too late.

Blaze threw himself at Gabe. Gabe's jaw cracked when Blaze's fist collided with the bone.

One punch after another, Blaze swung his fists, not giving Gabe time to draw a breath, let alone counter his attacks.

He was going to kill him.

Then he was going to kill Matias.

And once both were done, Blaze was going to burn the whole House down, every member.

"Blaze!" Andro's voice came from behind him, but he ignored it. "Blaze, get off him!"

A pair of hands hauled Blaze off Gabe's body, and he thrashed against the hold. He whirled, ready to lash out at Andro, but his friend held up a hand.

"You'll kill him before it's time," he said, panting. Blaze regarded the guy on the ground, groaning in pain.

Then, he found Matias a few feet away, in a similar state. Andro's knuckles were raw and bleeding, and that calmed the beast inside Blaze for a moment.

He cleared his throat, and looked to the lake.

Alecto was a few feet away, perched on that damn boat that was third filled with water, staring at them.

There was blood everywhere.

Blaze stormed forwards, but before his feet could even hit the water, both Jolene and Andro grabbed his arm and dragged him back.

"Have you fucking lost your mind?" Andro screamed into his ear. "You have to turn on your fucking brain and start using it!"

Blaze got a hold of himself and the rage that was threatening to suffocate him.

Andro was right.

Blaze yanked his arm away.

"Did you get the Book?" Alecto called, and they all turned to her.

"Val is on it with the rest of the Snakes. Don't worry about it," Andro called back, pacing the shore. "You stupid bitch! You almost died, and what you're concerned about is the Book? Really?!"

Alecto rolled her eyes.

Blaze wasn't sure whether he wanted to laugh or grab her and shake her until she realized the severity of the situation.

Alecto could have died.

The boat rocked again, water around it swirling as heads popped up, one by one.

"We need to get her out, now," Jolene said. "Alecto put up a shield!"

Alecto stared at them for a moment, face blank. Then she blinked, cursed under her breath, and nodded, looking around.

She'd probably forgotten about it in the heat of the moment.

Soon, Alecto pulled up her protective shield, the red tendrils swirling over her skin.

Apparently she had been practicing. Her shield technique was more advanced than any of theirs.

Thanks to me.

Of course, Alecto perfected her shield after he dumped her in the Cursed Forest and left her to die.

The sirens were gathering around the boat, their scaled tails swishing in anticipation.

"Guys," Alecto called, gripping the sides of the boat. "Tell me you know how to get me out. I can't row. They're holding me in place."

"Yes, don't worry," Jolene called. Blaze and Andro looked at her. "I do have a plan. Almost."

"Care to share it with us?" Andro asked, glancing back to where Matias and Gabe lay on the cold ground.

"Fire will annoy them," Jolene said. "It'll keep them away, but it will also piss them off, so we'll have to be very quick and precise."

"Okay," Blaze replied. "I'll keep them at bay with fire. Can you and Andro muster a spell to get the boat to the shore?"

"I don't know about the spell, but how about this?" Andro said, lifting a hand with a band of rope he managed to scrounge from inside the boathouse nearby.

Jolene cracked a smile. "Perfect. We'll just need to make sure the rope gets to Alecto."

"But the sirens are holding the boat in place," Blaze reminded them. "What if you can't move the boat?"

Jolene stayed silent for a moment, then she brushed a hand through her pleated skirt and lifted her chin.

"We'll make them let go," she said.

Blaze smirked at the determination on Jolene's face. He grabbed for his bones, conjuring the fire in his mind.

When the flame flared in his palm, Blaze went to the edge of the lake and threw the first flame at the sirens gathered on the left of Alecto's boat.

The fire died the moment it hit the water, but not before it had the sirens hissing and scattering away. They turned their attention to Blaze, black eyes gleaming with hate.

Blaze didn't waver. He threw one flame after another, targeting every siren's head he could see above the surface.

By his side, Jolene and Andro both worked the rope, letting it float in the air towards Alecto, so she could hold on to it as they towed her to the shore.

When he sent a larger flame towards a group of five sirens climbing over the edge of the boat, the flame caught the boat, setting it on fire.

"Blaze!" Alecto gasped, moving away from the side of the boat, crackling with fire. "Now is not the time to fucking try to kill me again!"

"My bad," Blaze said.

"Again?" Jolene turned to him and the rope she was working on came to an abrupt stop. "What the fuck does she mean by *again*?"

Blaze pushed his tongue into the cheek, glancing at Jolene.

"I thought everyone knew."

"Jolene, help me!" Andro urged, and Jolene returned her attention to the rope.

But from the look that she gave him, Blaze was sure this wasn't the end of it.

The flame was spreading fast, but Jolene and Andro finally managed to get the end of the rope to Alecto.

She scurried forwards and grabbed tight to the rope.

"Pull me in!"

Blaze grabbed for the rope, and with Andro's help, they pulled her in.

"Did they leave?" Alecto asked, her eyes wide.

Just three more feet left. And she'd be safe.

Two more.

The water behind the boat swirled, a dozen heads popping from underneath the surface.

One more foot.

The sirens plunged forwards, hissing as they advanced.

But they were too late.

Alecto's boat hit the shore, and they all rushed towards her to pull her in and far away from the lake.

The sirens stopped, not daring to climb to the shore, and reared back to watch from the water.

Alecto was shivering all over, from the cold and probably from the shock.

"Oh, you're alive," Val's voice came from behind them, and they whirled.

She was jogging down the hill, the Book under her arm.

There was also a battered body dragging after her, heavy iron chains wrapped around its wrists and neck.

It was Jack Riverblood being dragged by the enchanted chains towards them.

"Oh, for fuck's sake," Andro said. "Tell me that's the *real* Book?"

Val snorted. "Yes, it's the real fucking thing, asshole. And I even brought the man behind all of this with me."

When she finally approached them, Blaze noticed the black smears over her face and outfit.

"What happened to you?" Blaze asked, looking her up and down.

"They sent the Grothics," Alecto answered, wrapping her arms around herself. "They never intended for us to get the Book back, did they?"

Val shook her head. "They carefully planned it so that the Inner Circle would be cut tonight. And without the Inner Circle and the Book, the rest of the House would crumble. Isn't that right, Jacky-boy?"

Val flicked her wrist, the chains tugging Jack forwards so hard he lost his footing and fell on his knees.

"Motherfuckers," Andro said.

"Now, the question is—what are we gonna do about it?" Jolene asked, throwing a glance at the other two guys on the ground.

"We have to make sure that the Tigers know they fucked up," Val said. "And we also need to make sure that the other Houses understand what happens when you follow in their footsteps."

"They die," Alecto said, her voice hoarse. "I don't care what we do about the other members or Riverblood. But those two are not leaving here alive."

"I like the way you're thinking, Black," Val said. "I really am glad you're alive."

"I'm glad you're alive too, Lang."

"So," Val said, turning her attention back to Gabe and Matias. "I say we give them the taste of their own medicine."

"I'm in," Jolene agreed.

Andro nodded. "Count me in."

"Let's not make it quick or easy," Blaze added.

Without another word, the girls gathered the rope, and they tied their legs and hands. Alecto even shoved rope into their mouths, just in case they screamed for help.

Then, they dragged them over to the pier, dumping each into a separate boat.

Gabe and Matias were both twice as big as Alecto, so they took up almost all the space in the small boats.

It would make it easier for creatures to devour them.

Then Blaze and Andro pushed the boats into the water, ignoring Gabe and Matias thrashing.

"If you keep moving, the boat will tip," Blaze shouted before curling his fingers into a small wave goodbye as the boat floated further away from the shore.

The sirens were still waiting.

Right then, the thunder rumbled, and the rain broke.

"Oh, the serpents are going to be here soon," Andro said as they gathered at the edge of the lake, watching the boats.

And surely, a few moments later, long thin snakes were making their way over the water.

Val walked over to Jack, still kneeling where she had left him. Not so gently, she fisted his hair in her palm and jerked his head towards the lake.

"We wouldn't want you to miss this, Jacky-boy." Val leaned in to whisper the words into his ear. Jack lifted his eyes to the lake, his jaw tight. "It seems you'll be short two members this year. It's gonna be hard staying in the big four."

Blaze smirked, satisfaction seeping into his bones at the desperation blooming in Jack's eyes.

The House of Tigers was done.

"I saw Genevieve," Alecto said.

Blaze stiffened.

"She's a Water Bride."

For a moment, none of them said anything.

What was there to say, really?

"We couldn't anticipate she was going to kill herself," Val finally said, her voice light. "I'm surprised she chose the Blood Lake to do it though."

"Yeah, why would she want to linger here, so close to the place that ruined her?" Jolene asked, frowning.

"Maybe it was a deliberate choice," Alecto said. "Maybe she did it because she knew she'd get to haunt us while we're here. She sure as fuck almost got to kill me."

"Fascinating, isn't it?" Val shrugged. "Let's remember to never set foot by the lake again."

"You really don't have to tell me that twice," Andro said.

"Let's go," Val urged, starting the climb up the hill back to the campus.

"*No*," Alecto said, her voice cold as a stone. Her eyes were still focused on the boat. "I'm going to see this through." She turned, locking eyes with Blaze. There was nothing but icy rage in them. "Just to make sure they won't survive."

So, they all stayed.

Blaze wanted to reach out and take her hand, linking their fingers together.

But he couldn't. He wasn't sure she'd want that.

He wished he could pull her into his embrace and squeeze her until she knew that she was safe.

He was sure Alecto wouldn't want that.

He had lost the privilege of touching Alecto.

But they had come for her, even if barely.

So, they just stayed, all five of them, hoping that it was enough of a promise to Alecto and each other that they'd come for each other one way or the other.

Even if barely.

60

"Girl, you're battered," Jolene observed as her hand moved to clean the wounds covering Alecto's face.

"You think?"

Jolene cracked a smile, her eyes focused on the nasty cut over Alecto's eyebrow.

"It was Blaze that night at the House of Dragons, wasn't it?" she asked, her voice gentle and soft.

At first, Alecto didn't answer, just stared at the wall behind Jolene's shoulder. It had happened so long ago, it seemed right now. Was there any point in even talking about it anymore?

But her friend was waiting for an answer.

With a sigh, Alecto said, "Yeah. That was on him."

"Why didn't you say something?" Jolene demanded, suddenly angry. Her hand dropped from Alecto's face, and she crossed her arms.

Alecto blinked, frowning. She opened her mouth to answer, but no words came out.

She knew exactly why she didn't say anything, but she couldn't tell Jolene. Her friend would be devastated, especially after what went down tonight.

They had come. All of them, even Val.

They came to save Alecto because she was one of them, half-mortal or not.

Alecto knew it now. But she didn't know it back then.

"I just didn't want anyone to know," Alecto answered finally. She met Jolene's brown eyes. "I didn't want anyone to know that I'd been stupid enough to walk into the same trap twice."

Jolene sighed, her shoulders slumping.

"Alecto," she said, exasperated. "I would have come to you if I'd been the one to step into the same shit twice."

Alecto huffed a laugh, even if everything hurt. Jolene smiled.

"I would hope that you'd do the same," she added.

"I would," Alecto said after a moment. Jolene resumed working on finishing cleaning her wounds.

"Good."

The door swung open, and Alecto turned to see Blaze's wild eyes as he entered her room.

She didn't say anything, glaring at him, and he did the same.

For a long moment, they just stayed like that, neither of them willing to be the first to speak.

What was there to say anyway?

Even if he had helped save her, he was still a fucking asshole.

Jolene was the first to break the silence. "All right, I'm going to leave you two to it. Alecto, your wounds are wrapped up. I'm going to bring you the salve you'll need to apply daily later."

Alecto nodded. "Thank you."

Jolene offered her a smile, her thumb caressing Alecto's cheek before she was up and gone from the room. Right before she left, though, she said to Blaze over her shoulder, "If I hear about *another* instance where you threaten her life, I'll cut your balls off, *Blazy*."

Even after Jolene left, Blaze still hovered by the door for a long moment.

Alecto crossed her legs, tugging them under her as she refused to look at him.

Finally, he came over and sat on her bed, so close to her that she could smell the leather and smoke and the damn lake on him.

He shifted towards her, bending his leg so their knees touched.

Alecto glanced at him. She barely had time to wince as his hand crashed behind her head, cupping her neck, and then, his face was mere inches away, dark eyes searching her face.

"You almost died."

Alecto blinked, trying to calm her thundering heart. "Yeah, I know. I was there."

Blaze sighed heavily, bringing her forehead to his. "I didn't like it."

Anger bubbled so suddenly inside her, she barely registered her hand, moving to slap his cheek, sending his head to the side.

"*Fuck you*," she snarled, moving away from him.

His hand on the back of her neck locked her in place.

"When are you going to understand, Alecto?" Blaze growled, bringing his face to hers once more, a red print of her palm blooming on his cheek.

"Oh, I understand everything very well," Alecto snapped, fighting against his grip. "I understand that you're a fucking asshole. No, you know what, *asshole* is a word that's not colorful enough to describe what you are."

Blaze stayed silent, glaring at her, so she continued as she buried her palms in his chest.

"You don't fucking have a heart. Or soul, for that matter," she hissed. "If you were to offer a demon a deal, they wouldn't fucking take it because even in Hel, there's not a place dark enough for your rotten fucking soul."

"You're right about that."

Alecto was thrown off by that for a moment, but then anger surfaced once more, and words spilled out against her will.

"You think knowing that you're evil makes you better? It makes you even worse because you know how fucking malicious you are, and yet you still refuse to do anything about it. You feed on the pain and misery you inflict on others. There is nothing that's off-limits. In fact, the worse the act, the more satisfaction it brings, right?"

Blaze didn't answer.

Alecto's breath was ragged, her chest burning, but she didn't stop.

"How fucking empty do you have to be to only feel satisfied when someone else suffers, huh? How fucking broken must you be to only thrive when someone else is suffering? But I suppose it's a Leveau thing because it sure as fuck isn't a *witch* thing."

Blaze released a heavy breath, bringing his forehead to hers despite her trying to push him away. Alecto didn't have the power to fight him off.

"I am all of those things," he admitted, his voice a whisper. "And I am probably much, much worse than that because there are no lengths I wouldn't go in order to punish someone or to get what I want. But you can't sit here and pretend like all of these things aren't the reason why you are drawn to me."

Alecto pushed at him once more. "I don't—"

"Don't give me that bullshit," Blaze cut her off. "You know you can't stay away from me the same way I can't stay away from you. For fuck's sake, don't tell me that you don't feel the way your pulse spikes around me, the way your senses sharpen."

Alecto inhaled a breath, grinding her teeth.

She was done admitting anything to Blaze. He already had crushed her the moment she let her guard down.

"And do you know why that is?" Blaze asked, his breath hovering over her mouth. "Because you're just as fucked up as I am. You have a pit as deep as Hel inside you, and it is filled with a rage so potent, it could ruin the whole of Inathis if unleashed."

Alecto tried turning her face away, trying to put distance between them because it was getting hard to breathe.

Blaze's hand slipped from the back of her neck, coming to grip her face so that she couldn't escape him.

"You don't bother cutting others off whenever they wrong you. You walk over anyone that threatens you, no matter what reason they have for it," Blaze continued. With each word, Alecto's heart raced faster. "And while you think that being half-mortal gives you a better sense of remorse, I bet you have absolutely no fucking idea what guilt tastes like because you've never experienced it before."

Alecto wanted to dig her nails into his throat, scratching and tearing through his flesh to stop those damn words from coming out of his mouth.

She hated Blaze. And she hated that he was right.

Alecto might have been born half-human, but she never accepted that side of her. Recent months had shown Alecto that she was as horrid as the rest of them. She was just as cruel as Val, Andro, and even Blaze.

And Blaze was one of the few who had noticed it.

"I *hate* you," Alecto bit out, but it didn't sound as convincing as she'd intended. "I sure as fuck wouldn't hesitate before ripping your heart out for a spell if it ever came to that."

"And I'd fucking let you, Black."

A shiver of desire went through Alecto's body at the sound of his voice, the way he said those words as if he'd truly meant it.

Finally, she met his eyes, the obsidian gems flickering with every emotion she was feeling—anger, desperation, desire...

They were so close, their breaths mixed, and Alecto dropped her eyes to his lips.

It was a mistake, but she craved them just as much as she craved seeing him brought to his knees in front of her.

Alecto wanted to ruin him. And she wanted him to ruin her.

Blaze released a soft moan as Alecto's lips crashed into his. She pulled him onto her as her back hit the bed.

Immediately, her body heated, flames of desire licking her everywhere as the heaviness of his body over her sunk in. Blaze wedged himself between her thighs, his cock already hard and pressing right into her core through all the clothing separating them.

Alecto moaned into his mouth, her hands gripping his shoulders, sliding down his back, and fisting the cotton T-shirt he was still wearing.

Blaze's hand traced a path down her neck, down the side of her breast, making her arch for him. When it found her hip, he dug his fingers into her flesh. Alecto jerked at the pain that was too intense to be caused only by his grip, and Blaze immediately moved away, looking down at her.

Panting, Alecto shook her head and pulled him down. "I'm okay. It's fine. I probably have a bruise from before."

Blaze blinked, the haziness clouding his black eyes clearing as he inspected her body. And then, the weight of him was gone, and Alecto pushed herself on her elbows, her cheeks burning.

Before she could say anything, Blaze pulled her by her knees to the corner of the bed, and then he lifted her to his chest, heading towards her bathroom.

"We gotta clean you up and bandage you," Blaze explained when he noticed the look on her face. "Jolene is going to cut my balls off if tomorrow you're more damaged than today."

Alecto let him set her on the tiles near her bath, and she watched him intently as he turned on the tap, adjusting the water temperature.

While the tub filled, Blaze undressed her, carefully peeling layers of still-wet clothing clinging to her body. Only when Alecto was in her underwear did she remember how much everything hurt, and one glance down her naked flesh explained why.

Bruises and scratches lined her ribs, her sides, and even her hips and legs. Alecto wasn't sure how she had gotten so banged up, but suddenly, her limbs were heavy, and all she wanted to do was sleep.

She didn't argue when Blaze took off her bra, dropping it on the floor, but when his fingers hooked beneath her panties, a breath hitched in her throat as warmth pooled between her legs.

Blaze hesitated for a moment but then dragged the panties down, leaving Alecto naked in front of him. He helped her into the bath and let her lie down in the hot water, which immediately relaxed every muscle in her body.

Alecto frowned when instead of getting undressed, Blaze kneeled beside the tub, reaching for the sponge and the shower gel. The smell of mint and oranges filled the bathroom as he lathered the sponge generously between his palms.

He hooked a hand under her knee, lifting her leg out of the water, and then he dragged the sponge over her skin.

Wherever there was a bruise or a scratch, he lessened the pressure, gently swiping the sponge as if he was truly trying to avoid hurting Alecto more.

Alecto allowed him to clean the fear and the stinking scent of the damn lake off her, but she couldn't look away from those hands working her body and the way his eyebrows were drawn together as he concentrated.

Somehow, this felt more intimate than anything else they had done before. And Alecto wanted nothing more than to recoil because it was uncomfortable just as much as it was divine.

The worst part of it all was that Alecto could see herself like this more often. With Blaze caring for her body, his hands greedily exploring every inch of her. She could see herself belonging to him, spending nights curled in bed with him by her side.

For a moment, she could see them actually being something more if both of them allowed themselves to be this raw more often. She saw right through him, and he did see right through her.

There was not a single ugly thing Blaze wasn't aware of in Alecto, and that gave her comfort.

They could be together if they truly wanted to.

But no matter how much Alecto craved comfort only he could provide, the warmth of his embrace, she could never be able to trust him again.

Blaze was a volatile, ever-changing being that one moment promised you the whole world, while the next, he was the one burning it to the ground.

His hand with the sponge moved higher up her thigh, and Alecto released a soft breath, leaning her head back on the tub. There was a smirk dancing on his face as he stole a glance at her through lowered lashes.

"Yes, Black? Have anything to say?"

Alecto licked her lips, narrowing her eyes.

She had plenty of things to say. Most of them filthy and horrible, filled with longing and desire even she wasn't fully comfortable with.

"And what if I do?" she asked, shifting her hips. This drew his attention back to her, and Alecto's heart raced as his hand hovered very close to her core.

One touch, and she could be on fire.

There it was, written softly on his sharp face, the truth of his feelings, of how his heart truly felt for her. It only lasted a moment, and when he blinked, only thick desire was left in its wake.

But that was enough for Alecto. More than enough.

She could never truly forgive him and forget. Blaze had tried to kill her. He had tried shattering her heart and soul. A few stolen moments of pleasure and peace couldn't fix that.

If she were honest with herself, Alecto wasn't sure anything could. But she was determined to try to see if vengeance could bring her satisfaction.

Alecto bit her lip as she arched her back, a clear invitation for Blaze to touch her, give her those clever fingers and let them explore.

But she was done playing his games, according to his rules. It was time Blaze started playing her game, even if he didn't know it yet.

His fingers found the throbbing spot between her thighs, and Alecto's fingers wrapped around the edge of the tub as she welcomed the warm waves of pleasure surging through her. She could feel his dark gaze on her as she let her eyes fall shut, and it gave her enormous satisfaction.

When Alecto was done with him, Blaze would know firsthand what it felt like to be the half breed amongst the pure bloods. He'd know what it felt like to walk into the room and have every pair of eyes on you, burning with hatred so strong you could choke.

And when finally he was the one broken and damaged, then Alecto would consider forgiving and forgetting.

61

J ack Riverblood didn't dare raise his eyes when Blaze and the rest of the Inner Circle entered the auditorium.

Good for him.

As they made their way up the stairs on the side of the hall to their seats, many eyes were on them. The results were not in yet for the first trimester, the Dean waiting for everyone to take their seats before announcing the end of the first round of the Game.

But the poor souls knew. At least most of them.

They weren't expecting the Inner Circle to be there today.

As Blaze took his seat, Andro settling on one side, Val on the other, he couldn't help but smirk to himself.

There was nothing better than proving the haters wrong.

"Where's Rogue?" Blaze asked, leaning in closer to Val.

"Taken care of."

Blaze trailed a finger over his jaw, his tongue poking the inside of his cheek.

With a heavy sigh, she turned to face him. "He's back in Hel, where he belongs. As I said, taken care of."

Blaze didn't push for any more answers, but he was pretty sure it had something to do with the Imp Queen.

A creature like her having their backs was indeed a huge advantage.

Still, Blaze wasn't sure whether it was a good thing or a very, very bad thing.

Finally, the Dean entered the auditorium, and the chatter died as everyone stared at the man in front of them.

"Welcome to the first meeting of the year," the Dean said, his voice carrying over the whole hall, strong and hard. His eyes scanned the crowd of students. "I'm happy to announce that the first round of the Game is over. The win hasn't been claimed yet, but there is plenty of time left. Congratulations to those of you who made it through."

A round of applause and a few hollers and howls went around before the silence settled once more.

"This year's Game had started off eventful," the Dean continued. For a moment, he locked eyes with Blaze before moving on quickly.

Andro chuckled. "I'm pretty sure you put the fear of the Gods into the poor man."

"You're welcome," Blaze said.

"Miss Bellthrove will do the honors," the Dean said, glancing back at his secretary, who immediately hurried to the board on the back wall, as always, a cheery smile curving her lips.

Blaze stopped listening.

"Have you ever seen that bitch not smiling?" Andro asked, wrinkling his nose. "I love a good positive vibe, but she's too much even for me."

Blaze and Val both chuckled, exchanging glances.

"She must be high or something," Jolene said over her shoulder from her seat in front of Blaze.

Alecto sat right next to her, but she didn't turn to participate in the conversation. Yet Blaze's gaze traveled to her anyway.

She had pulled her hair up with that vintage clip, letting long strands hang messily around her face. Her fingers were working the pearl necklace around her neck, and Blaze took in the view of the curve of her neck, the soft skin his lips explored last night.

He had been good, making sure he didn't leave any marks behind. Alecto had enough of them as it was.

The memories from last night still lingered, and Blaze's cock twitched as his skin tingled, reacting to the memory of her under him, moaning and grinding against his hard body.

Ah, Alecto was as sweet as sin.

And that made things difficult for him this morning when she wasn't there next to him when he awoke. Alecto had let him sleep in her room, and he wasn't sure when she got up and left him there.

Blaze waited, lingering in her bed as he caressed the fresh white linen sheets, cold where she'd lain last night. He soaked in her scent, which was everywhere around him.

Yet Alecto never returned.

Which could only mean one thing. It was never going to happen again, or even if it did, Blaze was only allowed access to her body, and that was it.

He could only blame himself, of course. He had fucked up without anyone else's help, and now he'd pay for it.

Would Alecto's body be enough though?

It should be.

If it were just an obsession, then the illusion of her belonging to him, even for one night at a time, was more than enough to feed the beast.

Alecto turned her head, as if she could feel him staring.

There wasn't any malice or hate in that sky-blue gaze, but there wasn't any warmth either. Blaze could feel the icy grip tightening around his chest, so he averted his gaze first.

He focused on the Dean's secretary at the front of a floating chalkboard. At the very top, there were twelve marks representing twelve Houses.

"Fuckers," Val muttered as Miss Bellthrove announced that the House of Dragons were close to stealing the Book from the House of Monkeys.

Norse, sitting a few rows ahead of them, glanced over his shoulder.

Anger and something else pinched Blaze's chest when he realized the leader of the Dragons was looking at Alecto.

His hands fisted against his will, and Val didn't miss it. She narrowed her eyes as she took in the scene, but she didn't say anything.

Blaze ignored her.

When Miss Bellthrove announced that the Snakes almost had the Tigers' Book and the Tigers almost had theirs, a wave of chatter went around the auditorium.

It was no secret anymore why the Tigers were missing two members.

Hatred.

Disgust.

Admiration.

Fear.

Blaze could smell other students' emotions in the air.

"Guess who's the most hated bunch of all?" Val snickered, clearly pleased with everyone's reactions.

Blaze smirked as he exchanged glances with Andro.

"Maybe we shouldn't have left Riverblood alive," Andro muttered.

"I thought you were against getting other witches killed," Blaze teased.

"I'm against killing *innocent* witches. Riverblood is anything but that."

Were any of their kind innocent though?

They were birthed by the Gods out of the blood of mortals and demons, their souls twisted and dark, destined to be the ruthless rulers of all three realms.

Didn't that make them all *equally* sinful?

It took a while for Miss Bellthrove to finish her speech.

"Thank you for your participation this trimester," the Dean announced.

Cheers and applause, followed by shouts and howling, erupted around them.

The Dean's gaze settled on their little group as he said, "Once again, congratulations to all who survived this round, and best of luck in the next one. May the best House win."

"May the best House win!" the crowd cheered, and the meeting was over.

"Well, that was uneventful," Andro sighed with disappointment, rising to his feet.

"Very," Val agreed.

Andro stretched his long body, yawning as he turned away, eyes scanning the crowd. They waited for the other students to scatter.

Blaze leaned back in his chair, resting his arm over the tops of Val's and Andro's when a hot breath tickled his neck.

"What happens when a King's head is cut off?" a hoarse voice whispered into his ear. The hairs on the back of Blaze's neck rose as his muscles stiffened. "You're next, Leveau."

WHAT HAPPENS NEXT

If you want to continue the journey, the second book in the trilogy, House of Ruin, is available for pre-order.

PRE-ORDER HOUSE OF RUIN:

https://www.karolinawilde.com/house-of-ruin

Don't forget to submit your pre-order receipt to receive the special pre-order goodies.

YOU CAN ALSO READ THE FIRST CHAPTER OF HOUSE OF RUIN:

https://www.karolinawilde.com/house-of-ruin

DISCOVER THE REALM OF INATHIS WITH THE FREE NOVELLA

INATHIS IS THE REALM OF MAGIC FULL OF DANGER, ADVENTURES, AND WICKED WITCHES.

One night. Two academic rivals. A mystery to solve. What can go wrong?

When Lorelei Moonfall returned to the town she grew up in for one last fun Litha celebration, the last thing she expected was to see her high-school academic rival, Rune Cedar. Let alone have to work with him to save their friends' little sister.

But when the child goes missing on one night of the year when children disappear to never come back, Lorelei and Rune have to put their differences and old wounds aside and work together to uncover the centuries-old mystery that will change their lives forever.

On their way to solving the mystery, Lorelei and Rune find themselves confronted with their feelings for each other. And both are surprised when their mutual dislike turns into something either expected least.

If you're looking for a spicy one-night story packed with the tension between two academic rivals fighting each other and their attraction for each other, then download the Children of the Wicked for free: https://www.karolinawilde.com/ newsletter

ACKNOWLEDGMENTS

Thank you:

Reader, because without your support, these characters wouldn't be able to go on this journey.

Lauren, for helping me shape this book into a decent plotline.

Beth, for making sure everything is perfect and polished.

Lena, for the gorgeous cover, which I couldn't have imagined myself.

Dara, for bringing my sweet Alecto and Blaze to life with your breathtaking art.

Anastasiya, for capturing Darly on paper perfectly.

E, for always being there for me and believing in my writing. And in this book.

ABOUT THE AUTHOR

Karolina Wilde is an author of House of Pain, the first book in a seductive dark fantasy romance trilogy, and a sex-positive freelance writer who worked with some of the biggest brands in the world. She has a serious obsession with chocolate (dark or milk, never white, and always with salted caramel), and when she's not writing another book or another client article, she can be found playing World of Warcraft or trying to conquer her never-ending TBR pile. Find her on social media @karolinawilde or on her website at www.karolinawilde.com.

[g] goodreads.com/karolina_wilde

[d] tiktok.com/@wildekarolina

[o] instagram.com/karolinawilde

[f] facebook.com/karolinawildebooks

[y] twitter.com/karolina_wilde

[a] amazon.com/~/e/B0B86MR4W4

Lightning Source UK Ltd.
Milton Keynes UK
UKHW030755270822
407893UK00001B/2